W9-BWN-844

BAMBOO AND BLOOD

Also by James Church

A Corpse in the Koryo
Hidden Moon

BAMBOO
AND
BLOOD

JAMES
CHURCH

Thomas Dunne Books
St. Martin's Minotaur ✿ New York

This is a work of fiction. All of the characters, organizations, and events portrayed in this novel are either products of the author's imagination or are used fictitiously.

THOMAS DUNNE BOOKS.
An imprint of St. Martin's Press.

BAMBOO AND BLOOD. Copyright © 2008 by James Church. All rights reserved. Printed in the United States of America. For information, address St. Martin's Press, 175 Fifth Avenue, New York, N.Y. 10010.

www.thomasdunnebooks.com
www.minotaurbooks.com

Library of Congress Cataloging-in-Publication Data

Church, James.
    Bamboo and blood : an Inspector O novel / James Church.—1st ed.
        p. cm.
    ISBN-13: 978-0-312-37291-0
    ISBN-10: 0-312-37291-4
    1. Ballistic missiles—Korea (North)—Fiction.   2. Korea (North)—Military policy—Fiction.   3. Pakistan—Fiction.   4. Koreans—Fiction.   5. Women—Crimes against—Fiction.   I. Title.
    PS3603.H88B36 2008
    813'.6—dc22

                                                            2008030116

First Edition: December 2008

10 9 8 7 6 5 4 3 2 1

Note to Readers

Many of the events mentioned in this story actually happened, though not necessarily at the time, in the sequence, or exactly in the way they swirl around Inspector O. For that reason, and many others, this book is a work of fiction.

PART I

Prologue

Each note was a bell hanging from its own brass hook, an infinity of them cleverly attached to the smooth and rounded edges of the sky. When streams froze, when branches on the trees were solemn and stiff, when every single thing was wrapped in the brutal hush of solitary survival, it was then her song would come to me from where she stood alone on the wooden bridge. No matter how wide I spread my arms, I could not hold the music of her voice. It echoed from the hills, and danced the icy stairways that led, at last, to the emptiness between the northern stars. Strange, what the senses do to each other—how a raw wind against the skin makes the heart uneasy, how in the crystalline black of long nights, memories become voices close beside you. The Russians love to write about it. They think they are the only ones who know the cold.

Chapter One

The muffled whiteness fell in thick flakes, a final quickening before winter settled into the cold, hard rut of death. Halfway up the slope, pine trees shifted under their new mantle. A few sighed. The rest braced without protest. In weather like this, tracks might last an hour; less if the wind picked up. If a man wanted to walk up the mountain and disappear, I told myself, this might be his best chance.

"Fix these lenses, will you, Inspector? They've iced up again. Where are the lens caps? Every damn time, same thing—the caps vanish."

I brushed the snow from my coat and glanced back. Chief Inspector Pak was scrambling up the path, the earflaps on his hat bowed out, chin snaps dangling loose. No matter what, the man would not fasten those snaps. They irritated him, he said; they cut into his skin. Unfastened, they also irritated him. Gloves irritated him. Scarves irritated him. Winter was not a good time to be around Pak, not outside, anyway.

The binoculars hung from his neck by a cracked leather strap already stiff with cold. Twenty years old, maybe thirty, East German made, and not very good because the Germans never sold us anything they wanted for themselves. The focus wheel stuck, even worse in cold weather, so objects jerked into view and then out again. We had bought ourselves two choices: blurred or blurred beyond recognition. Cleaning the snow from the lenses would make no difference.

"Here." As soon as he caught up, Pak thrust the binoculars at me. "Can't see a damned thing." He fiddled with the snaps on his chin strap. "I don't like snaps, did you know that? Never have. Too damned difficult to undo in the cold, especially when you're wearing these damned gloves. If you have to take off your gloves to work the snaps, what have you gained? Who invents these things? Does anybody think anymore? Does your scarf itch? Mine is driving me crazy. Do something with these lenses, would you?"

I felt around in my pockets for something to use. There was nothing but a few sandpaper scraps and two wood screws, one a little longer than the other. They both had round heads, with slots that didn't fit any screwdriver I could ever locate. Not useful, I thought to myself. So why had they been in my pockets for years, transferred from one coat to another? The coats would each be discarded over time, but the contents of the pockets were impossible to throw away. "Simply because you don't need something at the moment," my grandfather would mutter when he found whatever I'd put in the trash pile, "doesn't mean it's worthless." I could hear his voice. "Look ahead," he'd say as he carefully examined the discarded object before handing it back to me. "Don't forget—bamboo scraps and wood shavings. Even two thousand years ago some damned Chinese carpenter knew enough to save them. When the kingdom ran out of everything else, he used the bamboo scraps to make nails. Got him in good with the Emperor. Do you suppose you're smarter than he was, do you imagine the present is all you'll ever have?" I never knew what to say to that.

Maybe that was why so many things ended up in my pockets—a subconscious bid not to run afoul of my grandfather, but also a bid for an unknown future, a sort of materialistic optimism. Maybe even Marxist in a way, a pocket theory of labor. After all, *somebody* made those two useless screws, though they were metal, not bamboo.

"Inspector." Many animals hibernate in cold weather; I drift into philosophy. "Inspector!" Pak pointed impatiently at the binoculars I was holding. My thoughts drifted back to the lenses. With what was I supposed to clean them? There was nothing I could use in my pockets. Did I have dried grass in my boots? Was I expected to use my hair, like one of the heroines in a guerrilla band of old, scouting for signs of the Imperial Japanese Army in the icy forests of Manchuria? I stamped my feet to restore a little feeling. The real question was, what were we doing here, hours from anywhere, squinting up at a mountain of frozen rock and groaning trees, our ears burning as the temperature plummeted? Mine were burning. Pak's earflaps were loose, but at least they were down.

"Never. Mind." Pak was right beside me, yelling to be heard over the wind that suddenly swept down the slope. The first blast tore his words apart. A second blast hit just as he tried again. To keep my balance, I turned sideways, which may be why I could hear the wind and nothing else. I thought my right ear might be ripped off in the gale, but not before it froze solid. I imagined an ice cube with my ear inside skittering along the ground, bouncing against trees and rocks, until at last it came to rest at the foot of the mountain. It might be deemed a new listening post of substantial value. "Good work, Inspector," someone in the Ministry would say months hence, after all the paperwork on my commendation was complete, but I would only hear ice melting off the rocks, since my ear would not be in range of commendations.

"No, I'll do it. I'll do it," I said to Pak when the wind died down for a moment and I could feel that my ear was still attached. I brushed more snow off my coat and tried to use the sleeve to clear the lenses. "But we might as well quit. Really, being out here is not healthy." Then the wind started again, furious at something, howling, smashing any words that dared emerge. The last thing in the world we needed was to climb a mountain in this weather. We weren't dressed for it, not through lack of foresight on our part. The Ministry just didn't issue anything fit for climbing mountains in the middle of a blizzard. "The only thing we're going to find is frostbite," I said. The lenses were still frosted over, though at least now they were glistening.

Pak hunched his shoulders. "Relax, Inspector. Don't get in a sweat, or you'll get frostbite for sure." He reached for the binoculars. "You know, your ears don't look normal, especially the right one. Funny color for flesh." He cocked his head. "Are you alright? Pull down those flaps, why don't you?" He tugged down his own and pointed to his ears. "That's why they put them on these hats. Costs us extra, you know. Might as well use them, snaps or not."

To hell with earflaps, I thought and put my hands back in my pockets. To hell with standing in the cold. "This is ugly weather." I was shouting at the top of my lungs, but from the look on his face, I didn't think Pak could hear me. "We can't even see our boots in this wind!" It surprised me that I could still form words; my cheeks were numb, and the feeling had practically drained from my lips. "We'll be stuck in that miserable hut back there for days." I jerked my head in the direction of the peaks, made nearly invisible by the snow, unless the wind had become so strong it was actually blowing apart the light. "He'll freeze to death up there." I didn't point because I didn't want to take my hands from my pockets again. "We'll be lucky to find him next May." Pak gave me a blank stare. I shouted louder. "If he's down here in the next few minutes, we'll invite him to dine. I'll warm my ears in the soup." The wind shrieked and knocked me sideways a step.

Pak shook his head. "What? I can't hear you with these flaps down."

2

A figure emerged out of the driving snow, and the three of us were blown back to the hut. Even in the midst of a blizzard, the foreigner's face held an easy smile, a sense of subtle mischief on his lips. There was something about him that made you think he was far away in his own mind, that he wasn't buffeted by the same concerns and worries as everyone else. Halfway through the most serious conversation, he might erupt in rich laughter, throwing you off stride. "Sorry," he would say. "Something struck me as funny."

His forehead was almost hidden by a lock of black hair; combed back with his fingers, it always fell down again a moment later. The lines on his face creased when he listened, or pretended to listen. The effect was nothing dramatic, but enough to suggest he was paying attention, concentrating on your words even though he was already four moves ahead of where you imagined you were leading him. At odd moments, seemingly out of sync with anything else, his eyebrows arched and danced, sometimes to show pleasure, sometimes not. Just as he slipped into an ironic observation, one eyebrow would leap straight up. A moment later, his mouth would tighten, a bit, not much. He would puff out his cheeks and look down, as if he regretted his words, or at least their tone. That impressed me probably most of all. He paid attention to delivery; there was never anything unguarded in what he said or, more important, how he said it.

When he felt anxious, which was rare, his right hand held the fingers of the left, a source of comfort, perhaps, or an unconscious effort to hide them from harm, maybe a habit from difficult times. After watching him for a few days, I realized that when he paused to think, he always lined up his hands against each other, one finger at a time, meticulously, deliberately. Once everything was perfectly aligned, five fingertips against their twins, it meant he had decided what he wanted to say. Then he put his hands down on the table again, where they lay still, completely comfortable and at ease.

"I thought I was going to die up there." The foreigner spoke English with a slight accent. Even after two weeks accompanying him several hours a day, I hadn't been able to place the source. I had heard all sorts of accents before, but none like this. It nagged at me, not being able to place him. His documents said he was from Switzerland. Maybe, but somehow I doubted that was the whole story.

From the beginning, as we stood around waiting for his bags at the airport, he spoke in a soothing cadence, a voice so smooth I wondered if he swallowed a bit of silk every morning—silk pills, maybe. Without fail, he turned complex thoughts into short, simple sentences so I could translate for Pak. That alone told me he had done this many times before. It was not the mark of a tourist, or even a businessman. Western businessmen sometimes spoke slowly, like we were idiots, but there was always an aura of tension around them, a slight odor of calculation. They couldn't help themselves. Not this visitor. He stood casually in the immigration line, he shook our hands casually when we introduced ourselves, but this was not a casual visit. In the dreary, dangerous winter of 1997, he had been put in our care, under the protection of the Ministry of Public Security. This was inexplicable, at least to me. We didn't babysit foreigners, we followed them at a discreet distance. If Pak knew anything, as usual he wasn't saying.

"The wind never let up." The foreigner took off his scarf. "From down below maybe you couldn't tell. The trees lower down didn't move much from what I could see, but the wind near the top was like a knife." He laughed. "That's a cliché, isn't it? I'm sorry. But it cut through my coat, cut through my gloves. You people may be used to this weather. I'm not."

A worse place to hold a conversation, I thought, would have been hard to find. The hut was small, cold, and dark. The only light came from what little remained of a slate gray day seeping through a tiny window on the far wall. The three of us stood bunched together in one corner, squeezed by a square wooden table with one chair. Normally, I would have looked to see what sort of wood the table was. I was too cold to care.

Who would have put furniture in a room so tiny? There was a piece missing from the side of the table, the side closest the window, as if something had stuck its head in and taken out a bite. Not a rough cut but a clean, symmetrical bite. I looked again at the wood. It was only pine, and not very good pine, either. I was going to freeze to death under a lousy, sappy pine table. I looked more closely. Maybe it had been gnawed, though the light was fading so fast I couldn't tell for sure. Who ate tables? I thought back to woodworking tools my grandfather had used—cutting tools, chisels, planes. Every night, they were lined up on the wall of his workshop. It was a pleasant, peaceful place, cool in the summer, fragrant with resin that seeped from the pieces of newly cut wood. "You have to keep things neat," he'd say as he finished putting everything in its place. "Life may not be like that, not for humans, anyway. You'll find that out someday, to your sorrow. But there is order everywhere else around us. You'll never come across a disorderly forest, and I'm not talking about trees standing in rows and saluting, either." He'd point to the tools. "Put them back where they belong," he'd say. "Let them get a rest, refresh their spirit." Once the implements were in place, he'd brush the sawdust into a pile and put it in a barrel that sat in the corner. "People don't treat things right anymore," he'd say, "don't ask me why."

The foreigner's voice brought me back to the hut. "Why are we standing?" I'd never heard someone sound so friendly even though he was shouting. We had to get out of this place. Everything about it was wrong. We had no psychological edge in here for making this man explain—without games or irony or coatings of vocal friendship—what the hell he had been doing on the mountain in this weather. Trying to start any sort of a serious interrogation, even a short one, was impossible. We might as well be on a minibus in a gale. I had the feeling the foreigner thought he could leave anytime he wanted, just get off at the next stop and disappear into the swirling darkness. There wasn't even any way to lock the door. It barely shut, and the wind made it rattle and shake the whole time he spoke. "Why are we standing around? There's nowhere to go for the moment," he said. It was his way of making sure we knew the score was even—we were trapped just like he was, all equally uncomfortable, and nothing would change that. He looked at us and smiled faintly. It might be two against one, but minus ten centigrade was a good leveler of odds and he knew it. When neither Pak nor I moved, he squeezed himself into the chair. I watched him put his fingers together. He had something more to say.

"Presumably, you'll kick me out of the country. Just as well, you'll hear no complaints from me. To tell the truth, I'm anxious to get back to where it is warm, maybe stretch out on a beach and have suntan oil rubbed onto my chest by someone." He held my eye for a moment and smiled as the wind tore at the roof. Then he turned to Pak. "Someone wearing a bikini."

Pak moved from one foot to the other. The floor was radiating cold up through the soles of our boots so that my shinbones were starting to ache. "If it were up to me," Pak said, "you'd be on a plane right away. Even better, you'd have been gone yesterday. But that won't happen. So your beach will have to wait. You'll need something warmer than a bikini back in Pyongyang, because they say it's going to be a cold winter. There will be lots of questions, and they won't be politely asked, not like the inspector here does. Questions every day, all day, morning, noon, and night. Sun? Even in the unlikely event there are windows in the room you'll get, you won't see much sun." Pak took off his hat and fiddled with the snap for a moment. I knew he was figuring out exactly how to phrase what he wanted to say next. "You were supposed to stay close. That was the agreement. You stay with us; we keep you safe. That's how it was going to work. An hour here or there out of touch we could explain if we had to. But this time you went too far, disappearing all day long. They'll be waiting when we get back, believe me, and there's nothing I can do about it."

The left hand moved for its shelter. The foreigner shrugged again but offered nothing.

"Don't be a wise guy," I said. "You say you're from Switzerland. That's nowhere near the Mediterranean, so why don't we drop this image of suntan oil and bikinis?"

"Ah, very good, Inspector." He threw back his head and laughed. "As always, perceptive and to the point. You're right, I was born in Lausanne, but I'm still a Jew." He paused, calculating the moment of maximum impact. His eyebrows wriggled, just enough to be noticed. "Genetic heritage, sunshine in my bones, a thousand generations in the desert. Can't deny our genes, can we? What do yours tell you?"

"They're off duty." I glanced at Pak. He hadn't changed expression, but I had no doubt he was digging himself out from the wreckage. A Swiss Jew? A Jew of any sort roaming around Pyongyang? Not just roaming around, but under the protection and observation of the Ministry—our little unit of the Ministry, to be precise, and there was no reason to doubt the precision that would ensue. Maddeningly sarcastic questions, sharpened to a fine and precise point, recorded in painful detail, asked again and again. Fingers would point, and I knew where.

Pak was still chewing things over. I could see his jaws working. The prolonged silence only intensified the cold.

"It could have been a Swiss gene that impelled our guest up that mountain like a goat in this weather," I said, trying to keep some words aloft. Maybe they would push the air around, keep it from freezing solid. Maybe a touch of anger would help. Anger was heat in another form, after all. Pak didn't join in. Normally, he would follow up my opening, keep things moving. Fine, I thought, let him come up with something better to get us out of this mess.

Or was it not a mess? Did someone else know exactly who this fellow was? It wouldn't be the first time someone higher up left us hanging out to dry. I looked at the foreigner. Now there was no choice. Bad place for an interrogation or not, we had to find out something more about him. We needed answers before we got back to Pyongyang.

There is no sense questioning a man when you are wearing a hat, however, especially a hat with earflaps. It undermines all sense of authority. I took off my hat, and regretted it instantly. "Why do you wander around all the time? I've never seen anything like it. When it rains, you go for a walk. When it's freezing, you go for a drive. Now it's storming, it's miserable, it's getting worse by the minute, and what do you do? You go mountain climbing? What the hell did you think you'd find up there?" The wind screamed at the door, pulled it open and banged it shut again.

The temperature was still dropping. I didn't want to be in this storm another minute. We might die, literally where we stood. They'd discover us months later, a threesome frozen in place, a perfect revolutionary tableau to be labeled "Interrogation of an Enemy Spy" and then visited by lines of schoolchildren ever after.

"Where's your car?" I demanded. It was hopeless; the wind was slamming against the side of the hut. In another second it would send us swirling into the winter sky, earflaps and all, and take our cars with it. Pak looked at the ceiling, which was showing signs of giving way. The foreigner sat unperturbed. I put my face close to Pak's and shouted, "Didn't I tell you, letting him have his own car would be trouble?" This self-assured, wandering Jew in Pyongyang had been put in our charge, and what did we do? In response to his silken request, we'd gotten him his own car. His own car! Nothing fancy, but that wouldn't count in our favor, not in the least. Already I could hear it, the lame route the conversation in the State Security Department's interrogation room would take. At least I had to hope it would be SSD. Their interrogations rarely got anywhere with us; the plastic chairs became unbearable after an hour or so and no one could concentrate after that. But they would keep hammering on the same point—he had a car, he had his *own* car, and we had gotten it for him. "Well, how were we supposed to know?" I'd say when they finally gave up and told us to go home so they could stretch and get something hot to drink. "We're not paid to be mind readers, are we?"

The foreigner looked at me oddly. Something I hadn't seen from him before, a touch of anger, started across his face, but after a moment the familiar half-smile settled back on his lips. "Let me guess, you're about to begin asking me questions that could get me into trouble." One eyebrow waltzed toward the other. "You don't want to get me in trouble, do you?"

The wind stopped suddenly, leaving nothing but silent, burning cold in the hut. "Questions don't cause trouble." Pak shifted his weight again and slapped his arms across his chest. "Only answers do. Save it, would you? We have to walk a kilometer back to our car, and we'd better get there before the temperature falls any more, assuming it has anyplace left to fall. The Ministry will send someone for your vehicle in a day or so if the roads are passable. You won't be needing it anyway."

"Let me guess, you're afraid yours won't start in the cold." The foreigner stood up and put his hand on Pak's shoulder. "You wouldn't let me bring back a good car battery the last time I went to China. I offered, did I not? But you refused. So stubborn, so stubborn. It must be in the genes." He didn't seem fazed by the warning that people—unfriendly, nasty, thick-necked people—would be waiting when we got back to the city. Maybe something had been lost in my rendering of what Pak said. He could be a difficult man to translate. The edge on his thoughts didn't always survive the journey between languages.

I could see that the more Pak mulled things over, the angrier he was getting. The thought had occurred to him, too. Someone had used us. Pak could forgive almost everything, but not being used. His lips had tightened into a thin line. I wondered how he could accomplish such a feat in this icebox. My teeth had started to ache. Our quarry smiled radiantly. "Is there any coffee, some way to heat water?" he asked. From the look on his face, you'd have thought we were waiting for the menus so we could order dinner and a bottle of wine.

"The warmest things in reach are those genes of yours. Crank them up full blast, because we're going to need something to keep from freezing while we walk to the car." I looked at his naked ears. "Here, take my hat."

Pak shook his head and frowned, but I wasn't interested.

3

Two men from the special section were waiting when we stumbled into the office, past midnight. One was asleep, his head slack, chin bumping on his chest. The other one was awake, his long, ugly face fatigued and angry. "My, my, look who has returned to the nest." He pointed at two cups on the desk. "You don't mind? We helped ourselves to some tea. Maybe you could clean those once in a while. They were all greasy-like." This was directed at me, an opening shot. People from the special section like to get under your skin first thing; they think it makes them look tough. I was tired and numb beyond saving, but I smiled. "Whatever you say."

Pak slowly took off his coat. He stood rubbing his hands together for a moment, then pulled out the chair behind his desk and sat down. "I don't remember setting up an appointment with you two." He looked from one man to the other. "Or is this a friendly call? Maybe you want to repay the money you owe me. You do, you know. You both do. I haven't forgotten. And, oh, say, is that your car down there? It's in my spot." Pak slammed the flat of his hand down on the desk. "Move it."

The man who was sleeping yawned and opened his eyes at the sound. He glanced at me without interest. "Yeah, well, we'll take custody now, so don't worry about your parking spot." He stood up and moved toward the foreigner.

"No one is going anywhere until I make a phone call." Pak rarely balked at surrendering custody. There was something funny in his manner; it made me uneasy when he acted strange like this. "We've been tramping around in the snow for hours. I'll be damned if the two of you will just take over after sitting here and napping all night. You want to play, find yourself some orders, and they better be written orders," he paused. "Pretend to be useful for a change instead of just pushing people around." Pak picked up the phone, listened for a moment, then put it down again.

The two of them smiled together, as if one were a mirror image of the other. A moment later, the first one's face fell back into anger. His mouth moved a few times, but nothing came out.

"Phones are down," the second one said and yawned again. His overcoat had a nice fur-lined hood on it. "You know you can't keep him, and you know why. So don't be a dope."

Pak pulled a clean sheet of paper out of a drawer and slapped it on his desk. I'd never seen him make such grand, noisy gestures. "There's nothing that says I can't keep him, and there's nothing that says you get to take him. You're in my office, this is a Ministry building, and I say nothing happens until I get something with an official stamp that tells me I don't have jurisdiction. Meantime, go fuck yourself."

They both looked at the foreigner. "He doesn't move; he stays here. If he leaves this building, he'll be sorry. If he talks to anyone on the phone, he'll be sorry." The first one had found his voice again. He turned to Pak. "And you'll be sorry, comrade, believe me. Real sorry. We're going now, but we'll be back." He picked up one of the cups and tossed it to me. "Wash these, why don't you?"

They smiled again, in stereo, and slammed the door on their way out.

The foreigner applauded. "Bravo, bravo. A man of principle! I thought you said you were going to toss me into their jaws."

I put down the cup and rubbed my ears. "Almost thawed out, but I still can't believe what I just heard. Are you crazy?" I looked at Pak. "They'll tear us limb from limb. Especially the ugly one."

Pak shook his head. "I don't like people helping themselves to my tea, and I don't like them parking in my spot. Besides, they don't scare me. I don't care what they look like. It will take them a couple of hours to find the right person to supply written authorization. No one wants to commit anything to paper these days, too dangerous; there's no paper trail if there's no paper. Everyone wants everything verbal. Well, I don't. I don't have to take verbal orders from them, and they know it. Meantime, I'll call the Minister, and we'll figure out something else to slow them down." He turned to the foreigner. "You were under my care. You still are, as far as I'm concerned. I don't sacrifice people under my care, it doesn't matter how foolish they are."

"Where does all this leave me, if you don't mind my asking?" The foreigner did not look grateful or concerned. He sounded even less so.

"You?" Pak stared at the man for a moment. "Where does it leave you? You can go back to your hotel if you want. Pack your suitcase. Sit tight."

"What if they come for me at the hotel?" Still no note of concern in the voice.

"No problem. The inspector here will look stern. He will be implacable until they back off and go home."

"And if they don't?"

Pak looked surprised. "Do I detect a note of worry? I wouldn't have thought so, you getting worried. But if that's the case, if you'd rather hide, you can stay here. We'll dump you at the airport later this morning, and you take the next plane out." He pointed at the calendar on the wall. "It's Tuesday, you're in luck. The plane leaves early, assuming they get the runway cleared and the ice off the wings."

"What if things play out differently, not so propitiously? It's not that I'm worried, just running down the options."

"I'll bet you have contingency plans." Pak scratched his head. "*Deigeh nisht,* I think was the term you used. It's Swiss, you said, for 'never mind, it's covered.'"

The foreigner laughed even before I finished translating. "You were so drunk that night, who could believe you would remember anything. But you did! Maybe my efforts here were not in vain." He laughed again. "Look, I can get you honorary citizenship someday, if you need it. You and the inspector, both. Who knows, your Korean genes might like the beach, and a little oil, eh, Inspector?" He patted me on the shoulder. "Is there a bed in this place?"

Pak pointed down the hall. "No bed. You can sleep on a chair in the empty office. The bathroom is downstairs; there's no lightbulb, so try to wait until the sun is up to use it. You need something to eat, but I don't know where we can find anything right now. Maybe they have some food at the airport. We'll see what's possible later this morning. You have your passport with you?"

"No."

"It figures." Pak turned to me. "Go get it before those stone heads think to collect the damned thing from the hotel."

"The clerks won't hand it over." I didn't bother getting up. "'You lack authorization,' they'll say, if I can even rouse them at this hour of the morning. I may not even be able to get in the door. They lock it, and there's no bell."

"Be charming, Inspector." The foreigner handed me a hundred-dollar bill. "Be very charming and give them this as authorization. It might even open the door."

Pak grunted. "They might not take it . . ."

I put the bill in my pocket. "Though, then again, they might. Of course, as soon as they give me the passport, they'll make a call to our grinning friends." I stood up to go. "Incidentally, keep your honorary citizenship." I looked at a notch at the top of the window frame and said very deliberately, "I don't need it."

"You know, O, you might have been a Jew." The foreigner craned his neck at the corners of the ceiling and then settled his gaze on the top of the window, which was rattling in the wind. "You see Cossacks everywhere."

4

Wednesday morning, the two men from the special section were back, carrying a piece of paper and accompanied by two other men, from where they wouldn't say.

"What do you mean, he's gone?" The ugly one growled and narrowed his eyes. "I told you, if he left this place, you'd be sorry."

Pak tipped back in his chair. "Did you? I don't remember that. Do you remember that, Inspector?" I was standing in the doorway.

"No. I don't recall."

The others turned to look at me. One of them licked his lips. "You, of all people, O. It figures, our paths would cross again, someday." I didn't recognize the face, but his left hand was missing two fingers. He held it up for me to see.

Pak gave me a look, halfway between "You know him?" and "Let me handle this." I leaned against the wall, a little out of sorts. The man with the left hand had died a long time ago. Fifteen years, maybe more. I remembered the day precisely. I just couldn't recall the year.

"Where is he?" The ugly one turned back to Pak. "And don't say you don't know."

"I don't know." Pak took a nail clipper from his drawer. He clipped the nails on his left hand, and put the parings in a neat little pile on the desk. No one spoke. This is what it is like inside an atomic bomb, I thought to myself. In the millisecond before it blows everything to hell.

Finally, the fourth man laughed. "When we're through with you, you'll be lucky to have anything left to clip." He was taller than the others, older. "But I don't want to get ahead of myself. So, I'll give you another chance. Where is the foreigner?"

Pak swept the parings into a trashcan beside the desk before looking up. "He's gone. I assume he took the flight out of here back to Beijing. From there, your guess is as good as mine."

"You decided, on your own, not to hold him?" The tall man looked around the office. "Since when do shitty little policemen make decisions about national security matters? Beyond your writ, wouldn't you say?"

"He had a valid passport, a valid visa, a valid residency stamp, and an airline ticket that didn't look like it had been forged." Pak counted on his fingers as he listed each piece of evidence. "As far as I know, he went through the immigration line, looked at the officer in the booth, you know, the girl with the lips like roses in bloom, and was passed. No one said boo. You had a lookout for him, did you?"

"We had reason to hold him. You let him slip away. Tell me why."

The man with the left hand hadn't taken his eyes off me. There was no expression in them, but you wouldn't call it a blank look. I felt pinned to the wall, like a bug. Alright, so he didn't die fifteen years ago. Good for him. He nodded for me to step outside.

5

We went down the stairs without speaking. When we got outside, he kept walking to the front gate. The guards looked at him and then at me. I shrugged and followed him to the street. Finally, he stopped and turned around. "If I shot you right here, do you think anyone would mind?"

"Nice to see you, too."

He lit a cigarette. "You still don't smoke, I assume. No problems of conscience. Just left me for dead and danced home. I wondered what I'd say if I ever saw you again."

"What did you decide?"

"I forget." He threw away the cigarette. "You didn't even look surprised when you saw me."

"It crossed my mind." I started to walk. "Let's keep moving."

He fell in alongside, but didn't say anything.

"Where have you been in the meantime? We'd have run into each other sooner if you'd been in-country."

"Here and there. It took a few years to recover. Pretty good job, the way they put me together again. Good doctors. Very dedicated." He held up his hand. "Too bad I'm left-handed."

"Must make it hard to count."

He stopped. "I think I'll use two bullets. The first one so that it hurts, really bad. And the second one, so it hurts even more." He paused. "I can still count to two."

"You should be able to make it to three, but you're not even armed, so maybe we can skip through the tough talk." He'd lit another cigarette; his good hand was shaking a little, not much. "What did your crowd want with the foreigner?"

"Doesn't concern you." The smoke from the cigarette drifted slowly out of his mouth, as if he weren't breathing. "I'll tell you this, though. There's going to be hell to pay that he got out of the country. You know where he's from?"

"He says he's Swiss." That was true, as far as it went.

"You believe him? He's not Swiss. His mother is a Hungarian, that's why he has a Hungarian name. What did you think Jenö was?"

Actually, I'd checked that with the name trace section. I put in the request on a Wednesday morning, the day after our foreigner arrived. When nothing was back by Friday, I called. Real simple, they said. It's Italian. "You sure about that? His papers say he's Swiss." Don't worry, they said. We know names; it's Italian.

"So, maybe his father is Swiss." I avoided looking at the man's hand and concentrated on his face. There was nothing in it I recognized.

"His father was Israeli."

"Was."

"Dead."

"Is that so? You seem to know quite a bit."

"You'd be surprised." He threw away the second cigarette. "Let me ask you a question. Nothing complicated. Why'd you let him go?"

"We had our orders to be nice, show him around, keep him comfortable. Ending up in one of your holes didn't match the description. Anyway, he hadn't done anything wrong."

"Not in your book."

"Not in my book." I stepped off the curb. "You hungry? I'll buy you lunch." There hadn't been food for lunch for a long time, but we still made the offer sometimes, out of habit.

"No, thanks." He turned around and started walking back toward the gate. "I'd rather choke."

6

Pak didn't look up when I stepped into his office. "We're in a lot of trouble, but you know that. Where you been?"

"I spent some time thinking about noodles. Then I did some walking around. I wanted to clear my head, that sort of thing. Another cold day, we're due for a little break, wouldn't you think? Not that I mind. Cold is good for clearing my head." The cold did nothing for my head besides making my ears ache. Pak knew I was only throwing up chaff in hopes of avoiding the question he was sure to ask.

He asked it. "You know that guy with three fingers?"

"Two fingers, actually; the other one is a thumb. Yes, I do." I sat down and looked out the only window in Pak's office. The view wasn't much, an inner courtyard and, across the way, the Operations Building. It was snowing again, though just a few flakes. Maybe if it snowed more it would warm up a degree or two. My ears still burned from being outside without a hat. This sort of cold gave me an awful headache. "We used to work together."

Pak said nothing, but he didn't go to sleep, either.

"He was in an accident." I didn't think that would end the conversation. It didn't.

"And?"

"And it was a bad accident."

"And?" Pak was going to pull at this, no matter what. He was in that sort of mood.

"The man died. But apparently he didn't."

"To review: You worked together. Somewhere, not to be discussed, he was in a bad accident that killed him, but didn't. And you haven't seen each other since then. Shall I guess the rest, or are you going to tell me? Normally, I wouldn't ask, but this nondead friend of yours seems intent on causing us grief. He was standing in my office this morning, and as far as I'm concerned, that means he has crossed the line from the unmentionable past to a place where none of us want to be—the present. Where was this operation you two were conducting?"

"We were where we weren't supposed to be, not officially, though we had good reason to be there." When I'd left that group, my final orders on leaving were to tell no one what we did—no one, not ever. So far, I'd stuck to that. But this was different. Resurrection hadn't been mentioned as a contingency, one way or the other. "It was supposed to have been worked out ahead of time, our entry into the place we were supposed to visit. Only it wasn't. I thought he was dead, there wasn't anything I could do."

"That's all?"

"More or less. When I got back, they debriefed me, kicked me in the pants, and told me to forget the whole thing. They told me the chief of operations was unhappy, and that if I knew what was good for me, I'd stay as far away from him as I could. We never saw him, so I just assumed that was a fair description of his mood. The man with the fingers must have been overseas until recently; otherwise he'd have shown up sooner on my doorstep. Strange, isn't it? His appearing at this moment? It gives me a funny feeling."

"A funny feeling. Unique investigative technique, we'll have to tell the Minister. These feelings, you get them often?"

"Did I use up my quota for the month already?"

The phone in my office started ringing. I walked down the hall to answer it. "O here."

"Nice to hear your voice." It was the dead man. "We need to meet. I'll see you at the Sosan Hotel, in the coffee shop, let's say at 4:00 P.M."

"How about four thirty?" I hung up the phone because he was no longer on the other end. "Perfect," I said to no one in particular. "Four o'clock is fine." This meant getting the keys for the car from Pak.

Pak was examining his teeth in a small mirror when I walked in. After a minute, he put down the mirror and looked at me. "What?"

"I need the keys to drive over to meet someone."

"Who?"

"The dead man."

"Where?"

"You want to come along? That way you don't have to ask questions, you can see for yourself. In fact, you can take notes. But you have to pay for your own coffee."

Pak picked up the mirror again. "No, you go alone." He smiled into the mirror, a big, phony smile with a lot of teeth. "See, Inspector, with the wrong diet, you can lose your teeth, incisors, molars, the whole works. I'll probably lose mine by the end of the winter. They're already getting loose. I think it's scurvy. And then what will I do? Looks count for a lot, even these days. Everything is in the packaging, you know? At my age, the package isn't doing so well."

"You might be right; I hadn't heard. People in my neighborhood don't talk much about packaging. They don't talk much about anything. Things are very quiet these days." This was a bad conversation to be having. The weather was bad. News from the countryside was bad. I tried to lighten the mood. "I heard somewhere that eating tree bark is healthy for the gums."

Pak opened a drawer and put the mirror away. "Something wrong with tree bark? Or do you have your own stash of rice somewhere?" He closed his eyes. "Forget it," he said quietly. "Let's change the subject."

"Pick a topic."

"How about getting back to your friend? His name is"—Pak looked at a paper on his desk—"Mun." He paused. "That's the name he uses now, anyway. You knew him as something different, one assumes."

I reached in my trousers pocket and found two small pieces of wood. One was junk pine. The other was chestnut. Pak's eyes narrowed.

"Whenever I ask you a question and you reach for that damned wood, I know you are about to hide something from me."

"Not so."

Some people think I use wood as worry beads. I do not. Beads are generic; wood is particular. Every type of wood has its own personality. I generally do not say this in the presence of strangers because it is not something they like to hear. They find it offensive, or walk away convinced I am being sarcastic. The truth is, with complete access to every type of tree on the planet, you could probably find a wood for every hue of emotion and then some. My grandfather believed wood was as close to goodness as a person could get. He never said it quite that way. What he said was, "You never saw trees abuse each other, did you?" He'd mutter this to me when we walked on summer afternoons, when the road was dusty and the sun was still hot. "Do they speak meanly? Do they lie? Do they grab more than their share, or sit in the shade while others do their work for them?" He'd walk a little more and then turn to me. "Well, do they, boy?"

"No, Grandfather, they do not." No other answer was possible, or so it seemed to me at the time. It was manifestly true, the wood he worked with, the furniture he made, none of it ever caused trouble in the village or to our neighbors. The only problem I can recall happened one autumn. A visiting political cadre, a young man with a thin-edged smile, looked into Grandfather's workshop and said, "This furniture of yours is too ornate. It must be cleaner, simpler to match the lives of the people." My grandfather continued to sand a piece of wood, a piece for a small writing desk that had been commissioned by an official in Pyongyang, an old friend from the days of the anti-Japanese war when they were guerrillas in the mountains near the Amnok River. The sanding seemed to go on for a long time. The cadre looked at me and pointed to his ears, as if to ask whether the old man was deaf. At last my grandfather raised his head. "It isn't me that makes the shapes. They come from the wood. There's a certain truth to wood." He fixed the cadre with a long, level gaze. "Or would that be the responsibility of another department?" The young man nodded slightly. "You'd better find some simpler truths somewhere, or we'll have to get rid of these trees you're using and plant new ones, simple ones." My grandfather returned to his sanding. The cadre went away, and the neighbors walked over, one at a time, to say hello and comment on the desk. We all watched the road for a few months after that, but no one ever came to touch the village trees.

Pak knew I kept a supply of several varieties of wood, small scraps, in the top drawer of the desk in my office. He sometimes complained, but he never told me to get rid of it. When I needed to calm down, or think, or let my mind go free, I'd go into my desk and search around for a piece of wood. Lately, I had started carrying a couple of pieces with me, in case the duty car broke down when we were out of town. We were being called out of town more and more, to manage crowds at train stations or help out if a local security man became sick, or disappeared. The car wasn't in good repair, and there wasn't much maintenance going on. I knew we'd get stuck sooner or later. That's why I had the piece of chestnut. It was cheerful, in its own way. Chestnut could take your mind off of things. It was a treat I had been saving for a bad day. This had all the makings of a bad day, and I hadn't even been to the Sosan Hotel yet. I put it back in my pocket.

"No," I said to Pak. "Mun is what he called himself then, too. We didn't know each other very well. We met just before the operation started, read the file, asked a few questions. The training was only for a couple of weeks. We didn't talk much. He kept to himself, and so did

I." I shouldn't have been revealing even this much about an operation, even an old one that didn't matter anymore, but Pak could be trusted.

"You weren't interested in knowing more about someone who might soon have your life in his hands?"

"Nothing seemed very complicated in those days. Just in and out, they said. The less we knew about details, the better. That's what they said. Like teaching someone enough to jump out of a plane only one time."

"Not good."

"Awful. I think about it sometimes. I wonder if we were set up. Nothing went right from the start, nothing. When we got to the target, someone was supposed to have left a door open for us. They didn't. It was locked, and no one had bothered to teach us how to get past a locked door, not one like this, anyway. We managed to work the lock, but it took extra time we didn't have to spare. Guard schedules, that sort of thing."

"Why didn't you abort? I thought there were hand signals or something."

"You never went on one of these, did you?" I thought I saw Pak move in an odd way, nothing much, but something suddenly surfaced and then dove back into the deepest part of him. I let it go; it wasn't my business. He never spoke about what he did before he joined the Ministry, and I never pressed him to find out. Anytime we got to the edge of the subject, he found a way to steer the conversation onto something else. "The one thing they emphasized over and over to us was that there was only this single chance. Miss this and it would never come again, they said. The chief of operations wanted this done, they said, and he wanted it done right away. They never mentioned anything about aborting the mission."

Pak snorted. "Bunch of crap. There's no such thing as only one chance."

"You sound like my grandfather. One of your definitive bugle calls would have been helpful at the time. But you weren't there, as I recall."

"Neither was your grandfather." Pak mused a moment. "What happened to your friend Mun?"

"Something exploded. We finally got in and were looking around.

There were some wires I had to cut, and I was concentrating on that. Red wire this, green wire that. Or the other way around. It's not the sort of thing I'm very good at."

"Details, you mean." Pak swiveled his chair to gaze out the window. It never bothered him, that there wasn't much to see. "No, actually, you're pretty good at details, Inspector." He sat for a moment, as if he might want to say something more, then turned his chair back and gestured for me to go on.

"Mun must have spotted something, because he moved a few steps to my left. I remember it was to my left, because I had the red wire in my right hand. One minute I saw him picking up a small box, the next minute he didn't have a face anymore, or a neck. No hands, either. He dropped like a cow that's been shot in the head. No moaning, nothing. Just a lot of gore that wasn't moving. Funny thing, whatever it was barely made a sound. No explosion, none that I remember, anyway."

"So you left."

"Not right away. First, I located what we had been sent in for, most of it, anyway. On the way out, I checked again, but he was dead. I stepped over him and walked back to where the escort team was supposed to be waiting. They weren't at the primary point so I had to go to the backup, which was not easy to find. I cursed the whole way. When I got there, I was sweating buckets. They were sweating, too, looking at their watches and mopping their faces. They didn't ask why I was alone."

"Why bother? They could see you were in no mood to talk."

"No one was, believe me. They were nervous, real edgy. The whole way back they wouldn't look at me, not even at each other."

"Now your dead teammate shows up again. In pursuit of this Israeli who tells us he is a Swiss Jew."

"What makes you think he's Israeli?"

"What makes you think he's not?"

"His mother is Hungarian," I said lamely, "that's why his name is Jenö. It's not Italian, by the way."

"Who cares about his mother? He's an Israeli as sure as I'm Korean, and he was up here in the cold where there isn't a camel for a thousand kilometers."

"I don't think they have camels in Israel."

"You know what I mean. He was way out of his territory, and so is your old friend Mun if he's come back from the dead. You think it's strange?"

"No, more like fearful symmetry."

Pak looked thoughtful. "Your phrase?"

"Borrowed."

Chapter Two

The weather got better for a few days, not so cold, and finally, a lot of sun in the mornings, though the sun was still weak, like a dying man's eyes. Every afternoon the clouds came in, but that didn't matter much because it got dark early this time of year, so it wasn't as if the afternoons were much use anyway. Pak was jumpy. He drifted down to my office every couple of hours. Half the time, he'd just stand there, looking into space. Sometimes, he'd ask if everything was going smoothly. Nothing more specific than that. I pretended not to know what he was talking about. I just said, "Fine, everything's fine."

That was true, if a meeting in the Sosan with the long-dead Mun could be construed as "fine"; if listening to Mun recite a litany of complaints and threats from the special section could come under the rubric of "fine"; if "fine" could be stretched to include a final warning that I should consider myself as being on notice that "some people" were waiting for one more incident to bring down the hammer and shatter my status as the grandson of a Hero of the Republic. This sort of thing didn't bother me too much. It just wasn't what I would normally label "fine."

But I also didn't want Pak to know. He had enough to worry with. This was my business, old business, unfinished business. If there was a problem, it was mine to solve.

Pak's too frequent visits went on for several days. It got on my nerves. Someone constantly asking you if everything is all right, it can get wearing. Pak didn't think things were fine, I could tell. He thought things were going to end up in a train wreck. Pak knew plenty, he had good sources, and they must have been warning him. After being surprised once, he was going to make sure it didn't happen again. He must have dug up every contact he ever had to check what was going on. He wouldn't come out and say anything though. That wasn't how he did things. Each time, after I told him things were fine, he'd shake his head and walk back to his office, clucking his tongue.

It was a little curious that he never asked about my meeting in the Sosan coffee shop. I figured there must be a reason he didn't want to know, something more than his well-honed instinct against delving into things that couldn't bring anything more than another basketful of bad news to an already bad situation. If he asked, when he asked, I already knew what I'd tell him.

"So, what happened at the Sosan between you and your no-longer-dead friend?" He made sure to be looking out my window when he finally asked, so I couldn't see the expression on his face.

"Nothing." I'd practiced saying it out loud. It still didn't sound convincing.

"Is that a fact? You just sat there and laughed about old times and drank hot water?"

"I certainly didn't laugh."

"And him?"

"He sneered, mostly." Which was true. "I still can't figure out why he wanted the meeting." Also true.

"Not good." Pak had come away from the window and was rearranging a pile of papers on my desk. "Whatever he's up to, it's not good, we can assume that, but what else? He must have asked you a few questions."

"That's what I was expecting, questions. At least some probing for what we knew about the foreigner. But no, nothing like that. There is one thing, though. He said he wanted to get in touch with some of the people from our operation, the one he and I were on when everything went wrong." I glanced at my desk. Pak had put everything in two neat piles. I'd known where every piece of paper was before. The latest Ministry reports had been on the edge of the desk closest to the window, in roughly the order they came into my office; interrogation reports were more or less in order of priority along the the opposite edge of the desk, nearest the door; laterally filed field reports from other sectors in the city were pretty much everywhere else. "You might as well take those piles to your office," I said. "I'll never be able to find anything anymore."

"Why? Why did he want to get in touch with those people?"

"How should I know? I told him I had no idea where anyone was, and he sneered."

"Did he ask for another meeting?"

"No. But I'm sure of one thing."

"And what is that, Inspector?"

"I'll bet we haven't seen the last of him."

2

Winter was never busy. In bad weather, people stayed off the streets if they could. The worse the weather, the more they stayed indoors, even if they had no heat. We may have been the only ones in the city who were glad when it snowed heavily. Fewer people outside, less chance for trouble—everybody knew it. Anything that happened on the street pretty quickly got thrown our way. But if something went wrong in an apartment, it was rare for us to be called. Even if people phoned, Pak's inclination was to tell them to settle it themselves. Have the neighborhood committee deal with it, he'd say and hang up. The neighborhood committees liked that sort of thing; it bolstered their sense of importance and gave them another reason to meddle. Occasionally, one of them would write a nice note to the Ministry pointing out Pak's "good judgment." The note would be put in his file, and that would keep the Ministry off his neck for a few months. That was fine by me. If the Ministry was off his neck, it was easier for him to keep them off mine.

Just to keep a hand in things, I'd walk through my sector a couple of times a week in winter, even on icy days. Mornings, there would often be a street gang out clearing sidewalks. At least a couple of people would be working; the rest liked to loll around and chatter. The girls fixed their scarves when they saw me. The boldest ones sang out, " 'lo, Inspector, it must be quiet in your office today." In years past, their eyes would sparkle. Their cheeks ruddy with cold, they would whisper among themselves for a moment, and then one of them, the boldest, would walk up and say, "We've got tea across the way. Stop by and we'll bring it down to you." She'd wave toward an apartment house on the corner. "Or you can wait inside," something that always brought more laughter.

"No. Thank you, but no," I'd say. "These sidewalks need more work, don't you think?"

And one of the men, sweating with exertion, would look up and shout, "What are you girls doing there? Get your shovels working, why don't you, instead of standing around bothering the police. Let him go about his business, you hear?" He'd nod to me and then go back to chipping the ice. None of them would pay any attention to him.

But this winter things were different. The work gangs were smaller, and nobody spoke when I walked by. Sometimes, one or two would follow me with dull eyes, too weak or dispirited to move their heads. I had the feeling I was moving past ghosts.

On rare occasions, I drove over to the university. I didn't like being there. Schools belonged to another security unit, not even to the Ministry, and in those days it made me nervous to be on someone else's territory. But Pak had worked out an understanding to let us peek in from time to time. When Pak needed an understanding, he could usually get it. We should have access to the campus, he'd say, just to keep an eye on things. Just in case the situation started drifting toward some unknown event, a potential trigger. No one would talk about it openly, and the Ministry wouldn't put anything on paper, but we all knew what was happening, and we all knew that the students might get in front.

"I don't think I should be over there," I said to Pak.

"Don't worry so much. It's all arranged, just keep a low profile. If anyone asks, you're thinking of going back to school, technical training, something." Especially now, when classes were held only sporadically, with so many teachers too weak or tired to lecture, and the students too hungry to concentrate, Pak was keen on our keeping up good contacts on campus. I dodged as best I could, but I always ended up going.

"Get to school and check in with the ears, Inspector."

"Busy day, Pak, not sure when I can make it. Send someone else, why don't you?"

"All you're doing is staring at the molding on the ceiling. You're not going to paint it, so leave it be. I need you over at the campus. You're good at it; you give off the right vibrations. Students don't clam up when they see you coming."

"Yes they do. If looks could kill, I'd be scattered to the winds by now. They hate our guts, and you know it. Things haven't calmed down from when they chased that SSD fool off of the campus."

"Served him right, trying to break into a student meeting like that. Don't worry. As long as you stay in the shadows, they won't bother you and we can keep away from Tiananmen. Just check in with that kid you have on a string."

"She's not on a string. Why don't I do it off campus somewhere?"

"The whole idea, Inspector, is to show the flag."

"In the shadows?"

"You don't have to wave the flag, Inspector, just unfurl it a little. Stroll around, sit on a bench, rattle a doorknob, let them know you're there."

3

The room was frigid. It hadn't been heated since the last time the sun shone directly in the windows, and that had probably been in September. The girl was young; she might be pretty one day, but it was far too soon for that. She kept her hands in the pockets of a thin blue coat that couldn't have done much against the cold. She shivered once or twice.

"I thought you weren't going to come here anymore, that's what you promised." She kept her voice toneless, though it was with some effort. She was holding back. "The last time you showed up, someone almost saw us. If anyone catches me talking to you, I'll be ordered to leave. You say it's all been worked out, but that's not true. Local security will report me, and then I'll be sent home. You know I'm only supposed to talk to the assigned security people. Why can't you stay away from campus, like you promised?"

I considered this for a moment. It was gutsy of her, telling me off. Maybe that's why I picked her to begin with. Her file said she was always outside the group. She'd only been accepted at the university from a nowhere village near Hamhung because she was good with languages, and because she was considered an exceptional pianist. Where she found a piano to play out there in the countryside, I couldn't imagine. "You like Rachmaninoff?" I looked around the room. The walls were bare. The instructor's desk had been moved to one side, and there was a three-legged easel with a piece of gray cardboard on it standing at the front. The cardboard had several names printed on it. The last one was Rachmaninoff. I figured she'd like whatever was listed last.

"I do. I want to play his music someday."

"Which piece?"

"What's it to you?"

"You think I don't like music?"

"Do you?"

Four questions in a row. With her, I could keep it up all afternoon, all questions. It would be interesting one day to see how long she could play the game, until she slipped and actually said something. This afternoon, though, I didn't need anything from her. I just needed to be here. It bothered me a little that someone might see the two of us together. Sent back to the east coast, she might not survive, or she'd leave for China and end up selling herself. I moved away from the window. "This may surprise you, but I have been known to listen to music. More than that, I've heard some Rachmaninoff."

She took one hand out of her pocket, her left one, and looked at her nails. They were broken and dirty. She flexed her fingers. She was aching to get out of the room, but her hands were important. If she took them out for me to see, it was a gesture. She might not know it, but that's what it was. It wasn't trust, exactly, but it was coming close.

"Which piece? You have a tape? I like him a lot better than Shostakovich. That's mostly what we listen to. I think he's overrated."

She said it as a challenge, but I didn't pick it up. She sighed. "We had a German conductor here a couple of months ago. All of a sudden he appeared, like he dropped from the sky. He brought some music for us to play, tapes for us to hear. One of the pieces was Rachmaninoff. I cried when I listened to it. How could anyone imagine anything so beautiful? How could he have heard something like that in his head?" Her voice wasn't toneless anymore. "I want that, I want to know something that beautiful." She stopped suddenly and looked at me intently. "He left Russia, you know, after the revolution. Do you know where he went?"

That's my girl, I thought. Smoldering like a pile of juniper branches. If I didn't say something to cool her down, she might burst into flames right here in front of me. Maybe she would survive after all. "Musicians are strange," I said. She frowned, and I hurried to cover my mistake. "What I mean is, they aren't moored to one place. Art is universal, isn't that what they say?"

She hummed something.

"Rachmaninoff?"

I was rewarded with a quick smile. "You guessed that, didn't you? It must be your security training." The smile disappeared. "Well, you left your spoor. That's what you wanted to do, wasn't it? You see, Inspector, I've figured you out." She pulled her hands out of her pockets and walked to the door. "I have, you know."

"I know." I waited until she had left the room and I could hear her footsteps in the cold hallway. "I'm betting on it."

Both hands out of her pockets—maybe not trust, actually; maybe defiance. It came down to the same thing.

4

It wasn't a long drive back to the office, but I needed some time to think. I could think in my office, except for Pak coming down and asking if everything was fine. I couldn't think when he did that; I couldn't think once he left because I knew he would be back. If I drove around my sector, I could keep the car heater on. There wouldn't be much to see, the streets were almost deserted, but at least it would be warm.

No one had mentioned the subject of the Swiss visitor again, a silence that had nothing good to recommend it. No one at the Ministry raised it when I went by to look for a file on an old case. The special section team stayed away from our office, though every day we expected them to pay another call. Pak was sure so they'd be back, he gave me explicit orders not to clean the cups. Most disquieting of all, during our brief meeting at the Sosan Hotel, Mun hadn't raised the subject even once. Out on the street, he had hinted he knew quite a bit about the visitor, but at the Sosan, he clammed up. He'd repeated the warnings about how much trouble I might be in, but didn't let on any more about what he knew. From the way he had asked me if I still had contact with anyone from our operational days, I didn't think that's what he really wanted to know. It seemed more like he was trying to figure out what I remembered from the past, and what I was willing to talk about. I told him I didn't remember anything, and hadn't seen anyone, which was mostly true. I didn't like his sneer, but paid for his drink anyway. I figured if he went away and never came back, it was worth the investment. Not that I thought he'd go away. It wasn't, as I'd told Pak, a good bet that we wouldn't see him again.

That still left one burning question mark hanging over us—why the Swiss visitor had become a nonsubject. Pak seemed to think that the subject was something being discussed somewhere else and that it would eventually crash down on our heads again. This wasn't like Pak, to be so jumpy and off-key. Pak was the polestar, the fixed point. If he started to wobble, there was no telling what would happen to the rest of us. I didn't blame him. The situation was bad. Pyongyang was awash in rumors, most of them true, about how conditions in the countryside had fallen apart. We were ripe for something, I just didn't know what.

Chapter Three

"Life, existence, whatever you want to call it these days—it's all made up of layers, am I right? People speak in generalities. They constantly sum up existence, apply a necessary shorthand. They say 'one' but they actually mean 'many.' If you say 'morning,' Inspector, what do you mean?"

I was standing in Pak's office, wondering what had brought this on. "I mean morning, like now. This is morning, which is when I generally come in to report what happened the day before. So here I am. I came in to give you a report on the meeting I had yesterday with the student. Yesterday afternoon. This"—I pointed out the window at the darkness—"is morning."

Pak waved away the idea of the report. "No, you don't mean morning. Morning is shorthand. What you really mean is that the sun is at a certain spot at or below the horizon, the sky a certain shade, the early breeze bringing the smell of earth, someone groaning after not enough sleep. It's the same with happiness, or sorrow, or boredom, isn't it? All layers, everything layers. Layers and intersections."

I could never fathom what set Pak off like this, climbing to these philosophical heights. Whenever it happened, the only thing to do was to follow along and try not to fall too far behind. "Intersections," I said and nodded, but he wasn't waiting for my reaction. He was already on the ledge above me.

"If you start to strip things down too much, get at their 'essence,' what do you suppose happens?"

This time I didn't bother to nod. It wasn't a real question. Pak pointed a finger at me. "I'll tell you what happens. If we aren't careful, things that matter disappear because we reduce them to bits and pieces, smaller and smaller, to the point where they become nothingness. Abstractions take over. Pretty soon, we start thinking that the only difference between day and night is the amount of light. 'Essence is everything,' people start thinking. So they keep searching for essence, some sort of first principle, but essence isn't anything. Sometimes, it's nothing."

This was fast getting to be unprecedented. A change, not yet defined, was coming over Pak. First he had been unusually confrontational with the special section, and now he was soaring into philosophy, far beyond the boundaries where he usually stopped. In another minute, we might need oxygen bottles, we'd be so high in existential clouds.

If Pak was suffering from the altitude, he didn't show it. "We can say exactly the same about sight," he said, and he smiled expansively. I looked around the office. Was there nothing I could use to slow his ascent? Some sort of cord to keep him from drifting completely beyond the boundaries of space?

"You think you see something, O. No, what you really perceive is movement and change; what you perceive is the changing light, light off one object in relation to something else. If there's no change, if things are totally static, there's nothing to see. That is a fact. Provable fact." That must have been the apogee, because he stopped and leaned back in his chair.

I took a breath. "Then I'm surprised anyone can see around here. Nothing ever changes."

Pak pretended he hadn't heard. He stared out the window into the darkness and the empty courtyard. "It's exactly the same with sound, you know. Constant complaining—almost impossible to hear after a certain point." He swiveled back to his desk and took a piece of paper out of a folder. He studied it a moment. "A woman was murdered last month. We're supposed to find out why." He glanced up to see my reaction. I started to speak, but he cut me off. Pak rarely cuts anyone off; he always defers to another speaker, even when someone interrupts him. "Not 'why,' actually. Not 'why' in the traditional sense. We're just supposed to gather information about her, background, family, friends, political reliability, education. Gather them up, all the things that might have a bearing on the 'why.'"

"Sex life?" Right away I was on guard. Cutting me off was another example of aberrant behavior. He was worried about something. If he wasn't going to share with me what it was, then I'd better worry, too.

Pak observed me with a kind of smoke in his eyes, a hazy, far-off look meant to avoid giving anything away. "If it's relevant, yes."

"You don't think it's relevant?" I never liked it when he gave me that hazy look.

"It might be. But there is a complication."

"A complication. Let me guess. She had odd appetites."

"No, she was murdered overseas."

I gave it some thought. "That's a few hundred kilometers out of my district, isn't it?"

"We have less than a week. They want a nice thick dossier prepared. We hand it over, then it's not our business anymore. It goes to the Ministry, but I have a feeling"—he paused for the downbeat—"I have a feeling it doesn't stop there. You'd better get moving."

"How do we know she was really murdered?" Getting moving, as Pak put it, was not high on my list until he let me know a little more about what I was supposed to do. A person could fall into a deep hole unless he asked question or two before he got moving. "Maybe she just died. People do that."

"We don't know anything other than what it says on this." Pak held up the piece of paper. "I'll assume it's right, and so will you. It doesn't matter anyway. The facts will be the same on this end, no matter what happened to her or if she liked . . ." Pak paused. "It doesn't matter what she liked. All we need is a collection of the facts on this end. That's it. Nothing fancy, no hypothesizing, no grand framework. No essence. Just facts. Fact one, fact two, fact thirty-four. Sweep them up with a broom. Just think of yourself as a broom, Inspector. Now, go sweep. Most of it should be in files somewhere, so you can sit and keep your shoes dry." It was raining again, needle drops with icy tips that clattered against the window. "Don't bet some of the files haven't already been fiddled with, though. And where there are gaps, you'll have to go out and fill them."

"Isn't this a little odd? I can't remember being put on something like this before, worrying with events so far outside our jurisdiction."

"An unquestioning broom, a dumb, unthinking, uncomprehending broom. Shut up and sweep, can't you?"

"You don't think this smells right, I can tell. What do you know that you're not sharing?"

Pak got up and closed the door. When he sat down again, he crossed his arms. It made him look weighty—weighty and obdurate. He wasted another minute or so, hoping I would turn into a broom. I didn't, and finally he shrugged. When I first started to work in Pak's section, I thought that shrug was dismissive, a gesture meant to show that he was top dog and I wasn't. If I wanted to shrug, I thought, I'd have to find someone lower down the chain. Over time, though, I realized it wasn't deliberate and it wasn't aimed at me. It was part of a conversation Pak carried on within himself, an internal argument he had before deciding he didn't want to debate a point anymore. Some people grimace after they've made a decision they don't like. Pak shrugged. "The word is, this isn't just a simple murder. There are overtones. Or undertones. The sort of thing I don't like, and I tried to make the same argument you're making—that it's outside our jurisdiction. No luck."

"Not simple." I moved over to the window. "Murder may be a lot of things, but it's never simple." The icy rain had changed to snow, and would soon be piling up against the three ginkgo trees that stood in the courtyard. Pine trees took winter with a touch of grace. Not the ginkgoes. They endured in a stolid, flinty sort of way, pursed lips, rigid and annoyed. One of the three was sick. It probably wouldn't last much past spring. It would never be replaced. We'd be down to two, and that would change the entire tone of the courtyard, change the light coming into the office, change everything. "You can't nurse a tree," my grandfather would say. "All you can do is say good-bye."

"I don't know how, but the whole thing seems mixed up with that funny group that works out of the party, you know, whatever they call themselves these days," Pak said. "The ones who deal in special weapons, and I don't mean infantry rifles or pistol ammunition. They're hooked up with this somehow, that's what I'm reading between the lines." He held up the paper again. This time I got a better look. There weren't many lines on it.

"Where did this assumed murder take place?"

"How should I know?" Which sometimes meant he knew exactly.

"So, we can assume they don't want us to guess where, and they certainly don't want us to find out. Agreed?"

Pak fiddled with his pencil.

"In this case," I said, "I'm going to take silence as assent. But you must realize, I'll certainly find out sooner or later some of the things we aren't supposed to know. It's inevitable. Maybe even by tomorrow. I mean, it won't be very hard to figure out where she was sent, and if we're unlucky I'll stumble over a lot more."

"You might, unless they've already pulled all of the files, not just fooled with them but pulled them and warned people to clam up."

"No, not 'might.' I will. Even if I try not to, I'll find out. And when I do, we'll know too much, won't we?" It suddenly occurred to me that whoever ordered this assignment either didn't understand much about investigations, or knew more than we realized. First the visitor had showed up, then Mun, and now this.

Pak opened a drawer and took out a piece of paper. "You don't mind if I doodle, do you?"

"You want to know what stinks about this? If it is really connected to that funny weapons group you just mentioned, then the investigation belongs in other circles, not with us. There are plenty of units outside the Ministry to handle something like this. Why not those guerrillas from the special section? It has nothing to do with us, does it, if a woman is killed in Pakistan?"

Pak's pencil stopped on the paper. He looked up and frowned. "Why would you think that?"

"That it has nothing to do with us?"

"Don't be coy, Inspector."

"Pakistan?" I thought about it. "I don't know, no reason, I guess."
Pak didn't look like he was going to take that for an answer.

"Alright, just thinking out loud. Why? Am I getting close?"
Pak's expression didn't change.

"Three Fingers, actually." I really didn't know for sure why I'd mentioned Pakistan. Maybe it was on my mind. Seeing Mun had brought back a lot of memories.

"Is that where he left the other two? Is that where someone didn't prop the door open for you?" His eyes bored into mine. "That's all? Just free association?"

"You mentioned something about special weapons. I've heard a few things about that, not much. When foreign visitors come through my sector, I get reports. I don't file everything I hear, you know that, but lately we've had some curious comings and goings. Even if I look the other way, people like to tell me things. Pakistan keeps coming up in what they say. Special weapons come up sometimes. I figured it was cracked, garbled, I don't know. It's cold and people are hungry, a lot of stuff is going around on the streets. Some people talk more than they used to."

"Forget whatever you've heard; forget it." Pak began to draw jagged lines on the paper. "Inspector, let's not make this any more complicated than it has to be. Empty your pockets of all of this speculation." He glanced up. "Never mind, forget what's in your pockets. You just gather a few facts for us tomorrow. We'll put them on a form, seal it up in a nice new envelope, and drop it into the bureaucratic river that flows through the whole of mankind's existence. It unifies us as a species. I think bureaucracy preceded speech. It may have even preceded sex, normal sex, anyway." He gazed thoughtfully into the courtyard for a moment. "Do us both a favor, O, and for once take my advice: Just be a broom."

"I don't think a broom is what we need."

"You don't." Pak sighed. "Naturally, you don't."

"No, I think we are in the realm of the shovel."

"You planning to dig?"

"If necessary. I do that sometimes, you know."

2

As soon as I knocked on the door, I knew things weren't going right. From inside I could hear sounds, furniture scraping, someone clearing his throat, then footsteps.

"Who is it?" It was a man's voice, an old man. According to the file, this was her father, a widower, a former air force general. Leave it to a general not to open the door. "I said who the hell is it? You hard of hearing?"

"No, sir. I'm just waiting. Would you mind opening the door so we can talk? It's cold in the hall."

Laughter. "Not any warmer in here, sonny." The door opened. He was old, sharp eyes, grizzled is probably the right word for the rest of him. "Say what you want and say it quick. I'm sick." He coughed and wiped his nose with the back of his hand. "Well, say it, what do you want?"

As soon as I'd left Pak's office, I got started on the investigation. I rummaged around in the Ministry's file room, traded an insult or two with the clerks, and then made a list of facts to sweep into a big folder to put on Pak's desk as soon as I could. No shovels, no digging—I heard a little voice repeating. The sooner I start, I told myself, the sooner it's done.

First on the list was the woman's father, the old general. "I've got to ask you a few questions, that's all."

"The hell you do. You tell me who you are first, then we'll decide what comes next."

"Inspector O, Ministry of Public Security. I'm sorry about your daughter, but I have to ask you some questions, General."

He frowned. "You alone?"

"I am."

"Come in. Keep your coat buttoned, it's cold as hell in here." He stood aside, and I walked past him into a dark room.

"Should I open the curtains?" I bumped into a low table. "It will give us some light."

"I don't want any damned light, what do you think about that? I want it dark. I want to sit in the dark and think. That meet with your approval, Inspector?"

"Fine. Mind if I sit?"

"Ask your questions, why don't you?"

I sat down and tried to figure out how to deal with the man. The air in the room was so laden with grief, it was hard to think. I wasn't going to get much out of him, no matter what tack I took, and he wasn't going to give me much time. Since he wouldn't tell me what I needed to know, even if he knew it, I might as well not even bother to ask him directly. Just take it easy, I told myself. Stay in control. "About your daughter. Did you have any communication with her in the last few months?"

"The last few months? No."

"Few means many, several, something more than two but less than six. Does that help?"

"We spoke once or twice."

"On the phone?"

"Stupid question. Yes, on the phone. How else would we speak? Once, she was in an embassy; she called my office. The other time"—he said this very softly—"was from New York. She was real excited. She didn't say much, but I could tell by her voice. She said she was happy. I told her to be careful, to listen to the security people."

An embassy. Well, it was a start. Curious, that hadn't been in any file on her I'd seen so far. No mention of being attached to the Foreign Ministry. "At the embassy, she was happy with the surroundings? Weather was okay, food alright, and so forth?" I didn't want him to realize I had no idea where the embassy was. Maybe it was Pakistan, maybe it wasn't. If he sensed I was guessing, he certainly wouldn't tell me. If he smelled a hunch, he'd smile grimly and sit back, as I imagined he used to do in a roomful of generals—each one suspicious of the next and all of them scared of him. He'd go silent all of a sudden. Nothing would make him open up then. I softened my tone a little. "Did she mention anything that caught your attention? Insects, trees, trouble sleeping? Anything?"

"Pretty fine-grained questions for a cop. You sure you're not one of those security snakes?" I shook my head and pulled out my ID. He didn't bother to look. That wasn't what generals did. Other people, guards at the gate, checked IDs.

"We didn't talk long." He was changing the subject. "She just wanted to know if I would send her something."

"What was that?"

"Got your attention now, don't I?" He went silent, so I waited. I could wait as long as he could. We stared at each other for a couple of long minutes. Finally, he walked into the next room and emerged with a book. "She wanted one of these. One of her books." He held it out for me to see. "Something about music. By the time I found someone to carry it out to her, she was dead." He felt bad about that, I could tell, but he wasn't going to say to me that this or anything else on earth bothered him. "Dead," he said again. "I don't remember where I put the damned book, if that's what you're going to ask me next."

"That's not the book?" I pointed to the one he was holding.

"I told you, I can't find that one now. I put it somewhere when I heard she was dead. I have this one, that's all. It was hers. I look at it sometimes."

Time to change the subject. If he sank any deeper into melancholy, I'd never get him back on dry land. I should have seen it coming as soon as he said he'd told her to be careful in New York. "You still go to the office? I thought you were retired."

"How long you been at this job, Inspector?"

"A while."

"A while. You were in the army?"

"I was."

"They boot you out?" The melancholy had been vaporized.

"No."

"Why'd you leave? Army not interesting enough? Too tough?"

"Maybe I should go out and come back in, so we can start this all over."

"Maybe you should just go out and not come back."

I looked around the room. "No, I don't think so. I think I have some more questions to ask, and I think you're going to answer them."

"If I don't?"

"But you will. Sit down, General. I don't really want to be here, and you don't really want me here, so we're on equal footing. I said sit down."

The old man squinted at me. When he was younger, it was a steely look; now it was just a squint. "You have a hell of a nerve." He paused. "No, I'm not going to sit. But I'll answer three questions. Then you're done. And don't think I'm not serious, because I am. People in the army still stand at attention when I break wind." He grinned. "You want to test me?"

"No. Three questions are fine, for now." I let that sink in for a moment. "First, when you spoke to your daughter, you said she sounded excited. Do you mean agitated? Did she sound worried about anything, anything seem to be bothering her, any concerns she voiced to you about her personal safety? That's all one question, by the way."

"No, she said everything was fine." I thought he might just shrug off the question again, but he seemed to take it seriously. "Something funny that I recall: When she called from New York, she said she'd walked in his footsteps and now she could die happy. That's all she said before we were cut off. The second time, it was a few months later. It wasn't a good connection, but I'd say she sounded tired. Trouble sleeping. The chants or singing, whatever it was, woke her early. It made her edgy, she said, everything being so foreign. One more thing, she said that fool husband of hers was going to get her in trouble with the locals. I'll save you a question. No, she didn't say why and I didn't ask."

"You saved me two."

The old man grunted and walked over to the window. He moved one curtain to the side. The light didn't exactly spill into the room—it was already late afternoon and there wasn't much left—but the gray from outside crept along the walls until I could see that the place hadn't been cleaned in a long time. We fell back into silence. I figured I'd give him a chance to say something else, if that's what he wanted to do.

Finally, I stood and walked to the door. "I have a few other things to check, but I'll be back for the last two questions. If you remember something that you think you ought to tell me, something you forgot, let me know."

"Don't bother coming back. There's nothing else. You'll be wasting your time." He closed the curtain again. "I told her not to get into this stuff, but she wouldn't listen to me."

"What stuff?"

He moved over to the door. "I'm done talking to you, Inspector. Your people want something from me, tell them to put it in writing."

3

I spent the rest of December sweeping up a few inconsequential facts about the woman who had been murdered. Or not murdered. Anything was still possible, based on what little I knew. Maybe she'd just dropped dead. I didn't actually have a single fact about what happened to her, and the paper we had on her case told me exactly nothing. It asserted she'd been murdered. That didn't mean anything to me. But I was starting to lean. That happens sometimes. A few facts here and there, a feeling stirs an intuition, and the next thing that happens, I'm leaning in the direction of a hypothesis.

Her father told me she said she couldn't sleep because of the chanting in the morning. She wouldn't tell him it was the call to prayer, but that's what it could have been. This was circular, I knew. I assumed that what she was complaining about was morning calls to prayer for no good reason other than that Mun had suddenly shown up. Circular logic isn't wrong, it's round. If it was a call to prayers, it could have been any Islamic country, but again, not if I threw Mun into the equation. True, I didn't know where Mun had been for all of these years. I knew where he and I had been, though, and it wasn't a cosmic coincidence that he had suddenly appeared and wanted to talk over "old times" with me. Or that he had showed up just after someone had delivered an Israeli or a Swiss Jew, or whatever Jenö was, on our doorstep. If I had to choose, I'd choose circular logic over cosmic coincidence.

This is how I get when I start to lean, even when I know it would be better to assume things are unconnected. I looked, I swept, I dug into the woman's background, but there wasn't a lot of information about her where there should have been, and every time I found a gap, even a little one, I leaned a little more. She was dead. People had a habit of doing that, and afterward, there were always gaps. Some gaps are natural. That's how people live their lives—gaps, empty places, silences. But not like what this woman left behind.

I had no description of where she'd been when she died, or what time of day it was, or what color clothes she was wearing, or which way her legs crumpled when she hit the ground for the last time, assuming she'd been standing just then, at that moment. If I knew some of that, I might have some sense of where to start filling the gaps. So I dug into holes that already existed, and swept small voids into bigger ones. That's when it hit me, the pattern. Someone had given us this assignment, and then nothing. No pressure to finish the report. None. Mun had showed up out of nowhere, then disappeared again. No more contact. The special section had paid us two visits, and then they were off our backs. Not even a phone call. Gears were turning somewhere and then getting stuck. Not my business why, and as far as I could see, Pak didn't think it was his business, either.

To my surprise, it didn't turn out to be such a bad way to spend the end of the old year and the first weeks of the new one, poking around files, gathering odd facts, staring into the blank spots in the dead woman's life. There wasn't much else to do, and I wasn't in the mood to do nothing. The folder I was supposed to be assembling was still on the thin side, and I was wondering how to make it appear fatter one morning when Pak walked in and dropped some orders on my desk. Normally, he says something when he gives me a set of orders. This time, he walked out again without saying a word. Not happy, I thought as I tore open the envelope.

I read the paper three times before the thought formed clearly in my mind: crazy. I was to go to Beijing to meet Jenö at the airport and escort him back to Pyongyang. It was beyond comprehension, given the thinly veiled—nearly naked, actually—threats from the Man with Three Fingers about how we shouldn't have let Jenö out of the country to begin with. The man had barely got out, and now I was supposed to fetch him back? I walked over to Pak's office and stuck my head in.

"Just do it." He said without looking up. "Don't ask me what is going on. I don't have a clue."

4

At the Beijing airport, Jenö smiled and followed me onto the plane. Considering the run-in we'd had in Pak's office with the special section, the man seemed unnaturally calm, even for him. There wasn't a drop of tension evident in his bearing, no cloud of concern on his brow, no spark of apprehension in his eyes. Someone watching us—and for sure there was someone watching us—would have thought I was more nervous than he was. Neither of us spoke for a while after takeoff. Finally, he looked out the window as the plane banked and the view opened up in a break in the clouds. "More snow than before, a lot more. January must be a bad month here, and it's not even half over." He pointed and his finger tapped the oblong window. "See that?" I leaned over his shoulder. "That's the plane's shadow playing across the ground. The snow is an odd color, isn't it? Looks like butterscotch pudding spilled from the hills."

"I wouldn't know," I said and moved back in my seat. "To me, it looks like pumpkin porridge dripping from the rim of a pot." No one made pumpkin porridge like that anymore. My grandfather made it in the autumn, from pumpkins we gathered off the vines that grew on the fence behind his house. He said he learned to make porridge from his father, and that I should learn it from him. After I moved to Pyongyang, I couldn't get pumpkins. Or when I did, I couldn't find the time.

"Sounds delicious, pumpkin porridge. Can you make it?" Just then the pitch of the engines changed. Jenö glanced around nervously, straining to hear what might come next. The engines dropped back to normal, and he relaxed. "I am very sensitive to sound, Inspector. Some people respond to visual cues. I am hypersensitive to sounds of all types."

"I'll keep that in mind."

"The people behind us, incidentally, are Israeli." This he said in Korean, accented, but perfectly understandable. In fact, too good; it was as if the sound were coming from a machine. It nearly knocked me off my seat.

"You speak Korean? Why didn't you let on before?" I had meant that to come out as complimentary, but the annoyance was quicker on its feet.

"Surprised? Your language isn't so difficult, no worse than Hungarian. Besides, they're related. Come to think of it, maybe we're related. Wouldn't that be something? Ancient brothers from tribes that wandered apart in the misty past."

"I don't think so. I don't like paprika."

The trolley with drinks stopped beside us. The stewardess looked down at me. Why don't these good-looking girls work in my office, even near my office? I thought. Why are they confined to this ancient Russian tube ten thousand meters above the earth? Jenö nudged my arm. "Don't pant. Just tell her what you want."

"Nothing." I nodded to the stewardess. "Nothing for me. Perhaps our guest would like something, though. Go ahead, ask him in Korean. Or Hungarian. No, wait, try Hebrew."

"You really shouldn't refuse me, Inspector," the girl tossed her head back, just a little, just enough to notice, then she smiled at the foreigner. "Drink?" she asked in English.

He took a cup of tea; the trolley moved on. I looked around the cabin and then settled back. I closed my eyes, pretending I was some-where pleasant. An elbow nudged me.

"I'd rather not be poked," I said. "Please, don't poke me like that, I don't care whether we are tribesmen or not."

He paid no attention. "You might get up and stroll into the first class cabin. There are some interesting passengers beyond the curtain. You'll find three more, just like that group behind us. Say 'shalom' to them and watch their eyes pop out." I didn't move. "Go ahead, have some fun, what can it hurt?" He poked me. "Eh?"

I sat up. All of a sudden, existence was awash in Israelis. A few weeks ago, I'd never met one in my life. Now they had me surrounded on, of all places, an airplane. I wondered if they were planning to hijack the plane. These were the people who had carried off Entebbe. They were larger than life, tougher than nails. I didn't like traveling by air in the first place; I hadn't wanted to go on this assignment to Beijing; and now I was being poked relentlessly, surrounded by a commando flying squad.

"I'm not going up to first class," I said. "I never walk on an airplane when it's aloft. It's not right. Movement could disturb the balance, or the trim—whatever it is."

"You don't go to the toilet?"

"I make it a point to take short flights."

"How about standing? Can you at least stand?"

"Standing is possible, as long as it is done gently," I said. I stood up carefully and looked back at the trio seated three rows behind us. Business suits, European, but slightly off. They were reading papers in an alphabet I'd never seen.

Jenö reached over and tugged at my jacket. "The papers are in Hebrew. They think no one can understand. Classified documents, I'll bet."

I sat down again. "You know these people, I take it. And the ones up front, too?"

"Not personally, I don't know them." His eyebrows went into the first few steps of a gavotte and then stopped, as if the orchestra had abruptly gone out for a smoke. "I heard them talking while we were in line at the check-in counter. They're from the Foreign Ministry, apparently. Chatting away, making snide comments, convinced no one could possibly understand Hebrew. Can you believe it? What are they coming for, do you think?"

"How should I know? And if I were you, that would be the least of my concerns. You're in enough trouble. The real question is not why they are on the airplane." Actually, that *was* a real question, it just didn't bear on my immediate problem. "The real question is, why are you coming back? And why the hell didn't you let on before that you knew Korean? It would have saved me having to translate through frozen lips when we were in that hut in the mountains." I shut my eyes again. There were two questions that loomed, and I had no doubt that if I ever found the answers, they would be intertwined. First, exactly what I asked him—why was he coming back? And second, which was my problem more than his—who approved the visa after the trouble we had keeping him safe from the special section last time? A normal person wouldn't want to come back. A normal visa request after what had happened would have been turned down instantly. It would have provoked gales of laughter before being stamped: DENIED. This return trip wasn't normal in any respect. It even went beyond abnormal. So where did that leave me, other than accompanying a foreigner on the wrong side of unfathomable?

Jenö unleashed the familiar smile. "No games, Inspector. I appreciate your coming to get me, but it was unnecessary. I don't need an escort; no one is going to touch a hair on my head." The pitch of the engines changed abruptly again, too abruptly for him, because he paled and gripped the armrest. Apparently, he hadn't been at Entebbe.

"Don't let it worry you," I said. What happened to his hair would get sorted out after we landed. "Probably just some dirt in the fuel line. It usually clears." I watched him pale a little more before poking his shoulder. "Look, would I be here if I thought there was any danger? Don't worry. This plane is indestructible. If it hasn't crashed by now, it never will—that's what you have to keep telling yourself. Don't pay so much attention to sounds. You have to train yourself not to hear things sometimes. Like the thudding of Cossack hoofs."

"Very stoic." His voice was a little strained; maybe he was low on those silk pills he took every morning, or whatever it was that kept his voice so damned smooth. He craned his neck to look out the window.

"Do you want to switch seats?" I said. "You'll feel better if you don't have to look at the earth. It confuses the horizon, makes you dizzy when we bank or go bump."

"Not at all. I just hate landings. Do you mind if I shut my eyes and sweat for the next twenty minutes until we're on the ground?"

"Suit yourself." The landing gear made a loud thump, and the pilot pushed the plane into attack mode. I checked to make sure the wings were attached, and spent the rest of the way down wondering how big a crowd from the special section was already assembled on the tarmac.

5

The next morning, Pak sat at his desk and pulled his ear. "This is complicated. No, I'm wrong, it's not complicated. That's too simple. It's unbelievable, completely unbelievable." He shook his head. "I still don't believe it. Tell me you are joking, Inspector."

"I stick to facts, and the facts are these. The first group, in the front of the plane, didn't know the second group was in the back, and vice versa. They come from separate parts of the Israeli government. They don't communicate, very secretive; one hand doesn't know what the other is doing, if you can believe that sort of thing happens."

"So what are we supposed to do? Keep them apart? Bring them together? Put out name cards in the hotel dining room so they don't get mixed up and share a table with each other?" Pak motioned for me to sit down, but I didn't want to. If I sat, we'd start talking about things we shouldn't be discussing. Inevitably, the subject of how bad things were in the countryside would come up, people moving without permits to find food, bodies on the side of the road, trains with old women riding on the roofs of the railway cars and falling off. We'd talk, one thing would lead to another, and we'd both be depressed for the rest of the day.

"I'm not going to worry about their seating arrangements," I said. "Let whoever signed for them at the airport clean up the mess. We have one visitor to look after, and that's enough for me."

"Even one is too many. I don't have the manpower for visitors of any stripe. I don't have any manpower at all. You're supposed to be putting together a file on that woman. It should have been ready a week ago. I haven't even seen a draft, not a word."

"I'm not the one who okayed the orders for me to fly to Beijing in the middle of everything."

That was unfair; Pak hadn't wanted me to go. "People do write on airplanes, you know, Inspector. They have those little trays that come down. I've seen them."

"I thought you didn't like to fly." I started edging toward the door.

"I don't. I had to board a plane at Sunan once to search for something." He turned the memory over in his mind. "Never found it."

"Maybe some people can write on airplanes; not me. I can't even think on a plane. Something about the noise and that sense of being disconnected from the earth. I'm not one of those people who likes to hurtle through the air."

"You sleep?"

"Sleep? Don't be crazy. I concentrate." Pak looked dubious. "The engines need a lot of attention. Sometimes I concentrate on the wings, but mostly the engines. At that height, you don't take anything for granted. There's no way I could work on finishing up the file. Besides, the stewardesses are always interrupting, going up and down the aisle."

"Brushing against you, I suppose. You got an aisle seat, naturally."

"They're assigned." Pak's face indicated he was dubious. "I could keep better control of him from the aisle seat." Pak remained silent. "Okay, yes, the stewardesses are friendly girls."

"I leave such things to you, Inspector. Now, when do I get that report?"

"After someone tells me what to do with our visitor."

"He stays with you. That's why you were sent to get him."

"Did you know that no one from the special section was around to meet us at the airport? They weren't even lurking in the shadows. The dogs have been called off. Even the immigration people didn't blink twice when he came through. Don't tell me they hadn't been alerted."

"Apparently not."

"So you are going to try to convince me that this is all normal?"

"No. I don't know what normal is anymore. Do you?"

Discussions about normality were out of bounds as far as I was concerned. I didn't care about normality right now. My priority was to get rid of this foreigner. I needed to hand him off to some other section and then get out of the way before they knew what hit them. For that, I needed some facts, not the least of which was who had approved the reentry visa. I didn't care if Pak wouldn't always tell me what was going on, as long as he knew. But in this case, he didn't know. The news about the two Israeli delegations had surprised him. If Pak was surprised, it meant we didn't know where we were going, how far away from the edge of the cliff we might be.

"By the way, our visitor has a long list of places he wants to go," I said. "He gave it to me while we were waiting for the bags. Some of his requests are way over on the east coast. And I don't mean places for sightseeing. He doesn't care about Kangwon and snowy peaks. He's interested in North Hamgyong. He asked if I knew anything about Hwadae county." As soon as I heard myself say that, I knew where the edge of the cliff was.

"Really?" Pak also sensed a cliff. "How interesting. Is there anything else we can get for him? Caviar, perhaps? A harem? Do you think he knows he has to pay double for a car this time of year, and that he can't drive himself anymore? A driver will cost more than the car. Assuming I can even get him a car. Assuming, of course, I can get him a driver from somewhere for a car that probably doesn't exist. Believe me, he's absolutely not getting our last and only duty driver, not if I can help it. And you can be sure he's not going anywhere near Hwadae county."

For some reason, I decided to ask a completely pointless question. "Something going on up there?" Of course something was going on, why else would anyone want to go to North Hamgyong, especially in January?

"Nothing either of us needs to know about."

"But he does?" Another pointless question, but one that, I had no doubt, would eventually need an answer.

"I'm not going to start guessing about his agenda," Pak said, "and neither should you. Don't let me hear that you've started checking around, either. Stay away from the subject. Our visitor isn't getting out of the city, not unless he can pay off a lot of people. I don't care who he has behind him." He stopped. That was all he wanted to say about what or who we couldn't see. "At the moment, the man is not a police matter. We are assigned to wipe his nose if he sneezes, that's all. Anyway, the roads are piled with snow and no one is around to clear them these days, which for a change is a blessing. If he asks again, tell him about the bad road conditions."

"None of that will worry him. He can pay off whoever he needs for permission and still have enough left to pay his own road crew. He has plenty of money, a wad of dollars. I saw it, and I don't think he declared it all when he came through customs."

"How much has he offered you?"

"Nothing. I think he's waiting for me to ask."

"So ask."

"Maybe later, not yet. I still have some dignity left."

"That's good. Dignity is good. See how much rice your dignity will get you."

I kicked myself for standing around and talking. The conversation had just lurched onto the subject I most wanted to avoid. Pak frowned. "You know, this morning I ran across an old friend in the Ministry, someone who has been stuck in the mountains in Yanggang for the past year. He looks like a skeleton."

"That bad?" I could sense huge cloudbanks of depression looming over us.

"It's worse than bad."

"Construction unit?"

"Not anymore. The unit was so depleted they had to disband it. Everyone was out looking for food. He told me that the country- side . . ." Pak shook his head again. "It's bad. Very bad."

I sat down. We were in the thick of it; there was no sense trying to avoid the subject anymore. "Are you alright? I mean, the family?" Pak had a young son. His wife was sick, and his mother was getting weaker by the day.

Pak stared out his window. The view was enough to depress any- body, especially in the middle of winter. "Two meals a day, very healthy. Isn't that what they say on the radio? If two is healthy, what do we call one meal a day? Or does hot water count as nourishment now?"

"I hear that the radio doesn't operate in the provinces most of the time. Not enough fuel for the generators. Not enough technicians left to fix the transmitters that still have fuel."

"Careful what you repeat, Inspector," Pak said quietly. Then even more quietly, "Most of the time, neither do the trains. Almost nothing moves out there these days."

"And?" The situation in the countryside was not a secret; the local security offices had stopped trying to prevent the stories from circulat- ing. One Ministry officer who was in town to plead for backup support told me it was like trying to blot out the sun with a rat's turd. When I told him to come up with a better image, he grinned quickly. "It's a joke, Inspector. We've eaten all the rats. There aren't any rat turds left."

"And?" I repeated the question.

"And, and we do what we do," Pak said. His voice was back to nor- mal. "That's all there is to it. A couple of the other districts in Pyongyang are running short on people; some of the shifts have been lengthened." I'd heard officers were disappearing for days at a time without notice, looking for food, sick from the cold, but there was no use mentioning it. Pak cleared his throat and looked away. "You going or staying?" He didn't want to ask because he didn't want to make me answer. Just posing the question was an admission of where things stood.

"I'm here, aren't I?"

He nodded slowly. I didn't say anything else, and neither did he. In the silence, there was no doubt we were both thinking the same thing. I knew better than to mention it, but I kept wondering. Suddenly, I realized Pak was looking at me in horror, because I had just said it out loud.

"Is he going to make it?" The words hung in the cold air. In summer they might have vanished quickly, but in the cold they lingered, fed on each other, grew like a wave that swells until it swallows the sky.

Or maybe I didn't really say the words; maybe it was just that my lips moved. "Is he going to make it?" Even if it's just your lips moving over that question, it booms around the room. Loud enough to rattle the windows, and paint itself on the walls so that anyone who comes in a week later will see it.

He. Him.

With a slight lifting of the eyebrows, say *"him"*—no one had any doubt that you meant the new leader, still mourning his father as the rest of us drifted. We all knew that we were drifting, and we knew where. A nation of shriveled leaves floating on a doomed river toward the falls. A winter of endless sorrow.

The horror on Pak's face dissolved again into weariness. I knew his body was soaked in fatigue, functioning on momentum, getting up each morning with regret that morning had come at all, not knowing why each new day arrived, unbidden. Each night he fell asleep while he posted the signs on the four corners of the darkness, "Tomorrow is canceled, please, no more. No more." But dawn ignored the pleas, dawn brought nothing, no hope, no light, nothing but a selfish insistence that it would inflict itself, empty-handed, the burden of new hours grinding down even the strongest until they imagined death itself had abandoned them, taking friends and family but leaving them.

I lived alone, but loneliness was no burden, not like people sometimes imagined. It was a matter of indifference to me if a new day came. Dawn brought nothing, but I didn't care. If the new light of day had ever meant anything, I had forgotten what it was.

"How is your mother?" I asked Pak. Once, that was a simple question, a question from normal times, when the answer was normal, in a normal conversation. It wasn't simple now, but if I didn't ask it, it would mean there was nothing left for us to hold from before. It used to be a simple question because the answer was simple. No more.

Now, Pak might tell me to mind my business. If he was as weary as he looked at this moment, he might simply walk out the door, down the stairs, and never come back. I waited, and the waiting spoke to how far from normal we had drifted. He sat and didn't answer, not with words, not with a gesture, not with his posture. That void told me what he didn't have the will to say. No, he wouldn't leave. He wouldn't leave, though there were people we both knew who had done that, leaving family, leaving everything, walking into the cold and disappearing. A query would come down from the Ministry once a month—"Where is so-and-so? Anyone with information about so-and-so should report immediately to the chief of personnel," which was almost funny because the chief of personnel had disappeared. Someone had been assigned his job but not given the title lest that person disappear, too, and the job have to be filled again.

"She rarely eats." If he was going to stay, he had to speak. He knew it. He had to talk to other people and read his files and draw one breath after another. "She says her food should go for the boy. We've argued until I can't say the words anymore."

"I have more than I can use."

"No, Inspector, you don't. I need you healthy."

"Just let me know." He nodded. That meant the subject was closed, and it was time to move things back to business. If you had to breathe, you might as well get back to business. "That background report may be delayed a little more," I said. "Some of the people I have to interview in order to finish it aren't around."

There it was again. I didn't say where they had gone. I didn't have to. Pak knew what I meant. I could see in his eyes what he was thinking. He was imagining what he would never do, being one of the gone. Leaving everything, avoiding tomorrow.

6

After a session like that with Pak, I wasn't going to my office and stare at the walls. A long walk would do me good. If it got cold enough as the sun went down, it would drive everything from my mind. I could get back to the office after dark, finish a little paperwork, and then go home.

"Don't take my car," Pak said. "I need it later to get to some meetings. Take the duty vehicle. It's back from repair, guaranteed to start. Just in case, don't go too far."

The Potong River wasn't too far, and I liked walking there. By then, there wasn't much left of the afternoon. It turned to dusk, but dusk didn't hang around; nothing wanted to linger at this time of year. That was why I didn't see her coming.

"Hello, Inspector."

"Hello, yourself." There wasn't much else to say. She was the last person I expected to run across. Then it occurred to me, maybe it was fate. Why not? I was due for some fate. "I was just thinking about you."

"Is that so?"

"I've been wondering, what if I want a transfer?"

"Something wrong between you and Pak? You finally exhausted his patience? The man has a reservoir of patience deeper than the ocean, but you have drained it."

"No, Pak is fine, still putting up with me. I'm just thinking ahead. A whole career in Pyongyang, it might not look so good when it comes time for my promotion."

"If either of us lives that long. Face it, you're not ever going to be promoted, O. Besides, when did you start craving advancement? 'Don't make the offer,' you said the last time the subject came up. 'I won't take it. I'm fine where I am.'"

She was a woman I'd met in the army; "an old friend" is how I described her to people when they asked. A few years ago, she had been made a deputy in the Ministry's personnel section. It was her chief who had disappeared. The whole section had been put on report for not predicting that the boss was going to defect. No one knew for sure if he had defected, but he was gone, and it was pretty clear he wasn't on vacation in Cuba.

With the day finished, the temperature was looking for a place to spend the night. It would be good if we could go to her office to talk. As head of the section, she'd likely have some heat. If anyone had heat, she would. No one wanted the acting chief of personnel in a bad mood, whether she was on report or not. Little presents came her way, small bags of rice, pieces of fruit. She also had a lot of people slithering under her door in hopes of getting a good assignment. I wasn't one of them. Once, we had been very close, but things had changed. I had forgotten why.

"Well, then," I said, "let's just pretend. If I *was* going to get promoted, wouldn't I need to serve outside of Pyongyang?"

"What is this about? I don't have time for games, O, not these days. They're crawling up our backsides, trying to figure out where he went."

"I assume that's the one place he isn't." I smiled in the dark; she looked at me with ice in her eyes. Even in the blackness, I could see that. That look, it started to jar loose in my memory what had gone wrong. "Let's just say I wanted the toughest, most undesirable post you could find. Let's say I got headquarters really mad at me, and they decided it was time to exile Inspector O to teach him a lesson. Where would they send me?"

"You don't want to go to North Hamgyong, and I'm not sending you. It's suicide these days. You never struck me as suicidal. Obtuse and heartless maybe, but not suicidal. This isn't about postings. What is it?"

"I need your help."

"You need my help, you bastard?" She laughed, the way an axe laughs at a piece of kindling. "After all this time, you knock on my door and say you need my help? How, specifically?"

"Hwadae county." Might as well get straight to the point. Romancing her up to the question clearly wasn't going to work.

"Are you crazy?" She considered. "No, you're not crazy, you scheming bastard. I'll tell you what I should do. I should put you in the coldest, deadliest, sickest, hungriest place I can find. I should make you a mine guard, a camp guard." She took a deep breath. "I might still do that, don't push your luck. But I won't send you to Hwadae."

"I don't want to be assigned there. I need to know what's going on."

"Of course you do. Every crummy sector cop in the capital needs to know what is happening in an isolated, out-of-bounds county on the east coast." She snorted, which was never her best noise. "Don't ask me. It's military, and they keep us out. That's all I know, and if I knew anything else, you're the last person in the world I would tell." She was lying, very openly, which was the only way she could tell me what I wanted to know. Amazing! As angry as she seemed to be after all of these years, she was willing to help. Maybe she still liked me. Not bad, having a chief in the personnel section, even an acting chief, with the hots for you. It was more than I had a right to ask; but it was exactly what I needed.

"There's a visitor who wants to go there," I said and put my step in cadence with hers. "Body rhyming," we used to call it when we went for walks. That popped into my memory from somewhere. I shut the door in a hurry. "Should I take him?"

"You couldn't get him past the first barrier. He'd need special orders. So would you, incidentally. A Ministry ID doesn't go as far as it used to."

"He's an Israeli."

I could tell that stunned her. She took a half step out of rhythm and then stopped abruptly. "Well, well, well. He'll have some interesting company if he gets in there." No reason she should know about a visitor under our protection, but still, it surprised me that she didn't. I would have thought the news had gone up and down the corridors by now.

"Interesting company?" I thought my voice had just the right lilt of disinterest. "Like who?"

"Maybe Pakistanis. Maybe Iranians. Maybe Bolivians."

"Bolivians?" It was hard to sound uninterested.

"Why not? If I were from Bolivia, I'd want missiles to protect me against Venezuela."

"Venezuela isn't near Bolivia."

"My mistake." She walked away, down the path to a waiting car. Her engine probably got maintained pretty regularly.

7

I didn't go back to the office as I'd planned. I needed to walk a little more in the dark, maybe head to the Koryo and let my thoughts fall into some sort of order. I made a mental list. The Man with Three Fingers, the general's dead daughter, a Swiss-Hungarian-Jew with a wad of dollars, and now, to top it all off, two Israeli delegations falling over each other. None of them had anything to do with Bolivia, but I'd bet they were all linked. Timing had everything to do with it. Pak hated it when I fell back on timing to explain a hunch. I never much liked it, either. The only thing I liked less than timing as an explanation was coincidence, cosmic or not. Even if I could accept coincidence now and then, there was no way that could cover two Israeli delegations. I thought about this for a while—whether timing meant something or whether it meant nothing—and then I realized I was completely alone. No one else was on the path; there was barely anyone around. It wasn't that late; there should be at least a few people still outside, hurrying home. The city had become eerie, much too quiet. There was no pulse left, no spark. The stores were empty, the streets were deserted. The whole way over to the Koryo, I kept wondering where the hole was that had swallowed the population. By the time I got to the hotel, I was practically frozen.

Once my fingers thawed, I found a phone and called up to Jenö's room. "I made it here, barely. Meet me in the coffee shop. I'll be the one pouring hot water over his head."

I was the only customer, so I picked the warmest-looking table and sat down.

Jenö showed up a few minutes later. He didn't even say hello. "How did the first group react when it found out about the other one?" It sounded like the beginning of a bad joke. The two Israeli delegations were staying in the hotel, but apparently he was steering clear.

"I haven't talked to them."

"You must have seen a report."

"Let's just say one of them spit bullets and the other two laughed until they cried."

Jenö leaned back and smiled, content. It seemed a good time to break the news to him.

"All your requests for meetings have been denied," I said matter-of-factly. We weren't on a beach. We were both wearing our overcoats. The coffee had gone cold almost immediately, not that it mattered. "All denied but one. You can go to the Trade Ministry tomorrow morning, assuming there's someone around to meet you. It's only a five-minute car ride from here. Other than that, you're allowed to wander around within the four walls of this building. You can look closely at the hotel lobby. When you get tired of that, you have permission to stare at the television in your room. As a fallback, go up and down in the elevator a few times."

"I protest."

"Then look out the window if you'd rather. I think you can see the train yard, or at least the tracks. I doubt you'll see a train."

"I mean about the appointments. I didn't risk that plane ride just to sit around this depressing hotel."

"Oh, really. You don't like the Koryo? It's not bad, once you get used to it. Besides, no one twisted your arm to come back. Why did you? We had a hell of a time getting you out safely the first time. You must realize by now that there are people who would like to get their hands on you. I'm still wondering how you got another visa."

"You don't know?"

"My Ministry doesn't issue visas. If we did, you wouldn't have one."

"I have money, Inspector. Your government is in rather desperate need. Tab A, slot B, so to speak."

"Well, your tabs don't seem equally compelling to everyone, as far I can tell. Your requests for meetings are denied. I'm supposed to make sure nothing happens to you, and the best way to do that is to keep you here."

"I see. Perhaps you are the one who has denied my requests?" The man looked off into space; his eyebrows twitched thoughtfully. "It really doesn't matter where I have my meetings, you know. People can come here. It's warm, relatively speaking. We can sit and talk, drink tea, have something to eat." He put his hand on my shoulder and his eyes lit up. "Brilliant idea, Inspector, brilliant. I should have thought of it myself. If I can't go to them, they'll be happy to come to me, right?"

"When do your friends leave?"

"Those two delegations? They aren't my friends. We have different goals, very different. I want to make money. They think I cooperate too much with people who should be stepped on."

"They think we should be stepped on?"

"They did think that before, but now they seem to have changed their minds. That's why they're coming by the planeload to see your officials."

"And what changed their minds?"

He shrugged and then smiled. It was one of those charming smiles that put my hackles on red alert. "That isn't something I would know, now is it? I just want to make some money."

I relaxed a little, it was so ridiculous. "Are you kidding? Money? Here?"

"Sure, why not? You have workers; they know how to obey orders. They're educated and can be trained. I've heard from others who have set up shop here that there are ways of making things work. If you had roads and electricity, I could be the richest man on earth." He paused. "But I can make do with a lot less. What sense is there in being the richest man on earth? A lot of unhappiness is all it brings. You ever hear of King Midas?"

"I slept through the English history classes."

He smiled. "Only one thing I need."

"Sorry, I already told you, your requests for meetings have been denied."

"I heard." He put a hundred-dollar bill on the table, stood up, and walked past the girl at the front counter without paying.

8

The next morning, we met in the lobby. It was so cold the staff all wore overcoats with the collars up and, if they had them, scarves. "Someone from the party will see you at ten o'clock," I said after we shook hands.

"What about the Trade Ministry?"

"It was decided you don't require anyone from the ministries. The party will do fine for your needs."

"And what are my needs?

"That is what you'll explain this morning when you meet someone from the party."

"I suppose this means you are no longer assigned to look after me. So, good-bye, Inspector, thank you for your help."

As we shook hands again, his eyes widened slightly when he felt the bill in my palm.

"You accidentally left something on the table yesterday," I said.

His hand went into his pocket. "It's not polite to refuse a present from a visitor. Every culture has that as a basic rule."

"Perhaps, but I heard somewhere to beware of Greeks bearing gifts. We don't see many Greeks," I said, "so I assumed that went for the Swiss as well."

He smiled, not the charming one.

"Maybe even Pakistanis." It didn't mean anything, or maybe it did. Pakistan was on my mind. Not on my mind, exactly, but just below the surface. Ever since my old friend the acting personnel chief had let me know that someone from Pakistan had gone to Hwadae county, I'd heard a rustling in my subconscious, something stirring, a Siberian wind blowing dead leaves along the frozen ground. Hwadae county was off-limits; we were supposed to report anyone overheard saying anything about the place. It was supposed to be a big secret that things to do with missiles went on up there, but plenty of people had relatives, who had friends, who knew former army buddies who drank too much and said something they weren't supposed to when their heads were lolling and their tongues were loose. If someone from Pakistan had gone to Hwadae, then it wasn't so far-fetched that the special section might have an unusual interest in what happened to a certain Korean woman who died in Pakistan—and something kept telling me that my first wild hunch had been completely right, it had been Pakistan. In the great wide world somewhere else, that might be a stretch. Not here, not in my little corner of reality.

Jenö didn't say anything when I mentioned Pakistanis, but the half-smile normally on his lips vanished into the cold. In that instant, he told me just what I needed to know. I left before his eyebrows slow-danced back into place.

9

After I left Jenö, I sat in the duty vehicle for a few minutes with the engine running and the heater on. Now I was pretty sure she worked at the embassy in Pakistan, or at least found access to a phone there. It was still officially a hunch, but it had become one of those hunches that don't want to get crowded out by other possibilities. Yes, if Pak wanted to argue I'd have to admit it might have been somewhere else; I couldn't prove she'd been in Islamabad. Actually, I wasn't even supposed to prove it; I wasn't supposed to worry about it. It wasn't the sort of fact the broom was supposed to sweep. If the Man with Three Fingers hadn't turned up and sneered, I might have dropped the whole thing, but I didn't want to leave another body lying around my conscience.

The problem was, where to go next? Her husband had an assignment, but doing what? For whom? Her father said she'd complained he was going to get her into trouble. If she was just a wife, how could he get her into trouble with the locals? It wasn't beyond possibility that she had an assignment, too. And if she'd had an assignment, maybe it was connected with why she turned up dead. In that case, there was only one place to begin checking—the Foreign Ministry. It wasn't somewhere I liked to go, but they usually had hot water for tea.

Outside it was frigid but clear, so I decided to leave the car at the hotel and walk. The less I had to drive on slick streets, the better I liked it. There were a few other people out walking, and even a couple of old trucks on the road. I watched them go by, which may be why I didn't notice that the sidewalk down the hill hadn't been cleared. Just as my feet left the ground, an army jeep coming up the hill spun its wheels and slid sideways into a nearby snowdrift. The driver climbed out and looked around. He spotted me on the ground.

"You! Give me a hand." It was an officer, a colonel. Just like I remembered from the army, a colonel always shows up when you least need him. When I didn't move, he bristled. "I said give me a hand. I haven't got all day."

Inquiring why he didn't have a driver didn't seem like a good idea, certainly not while I was on my back. I stood up slowly, careful not to slip again. "I'm on duty, Colonel, and on assignment." It was an assignment I'd given myself, but what the hell. "I'll give you a push, and maybe you can drive me where I need to go. It isn't far."

That bargain didn't seem to go down. "You think you can refuse a direct order from an officer of the People's Army these days? I can have you arrested. I can even have you shot. I can do it myself, if I've a mind."

"You want help on your jeep or don't you?" My feet were getting cold, and my back was sore. If I didn't get somewhere warmer soon, it would stiffen up and I would be hunched over until spring. I wasn't about to stand and argue for a whole afternoon, even a short one in January, with a colonel who didn't rate a driver. He might have me shot, but he didn't look the type to do it himself, certainly not here. There was more and more talk that the army had made a grab for extra status, but that still didn't dictate executing police in broad daylight with no one else in sight. Make sense, you strutting bastard, I thought to myself. Why shoot a monkey to scare the chickens if there are no chickens around to see you do it? Or was it the other way around?

The drive to the Foreign Ministry took less than two minutes. We roared up to the front steps so quickly it startled the sentry, who unfastened the holster at his hip and reached for his pistol. I was barely out of the jeep when the colonel backed into the street at high speed and slid into the square before he regained control, hurrying off in a spray of ice and snow.

The guard had seen me before. He didn't want to move again because if he did, it would disturb the warmth of the posture he had settled into. He flicked his eyes to the door. I went in and up the stairs to the liaison office. I didn't knock.

"Inspector!" The liaison officer had a small electric heater on. That was illegal, but warm. He nodded for me to come over and share the heat. "Is this a pleasant surprise, or have you arrested someone who is going to cause us trouble of a diplomatic sort?"

"I'm on heater patrol."

"Well, you came to the right place." The lights flickered once, then went out. So did the heater. "Funny," he said, "the other day on the radio they announced that the electricity workers had overfulfilled this month's quota."

"Perhaps they were rewarded with today off."

We stood around in the dark, wondering how long it would last this time. Sometimes it was only a few seconds; sometimes it was longer. A few people kept candles in their desks. Apparently, he wasn't one of those. "Don't move, Inspector," he said very softly. "If you move, you'll dissipate the warm air. Just stand still and let it waft slowly up to the ceiling. If we're lucky, Mr. Shin downstairs will do the same, and his heat will be arriving through the floor just as ours goes up to Miss Ban. Imagine the heat going up her legs, will you?"

"I'll do no such thing." I thought about it for a moment, and as I did, the lights went back on. "There, back from vacation. They probably just went out to read the paper. I need a favor—only you owe me, so it really isn't a favor. It's more like payment."

He rubbed his face with both hands, as if he were washing something away, maybe the memory of the last time I had twisted his arm behind his back to give me information. "Very well, though I don't recall your doing anything for me lately."

"Are you going to make me pull your cousin's file again? Selling copper from downed electric lines is still a capital crime."

"What is it I can do for you, Inspector?"

"I need a few facts, that's all."

He was impassive. Finally, he stirred. "If I can."

Just then the lights flickered again, but this time the heater stayed on. "It's the wiring," he said. "The heater draws too much power. You know what they say about this ministry—more heat than light. I'll have to jiggle something."

Maybe people said that about every ministry. "Forget the wires and the cute slogans. I need a woman."

The liaison man looked up, presumably to where Miss Ban sat. "You'll have to get in line, Inspector."

"No, I need information on a woman, a particular woman. She worked in the embassy in Pakistan until recently. Or possibly her husband did. One of them did, anyway. Before that she was in New York." Admittedly, I still didn't know for sure she had even been in Pakistan, but I felt as sure as I could be based on nothing more than a hunch. What I needed was a piece of paper that had it down in black and white. It did no harm to offer up what I thought I knew. If I was wrong, this man would be happy to say so. If I was wrong, I wanted him to smirk and jump in to correct me before he had a chance to realize that maybe it wasn't something he was supposed to do. It was different with the old general. They were like two trees that reacted differently to the same breeze.

"She has a name, I assume."

I wrote it down and pushed it over the desk. He looked, then blew out a puff of air. "A person of interest, apparently. Someone already came and took away her file."

"You saw it before it disappeared?"

"I didn't read it."

"You looked at it; it happened to open as you were retrieving it, and you happened to see something?"

"Some files have clasps on them. This one didn't."

I nodded. "What about the husband?"

"That will take me a while. It's hard to search files when the lights go on and off."

"Give me a call when you find something. If you don't call, I'll be back when you don't expect me, and I might have some wire cutters with me next time." He recoiled slightly. "Find a flashlight somewhere in this building. There's enough light to see the files with that. Maybe Miss Ban can help."

He looked up at the ceiling, but I couldn't see his expression because the lights flickered again and then gave way to the dark. I saw myself out.

10

"Are you actually so at ease with yourself, Inspector? I wonder if you are; or is it that you are as completely empty as always, void of all feeling?" My old friend the acting chief of personnel sat in my office. She didn't have the air of someone who had the hots for me. Her question might have been the start of a late-night argument, just like old times, but it was only noon. It should have been a warning when she called and said she needed to come over. So why did I ignore the warning, the ominous tingle in my spine? Maybe I was distracted by the glare of the sun off the snow on the street outside my window. If I had been wearing my sunglasses, the glare wouldn't have bothered me. If I'd had on my sunglasses when she walked in and sat down, I could have looked directly in her face and she couldn't have seen into my soul, where I was surprised to discover she still lurked. I would have had time to stop myself, to keep my mouth shut. "Me? Ill at ease?" I turned and did the only thing I could. I laughed.

She smiled, and I suddenly remembered she had several. One of them was real, pure starlight and moonbeams. This wasn't it. "Happy to see me again so soon?" She could keep her tone eerily even, the same calm surface that killer sharks love to cruise beneath. She did it before she ripped you apart, tore huge chunks out of your existence before you had time to shout for help. Even now, when her tone was so deadly flat, her face was round and her cheeks dimpled. The smile might be unreal, but the dimples weren't. The dimples killed me. They were mantraps.

All the conversations we'd ever had came back at me. On our walk the other day, I only remembered a few things, snatches of emotions. Now, with her sitting so close, everything was accessible. I frantically rewound all the tapes in my head, trying to remember with precision, to wade through the flood of memory onto something solid, to someplace where I couldn't see her dimples. She didn't help; she just sat and looked into my eyes. Walking beside the river, putting our steps in rhyme, I didn't really have to look at her. Anyway, she had been all business. Mostly all business. But now she was across from me, looking into my eyes. She read everything. Nothing escaped her. That was always the problem. That's probably why they put her in personnel.

There had been a time when I considered poking them out, my eyes, so she couldn't read me. It was the only solution that I could think of short of killing myself, which I didn't want to do at the time. Now this. First the Man with Three Fingers reappears, and now this. I should have done it; I should have poked my eyes out when I had the chance.

"No," I said and should have left it at that, but with her, I couldn't leave things. When she sat there, dimples and all, I was compelled. "I mean, yes, of course I'm happy to see you." I hoped that was all my eyes were saying. "Yes and no." I was talking too much. "No, I'm not empty. I just learned to let go."

"Really? And where did you learn that? After all those years, where did you learn that?"

"Self-taught. Maybe it comes with age." I stared at my hands. They seemed familiar, which was a relief. "You look good. It's nice to see you again. So soon, I mean. Twice in so short a time."

"You're a liar. I could always tell when you lied to me, especially when you were talking to your hands."

"You make it sound like it happened a lot."

"It was constant, only you didn't know it because you had no idea who you were then. And that's putting it nicely."

"And now?"

She stood up and moved closer, right next to me; I could feel myself filling and emptying again, like a minor star pulsing in a faraway corner of the universe.

"You just stopped." She was barely whispering. "All of a sudden, you never got in touch. It was like you had died."

"I was, sort of, dying. It was death, in a way." I didn't mean to whisper, too, but what else could I do? How can you talk normally when someone like her is leaning so close? "I thought about calling, but you know I don't have a phone in my apartment. I didn't know what to do."

"Your office doesn't have a phone?" She moved back and looked at my desk. I felt my face get hot. We used to talk a lot while I was at the office. I'd shut the door, and Pak didn't interrupt. If he passed by when I was on the phone, he'd listen for just a moment and then walk away. He never mentioned it.

"Private calls." My voice was returning little by little, but my face was still flushed, probably my ears, too. "They don't want us to make private calls from the office. You know that, it's in the handbook that your section puts out. Only official matters are supposed to take place on official phones. That's the rule." I sounded like the book of regulations that sat on the floor behind my chair. "Anyway, what we had to say to each other in those days was nobody else's business."

"So what was the other day?"

"That was official."

She didn't respond. Then came the question I hoped she wouldn't ask. "How close were we?"

I knew what she wanted. She wanted me to say we had almost made it, almost crossed the bridge in one sweeping, final move. She wanted to hear that we could have done it. "Close," I said.

A soft moan escaped her lips. Can a man dissolve? I looked away and considered how difficult and yet how useful it might be suddenly to become nothing more than smoke. When I looked back, she was at the door. She turned for a moment, long enough for one final word.

"Bastard." It seemed to be her word for me these days. It wasn't a word I liked her to say. I'd have to tell her that, if I ever saw her again.

I turned the word over in my mind a few times before I realized my phone was ringing. It was the liaison man from the Foreign Ministry. "Where have you been? I've tried calling and calling. We could meet for a couple of minutes, it might be interesting."

"Hot air?"

"Enough. Miss Ban is making pleasurable sounds upstairs."

"If the car starts, I'll be there in twenty minutes."

"Otherwise?"

"Give my regards to Miss Ban."

11

I drove out the front gate. An old lady and a small girl were on the sidewalk across the street. They walked alongside each other, their paces matched by the bow of time. For a while they held hands, then the child moved ahead, just a short burst of energy, a few steps alone, enough to make the case. She stopped and waited for the old lady to move up beside her. They started, paces matched again. Both looked ahead; the girl reached her hand up, the grandmother put her hand out. They walked like that for several steps, hands reaching for each other, not searching, sure that the space between them was nothing, that it was not permanent. Finally, one of them, you couldn't tell which, moved the extra centimeter; maybe it was both, but I didn't think so. They were joined and walked on—neither hurrying, neither lagging.

The car sat idling for another minute as I watched them. Which of them would not survive the winter? I hated the question. I despised myself for asking it.

One of the gate guards walked up and looked in the window. "Problem?"

"Nothing for you," I said and turned into the street.

Chapter Four

"No one in the building knew her. There is no record of the file. It never existed."

"What did you see, then?" It was amazing how much heat one little heater could put out. The only problem was, in order to avoid overloading the wires, he had rearranged things in the wall socket; the lights had to be off. In the morning, there was probably enough daylight coming in the window to read by; now, in the afternoon, I could barely see his face, except when he moved into the glow of the heater.

"Must have been a phantom, a place holder. It wasn't for her. It was for her husband. That's a guess, and I'm not going beyond that."

"This is why I came out of my office, drove through the snow, and sit here in the dark? For you to tell me you're not going beyond telling me you don't have anything?" I reached in my back pocket and pulled out a pair of wire cutters.

"So, forget I told you," he said quickly. "Don't think about it. We'll find something else." Upstairs, Miss Ban walked across her office. For a lithe woman, she had a heavy tread. The liaison officer looked at the ceiling. "She's been restless the past few days. It's not like her. Usually she just sits."

"What does she do?

"Some sort of research."

"Right, research. How come she has her own office?"

"I guess someone doesn't want her disturbed." He poured a cup of hot water for himself. "You want some?"

I did, but I didn't want to give the impression that a cup of hot water was a substitute for what I really needed from him. "Let's get back to the file." I put the cutters into my jacket pocket, where they would be visible. He bit his lower lip, calculating how much room he had to wriggle.

"Nonfile," he said.

"Nonfile. You have many of those, or are they kept in a nonfile room?"

The liaison man looked up at the ceiling. I followed his gaze. "Maybe I'll pay a call on Miss Ban."

2

"Miss Ban, I am Inspector O from the Ministry of Public Security. I would like to talk to you."

She stood in the doorway to her office, giving no sign that she was prepared to step aside. "You'll have to make an appointment through normal channels, Inspector. You shouldn't even be on this floor."

"Pardon me?" I couldn't remember why I imagined her as lithe. I should have trusted my instincts. Her footsteps sounded like someone solid, and now I saw why. She was tall, solid as a rock. Not fat, not heavy, just very solid. I knew elite guards who didn't have her build. Maybe that's why she had this job shuffling phony files. She looked like she ate small men. "I'm not here to vacation. I'm on assignment, and I need to talk to you. I don't make 'appointments' when I question people. You can consider yourself lucky you weren't ordered to appear at my office."

"I'll do that. Consider myself lucky. If that's all, I'm especially busy right now. Come back some other time, maybe in a month or two, when it's warmer. I look forward to spring, don't you, Inspector?" She smiled with her mouth, only it wasn't anything that warmed the heart. It was a serious warning, and I could tell she was a serious woman. She parted her hair in the middle, not a little to one side, but right down the center line so it looked like it was done with a machine. Maybe it was. Maybe they made such machines and she had been issued one in order to make it clear she wasn't fooling around, she was serious, and if you didn't think so, just look at that part in her long black hair. As soon as I left, she would phone in a complaint, and the guard at the front door of the building would be given orders to keep me out. He wouldn't try very hard, but I didn't need the extra hassle.

"On second thought, Miss Ban, let's just say I'm drawn to you. Let's just say I'm lonely, and you're lonely, and it's warm in here. Can I come in and share the warmth? Is that a problem?"

"Nothing personal, Inspector," she said and shut the door. I thought she might open it again, but she didn't. It was uncomfortable standing in the corridor, too similar to the meat lockers I had to visit during one investigation of a butcher who dealt in counterfeit loin. I normally don't wear my hat inside of buildings, but this corridor was testing the limits. I tried the handle, but it was locked. I thought of kicking the door in, but the amount of explaining and hours of meetings that would result from a complaint about destroying part of the Foreign Ministry building were more than I wanted to endure, much less Pak's looks of disbelief each time he glanced in my office over the next few months. Besides, she didn't look like a woman who was impressed by a man who kicked in doors.

I knocked once. "I'll be back, darling." I figured the last word would rocket the others along the corridor up from their desks, ears against their doors. There was a short, throaty laugh from inside, the sort of laugh a woman of Miss Ban's frame supports easily. When I got back to the liaison man's office, he was gone. So was the heater.

"He's out. Visitors from afar," a man said as he walked past me and into the next room. After a moment, he reappeared. "That one"—he pointed at the liaison man's door—"has a heater." He looked in the room. "He must have taken it, but he has one. It sucks electricity all day long."

"You trying to tell me something?"

"He's not supposed to have it, is he?"

"What makes you think I'm interested?"

"Nothing." The man's face was gaunt. "Nobody is interested in anything anymore. So, good, we'll all freeze to death, everyone but him, if we don't starve first." He looked at me closely, his eyes ablaze with something, not fear exactly. I couldn't tell whether he wanted to take back the words, or be assured that I had heard him.

"You have a family?"

He nodded.

"Then don't talk crazy," I said. "When some people get too cold, they become crazed; the words that come from their mouths become crazy. Remember that."

He put his hand to his forehead, a gesture of despair, and waited. "What next?"

I knew right then, he would not live out the winter. At this point it was a matter of will with a lot of people. His was gone, which saddened me for some reason. I didn't know him, but I didn't want him to give up. "Those with heaters will sit in front of them and curse every time the power goes out. Those of us without heaters won't notice the difference," I said. He didn't reply, but he didn't walk away, so I figured he wanted the company. "You know Miss Ban, upstairs?"

"Only her tread. I don't go up there," he said absently.

"You have your own office?" I pointed at his door.

"No, this one is for a team, but everyone else . . ."

"They've left."

He shrugged.

"But you stayed."

"They say it's an arduous march; all I do is sit in the dark. I won't get a medal for that."

"I don't suppose you've ever been to Pakistan? Served there? Made a trip?" Might as well start with the biggest shot in the dark and work backward.

"No. What's it to you?"

"Where have you been, then? I'm interested in leading a tour group."

"You ask a lot of questions." At least he could still fight back; maybe it would be enough motivation to stay alive, if he decided to fight.

"A question machine, that's me. I keep asking until I get an answer. Could be the switch is stuck or a connection is loose." Once again he didn't respond, but there was something new, an alertness that had been drained from him only a moment ago. "Where did you serve?" I decided to see how far the conversation would go.

"Middle East. Craziness. Libya. The man's a nut, as far as I can tell."

"You put that in a reporting cable, I suppose. Such forthrightness is much appreciated in this building, I hear."

"Reporting wasn't my job." He smiled, finally, for the first time. "Forthrightness wasn't my area of expertise. My job was making sure the ambassador stayed out of trouble."

"So, did he stay out of trouble?"

"He defected." The words seemed to stick in his throat, and it looked for a moment like I might lose him for good. I nodded for him to go on, and for some reason that seemed to blow up the dam. He didn't need any more encouragement. "The whole embassy was scared to death when the ambassador disappeared. People were angry with me; they said I should have been more alert, more aware, like I was supposed to know what he was thinking every moment, like I was supposed to be able to read his mind." His face took on some color, and so did his voice. "A security team came out in a hurry; they told us to pretend nothing had happened and to go about our business, but no one could think straight. I was convinced they'd shoot me, take me out to the garden in the back and shoot me, but after a lot of questions they said it wasn't my fault. Damned right it wasn't my fault. I'll never know what got into the man."

"That was in Libya?"

He looked at me strangely. "No." He didn't volunteer where, and I wasn't going to ask, not unless I needed to.

"You think they'll send you overseas for another assignment?"

"I don't think they even know I come to the office every day. I read the cables and put them in a file. This file, that file. Like I said, no one cares." The energy was gone again. It made me uneasy to look at him, wondering how long he would last.

PART II

Chapter One

"Give me one good reason. Go ahead, just one. I'm trying to do your country some good, so why am I being held prisoner in this hotel?"

"You're not a prisoner." It was exasperating, having to argue with Jenö. He kept pushing even though he knew I wasn't going to budge. "I already told you, feel free to wander around the lobby. Have you done that yet? Or you can go upstairs to the counter where they sell books. Have you seen volume twenty-two yet? Riveting. You can even play pool, if that is possible to do with gloves on."

"You're a strange man, Inspector."

"Thank you, or isn't that a compliment?"

"Surely you want things to get better for your country?"

"Don't worry, we'll survive."

"Oh, I'm sure you will. But I'm not talking survival. I'm talking progress. I'm talking"—he looked around the lobby—"a little more heat." For once, he kept his eyebrows under tight control. "You know what I mean?"

"I don't have to know what you mean. I'm not anyone you need to have a meaningful conversation with. I'm only here to make sure that you stay out of trouble, or better, that trouble stays away from you. That's possible as long as you do what I say. I suggest you just nap under the covers for the next forty-eight hours. Then I'll wave good-bye as you go through the immigration line at the airport. As far as I'm concerned, that will count as progress, you on an airplane, lifting off and flying away."

"Can we walk around the block?"

"You realize how miserable it is outside?"

"I know the temperature, Inspector. You can chain me to your wrist if you want. I'm not going to run away."

I laughed. "Very dramatic. We don't use chains. Okay, let's walk. You have on long underwear? Or are you still relying on those genes of yours for warmth?"

It was much colder outside than it looked, the dead cold that comes on clear, sunny days. There was no wind, but it was hard to move, the cold like an invisible weight, maybe gravity doubled. After we walked past the stamp store, I could see that he was having second thoughts about being outside.

"You had something to say?"

He was breathing hard, gasping from the way the air entered his lungs and filled them with ice, and I wasn't sure he could hear me. He turned his head slowly. "Why would you think that, Inspector?"

"No one is outside today unless they have to be. We don't have to be, so the logical conclusion, and the one of every person who saw us go through the front door, can only be that you want to talk and—more to the point—not be overheard."

"You'll record what I say?"

"No, I don't care what you say. I told you, I'm only supposed to keep you safe, and that means my main concern is that you don't slip on the sidewalk and break your arm. Watch where you're walking."

"Is there a place we can stop to get something warm?"

"As long as we keep moving, you won't freeze solid. I'll have you back in the hotel in twenty minutes, unless you plan to make a long speech."

"In other circumstances, Inspector, I might have taken my time edging into what I need to say to you. I would have stroked your ego, appealed to your manhood, perhaps. Then I might have looked for some vulnerability, found a way to snap your psychic spine."

"But you've decided not to."

"No, the temperature has given me no choice. I have to get straight to the point."

"Suddenly, I'm doubly not interested. Forget it. Whatever you are going to suggest, forget it."

He shook his head. "Listen closely. I need your assistance, and in return, you can have whatever you want."

"You're not serious. Only yesterday I told some fool that when it gets cold, people talk crazy. I thought I was making that up, but maybe it's true."

"I'm not trying to recruit you, Inspector. I'm not asking you to betray your country."

"Then why couldn't we stay in the hotel for this?"

"I don't want your brother agencies to know, that's all. There are people trying to prevent me from getting my work done. Some people want me to succeed. Some people don't."

"The latter group seems to be on top; tough for you. It's nothing that concerns me."

"Quite the contrary. You don't live in a bubble. Lots of things concern you, even if you know nothing about them."

I stopped. "Look at that line of trees over there, look at the tops, what do you see?"

"Let's keep moving. We're not talking about trees."

"You may not think so. What do you see?"

"The tops are even."

"Good. Now, look at the trunks, what do you see?"

"Inspector, I'm freezing out here. Can we get to the point?"

"The trunks, what do you see?"

He sighed heavily. "Some of them are on small mounds, some are on the ground, but the tops are all still even. Are we done with this?"

"Even, you say. None too short, none too tall. Now, let's move closer. What do you see?"

"The tops aren't even any more. Can we please go inside? I value my extremities. I'd like to keep all of my fingers." He looked at me oddly, but I pretended not to notice.

"Nice illusion, isn't it? The tops aren't actually even. You can see that with your eyes, but your brain insists on creating a sense of order where none exists. It's an illusion. What you see, and what is there—not the same."

"Have you ever seen pictures of those frozen mammoths in Siberia, Inspector? This is what they must have gone through in their final, excruciating moments. Listening to police-mammoths lecture until they turned to ice blocks."

"Ever since I was small, I noticed the illusion that trees gave, or rather that my eyes did. Things look uniform, only they aren't. We have a need to see uniformity, so we do. Eventually, I began to wonder if reality was someplace other than where I was. Ever have that feeling?"

"I have no feeling left. I think my lungs have begun to ice up."

"No, that doesn't happen for at least another ten minutes, don't worry. If you breathe through your nostrils, it might delay things a few minutes beyond that. In your case"—I looked at his nose—"maybe a little longer."

He groaned audibly. "I think I'm dying."

"The first time I can remember sitting on a train, staring out the window, I watched a farmer walk beside an oxcart along the edge of a field. The ox was plodding, the two of them barely moving. It confused me. The farmer was in sight for a few seconds, and then he was gone. Whose was the reality? His? Mine? Did he disappear? Or did I? Was he still there? Was I? I have that same feeling right now with you. If I look away, maybe you will disappear and not be there when I turn back."

"This is truly stunning, Inspector. How did I get mixed up with the only North Korean alive who imagines he is Spinoza? Stop worrying with metaphysical oxen. Pay more attention to the temperature."

"Don't you ever wonder about reality?"

"*Yes!* No! Who gives a damn about reality? We have to get out of this cold." I didn't move. "Do you know what absolute zero is, Inspector? It's the temperature at which I lose my temper. Forget the big questions right now. There are savage birds circling. We don't have time to worry about theories of existence."

I looked up, but there was nothing there. No birds. "Just suppose," I said. "Suppose this isn't reality. Suppose I'm actually somewhere else."

He stared at me oddly again. Then he shrugged. "The cold must be getting to you. Listen to me."

Chapter Two

Jenö talked, and I listened. He referred to his list of travel requests, said he could do without meeting anyone from the party, emphasized again and again how there were people who wanted him to succeed while he was here and thus it depended on me to help him do that. He mentioned that virtue was its own reward, but added that additional recompense was not beyond question. He threw in a few comments about bikinis and suntan lotion, but then his teeth started chattering so badly I decided we'd better get back to the hotel. At the front entrance, he repeated that there were dangers all around us, birds of prey circling and so forth.

I dismissed this as an exaggeration brought on by exposure to extreme cold. I'd seen it happen in the army when we were on guard duty for extended periods in winter. Frostbite of the brain, someone called it. I stuck around the hotel and kept my eyes open for the next twenty-four hours, nevertheless. I wandered through the lobby; I sat drinking tea; I shuffled into the hotel store and chatted with the salesgirls. I went up to the front door and looked outside. Nothing untoward occurred; nothing even looked about to occur. Day moved to night and back again without a hint of the unusual. There were no signs of bodily harm in preparation. People weren't hanging around the vicinity of the hotel where they shouldn't be. That was easy enough to see because the streets were empty. No one could be inconspicuous in this weather. Just in case, as I left to return to the office, I told the chief security man at the hotel to keep tabs on Jenö, something beyond their normal routine. I didn't completely trust the hotel staff or the SSD men hanging around, but there wasn't much I could do about that. We didn't have enough people left in the office to assign against phantoms, not new phantoms, anyway. The old phantoms were taking up all available personnel.

When I got back to the office and told Pak what Jenö had said, I thought he would laugh. He didn't. "That's all of it?" he asked.

"Every word." Some of what Jenö told me had been intended only for my ears, or at least that's what he implied. But I don't keep secrets from Pak, not when it comes to work. We don't always put it in the files, but I make sure Pak knows everything I know—almost everything.

"Go back there and sit around," Pak said. "I don't trust those security men, none of them. There's a reason they work at the hotel, and it isn't a good one. All I want is for our guest to leave in one piece. That's not too much to ask, is it, Inspector?"

I'd just spent a full day and night moping around the Koryo, watching the security men watch me. Why would I want to go back?

"The hotel has hot water," Pak said. This was true; they had more than the Foreign Ministry.

"The duty car is acting funny. You don't mind if I take yours?"

"Why should I mind? You take my car all the time." He tossed me the keys. "If you spin out on a patch of ice, don't call me, I don't want to know."

Back at my desk, I opened the top drawer and did a careful inventory. If I was going to sit doing nothing in the hotel, I might as well have a piece of wood that would help me sort through the case. Something pragmatic. Elm was good in that way. Most trees succumb to nonsense at some point in their lives. They get top-heavy. They forget their roots. Not elms. From beginning to end, they remain stately and pragmatic. I had a piece of elm somewhere.

"Get moving, O!" Pak yelled down the hall. "I don't want to explain to the Minister that something happened to our guest while my inspector was pawing through scraps of wood." I grabbed the first piece I could find. Acacia. Suboptimal for the work at hand, but it would have to do.

When I got to the hotel, I spotted Jenö sitting on a bench on the second floor. He waved but didn't make a move to join me. Well, I thought, if the molehill won't come to Mohammed.

"I'm tired of being in my room," he said as I stepped off the escalator. "There isn't a lot on TV at this hour, and I'm out of things to read." There was a book next to him on the bench.

Just then, three girls walked by in single file. The first one, pretending to be busy thinking, stared straight ahead. The second smiled and nodded, almost gaily. The last one looked away, a deliberate gesture. It was probably as close to haughty as she dared. They were all the same age, not more than twenty or twenty-one. The second one had her hair tied in the back with a blue bow. Otherwise, they were dressed nearly identically in bright-colored traditional Korean skirts and jackets.

"Did you see that, Inspector?" Jenö watched as the trio disappeared around a corner. "I love those dresses."

"I wasn't looking." Of course I'd seen it. Who wouldn't look at three girls floating by like ribbons in an April breeze?

"Nice to see something colorful for a change."

"Next week is Lunar New Year; that means the flowers can't be far away. It's built into people's genes, this sort of rhythm. You find it quaint, I suppose."

"Not at all. Beside the dresses, you know what I noticed? Three girls, three separate reactions when they passed by."

"Three. Were you expecting more, or less?"

"Why do you think the girl in the middle smiled? Why wasn't she afraid like the other two?"

"None of them was afraid. What do they have to be afraid of?"

"You tell me."

"Three girls went by. They weren't triplets. Is there any reason they should react the same? Are they trained dogs?"

"It was a simple question."

"Good."

"Only a harmless observation."

"Fine."

Jenö pulled out his wallet. "Let me show you something." He handed me a photograph of a group of schoolboys. Each confronted the camera in a different way. "This is my son"—he pointed at one of the boys— "and his friends. Look at them."

"I'm looking."

"Not trained dogs?"

"No."

"So what makes them react so differently, so individually to the very same instant in time, just when the shutter clicks?"

"You have a theory?"

"No, it just interests me. I wonder about it. I'd say you do, too. All the time, you wonder about reality. Why does one person stand here and not there? Who moves to the front in a group? Who hangs back? Who smiles? Who smirks? Who stares into the lens? And most important, the question that nags constantly—why?"

"And the answer is?"

"You're not following me, Inspector."

"I think I am. You're trying to figure out whether I'm the bird that flies off the tree first, or if I wait for the others. You're trying to figure out whether I'm the schoolboy who smiles at the stranger, or if I'm the one who looks away. Do I wave when your car goes by, or do I stare impassively?"

"Cossacks, you're seeing Cossacks again, Inspector. But thank you. I think you just answered my question. Now I have another one for you."

"I'm listening."

"Remember what I told you the other day? I need to make contact with someone. Can you help me?"

"No. I hate to be impolite to a guest, but absolutely not. I cannot help you do anything but stay out of trouble. Why don't we sit and wait for more groups of girls to walk by. They do that every so often. It passes the time, and as long as you only look, it's harmless. Besides, it's comparatively warm in here right now. Making contact with anyone means going outside."

Jenö passed me the book, his finger on the edge of an envelope between the pages. "They were sold out of volume twenty-two, but the lady assured me this one was equally as good." His eyebrows did that bouncy, energetic dance the visiting Russian troupes always performed near the end of one of their programs. They call it a country quadrille. I just wasn't sure what country.

2

In the midst of nowhere, in the middle of what should have been a small, narrow valley of rice fields backed up against a frozen river and lines of tall, ragged hills, a triple barrier cut across the land. On the outer perimeter, an electrified wire fence held up with thick concrete posts; inside that, electrified wires running close to the ground; finally, inside that, coils of barbed wire. The two electrified barriers probably weren't live. There wasn't any electricity out here, unless they had their own generator. If they did, it wasn't running. Generators hum, but everything was quiet. No birds, no people, no nothing.

A bridge stretched over the river, but I decided to park and go ahead on foot; the pilings didn't look strong enough to take the weight of my car. On the far side of the bridge was a wide gate. In front of it stood an army guard, sunken cheeks, sunken eyes. The eyes glanced at my ID.

"Wait," was all he said before he disappeared into a hut just inside the gate. I waited. It's best not to seem impatient when standing outside a military gate in the middle of nowhere. To pass the time, I flexed my shoulder. It was stiffening up, probably because on my way here, I'd had to back downhill nearly half a kilometer when one narrow road over a mountain just stopped. If anyone had reported the country was minus one road, it hadn't made its way to the Ministry's transportation office.

A second guard walked up and looked me over. He seemed more alert than his companion; maybe he wasn't used to visitors flexing at the gate. His expression was distinctly veiled. Not just one of those slack looks country people give you; this one was more careful than that. It was calculated, carefully designed to have no sure meaning. I remembered my conversation with Jenö. Which schoolboy would this have been? The one that hung back? The one that turned his head away?

Off to the side, about ten paces away, was an elevated guard post, big enough for one man and high enough for him to be a couple of meters above anyone at the gate. It was meant for a third guard to watch the other two and to make sure that if anything went wrong, there was backup with a clear line of fire. But it was unoccupied.

The first guard emerged with my ID. He handed it back without any reaction. No eye contact; no gesture that I should pass; no refusal. In my days in the army, ambiguity hadn't been one of our options. We told people yes or no; pass or go away. Those were the choices. Things apparently had changed. I decided the absence of a clear negative was positive enough, so I started through the gate.

"Halt!"

I stopped. Quick movements after a command like that were never wise. There was a pistol aimed at my chest. The man holding it had on a thick coat with a hood. It was the kind officers in special favor wore, but I couldn't see any insignia.

"A problem with my ID?" I glanced back casually at the two guards. Their weapons weren't drawn, which I assumed was a good sign—unless that, too, had changed.

"I want an explanation, and make sure it's convincing. Your ID tells me who you are, not why you want to get onto my facility." He didn't emphasize it, but he didn't have to—"my" facility.

"Official business."

"Official business." The pistol didn't waver. "Whereas, apparently you think I'm on holiday." The officer took a step toward me. "This isn't the sort of place your ministry has any business, official or otherwise."

"Not normally," I said. This man was too self-assured to be a colonel. Colonels are jumpy, even senior colonels. He must be a general, though I didn't recall generals being so short on support staff—adjutants and so forth. It wasn't usual for generals to hold pistols on visitors; that's why the lower ranks existed. Whether he was the man Jenö wanted to meet remained unclear. If he didn't shoot me, we were off to a good start.

"Your ministry has no business out here at all, not ever." His tone was brusque, but his finger had come off the trigger.

"In this case, it is something important. Not normal important. Very important."

"Of course. Why would anyone drive out from the warmth and comfort of Pyongyang if he didn't have something very important to do?"

I hadn't seen any tire tracks on the road up to the gate. It was hard to imagine a general without a staff car, or a jeep. The colonel in Pyongyang didn't have a driver. This man didn't even appear to have a jeep. "Our conversation might be more productive if one of us didn't have a weapon pointed at his midsection."

The barrel dropped a hair. "Better?"

"I take it you're not going to allow me to carry out my mission."

"Very impressive word—mission. A solo mission, at that. Why are you by yourself? I thought the police traveled in packs."

"Maybe you're not the only ones shorthanded these days." I nodded at his empty guard post. Pointing would have meant moving my hands, and I didn't want to do anything that put his finger back on the trigger.

He didn't take his eyes off me. "I have to send some of them home. I've fed those I could with my own rations, but it's not enough. So I send them back to their mothers to cluck over them. As if their families have more food than we do." He holstered the pistol. "You can sit in the hut if you like while you try to explain why you're here. Then I'll decide what to do with you."

"Do you mind if I go back to my car to get something?" The general didn't reply, and the guards, after watching his face, stared at nothing.

3

When Jenö had asked me again to help him set up his meeting and told me who it was he wanted to meet, I drove back to the office and told Pak we needed to dump our visitor. Get rid of him, fast. He was going to get himself into serious trouble, and if we were standing next to him, we'd end up in the same pot. For the second time in the same day, Pak surprised me.

"We can't dump him. You'd better go out and see what this is about."

I was stupefied. "Are you kidding?"

"Sometimes, Inspector, it is better to bend a little. It's unusual what he wants, but everything is unusual these days. There are winds blowing from places you and I don't even know exist. Forget the Ministry; they don't have to know, and if they find out, I'll handle it." He glanced at the envelope Jenö had given me. "Don't open that," he said. He reached into his desk and took out a small book of red coupons. I could see it had never been used. He tore off the first two tickets and handed them to me. "These should get you access to special rations. Notice I said 'should.' This booklet is three years old, and who knows what's gone cockeyed in the meantime. I was told only to use the coupons in extreme situations. No one defined extreme, though, so I'm doing it myself."

"You have access to grain?" I squeezed every drop of surprise out of my voice.

"I've thought about it a lot, Inspector. I don't need your disapproving stare. I can't use these for personal rations. I can't, and I won't."

"But you can use them for this crazy foreigner?"

"Maybe the grain isn't for him. Maybe it's for something more important."

"Really? And am I to be let in on this little secret, or do I just follow orders? These mysterious breezes, are they why you stood up to the special section when they were here last month? Was it because you knew more about the foreigner than you bothered to tell me?"

Pak put the coupon book back in the drawer and slammed it shut. "Don't press me on this, Inspector. I've got a lot on my mind. Keep it simple. If those tickets really work and you can get a couple of bags of rice, throw them in the car and bring them out to your meeting. Take this along, too." He took a piece of paper from his desk, folded it in thirds, and put it in a tan envelope with a red stripe in one corner. Then he pulled a strip of white paper from the flap and sealed it. "Amazing, isn't it? The supplies some sections have."

"A red stripe? Isn't that a little melodramatic?"

"Just be glad it doesn't have a black stripe." Pak handed me the envelope. "This may come in handy. It's from someone I used to know. Apparently, he wants our guest to have that meeting."

"And we take orders from him? Since when?"

"Not orders, Inspector. Call it a favor."

"Do I know him?"

"If you didn't before, you do now." Pak nodded at the envelope. "Don't use it unless you have to. And try not to get yourself shot. You'll be a long way out in the countryside, and I'm not sure we have the resources to go looking for bodies."

At the ration depot, the red tickets only got me a few half-empty bags of rice and a sour look from the supply clerk. "I didn't know people at your level could get these tickets," was his only comment.

Chapter Three

I left the sacks in the trunk of my car and carried back a small bag to the front gate. The gaunt guard wouldn't look at me. He frowned at the bag and then waved me into the hut. The general sat alone at the table. He had taken off his parka, though it was even colder in the room than it was outside. I put the bag down in front of him. "It would please me if you shared my dinner," I said. He didn't react. I put down the envelope. I hadn't opened it; I wasn't even tempted. Jenö had passed it to me, but from Pak's reaction, I could tell it was from someone I had never met and didn't especially want to.

The general quickly opened the bag, divided the contents into six portions, and called out to the guards. As they came in, one at a time, he handed a portion to each of them. When that was done, he stood and carried the third portion along with the envelope through a doorway into a dark room at the back of the hut. With the door shut, I could hear no more than a murmur of voices, someone coughing, and a sound of a dog barking once, softly, as if muzzled.

"My adjutant," the general said when he emerged again. "He's not well." That left three portions. He nodded and gave one to me. The second he put in his pocket. "Come with me, Inspector," he said. The last portion stayed on the table.

Outside, as soon as we were beyond earshot of the gate guards, he stopped. "You seem awfully sure of yourself," he said. "Passing things to people you don't know. It's not wise." It was cold enough for the parka, but he'd left it behind. He was going to make it clear to me that he was tougher than I was.

"I'm not worried. In Pyongyang, a colonel threatened to have me shot."

"Son of a bitch!" he shouted so loud that the gaunt guard whirled around to see what had happened. "At our last staff meeting, we were told colonels couldn't shoot policemen. Only generals could." He laughed; it didn't seem to be something he did very often. "I wouldn't have shot you."

"I think I knew that."

"Even so, one of the guards might have pulled the trigger. They don't need my permission to shoot. Their standing orders are to keep out of this compound anyone—anyone—who doesn't carry special orders. You don't have anything like that. You don't even have regular orders. Out here, your ID is garbage."

"That's what I've been told. If you don't mind my saying, your soldiers didn't seem ready to shoot. They're surly enough, but not killers, I'd say."

"Only a few of them carry live rounds. You wouldn't want to find out which ones, believe me. Anyway, you don't know for sure that those were the only guards watching, or whether my weapon was the only one trained on you. All you know is what you saw."

"Ah, reality," I said. "You're right, I only know what I saw. I am fairly sure, however, that I saw you pick up that envelope and carry it into that back room. You didn't have it when you came back. So, can I see this facility or not, General?"

"You shouldn't be here." The general kicked a stone to the side and started walking. "No one should. Not even the army. The place is empty. It's falling down. And you still haven't told me what you want."

"Someone needs to look around, with your permission."

"Someone without authorization, obviously. What if I say no?"

I didn't reply. Of course he would say no. How could anyone in his right mind say anything other than no?

The general took a pair of gloves from his belt and put them on. He was tough, but he wasn't crazy, I decided. The cold was immense.

"Let me ask the question another way," he said. "Maybe it will help you formulate a response that goes beyond a dumb stare. What is this about?"

Jenö had been vague, and Pak, after he'd heard my account, hadn't gone beyond saying I should make the contact but not get myself killed in the process. I didn't think either of those explanations would be edifying.

"When a general asks a question, a general expects an answer. You must have learned that somewhere along the way. If it will do any good, I can repeat myself. This facility is off-limits. Very, strictly, completely, totally off-limits."

"That's why it was selected, one presumes."

"I'd be jeopardizing my men, not to mention myself, if I let someone visit here for purposes I didn't understand and that were never adequately explained. I'm not interested in what you presume. What do you know?"

"The contents of that note weren't enough?" I thought I felt one of the winds Pak had warned me about starting to blow across the open ground.

"That note isn't your business."

I didn't have any instructions or explanations on how to keep this going any further than I'd taken it. All I could say was what popped into my head. "Maybe no one need know about the visitor or the visit."

He shook his head. "Don't be a fool, Inspector. My men are loyal, but only up to a point. People can't simply materialize inside this compound. You and your visitor will have to go through the gate, past the guards. Even if they let you in, word will leak out quickly. Do you think the guard with the dull eyes doesn't see everything around him? People check and double-check. The political officers come through and ask questions. On occasion, the field telephones even work all the way out here." If there was a straight "no" in there, I didn't hear it.

"What if we came up with a story?"

"We?"

"General, this is important. Think of it as a hinge. A door won't open without a hinge." It wasn't a bad image, considering I had no idea what we were talking about.

"You're one of O Chang-yun's grandsons, aren't you?" If he had hit me on the back of the head, I wouldn't have been more surprised. It didn't come out of nowhere, though. We'd never met, he didn't know I was coming to visit, but somehow he had that piece of information, and he must have been waiting the whole time for the right moment to slip it in.

"Yes," I said simply. It wouldn't have done any good to ask him how he knew.

Now it was his turn to remain silent. He stared at me, but I wouldn't have called it a dumb stare.

It was now or never. "Show me around; we can talk."

"You inherited his guts, but not his brains. Alright, we'll walk. You talk, I'll listen." He straightened his tunic and patted his pistol. "And I'd better like what I hear."

We passed through an inner fence line. There wasn't any guard at the gate, but a soldier stood a few meters away with his back to us, looking out across the fields with binoculars. He didn't turn around to salute, though he must have heard the crack as I broke the ice that had formed over the puddles on the path. I saw him twist the focus wheel; it was obvious he couldn't see a thing.

"This is where the simpler components were assembled." The general had decided that he would do the talking after all. Maybe he'd had time to digest what was in the note. "Most of the important work was done underground, inside those hills"—he waved in the direction of the first line of mountains that rose a few hundred meters away—"but some of it was done aboveground, in these buildings. Don't ask me why. I don't plan these things. I don't construct them, either."

We walked another fifty or sixty meters over broken ground, littered with debris. The general pointed at a building several stories high, with all but a few windows broken. It was hard to imagine how that could happen. Who would break windows on such a secure site? "The place is unheated, and the roof leaks," he said. "In summer, the humidity drips from the walls. Anything copper has been stripped out; everything metal is rusting; all the wood has already rotted." We stepped through a door hanging from one hinge into a huge, dark room. He knocked on the wood. "Is this the sort of door you meant?"

I could smell acid and mold. A control panel sat against one wall—the covers on the gauges were cracked and water had seeped in, though it didn't much matter because the dials had fallen off. "They're frozen, as you can see, but there is nothing to worry about. The gauges have nothing to record." He led the way into a narrow, low-roofed, U-shaped passageway that led into another room, probably fifteen meters high and nearly twice as long, with two half-dismantled storage tanks lying on their sides.

"Is there another way out of this room?" I looked around. Sometimes I get nervous for no reason in dark, unfamiliar places.

"Only through those hatches on the floor."

"Leading where?"

"These were the waste tanks used for the chemicals that treated certain components. At the bottom of each tank is one of those discharge hatches."

"Big enough for a person?"

"A person? Not normally, they're pretty narrow. It would have to be a very skinny person." He shrugged. "Not normally, but these days, yes." I hadn't expected irony from him. "You need to see anything else?"

I followed him outside.

"That pair of buildings, over there." We had crossed a small field down to a point near the river. "They look interesting. Why are they so close to the water?"

The general shrugged. "Good for discharging chemicals, I guess."

"What's in front of the shorter one? From here I'd say it looks like a band saw."

"It will look the same when you get closer, because that's what it is."

"To cut metal?"

"No, to cut wood. You'd be surprised what went into these missiles."

Missiles, he said. What else did I expect?

We turned a corner and walked down a path lined with shivering, mangy poplars. Most of them were less than two meters tall, and more than a few of them had been stripped of most of their branches. "This may be the closest thing to a forest in the province. These trees would be gone in a day if I opened the gates. As it is, I have to make sure none of my men accidentally knocks one over. Because after that, they will accidentally sell the wood on the outside."

We came to another pair of buildings on either side of the path, both four stories high. They were joined by a trestle bridge that looked like it had been used to move small, narrow carts between the upper floors. Scattered on the ground in front of us were rusted steel beams.

"These were the assembly buildings. The one on the right is a complete wreck. When I got here last year, it was already in this state."

"And the other one?"

"Only a partial wreck."

"Does anything still function here?"

"That's not my concern. If it's inside the fence line, I guard it."

"I suppose the vegetables are worth something." I walked over to a small plot that showed signs of having been cultivated a few months ago. The rows were uneven and the soil was rocky. "I don't think they got much of a harvest, though."

"Did you need to see anything else? Or have we exhausted your curiosity?" The general stopped to retrieve something from under one of the steel bars. He held it up for me to see. "Cigarette butt."

"I recognize the species."

"My men don't smoke these."

"Cigarettes?"

"Not these." He sniffed it. "French. Gitanes."

"If you say so. I never smoked a French cigarette, so I'll take your word for it." I'd also never run across a cigarette butt that still smelled after sitting most of the winter in the snow, but there was no use pointing that out to a general. Besides, what a French cigarette was doing in his compound was his business.

He put the cigarette butt in his pocket and then reached for his pistol. "I'm going to escort you back to the hut, Inspector. It will look better if we don't seem to have become fast friends."

"Have we?"

"Put it this way: When you finally walk out of here, my men should not see you again."

Back in the hut, the general pulled off his gloves and threw them on the table. The last portion of food was gone.

"This is my headquarters. That is my headquarters staff." He pointed at the two guards who had moved from the gate to stand by the door. "After the incident with that corps on the east coast—" He stopped suddenly. "You know what I'm referring to?"

"I try not to pay attention to military matters, especially those outside the capital. It overloads my circuits."

"Someone in the Fifth Corps went crazy, or maybe they came to their senses. Anyway, it looked like the beginning of a rolling coup." He watched my eyes. "Don't pretend you hadn't heard. It was crushed, and the rest of us had to readjust to fill in the blank spots. My division has twice the area to cover and half the staff. I am to guard these facilities and a few others close by. They moan to each other at night across the emptiness. That's all they do."

"I'm still puzzled about the glass." That, and why I was out here in the first place.

"The glass? It's a mystery, isn't it? You're a policeman, why don't you find it for me?"

"Can't you replace it? At least board up the empty panes."

The general looked over as his adjutant shuffled out of the back room. He shut the door before I could see what sort of dog was in there. Not too many guard dogs are put up in staff headquarters, even if they're only huts. "The inspector thinks we should board up the windows, Major."

The major coughed weakly and sat down on a chair against the wall. "Are you the one who brought the food?" He coughed again. "Did you bring any cigarettes?"

The general turned back to me. "Fixing the windows will protect the overturned and rusted machinery, the rotted floors, and the corroded pipes from . . . from what?"

"Forget I mentioned it." The major needed cigarettes like Pyongyang needed one-way streets.

"No, please," the general said in a suddenly solicitous tone, "it is instructive to hear from Pyongyang. Always good ideas."

"To tell you the truth, General, I'm not here to comment on your facility."

"A relief to learn that, isn't it, Major?"

I didn't remember sarcasm as a strong point of military service. Maybe the times had brought it out. "My apologies. No one is in a good mood these days, and I should have been more careful."

The general nodded at a chair. "Sit down if you want."

"You said this was a component assembly point."

The major stirred slightly, and the general frowned. "It was what it was; it is now something entirely different. Let's call it a symbol and leave it at that."

"Whatever you call it, I'm authorized to bring a visitor here."

"This should prove interesting because I have no authorization to receive anyone."

"You received me."

"No, at the moment you're still under guard." He patted his pistol.

I took out the document Pak had given me and unfolded it carefully. "This is a special situation."

The general stared at the paper. "More notes. Are you mocking me, Inspector?"

The major coughed and put his head against the wall.

"Not at all," I said. "I'm serious."

"If I had a telephone that worked, I'd call the chief of staff," the general said. The major lifted his head. "Or perhaps not," the general continued. "Why not the first vice marshal?" He looked at the two soldiers. "Get me the first vice marshal on the double." Neither of the guards budged, though the major groaned softly. "No, wait. We ate the last dispatch pigeon a week ago, didn't we?" The soldiers smiled slyly.

The general took the paper, read it quickly, and tore it into small pieces. "Wonderful to see you, Inspector. Nice to break the monotony. Now get out of here." He put his pistol on the table. "Drive back to wherever you came from. Tell them that all is calm in the countryside, and that they can safely let us continue to sink into the earth."

The game wasn't over, and we both knew it. "There are several sacks of rice in the trunk of my car, General. I put them there for traction in case the road was icy, but it's clear, so I won't need the extra weight on the drive back. The lock on the trunk is broken."

No one moved a muscle.

"I need to be back in Pyongyang by sunset, so I'll have to drive fast."

The general nodded; the two soldiers disappeared. After a minute or two, I heard the trunk of my car slam shut.

"I hope to see you again, General."

"Have a safe trip," he said, but he didn't walk me to my car.

Going back, the roads were no better than they had been coming. There was no reason they should be, since most of them were one lane.

When I drove into Pyongyang, it was past dinnertime. I went straight to the Koryo. Jenö was pacing around the lobby. As soon as they saw me, the hotel security men disappeared behind the pillars and went for something to eat.

"Where have you been?" Jenö pounced. "I thought you'd be here hours ago. Do you have any idea how many times the electricity went off while I was waiting?"

I was hungry and tired from the drive. "Next time bring a flashlight if it bothers you."

"Did you get permission?"

"Can I at least have time to sit down before you start on me?" I went over to the doorman's chair and sat. "Hard to tell what we got. The military says no instinctively. In this case, it may have been less than categorical. The fellow on the scene is interesting, that much I can say with confidence."

"Now what? Do we go or don't we? Without seeing the place I'm not prepared to proceed."

"Proceed? With what?" He started to reply, but I stopped him. "Don't tell me, I don't want to know. That's your business, and you can have it. Give me a day to think over what comes next. It will take me some time to fill up again, anyway."

"With gasoline?"

"No, rice. This will cost you."

2

The next morning, Pak was writing furiously. He always wrote furiously. Before they stopped making requisition forms, he put in a request every month for a chalkboard. "I want to beat the hell out of something when I write answers to these idiots," he would say. "Chalk is good. A chalkboard is perfect. You can pound on it for hours, and then when you're done, you erase the whole damned thing."

He stopped and crumpled the piece of paper that had borne the brunt of his pen. Then he cursed, smoothed it out, and started writing furiously again. He didn't look up when I knocked on his open door. "Get packed," he said simply. He read over what he had written. "Damned craziness." He put the crumpled paper in a file folder with a black band around it. "Well." He finally raised his head. "Are you packed?"

"For what?" I hadn't gone back to the office that night after seeing Jenö. It was late, I was cold and tired, and the tale of my conversation with the general could wait until morning. Nothing, I figured, would happen in the meantime.

Pak pointed at the folder. "For this." Apparently, I had been wrong. Apparently, a gear somewhere had become unstuck overnight.

I looked at the folder. There obviously wasn't much in it. It must have been only a small gear. "I don't know what it says."

"Of course you don't. It's a secret, very closely held in the Ministry. I am even instructed to keep it from you. Can you believe that?"

"Do I have a choice?"

"You are ordered to New York effective immediately."

"What?" My mouth doesn't generally drop open, but for this it did.

"You have an aisle seat on Saturday's plane to Beijing. There you wait for a visa, which may or may not be forthcoming from the Americans, and then onward as soon as possible to New York. 'Onward as soon as possible.' I sound like a dispatch cable."

"I can't do that." I was thinking fast but not coming up with much. The last thing I wanted to do was to fly over the Pacific Ocean to New York.

"Give me one good reason you can't."

"I have to take our foreigner to that site he mentioned. Don't you want to hear a report of what happened when I was up there? I'm not sure whether the note you signed made a dent, but at least they didn't shoot me." I was going to have to come up with something better, much better. The only problem was, I couldn't think of anything.

"They can shoot you later, after you get back, if they want. Right now, we have no time to worry about the foreigner. You have seventy-two hours to tidy up your office, clear those piles of paper off your desk, and wheedle a decent pair of shoes from the supply clerk."

"I don't need shoes," I said. "I need an explanation. When I land in a city behind enemy lines, I like to have some idea of what I'm doing, don't you?" This sounded better; it even gave me momentary hope that I had found some firm ground on which to take a stand. Maybe Pak could turn it into something effective.

"No, you don't get to know anything." Pak had a better sense of footing than I did. If he didn't even pause to make a show of considering the argument, it meant there wasn't any firm ground on this one, only swamp for as far as the eye could see. "Obviously, they'll have to tell you something sooner or later. But nothing officially now, not yet, anyway."

"Nothing?" Paduk stones are given more notice of being put on the board than I was getting.

Pak shrugged. "You didn't hear it from me, but it has to do with the dead woman, the one for whom you were supposed to sweep up a few facts and then dump the whole thing back in the Ministry's file of 'cases-for-another-day.' We only needed some background information on her. Nothing elaborate, remember? Shoe size, preference in blouse color, eating habits. Anything to fill up a few pages. Maybe if you'd done that like I told you, we'd have been able to unlatch ourselves from this whole thing."

"You don't really believe that."

"Doesn't matter what I believe anymore. But, no, I don't believe that."

"So, why New York?" I already knew why, or part of it. Her father had told me.

"She was in New York for a short time before her final assignment. That much you've already discovered on your own, I take it. They want to know what she did, who she saw, where she went while she was there. They think it's important, why I don't know. I told you about those strange winds from strange places. This is one of those. Think of yourself as a seabird being blown off course to an exotic clime."

"It's January. New York isn't exotic; it's colder than it is here. I know, I read the reports from the security detail assigned to the diplomatic mission there. They say it's miserable."

"As if anything they write can be believed. Why you in particular were selected to go on this junket might seem odd, but these are odd times. You've been overseas before, so I suppose you naturally came to mind."

"Is this another one of those favors?"

Pak could be impassive when he needed to be.

"You volunteered me?"

"Don't be ridiculous. I protested being deprived of staff, especially now."

"You wrote a complaint?"

"No. But I crumpled the order a couple of times."

I smiled at Pak. He threw the file over to me. "Consider yourself doubly lucky. There's a big meeting here next week, one of those national sessions. Ten thousand extra people in Pyongyang with no heat, no electricity, and no food. We'll all have double shifts trying to keep them out of trouble. All of us but you. You will be happily away from the action, seeing new sights, dodging muggers and blond women with legs that reach all the way to heaven."

"I'm not going. They can't make me."

"And will you cite the muggers or the legs as the reason?"

Chapter Four

I would have rather flown anything else, even a Chinese airline, but the Ministry insisted that I take their advice. "We've booked you on the U.S. national flag carrier," the travel clerk said. "We know airlines, don't worry." So on Tuesday afternoon, I climbed into a middle seat and took my last full breath for twelve hours. The man next to the window was as big as an ox; the woman on the aisle had hips. The ox and the hips both ate their dinners without looking up. I left mine on the tray. When the lights went out for the movie, I listened briefly to the engines, closed my eyes, and tried to think.

New York. I was bound for New York, where I could expect orders that would officially tell me less than what Pak had already told me informally. The orders would be encoded, but try as the code clerk could, he would not be able to make them sensible because, at base, they would be meaningless, almost certainly designed to use what I already knew to lead me away from what I really needed to learn. Whatever I was supposed to discover in New York, I wasn't supposed to understand how it fit into a larger picture. Pak had told me as much as he knew. Well, almost as much.

This had not been a simple investigation to begin with, even if that is what Pak insisted we could make it. Simple investigations don't send inspectors to strange places, in such proximity to strange hips. Someone in Pyongyang was abnormally worried about the dead woman's fate, and was frantically searching for clues on at least three continents, maybe more. More and more, it looked like that "someone" was Pak's acquaintance, the one for whom he was suddenly doing favors. The one for whom I was only a paduk stone, put on the board wherever he needed. Nothing simple about it. Either the woman was extremely important in her own right—and what little I'd seen so far didn't suggest anything along those lines—or she was involved in something very sensitive. Or maybe none of the above. There was still that final possibility, the one that kept popping into line and wouldn't disappear. Maybe she wasn't really the focus of whatever it was that was going on.

Besides the woman, there was Jenö. No connection between the two of them that I could see, except that they dropped into my life more or less at the same time. Jenö had an inordinate interest in missiles. The woman might have been killed in Pakistan. I didn't know if there were tabs and slots in all that, but it was worth bearing in mind.

As long as there was nothing else to do, it would have been good to make a few notes, but there wasn't enough room to move my arm.

Chapter Five

"There was about the place the curious and companionable silence of men at breakfast away from home."

Pak seemed to be listening to me; I saw his head move to the side as it does when he is puzzled. But I was tired from the flight home, and he was slightly out of focus. Maybe his head hadn't moved to one side. Maybe mine had.

"It was a plain room, like the rest of the hotel. We all ate in solitary fashion. The waitresses kept their voices low. I suppose it might seem like a funeral, but it wasn't. It was oddly pleasant. Even though we didn't know each other, there was a sense of unity. We frowned together when one of the tables started a conversation. Bankers, I think. They were the only ones wearing yellow sweaters and big glasses."

This image of the breakfast room was still fresh in my brain. It was the only thing fresh in my brain. Otherwise, a brick occupied my skull, and had since I arrived back in Pyongyang around midday. The brick and I went straight to the office. "Don't worry," the customs official at the airport had said as he went through my bag absentmindedly, "it's jet lag. They say it goes away sooner or later." So far it wasn't going away. My consciousness was still over the Pacific.

"That's it?" Pak shook his head. "You were in New York for almost a week, and all you remember is breakfast?"

"I'll go back to my desk and write a long trip report once I figure out what time zone I'm in." If I went back to my desk, I could close the door and put my head down.

"No, I want to hear it from you directly, not on paper, not in your deadly prose. Come on, Inspector, I'll buy you a beer later, or something stronger if you prefer." He waited, but when I said nothing, he closed his eyes. If I dared do that, I'd be asleep where I stood. "It must have been amazing," Pak said.

"It was."

"I'm listening." Pak's voice had taken on a dreamy quality. He settled back in his chair, his eyes still shut. "Leave nothing out."

"It's just a city. A city is a city. Cities are all basically the same. They may be in better or worse states of repair, they may seem more or less orderly, but if the fundamental reality is straight in your mind, you don't get overwhelmed."

"The point?" Still that dreamy voice, as if he were listening to me from somewhere else. That wasn't like Pak. Even when fully awake, I was the one who drifted; he was the anchor. If Pak began drifting, I'd float out to sea for sure, food for sharks.

"It's a city, with buildings, streets, and noise." I paused, irritated, sleepy, still not sure I could remember what I'd seen because I wasn't sure I had really seen it. That reality problem again. "Lots of noise—cars, people, construction equipment. They are always tearing up streets, from what I saw, even in the dead of winter. There must be some flaw in their road construction technique. Huge holes in some of the streets."

"There are always flaws. Maybe there's a shortage of asphalt."

"It is crowded during the day, but empty at night in most places."

"Unsafe." He stirred. "That's what a lot of people say, it's unsafe."

"Could be, but I walked around a good bit and no one bothered me."

"Were you followed?" As I should have guessed, the man was paying attention, he wasn't dreaming.

"I thought you were going to listen."

"Well, damn it, O, you're wading too long through the preliminaries. I'm just interested, that's all. So, were you followed?" He opened one eye to emphasize that this was a question that couldn't be avoided.

"There are always a few thousand people behind you, who can tell? I think I caught sight of a tail once or twice, but there wasn't much of an effort to disguise it. The same man came into every coffee shop and bookstore with me for an entire afternoon. When I sat down, he sat down. When I browsed, he browsed. It looked like they were pushing, trying to see what I would do. Either that or they share the same training manual with our special section."

"Skip it. You can describe the operational stuff for the files later." He sat up, alert again. The anchor was in place. "What was there to see? And don't try to tell me all cities are the same. They aren't."

"There are buildings—lots of brick buildings, most of them old, though they think old is a hundred years. Not all of them are that tall."

"Not tall? What are you talking about?"

"Some are pretty tall, of course, but not all of them." Building height didn't interest me that much. I didn't mind craning my neck to look up at a tall tree. After all, it had grown to that place in the sky; the topmost leaves felt breezes the taproot could only imagine. But buildings didn't know one floor from another, and didn't care. "You know what was fascinating?"

Pak groaned. "You're going to talk about trees, aren't you?"

"There were signs painted on some buildings. These aren't banners or rooftop signboards, but slogans actually painted on the buildings. And I don't mean political slogans. I started taking notes about them while I was walking around. They were odd announcements, advertisements for goods, mostly. I saw one for 'Undies.' No one in the mission had any idea what it meant. I did an informal study to see whether those signs revealed anything, you know, sociopolitical insights into economic superstructure. That sort of thing."

"I'm hearing, but I'm not believing. What do you know about economic superstructure?"

"It's a small island."

"Three and a half kilometers wide. Not even as wide as the demilitarized zone."

"You were following me around?"

"When I have an inspector far away, I like to keep him close. I just needed a mental map of where you were, so I did some checking. I trust that was alright."

"How long is it?"

"From the Battery or from South Ferry?"

Suddenly, I didn't feel so sleepy. "You've been there, haven't you?"

"I've been here in my chair, Inspector, waiting for you to return and regale me. And you were talking about the economic superstructure. Proceed."

"I was about to say, we have a North-South problem, right?"

Pak wagged a finger. "It's not a problem."

"You want to comment on everything, or do you want to listen?"

"Speak, o traveler." Pak settled back again and closed his eyes.

"They divide East-West, like Germany did." I waited, but Pak didn't stir. "I couldn't see any difference between the eastern part of the island and the western part, but they can. So I did a little survey and discovered it shows up in subtle ways."

"I'll bet."

"You know what I discovered? On cross streets—those are the streets that are numbered—most of the building signs are visible only for those coming from the west, walking easterly. On the avenues—the bigger streets that run north and south—there is a slight preference for those coming from uptown, moving south, but that may be a statistical anomaly, except on Park Avenue, which is, from all I could tell, a bastion of the rich. So ask yourself, who benefits? Who is supposed to be looking at these signs, and who is being disadvantaged?"

"Okay, I'm asking myself." He opened one eye. "And you are going to tell me."

"The conclusion is inescapable. It is wrapped in a subtle sociological and class message, a subtextual fly in what the Americans like to think of as their fabulous melting pot. Simply stated: If you come from the poorer section, the east side, and cross over to the richer west, you are on your own. There are few signs put up for your benefit. But do you think those on the east side simply accept this?"

"I have a feeling they don't."

"That's right, they don't. In protest, most of the signs on the east side are meant for east side eyes. There are plenty of signs on the backs of buildings not so far from our UN mission, along the east side of Lexington Avenue. Who are those signs for? Pilots on East River tugboats? Far-sighted people on the Queens waterfront? I don't think so."

"Queens?"

"Look on your map."

"That's it? The sum total of your report?"

I rubbed my hands together. "I'm only getting started. Maybe I should take up political analysis. How hard can it be? Let's go for a walk."

Pak sat up and looked out his window. "In this rotten weather? February is no time to stroll around."

"Cold is good for you, it helps the new shoots."

Pak laughed, finally. "Whatever works," he said, and put on his coat.

When we were on the street, Pak put his hands on his ears. "I forgot my hat. This is a hell of a cold day to be outside, O." He'd used my name twice in a row; it meant he was happy to see me back. "Walk briskly. Never give your blood a chance to stop moving."

For some reason, it didn't strike me as so cold. "You want to hear about New York, you'll have to slow down a little. I can't think when I'm slipping on the ice. All my mental energy goes into balance." I slid on a patch that Pak had stepped around. "What has happened to the snow-clearing teams? Isn't anyone responsible for keeping the sidewalks clean anymore? They do a pretty good job of clearing the sidewalks in New York."

Pak slowed long enough for me to catch up. "You might want to go easy on the invidious comparisons. Think before you say anything for the next few days, until your feet are back on the ground." He reached for his ears again. "What did you learn about our lady friend? That's why you were sent there."

"I thought you wanted local color."

"Sure I do. What's the sense of having you go halfway around the globe if you don't bring back tales of dragons and giants? But the vice minister has been badgering me for information on that lady. You and I know he doesn't actually give a damn. What really concerns him is that your trip came out of the Minister's special budget, and so he needs to justify it. Of more concern to us, the Minister is being squeezed for information about the case. Every morning after you left, I got a barrage of phone calls from him. Each one had exactly the same message: He needed the answer today . . . this minute . . . this very minute . . ."

I didn't care about the vice minister. He was a rat and sooner or later would be trapped like one. The Minister was another matter. Who was putting pressure on him? An inspector might bend in the breeze; the Minister had a more difficult time doing that. Big trees blew over more often than little ones.

"I don't think I found much of anything that is going to help. It can be summed up in a couple of sentences. She was there for only a few weeks, at which point she left suddenly. She barely gave any notice. The security man at the mission said she told him a couple of hours ahead of time, that's all. He was still mad. He'd never seen anything like it, he said. And when he sent in a negative note for her file, he was told to forget the whole thing. As far as I could tell, she didn't do much in the office. The wives complained she didn't fit in."

"For instance."

"They had a reception, and all of them were supposed to cook something. She didn't cook. She bought something already made and unwrapped it right there in front of them. There was an argument about it, but word came down to leave her alone. People pouted that she got special treatment, and no one was sorry when she left."

"They know she was murdered?"

"Some rumors. They figured that's why I was there. I got furtive glances but not much cooperation."

"Where was her husband?"

Her husband, the one who was going to get her in trouble with the locals. If she was so difficult to get a line on, he would be impossible. People seemed to know less about him than they did about her. "I got very blank looks whenever I brought him up. He was supposed to be there, they were expecting him, but he never showed up in New York. No one notified the mission that his orders had been changed. Guess where he went instead? Pakistan, or that's what a few people thought they'd heard."

"Maybe he's still there. Anybody bother to check yet?"

"Not me, I was only a local broom, remember? She arrived in New York at the end of June, hung around until July, and then one night packed her bags and was gone."

"She couldn't have just left on her own. Someone must have taken her to the airport."

"Well, she didn't walk there, that's for sure. The airport is too far away. But no one in the mission drove her. I looked at their logs."

"Nobody bothered to find out how she got there?"

"The security man told me it was on his list of things to do. It's a long list, he said."

"What was she doing in the city when she wasn't in the office?"

"Either no one knew or they wouldn't tell me. People said she went for walks in the park in the center of town."

"Not alone, she didn't. She'd be petrified to go out by herself in that city."

"Could be, though if she took after her father, I don't think she had a lot of fear. You think she knew someone there?"

"Don't you?"

"I'm not sure if she already knew someone, or maybe she met them by accident."

"But she knew someone."

"That's what it looked like, but I wasn't going to dig around in something like that. I had no authorization; the orders were a joke. Anyway, I didn't know the territory. The main thing is, she didn't act like a normal Foreign Ministry wife. And if she didn't act like one in New York, I'll bet she didn't do it in Pakistan, either."

"You were wrong."

"This was useful?"

"No. It was more than a couple of sentences." We stopped at a doorway. Pak knocked. There was no answer.

"It's dark, they must have left. Let's go back to the office." By now I realized Pak was right, it was a crazy cold day to be outside.

"Don't be so impatient, Inspector." He knocked again, two taps; he waited, then one more.

The door opened a crack, barely wide enough for us to slip through.

"Hurry up, you'll let all the heat out." A woman's voice. Then laughter. Inside was nearly as cold as it was on the street. The room held a few small tables; two men sat drinking morosely. The woman who had shouted at us appeared. "All the heat!" She laughed again. "You're welcome to sit as long as you want. If you want to drink, you can do that. No food, though. The shipment of twigs didn't arrive." At this, one of the men laughed, and the other stared into his glass.

"Good, here we are, warm and cozy." Pak looked at the candle on the table. He had his jacket zipped up all way the up. "Anything hot," he said to the woman. "Hot water with sawdust sprinkled on it, I don't care. As long as it's hot. Bring it, and then leave us alone."

The woman disappeared. When she returned, she had a tray with two bowls of soup and a pot of weak tea. "Don't worry," she said. "It's as hot as it's going to get. If I had some fish, it would be fish soup. But I found some salt, don't ask me where, and that makes it seem like there's fish in it. No charge for the leaves." She put the tray down and disappeared again; this time she closed the door behind her.

We finished the meal quickly and in silence. The two drinkers stared at us. Pak reached in his coat for cigarettes. "Tell me a story, Inspector, about a faraway place." He lit two cigarettes and gave me one. "Weave a magic carpet, take us to the land of fallen women and beggars. And if you can't take us there, take us to New York."

2

"It wasn't much to see." I looked over at the drinkers. They turned their attention back to their glasses. "Very simple geography. It's on an island, like Yanggak-to, only bigger." I waited.

"Three and a half kilometers wide," Pak said. "Or did I already mention that?"

"It sits between two rivers, both broad enough to keep the population from moving back and forth except for the bridges. There are a few boats, but not many that I saw; maybe because of the cold weather. The wind was fierce, and there was snow piled so high in some places I could barely walk across the street. The whole place is pretty flat, though they haven't leveled it completely. Some streets are steep going down to the river on the east side."

"Like San Francisco."

"I don't know, I've never been there. I didn't think I knew anyone who had."

Pak hummed a few notes.

"What is that?"

"Called 'Gone to San Francisco' or something. It was on the radio when we were out on operations sometimes, and we'd sing it as a joke because the boss said if we got good enough, one day they'd send us to steal the Golden Gate Bridge."

Again, I sensed problems with the anchor. Pak had never told me anything like that before, not even hinted it. Something was making him very bold, almost reckless. "Do you want to talk about San Francisco or New York?"

Pak smiled and studied his cigarette. "Go on, tell me a tale. What about the buildings?"

"Buildings," I said, relieved he seemed to have calmed down again. "You've seen enough pictures to know what the skyline looks like. But you can't really understand the traffic without being there. There's noise from cars, horns honking, bus engines straining, almost the whole day long. At night there are trucks. I don't know what they carry, but they are going fast and they make a hell of a racket. Most of the cars are old—plenty of speeding and not much attention to traffic laws. Hardly any traffic police, but otherwise lots of patrols in cars and some on foot. If we had that many police visible on the streets, there would be a revolution. There's always an emergency vehicle screaming up one street and down another."

"Pedestrians? Bicycles?"

"Hardly any bicycles. Must be banned, though you'd have to be crazy to ride a bike in that traffic. You can't walk down the sidewalk without running into some beggars; in fact, a lot of beggars. Some prostitutes, too. A considerable number of people who looked very rich, if you find yourself in the right neighborhood. Women . . ." I paused to collect my thoughts because I still found it hard to describe. When I had seen it I could barely believe my eyes. "Women dressed up but obviously not satisfied with what they have because they are shopping for more. Prices are crazy; the prices of some of that clothing must be worth several months' wages to the clerks. Countless restaurants and markets, plenty of vegetables. Even in winter."

"Vegetables." Pak nodded. "You journey to a distant civilization, and you tell me about carrots?"

"Wait, I nearly forgot. Where's our foreigner? I should get in touch with him; we have unfinished business, remember?"

"Don't bother. He left."

"Left? When?"

"The day after I told him you were called away on another assignment."

"Did he ask where?"

"He did."

"Did you tell him?"

"No."

"Strange that he should leave all of a sudden." It didn't sit right, somehow.

"Everything about him is strange. Strange is our byword these days. Get back to the buildings. You skipped over that part."

"Old, new, tall, short, no empty spaces, just wall-to-wall buildings except for a few parks and the banks of the rivers. They've never been in a war, so nobody flattened the place. They do it themselves, the tearing down."

"It doesn't sound like you were in the office much, interviewing people."

"The mission wasn't interested in cooperating. Once I started asking about our subject, no one wanted to talk to me except to register complaints about her lack of cooking skills. So I went out, tried to get some feel on my own for where she'd been, whom she might have met, what she might have seen. Routine stuff."

"And?"

"I got lost."

"Were you followed?"

"Didn't I already go over this?"

"Yes, but we're going to get asked again and again, so let me make sure I know your story."

"It's hard to be sure whether I was followed. That's my story."

"Not the best, but we'll work on it. You said you were followed into a bookshop."

"Who knows? I told you, the same guy went into four coffee shops with me. I suppose it's possible that he just liked coffee. I only went in to warm up."

"You want me to guess? I'm guessing you were followed. Besides him, anyone approach you directly?"

I thought about it. "I was walking up a street, very steep, right where cars come out of a tunnel that goes under the river, east something street. There was a man walking down the hill. He stopped and asked if I needed help."

"Strange. Did he stop everybody he saw, or just you?"

"I was looking up at the buildings. He might have thought I was lost, which I was. He said a few words of Korean that he seemed to know, but I pretended I was Chinese."

"You think it was choreographed?"

"Nah, just chance. Old guy, colorful coat, though—red and black and white and I don't know what else. He didn't seem to have much to do. He wasn't in a hurry to get anywhere like everybody else."

"You double-check?"

"Sure. I made a note about the episode and gave it to the security man. Don't worry, we're covered. No one of the old man's description rang a bell with anyone at the mission. They said he could have been any one of a thousand religious Jews walking around. There was nothing in the contact logs fitting his description or that sort of approach."

"Religious Jews." Pak repeated it slowly. We looked at each other. "Maybe she was followed, too, and maybe she bumped into a religious Jew and maybe she never reported it. She wasn't the type to fill out forms, as far as I can tell. Runs in the family, I guess."

"Have you been doing your own research?" I was trying to remember the face of the old man on the street. It was mostly beard, so I couldn't be sure of the rest of it.

"Her father called the Ministry to complain about you, and they told him to call me. We talked for a while, if you can call that research.

What if she was approached in New York? That could have some connection to what happened to her later."

Sure thing, I thought. The long arm of New York. "There is no way to know what she was doing. The local security man only had a chance to follow her two or three times. He thought she might have been tailed by the locals. Nothing subtle, as far as I can tell. How many relays of people in blue scarves can there be, he asked me. Each time, she lost them for a while, but they picked her up again without much trouble because she went to the same place each time, that park. Going there she'd walk using a slightly different route; but each time she took the same cab home. He was sure it was the same cabdriver, a female. I thought that might be something, but it wasn't. When I tracked the driver down, it turned out to be a young Pakistani woman whose father had sent her to the U.S. to go to school."

Pak nodded. "A young Pakistani woman. Sure, there must be lots of them driving cabs in New York. At least she wasn't a Jew. Tell me, please, O, that there are no Pakistani Jews." He paused, turning this over in his mind. Then he went on. "This driver, she told you a story, I suppose."

"She did. I got in her cab and told her to take me to one of the train stations. She said she was bored with school and started driving a cab. She was worried because her father was coming for a visit. If he found out she wasn't in school, she said, he would drag her home. She didn't want to go. Why not, I asked. Because he would arrange a marriage to a man who would treat her like dirt. He might beat her. What will you do, I asked. She turned around to look at me. 'If he beats me? I'll kill him.'"

"Maybe she was just making the whole thing up."

"Nope. All you had to do was to look into her eyes. This was real. She wasn't kidding."

Pak took a last puff on his cigarette. "Get some sleep," he said. "You should take up smoking again." He pointed at my cigarette, floating in the soup bowl. "Might help your jet lag."

Chapter Six

"His name is Sohn and he's from the party," Pak said. The next morning, we were in my office, and Pak seemed a little ill at ease. It wasn't unusual these days. All of us were that way—a little ill at ease all the time. Bad stories were coming in from the countryside. Here in the capital, people were disappearing from offices, food was scarce, heat was random, electricity was unpredictable and even when there was some, it didn't last very long. No one pretended things weren't bad, though we didn't talk a lot about it. The question was whether we would get through it.

"Am I supposed to be impressed with his party status? Because I'll tell you frankly, I'm not. Not these days. You know him, maybe?" As I spoke, Pak drummed his fingers on my desk. In better times, that would have meant he was impatient. Or in some cases, usually in the spring when it was possible to smell the earth again, that little gesture meant he was full of energy, ready to go for a long walk along the river. Now, more and more, he did it because he was nervous and depressed. "How much longer are we supposed to stand around and snap at flies?" I said. "He should have been here a half hour ago. I can't wait all day. I have things to do."

"Like what? That report you haven't touched? Just relax, Inspector."
I almost laughed out loud—him telling me to relax. His fingers had settled into a slow, steady drumbeat, sort of funereal. I realized he might
keep it up the rest of the week if I didn't figure out some way to get him
to move his hand. "Try not to antagonize him," Pak said, and his fingers
went *thrum thrum*. "You can annoy me all you want, but for him, I need
you to sit quietly and listen to what he says. Let him throw his weight
around." *Thrum.*

"I'm losing track," I said. "Who's on top these days? I can't keep
score. Is the party up or down? Is the army the army of the party, or
does the party emulate the military? Which is it this week? Why don't
you draw me a chart?"

"Forget that. This is no time to be choosing sides. Who knows
where things will be in another six months."

Six months, I thought. Long time. He must have been thinking the
same thing. We just sat there for a minute or so, wondering.

"I'm not going to like him," I said finally. "This Sohn character will
rub me the wrong way, and you know how I react when that happens?"
I'd just asked Pak if he knew the man. He'd heard me, but he hadn't
answered. I was getting a funny feeling about where this was headed. I
didn't need to look six months down the road to see trouble. It might
arrive in only a few minutes.

"Let's be clear, Inspector. Your personal evaluation of the man is at
the bottom of my list of worries. Very near the bottom. I need you to
let him say whatever he is going to say and then, without answering
back or doing anything more than nodding politely, let him leave.
Down the steps, out the door, good-bye Comrade Sohn. Got it? The
phone call I received this morning from the Ministry said you were to
be present when he showed up. You're present. I'm just making a tiny
addendum—behave."

I didn't have anything to say to that, so I looked out my window. A
car went by outside, and I listened to its tires on the snow. A cold, very
gray day. The sound of a car slowly driving down an empty street. It
was enough to put you to sleep, that and the drumbeat from the desk.
I almost didn't hear Pak. ". . . you're staring off into space again. I
don't understand these mood swings of yours all of a sudden, Inspec-

tor. Cut it out, will you? Things are bad enough without your constant moping."

"What do you want from me? I don't take to cheerful suffering." I instantly wished I hadn't said that. Pak's life was worse than mine. The only suffering I had was watching other people driven to their knees.

Pak considered for a moment. His fingers went quiet, then resumed. "Not to repeat myself, but let Sohn do the talking. All you have to do is listen. That's the sum total of what I need from you. Silence." He picked up a pencil, which ended the problem of the drum. "Or am I asking too much?"

"So, you do know him. Is he the someone for whom you're suddenly doing favors?" No response. "Alright, it's not a problem. I'll let him do the talking. I'll be mute. I'll be a stone. I'll stare at his ears."

"Don't." Pak looked alarmed. "Whatever happens, don't do that."

"Don't stare? Why, will he disappear in a thunderclap? Who pushed me into this, anyway?" Silly question—it was fairly obvious by now that this man Sohn was behind it. "The Ministry has a whole roster of inspectors, a lot of them in the senior ranks. Good ratings, high marks in loyalty and performance. Why me?" Also a silly question.

"How should I know?"

I didn't like the look that wasn't on Pak's face. "Ever since our visitor showed up, we've had nothing but trouble," I said. "You think that has something to do with this party guy?"

"How should I know?"

"How should you know? You keep saying that. You know plenty that you don't tell me. If you owe him something, that's up to you to handle. Don't drag me into it." A horn sounded as a car pulled into our building's driveway. I looked out the window. The car was black, and it had party plates. "It's Sohn."

"I need to be in my office," Pak said, bouncing out of the chair and hurrying down the hall. A moment later he was back, with a tired smile around his eyes. "I just realized, he'll be outside the gate for a while. The new guards are going to give him a hard time. He'll show them his party ID and they'll stare at it. There, see?" Pak pointed out my window. "One of them dropped it in the snow, and the other stepped on it."

"Mind if I watch, too?"

"No. I don't want him to look up and see you." Pak stepped away from the window. "Actually, he shouldn't see me, either. He'll get out of the car"—a door slammed—"and start threatening them. Then he'll demand to use the gate phone."

The phone on Pak's desk rang. Pak pressed a button and routed it into my office. He put the receiver carefully to his ear. "Yes, comrade. I'm happy to give them orders to let you in, but I don't control them, as you know." He listened, but not with any tension in his posture. "No, not at all; I'm not denying you entry. It's just that I don't control entry. They do. No, it wasn't my idea to have it done that way. Who can I call to fix it? I can call the Ministry, but then they'll have to call the army. That's the new . . . yes, of course, I'll be right down." He hung up the phone. "The guards will back off when they see me, at least I hope so. Otherwise my feet will get cold in all that slush."

2

It had started snowing again and was almost dark when I heard what sounded like a bear coming up the stairs. The door to Pak's office slammed. There followed fifteen minutes of angry words and sharp barks. I leaned into the hall to hear better. Suddenly, Pak's door flew open.

"There you are, Inspector." He motioned to me, a slight warning. "Come in and sit down." Pak walked back to his desk with that uneasy gait that meant he was going to tell me something I didn't want to hear. "Close the door while you're at it."

I half expected the bear would be sitting across from Pak, but when I stepped into the office, the visitor's chair was empty. Instead, in the far corner, a man lounged against the wall. If Pak wanted the door shut, it meant we were not going to have a conversation about the weather.

"Inspector." Pak cleared his throat. "This is Comrade Sohn. He is from—"

"Never mind where I am from." The man barked to clear his own throat and then coughed to make sure the job was done. His ears were exceedingly small and perfectly shaped. It was as if the old ones had been surgically removed, replaced by a new pair from a child, and pasted to the side of his head, but slightly too low. On a woman, they might have looked good. Like shells. On him, it made you wonder if he was underdeveloped from the neck up. I tried not to stare. No wonder Pak had been so upset at the mention of ears.

"We can skip where he is from." Pak indicated I was to sit in the vacant chair. "But I believe he has something to tell you."

As far as I was concerned, Sohn had stepped off on the wrong foot. "I'm all ears," I said. I cleared my throat, not to be left out.

The man looked closely at me, weighing whether I was going to be trouble. Then he grunted and glanced around the office. It wasn't exactly disdain on his face, but he managed to convey that he was not usually to be found in this type of unimportant setting. Maybe that's why he was standing, to make clear he didn't feel completely comfortable in such a place. "Normally, our conversation wouldn't be held in offices like this," he said at last and coughed. "Normally, your supervisor would have nothing to do with it. Normally"—he paused to emphasize how abnormal everything was—"I would just borrow you for a while. You'd be put on leave from your duties, and then when everything was done, you'd drop back into this place. If all went well, you wouldn't drop back from too great a height." He stopped to make sure he had my attention. He did. "But your Minister has recently made clear he doesn't want his people disappearing like that these days. 'Too disruptive,' he complains. Your Minister has a reputation for complaining overmuch sometimes, did you know that?" The little ears waited for either of us to respond, but we knew enough not to.

"Naturally." Sohn barked twice and then continued, "Things being what they are, I try to help out where possible. Your ministry is important to us in these troubled times. That's the reason, and the only reason, I'm including your supervisor in this conversation." So it wasn't that I was supposed to be present when Sohn talked to Pak, it was that Pak was to be present when Sohn spoke to me.

I waited for Pak to say something. It was his office, it was his status being knifed. He sat back, subdued, very unlike the way he had been with the crowd from the special section not so long ago. There should at least have been some tension in his eyes. There wasn't. All I could detect was a quiet amusement, as if over a joke told long ago.

"What do you want from me?" If Pak wasn't going to say anything, I might as well speak up.

Sohn looked at Pak and smiled. "Your Inspector has asked what we want from him. Will you tell him, or shall I?"

Pak looked out the window. "It's your game, comrade."

"Fine." Sohn turned to me. "Plenty, Inspector, I want plenty." He barked and grunted, which I figured meant he was going to say something important. "So listen carefully. Don't take notes; don't ask questions. Just listen."

I nodded and barked to show I was on his wavelength. Pak shot me a sharp look.

"These are perilous times. It is not clear that we will survive another year." Sohn said this in a normal tone of voice, like the one normal people used when they talked about normal things—the cost of bus fare, or the price of a movie ticket. "Does that shock you, Inspector? That I should be candid about something so sensitive? But, why? Everybody thinks we're on the edge of the precipice, don't they? Don't you?"

If the man imagined for an instant I was going to answer a question like that, he was crazy. "I'm still waiting to hear what you want," I said, with less humility than Pak had indicated he wanted from me during this session.

Sohn moved so he was standing over me. I tried not to notice his ears. "I know you, Inspector. Believe me, I wouldn't be standing here if I didn't know you inside and out, top to bottom. Your type worries a lot, but you also know how to act when the time comes. This is it—time to act. Things will get worse, maybe a lot worse. Those who cannot take the pain this winter, cannot drag themselves through the final few months, they'll fall by the side of the road. We're better off without them." From the corner of my eye, I saw Pak shift in his chair. "And I'm not talking theory, Inspector. I know what things are like in the provinces. I just got back from there. They are as grim as everything you've heard. They are as grim as our enemies say. This is the fight for survival. But do you know what? We will survive. Despite what everyone thinks, or fears, or hopes—we will survive."

"I hear they're shipping in food, our enemies," I said.

This time it was Pak who coughed. "Get to the point, Sohn."

"The point. Thank you, Chief Inspector. The point is we need more from them, our enemies. More food. More oil. More whatever they are ready to squeeze through the eyedropper they use to measure what they will give. As the inspector just said, they are shipping in food, but we must have more. That's where you come in." He leaned down slightly, so I was looking directly at one of his ears. "You will help us get it, Inspector."

"Me? What if I say no?"

"Ha! That you cannot do. You can't. You can't say yes or no, because no one is asking you to make that choice. You have no choice because there is none. You will carry out this assignment; it is what you are going to do. Period. We are down to the naked essence of existence, reduced to simplicity itself." I thought of Pak's lecture on "essence." He must have heard that line on "essence" somewhere. Maybe it had been in one of those cadre lectures I avoided; maybe it had been the theme in one of those newspaper editorials I never read. Or maybe Pak had regular meetings with Sohn, and this whole conversation today was a charade for my benefit. I looked hard at Pak. No, it wasn't a charade. The memory of amusement had left his eyes. His face was drained.

"This is not an order, Inspector." Sohn wasn't finished talking. He stood up straight again and leaned against Pak's desk. "Let's be as precise as a bayonet through the throat. This goes far beyond an order. It transcends an order. What shall we call it? I know!" He snapped his fingers. "It is an imperative. This is one of those times when the old concepts don't fit. We are past any notions of shirking or obeying. This is about the survival of the nation. Not this country, not this person or that individual, but the nation, *our* nation. And on that, you have nothing to say. We will survive, and you will make sure of it. Your grandfather ensured we survived; you will do no less. Not one drop less."

"That's it. I don't think I can help you, Sohn." I stood up and opened the door to leave. I didn't think, I just did it. Pak would be furious with me for this sort of insubordination. Who knows what Sohn would do? Anyone who put bayonets and throats together into the same image was tougher than the normal party hack. But if he was going to drag my grandfather into this, as far as I was concerned, the conversation was over. I could deal with hot water. I always had.

"Sit down, Inspector." Pak was no longer subdued. He didn't often issue commands to me, but there was no mistaking his tone. "You'll leave when I give you permission, and I haven't done that. And you"—he turned to Sohn—"you don't come in here and push my staff around. How many times do I have to tell you people to lay off? If there is any semblance of order left in this city, it is thanks to officers like Inspector O."

Sohn took in the surroundings again, four bleak walls and a window looking nowhere. "A little box for little men. Trust me, I'm not here to debate. Day after tomorrow, the inspector leaves on assignment. He's my body until that assignment is over. End of story." He threw a piece of paper on Pak's desk. "This is the order, signed by your minister. I heard you only liked signed orders. Go ahead, look it over."

3

The next day, Pak sat in my office, drumming his fingers on my desk again. Same march of the doomed, if anything at a more somber pace. We hadn't heard anything else from Sohn.

"I still can't even remember what century I'm in, and they want me to jump in an airplane again! How many days since I got back from New York?" I looked out at the empty street.

"Two days. Tomorrow will be three. The century isn't important, as long as you can correctly locate the planet."

"Maybe Sohn has forgotten us."

"Not a chance. He'll be back. Didn't I tell you something big was up?"

"Sure, always something big and important. And when it's not important, it's earthshaking. Trumpets every damned time you turn on the damned radio. Nothing ever says: 'This is beneath your notice, O, don't concern yourself with it.' I'm so low in the food chain, I'm expected to vibrate to everything." I sat down and put my ear to the top of my desk. "Wait! I hear far-off rumbles."

Pak stopped drumming. "Quit kidding around."

"Who's kidding?" I put my ear against the desk again. "Let's make it eight hundred kilometers to the west."

Pak motioned for me to get up and shut the door. There was no one else around, but shutting the door had become a ritual that Pak was reluctant to give up. "How did you find out?" He didn't want to know, but felt obliged to ask.

"I vibrate, remember?"

"Go on."

"There was a defector in Beijing a few days ago. High level. Very, very high level. Am I right?"

Pak gave me a noncommittal look. "Whatever happened, if anything happened, will be reported to us, all in due time, in proper channels, with proper vibrations, I'm sure. Someone just has to figure out the angle. This is bad, but it is good, precisely because it is bad. Things are less dangerous, and that means they're more dangerous. That sort of thing."

I continued. "This morning, on my way to the office, I stopped at District Headquarters. After my trip, I figured I should look in and say hello. I saw a lot of nervous people running around covering their hindquarters, erasing signs that they were ever in the same room with this defector person. I barely got over here and settled with my feet on my desk when I started receiving a lot of nervous phone calls from people who wouldn't tell me why they wanted to know what they wanted to know. The question that naturally occurs to me is, what does it have to do with us? I never saw the man."

"A party secretary who defects," Pak said, "cannot but have something to do with us. How can you be so sure you never saw him? Did he ever drive through your sector?"

"I'd guess he probably did. It's hard to get anywhere in the city without going through my sector."

"Did he ever meet with anyone, talk to anyone, smile at anyone, nod to anyone while he was passing through your sector?"

"How should I know? I don't follow people at his level. That's State Security's job, if they ever wake up long enough to look at their daily operational packet. It's not my worry."

"Well, of course, these things are beneath you, O. By no means should you worry about them. Keep on not worrying until someone comes a-knockin' to find out what you know, or don't know. And someone will.

Soon. They always do. This . . . situation . . . has rattled a lot of expensive teeth. At the Ministry last night I heard most of the special squad was sent in a hurry to Beijing. Of course, they made things worse. Bunch of thugs standing around the streets. Did they think he'd change his mind and come back home after he looked out the window and saw their ugly faces? Speaking of ugly, I wonder if your friend Mun tagged along with them. Maybe he'll be back to question you."

I thought of the man at the Foreign Ministry whose ambassador had disappeared. "So what? He'll find nothing, because there's nothing to find."

"Really? Mun already knows we recently entertained a visitor of dubious credentials."

"We didn't entertain him. He was assigned to us."

"And you didn't go out walking with him?"

"What has this got to do with anything?"

"Sometimes, Inspector, I think you must have been hatched in another galaxy."

"No, I meant, what does all of this have to do with being snatched by Sohn and sent away on another airplane? If I fly into Beijing, I'll be landing in the middle of this mess. You don't want that, do you?"

Pak went into statue mode: no response, not even any sign of comprehension.

"For the record, the chief inspector declines to answer."

"Ask Sohn."

"Do you actually think he will tell me anything?" I already knew what Pak would say, but I let him say it.

"Probably not."

4

The next day was the coldest on record. I read once that people in some countries get accustomed to the cold. Iceland, maybe. Not someplace I needed to go. I'd never convince myself to crawl out from under the quilt to go in to work in Iceland.

"Get something hot to drink," I heard Pak say as I passed by. He didn't complain that I was later than usual. He left me alone until afternoon, when he walked quietly down the hall and stood at my door. He must have been waiting for a few minutes for me to look up from the plans I was studying. The plans were for a built-in bookcase, which appealed to my sense of fantasy. Built into what?

"You'll want to keep those in the bottom drawer for the next few months. I think we're going to be busy."

I looked up. "What?"

"Sohn is coming back in a few hours with a more complete set of orders. The Minister personally rejected what he tried to push on us the other day. The Minister doesn't want to dip into his special fund anymore." Pak stepped inside. He leaned against the wall in an effort to appear nonchalant. "Try not to antagonize the man again. I know that's what I said before, but apparently I wasn't clear. Just listen to what he has to say, even if he raises something near and dear." Pak paused to let that sink in. "Let him throw his weight around, something you failed to do last time he was here. He is one of the few who has kept his balance during this push by the army. We may need his protection someday, so don't—*do not*—get under his skin."

"Why do I keep getting the feeling that you two know each other?"

"His skin, O, stay out from under it."

"I've forgotten again. Tell me again, whose backside do I worship this week?"

"The wind blows, we bend like one of your trees. Bamboo, maybe. Bamboo bends, doesn't it? Nothing too difficult. You should try it sometime."

"Bamboo. It's not real wood, you know." I didn't say the rest of what I was thinking.

"Bend, O, for once in your charmed existence, bend."

"I'll tell you the truth. I still don't like him. It's not a snap judgment, I've given it a lot of thought during my sleepless nights. He doesn't look very smart. The back of his head resembles an anvil."

"Inspector, I'm not interested in wood, or anvils, or even your exotic sense of the sublime. Whatever his physiology, he still is a key piece of the machinery of the Center. That means he has power. And to some people, there is nothing more beautiful." A car drove by. We both stopped to hear whether it was turning into our driveway.

"So, who's behind him?" The car had passed without stopping. "That's the question. The party is losing its grip, and the army is getting very cocky. Maybe I forget to tell you, I had a nasty run-in with a colonel a few weeks ago."

"Did he take down your unit number?"

"No, he was in a hurry. He only wanted to make sure I knew he could wipe the floor with me anytime it suited him." My thoughts trailed off. Another car went by.

"We'll worry about the army another time. Just let Sohn say his piece and go away. That's all I ask. I think I fixed things; don't say anything that will get them unraveled. It's delicate, but he has to show up one more time for appearance's sake, and then he won't bother us anymore."

"Nice thought," I said, "but it's hard not to stare."

"Don't think about his ears."

"I'm still so tired I can't see straight. Why did they pick me? I keep wondering."

"We've been through that, Inspector. Maybe they pulled your name in a random drawing—how should I know why you got tagged?"

A horn blared. Pak moved to the window. "It's Sohn."

"You stay," I said. "This time I'll go down to receive the man. I'll be humble and crawl behind him up the stairs."

"No, humble is not your strong suit. Anyway, I don't want him marching up here like the king of Siam. I want to be in my office when he calls from the gate. Same routine. He'll argue with the guards for a while, but then he'll have to ask me to rescue him."

The snow had started falling again, and it was almost dark when I heard the bear once more coming up the stairs. The door to Pak's office slammed. Was reality what I remembered had happened or what was happening now? What if they were the same thing? Angry words and sharp barks emerged, even sharper than the first time. Finally, Pak's door flew open. I was half dozing in the hall, just where Pak expected me to be. "Come into my office," he said. "There's someone here you may remember."

I started to clear my throat, but Pak shook his head, so I just coughed politely and stepped inside, meek as a goat about to meet a bear.

PART III

Chapter One

I had been relaxing on the bench only a couple of minutes when a tall, thin man sat down beside me. He wore a felt hat with a feather stuck in the band. It wasn't a whole feather, or if it was, it was from a very small bird. The hat didn't do much for him, but he didn't seem to care. The sun was up and the clouds were clinging to the western horizon, so it looked like it might be a nice day. Even so, the lakefront was practically deserted. Only a few people were out for solitary morning strolls, probably waiting for the cafés near the lake to open. Along the path where I sat there were several other benches, all vacant, but the man in the feathered hat clearly wanted to be on this particular one. This bench, and only this bench, would do.

Maybe it was his usual place to sit early in the morning; maybe he often put on that green felt hat and came here to think about his life. Maybe in taking up his normal spot, I was interfering with a rite that had by now begun to define his existence. It seemed churlish of me to do so, and I almost got up to move. On second thought, I told myself, maybe being overseas, in unfamiliar surroundings, was causing me to philosophize myself into a corner. I'd only been here a day; it was too soon to feel guilty.

The man didn't say anything at first, just sat looking out at the water with a completely relaxed air. He took off the hat and laid it on the bench so that it sat between us, the feather pointing at me. Then he pulled a croissant from his pocket and tore off a piece, which he chewed slowly. He stood up and threw the rest to the swans, who had assembled in the shallow water near the shore, about ten steps away. The strollers had gone past, and there wasn't anyone else around except an elderly couple with a child, very subdued and with a serious look on his face. I wondered if the child had been vetted, or maybe the swans. This was a setup. I could feel it in my bones.

The man sat down again; he didn't even turn his head when he spoke. "Against my advice, you were given permission to enter." His English was deliberate, like a person might speak to a dog whose intentions are unclear. "I don't control the border. But here, inside, you are mine. You understand? Your every move will be watched. If you enjoy the scenery, I will receive a report on what you looked at, how long you observed it, whether you took a picture. I'll even know what exposure you used on the camera. If you stop for a drink at a bar, I'll get word in a trice what you ordered, how big a tip you left, whether you stared at anyone, or made small talk, or winked at the Indonesian prostitutes hanging around at the entrance. I'm going to be all over you until you get back on an airplane and fly away—far, far away." An insect landed on his shoulder. He crushed it quickly, examined what was left, and then flicked the pieces onto the grass. "Fine weather for February." He stood up. "I wish you a pleasant stay in Geneva." He left the hat on the bench. I don't like green felt. As he strolled away, I had the feeling neither did he.

2

The entire team—all six of them—sat around a table in a small room that overlooked the entrance and the wide steps that came up from the driveway. The curtains were shut, and the air was stale, a little overheated, I thought, as soon as I walked into the room. Five heads turned and followed my progress to the one empty chair. Only the delegation leader ignored me. He sat hunched over an open binder of papers, occasionally marking a page or underlining a word. A tiny black notebook lay to one side. As I sat down, a young man across the table frowned. "You're late," he said.

His face rang a bell, but only faintly. "No one told me we were meeting until a few minutes ago," I said mildly. "A bit more notice might have been helpful. It certainly would have been polite." This was an awkward beginning to what already had all the hallmarks of an unpleasant assignment. They didn't want me around; that much had been made perfectly clear.

"Never mind," the head of delegation said, still studying his papers. Nice touch, I thought. Busy man, too busy to look up. He might not know me, but I already had become as familiar with him as I wanted to be. His file had been handed to me before I left Pyongyang, two bulging folders stuffed with irrelevant gossip and a nugget or two of useful information. There had even been a fair character sketch by someone who had watched him closely for years. The photographs, as usual, were old. He had lost weight, and maybe a little bit of hair.

"You're here. Exactly why or what you'll be doing on this delegation isn't clear to me. All we know is that your name was transmitted as a late addition. There aren't even any instructions on how I'm supposed to introduce you." He looked up and smiled wryly, just as he apparently had done hundreds of times before in situations he didn't like. I studied his face. The photographs in the file may have been old, but his eyes were the same—more observant than they first appeared. If you didn't pay attention, you'd think he had soft eyes. It was a mistake you didn't want to make.

A few days ago, just before I climbed the stairs to the airplane in Pyongyang, Sohn had emphasized that I was to keep close tabs on this man—our friend the diplomat, Sohn had called him. "Make sure you keep him in your sights," he said. "Don't forget, the Center considers the diplomatic mission in Geneva a sensitive place, for reasons that go beyond anything you'd be interested in knowing. In simplest terms, if our friend the diplomat doesn't return to Pyongyang from there, you're in shit up to your ears." I figured if Sohn mentioned ears, it must be serious.

At the moment, the delegation leader didn't look like he was in danger of going anywhere or doing anything untoward. I took out a couple of pencils and lined them up in front of me. Then I reached into my jacket pocket and found a small notepad, which I put next to the pencils. When I had everything straight and square, I looked up and studied each of the delegation members in turn. Most of them gave me blank stares, or what they hoped were blank. It's hard for people to keep up the pretense of disinterest when they are holding their breaths.

"Whatever you decide," I said at last, after I'd wrung the final drop of drama from the moment. The delegation started breathing again. At least they knew where things stood. Showing them I couldn't be pushed around was something they could understand. It wouldn't do any good to go beyond that, especially if I was supposed to keep close to their boss. Doing that would be easier if he didn't bristle every time he saw me.

"Good." The delegation leader didn't seem fazed by how long I had taken to answer him. In his universe, if he didn't react to an insult, it fell to the floor and could be kicked away. "I'll say you are Mr. Kim, a researcher in the Ministry. Can you remember that? They think everyone is named Kim, so it won't even register with them."

"Fine by me." Nice jab—can you remember that? I ignored it, but it didn't exactly fall to the floor. Everyone around the table had heard it and was scoring one for their side. I wasn't crazy with the title "researcher," either. It sounded like I brought tea in for the heavyweights.

"That's fine, then," he said evenly. "Everything's fine. I'm glad we settled that." Another smile. "Perhaps something will come in the overnight cable traffic that will tell us a little more about how we're supposed to deal with you." He looked around at the others, but none of them had anything to add, so he continued. "Sometimes we break for coffee during the talks. We do that to manage the pace. It has nothing to do with wanting coffee or one of those little cookies we've gone out and bought. You should hang back when we break. Don't mingle." He slipped the little book into the inside pocket of his coat. "Pretend you're working on your notes or something. If one of them comes up to you, act like you don't speak English. You don't, do you?"

"I know some." A little cookie now and then would be good.

The man across from me studied the top of the table carefully. Now I remembered. We'd had an entire conversation in English, standing in the hallway of the Foreign Ministry a few years ago. It was in the spring, and the windows of the offices were open to let in the breeze. Neither of us had said anything important, just a few idle minutes trying to come up with a vocabulary word or two the other didn't know. "At least, I think I can speak a couple of words. I used to."

"Well, forget whatever you knew. If they sense you understand English, they'll constantly be trying to draw you out. How about French? You don't know any French, do you? German?"

"No. Don't worry, I'm not here to get in your way."

This time his smile was broader, more encompassing. There was nothing I could do but get in his way, and we both knew it. "See that you don't, and everything will be fine. You probably have your own reporting channels." There was a sense that he was trying hard not to sound irritated. "I realize you'll write what you feel like writing, and it is unlikely you'll show it to me before sending it out. That's how these things usually work, isn't it?" He pursed his lips and took off his glasses. That had been in his file, how he pursed his lips when he was displeased. "An unconscious pout," one entry read.

"Do you need to see our reports as well?" His voice took on a mock-friendly ring. "Even if you read them, of course, you have no authority to make changes. I've already checked. The rules for outgoing telegrams from a permanent diplomatic mission are the same as those that apply to the embassies—the ambassador at post gets to comment on whatever goes through our channels if he wants to, but his is the last word. Especially"—he let that word burrow in nice and deep, and then repeated it to make sure there was no mistake—"especially here."

"Unless, of course, there are overriding orders." I threw that in the pot to see if it would unsettle him. It didn't.

"There are no such orders. If any do come in, let's deal with them then, shall we?"

It must have been something they taught in the Foreign Ministry. Never let a point go unchallenged. There were times we worked that way, too. But I wasn't in the mood, and this didn't seem like one of those times. Something about that episode on the bench earlier in the morning had set my teeth on edge. I wasn't ready to battle with one of my own diplomats over millimeters. "Actually, I don't need to see your reports; I'm not interested in reading fiction."

There was an intake of breath from the delegation, which stared at me in unison like a set of oversharpened penknives. Then they each turned away and began going through their script for the meeting. One or two sneaked a glance at me. The young man smiled to himself. He looked like he might know a thing or two. I made a mental note to talk to him later, when I could get him alone.

3

On the day I left Pyongyang, almost at the last minute while we waited in a special room that kept me out of sight of the rest of the passengers and anyone else in the terminal building, Sohn finally told me why he was sending me to Geneva.

"You'll be on the delegation to the talks."

"What talks?"

"The missile talks." He watched me closely. "Something the matter?"

"Nothing." Missiles. Hwadae county. Pakistan. The dead woman. A lot of tabs were fitting into a lot of slots.

The first round of negotiations, Sohn said, had been in Berlin. They had produced nothing, other than the estimate that the second round wouldn't produce anything, either. Just having another session was considered good enough. After some internal discussions in the Center, it had been decided that, off to the side during the next round of talks, there would be a chance to pass the following message: *Beware, you never know when starving people might do crazy, irrational, dangerous things.* They'd told Sohn to find someone who could do that, and after rummaging through the files, he'd selected me. I had been overseas, I didn't freeze up around foreigners, and I had a good revolutionary pedigree. They also wanted someone to keep an eye on the delegation leader, but most of all, my assignment was to deliver that message. The messenger was important, and I checked all the boxes, that's what Sohn said. I didn't believe him. It was all smoke.

"How do I deliver this message? Over drinks? Crudely handwritten on a piece of paper?"

"Up to you," Sohn said. "You're smart. You assess the situation. But however you do it, slip it in like an assassin's blade. Make sure they feel it. Make sure they don't forget."

Why not let the diplomats do it? I asked. It was their job, wasn't it? It's what they're trained to do, to circle around the bush, dropping hints here and there, shards and splinters to be reassembled in faraway buildings. Sohn snorted. "I don't trust them to do it right. Most of a message isn't content anyway, but context, tone, the play of light and dark across the mind. These striped pants have no sense of menace. They smile too much, they laugh." He laughed. "You see? It sets you at ease." Then he barked and cleared his throat. "I don't want the Americans at ease. I want them tossing at night, waking at odd hours in a sweat." He laughed again, as if he finally found something that pleased him. "What sort of message is that?"

"Why the drama, hiding me away in this little room?"

"You'll board a few minutes after everyone else. The plane will wait around with the door open until our sedan pulls up. The crew will know there was a last-minute passenger put aboard; they'll tell their friends. The story will seep in here and there. That's good. I'll get out of the car just long enough to wave good-bye. I want some people to wonder what I'm doing."

4

The delegation leader looked at his watch and stood up. "Time to get moving," he said. He turned to me. "We got off to a bad start. I apologize." He extended a hand. "Nothing is easy these days. It's hard enough to do my job under normal circumstances. We'll stay out of each other's way."

I went on high alert. I'd been with smooth characters before, but this one was going to be a champion, I could tell. I shook his hand.

"Once we go into the meeting room, please sit at the end, next to Mr. Roh." The young man, the one who had smiled to himself, nodded slightly. "If we decide to break for a delegation meeting, come out of the room with us. It's their turn to invite us to dinner, which they'll probably do just as we adjourn for lunch. I'll accept, but we'll make excuses for your inability to attend."

This was the first real sign of the game he was going to play, keeping me in a box. "I'm afraid I have to tag along," I said. "Where you go, I go, too." That card was on the table. I wanted to see what he would do with it.

He shook his head. "The instructions I received this morning said only that you were to attend the talks; there was nothing about the dinners." The man was a curious mix. One minute he was pliable, the next he was unbending. His tone of voice stayed calm throughout; even the look on his face didn't change that much. Somehow, though, he conveyed what he wanted you to know. On my being at his dinner table, he was adamantly opposed.

"Maybe not, but I'm afraid you have no choice."

His reply was cut off when the door opened and a woman looked in. "Their cars are on the way up the drive."

"Very well. We'll greet them in the entry hall. Everyone put on a pleasant face." The delegation leader turned to me. "It's how we conduct our business. We are pleasant. You don't object?"

I smiled at him. "Will this do?"

"It would be best if you came in at the last minute. If they see a new face during the initial pleasantries, it may put them off." He looked at my jacket and swallowed hard. "Your pin seems to have gone missing."

"It does seem to have done that." I hadn't even brought the pin bearing the leader's small portrait with me to Geneva. I was indifferent to wearing it, but I didn't like sticking my finger every time I put it on. Pak never commented on its absence anymore, and Sohn—though I was sure he had noticed right away—never said anything. I straightened my tie. "How do I look?"

The delegation filed into the front hall. I went over to the window and pulled back the drapes. A sedan pulled up, followed by a van. The press had been allowed in the compound, and the photographers were taking a lot of pictures of nothing. When I heard people moving into the meeting room, I slipped in the side door. No one gave me a second look.

Once we were seated, the introductions began. People nodded solemnly when their names were mentioned. "And finally, at the far end to my left is Mr. Kim." The faces across the table turned to look. "He is a researcher in the Ministry, assigned temporarily to our mission here." It sounded ridiculous, though the other side didn't seem to notice. A couple of them made notes; the rest stared at me for a moment, thoroughly uninterested or uncomprehending. Or both.

I didn't plan on picking up my pen during the session. No sense looking like a minor scribe; it was bad enough to be introduced as a researcher. When the time came to pass the message Sohn had given me, it was important that they thought I had credibility. I couldn't give off those vibrations if they considered me a table sponge. One member of our delegation had already closed his eyes. That wasn't something I could do. Sohn had told me I was supposed to keep my eyes open. I decided to sit back and frown, with an occasional glance at the ceiling. From across the table, maybe it would appear I was following the discussions with disdain. It only took a few minutes for me to realize that was impossible. I was bored to tears. My eyes shut, and it was pleasant until I heard Mr. Roh whisper in my ear, "We try not to snore in these sessions." He closed his notebook. "But we can petition for an exception in your case."

5

"You spend a lot of time looking at the lake." The next morning, the tall man sat down beside me. It was the same bench, but this time he wore a dark blue beret. He seemed more comfortable in that than in the green felt hat. "It seems it might snow. Nothing to write home about," he said, looking straight ahead, almost as if he didn't know I was there. "But then, you don't write home, do you? You don't write, you don't phone. You're almost always out by yourself. Why is that, I wonder? It's very odd. You're not thinking about defecting, I hope."

"Only if it gives you sleepless nights."

"Why did they introduce you at the talks yesterday as a ministry researcher?"

"It's an honorary title." I smiled. "I'm flattered that you were listening."

"It's not what appears on your visa application. I could have you thrown out for lying to immigration authorities."

"Why, what did it say on the application?"

"You didn't fill it out?"

"Of course not. Do I look like I fill out my own visa applications?"

"It says you are a third secretary."

I turned to him. "Third secretary? They could have done better than that."

"You are more interesting than I was led to believe. How about a cup of coffee? Let's get in out of this cold wind."

"No, thank you. I appreciate the offer, though." I thought that sounded diplomatic. A little oily, perhaps.

"Don't worry, you can spend some time with me. None of your people are watching."

"Someone is covering my back."

"No. They were, but their car was in a minor accident and they've been detained."

"I see."

"These things happen in Geneva. On the weekends, with all the traffic, the roads can be difficult to negotiate."

"Just the same, I think maybe I'll just walk back to my mission. I saw some chestnut trees along the street I want to look at."

"Your mission is on the other side of the lake, a long walk, especially in this weather. Perhaps you'd allow me to drive you? I could let you off a few blocks away, near the statue, the one of the woman whose lovely backside faces the road. No one would know."

"Why this change of heart? Last time we met, you wanted me out of the country."

"I did. For one thing, you people attract others. It's as if you are flowers, and the bees of services from other countries cannot resist. They swarm in here and do silly things. That complicates my life, and I prefer life to be uncomplicated, or as uncomplicated as I can make it."

"Let me know how it turns out."

"To tell you the truth, I thought you were here to deal in missile parts. I've had enough of that for a while. In the last few weeks, I've gone through stacks of blurry copies of bills of sale and shipping manifests until I nearly went blind. If you were dealing in missile parts, I'd have booted you out without a second thought."

"Why would I be dealing in missiles?"

He shrugged. "Why not? There's money in it. Arms go through airports all the time. We usually don't stop shipments unless they are labeled "Weapons"; it's bad for commerce. In fact, yours is the only one we've stopped in a long time. We were asked to intercept it, so that's what we did. The shipping form was unimaginatively filled out. 'Bulldozer replacement parts,' it said. I haven't seen too many bulldozers with stabilizer fins, have you?"

"I don't know anything about missiles. Or bulldozers, for that matter."

"That was my conclusion, but it leaves a question. Why are you here?"

"Ah, finally. Why didn't you ask before? It's not a secret. I'm here because my mother likes chocolate, and the store near our villa in Pyongyang ran out."

"Very good." He laughed and looked around. "That will be a great shot, the chief of the Bundesamt für Polizei, sitting on a bench and laughing with a North Korean agent. Would you like a print? Or would you rather have a video of you with one of the Portuguese girls that hang out in our bars?"

"I don't know any Portuguese girls. The other day you were pushing Indonesians." The chief of Swiss counterintelligence was following me around? You'd think the man would have more important things to do.

He stood up. "My name, in case you are interested, is Beret. Please call me Monsieur Beret. I will call you Monsieur O. Or perhaps you'd rather I call you Inspector." He watched for my reaction. I looked out at the lake and wondered briefly how much more he knew about me. And how he knew it.

"It will start to snow within the hour. Stay warm, Inspector, however you can."

6

It was Saturday, so there were no talks scheduled. That was fine, because I didn't want to go over to the mission and make faces at the diplomats. I wandered by the chestnut trees and watched for a while as they danced in the wind. You couldn't say they were graceful. A couple of big cars drove up to the hotel across the street and parked, but no one got in or out. It was getting too windy to stand around, so I headed across one of the bridges into a shopping district. I started down a covered passageway, and there was the Man with Three Fingers, examining watches in the window of a jewelry store. Somehow, I wasn't surprised he turned up again. I had been pretty sure that just paying for his drink at the Sosan coffee shop wouldn't be enough to keep him out of my hair forever. Maybe I should have bought him lunch.

"A chance encounter, I suppose." I walked up slowly and stopped a step behind him. He looked surprisingly at ease. At first I thought he hadn't heard me, but he wouldn't have missed my reflection on the glass. He moved, barely, to acknowledge my presence.

"I leave nothing to chance anymore. Maybe you shouldn't either." He pointed at a watch. "Do you see that? It costs twenty thousand euros. Why would anyone spend that amount of money on a watch?"

"Maybe they really, really want to be sure they know what time it is."

He pointed at another watch. "That one is ten thousand euros. Do we conclude it only tells time half as well? Perhaps it only tells time during the day, and you need another watch, one with diamonds, for night."

"Are you really supposed to be out all by yourself like this? I thought special police roamed in herds. Where are your pals?"

"You're my pal, O. Remember?" He finally turned to face me. "Or do you still just discard people when it suits you?"

I let that alone. It wasn't worth batting back. "The Swiss service is pretty good. They must have a bead on you already."

"I doubt it. They think I'm Mexican."

"Mexican? You know Spanish?"

"Don't worry yourself over what I know."

"I'm not. It's just that the locals are keeping tabs on me, and by now I would assume they have taken twenty pictures of us standing here talking. Since I don't know Spanish, they'll assume you must know Korean. That will interest them, a Mexican with a mastery of Korean. They aren't exactly kindred languages."

"Really? And what would you call a kindred language to Korean?"

I figured he wasn't really interested, so I kept quiet.

"Still the same, aren't you? Just like on the operation. When you weren't worrying, you were fussing. I guess you must have fussed all the way out of the room, with me on the floor. Of course, I wouldn't know. I was bleeding and unconscious. Practically dead. I guess that must have worried you, huh?"

"Mexicans don't speak Korean."

"We could be speaking English, or Chinese. Like I said, don't start worrying yourself on my account." He looked back at the watches. "No matter how much they cost, they all mark time the same way. The casing doesn't make a bit of difference; it doesn't go any smoother, or faster, or happier. It just goes, isn't that right? And sooner or later"—he touched my shoulder with his ruined hand—"it always runs out."

A black car cruised by, the windows open.

"Well," I said in a loud voice, *"adios, amigo."*

7

Sunday it rained, and when it didn't rain, it snowed. That night I had trouble sleeping. It was ten o'clock in the morning in Pyongyang, no wonder I couldn't sleep. So what if the Swiss clocks showed 2:00 A.M.? That wasn't the time in my head, or on my watch. I never changed my watch to local time. Who the hell cared what time it was in Switzerland? The message Sohn had given me kept running through my head. When was I going to deliver it?

I could see Sohn's face, grim and deliberate, as he had gone over what he wanted me to convey. "They must be made to believe that we are about to collapse, that they will inherit more maggots than they can count, more bodies than they can bury, more disease than they can cure, more chaos than they can stomach. They are convinced that we are weak, on our last legs, about to collapse? Let them; let them worry every night when they go into their warm beds that we are about to hold our breaths until our wasted bodies fall across their doorstep. That's good. We want them to think that, because it is the last thing they want. Do you imagine for one moment that they look forward to caring for us? Do you think they want the responsibility for twenty million beggars? Of course they don't. It would interfere with their shopping, their specialty foods, their imported blouses and ties. The last thing our southern brothers want is for us to crawl into their fat lives, and so they will pay to prop us up. Believe me, Inspector, they will pay whatever it takes, and we will not let them get off on the cheap."

"So," I said, "we show the Americans we are weak."

Sitting in that little room in the airport, I noticed that Sohn had rheumy eyes. That and his small ears did not make him look like a man on the way up. But appearance wasn't everything. These days it wasn't anything. Pak was right on this. The essential question wasn't how pretty Sohn was, but how much power was behind him. I couldn't be sure, but the more I thought about it, the more I had to guess it was plenty. Our ministry wasn't easy to kick around; snatching personnel to send on funny assignments took clout.

"No!" Sohn shouted. I had jumped. People with rheumy eyes usually didn't shout like that. "Haven't you been listening? Not weak. Crazy. We show the Americans we are crazy, crazy enough to pull the trigger. Still strong enough for that, and plenty crazy. If they think we're weak and rational, we're finished. They have to think we have weapons that can destroy them, because in fact, we do. For that, these foolish missile talks cannot succeed. If we end up making a deal with the Americans, they'll never deliver. And the people who actually can deliver will be dealt out of the game. And then, then we *will* be weak. Then they will walk over us, at which point you and I, Inspector, will be dead. So we will survive by looking like we can't survive. We will survive by looking like we can't be defeated." Then he had relaxed, the way a tiger relaxes when it's near a tethered goat. "You have your passport? Cash? Well, now you have your instructions, too. I have only one more thing to say: Don't screw up, it might be our last chance."

I remembered very clearly that final injunction. I turned it over in my mind. One of the roof timbers creaked in the cold, recalling something, and that's when I knew it for sure. It wasn't chance that Jenö had been assigned to our care. At two in the morning, there is a certain clarity that creeps around your brain. Tab A, slot B.

8

"I didn't know you were allowed to travel these days." My brother was never happy to see me, and certainly not by accident. I wasn't happy to see him, either. When I woke up in the morning after a few hours of sleep, my stomach was bad. The talks had gone on all day, and my stomach hadn't let up once. I wrote a cable for Sohn, but the code clerk wouldn't take it for a couple of hours and I couldn't leave it, so I sat around until almost 8:00 P.M., which was already 4:00 A.M. in Pyongyang. No one would read a message at 4:00 A.M., unless they couldn't sleep. If I were in Pyongyang, I wouldn't read a message at that time of the morning. If I had been in Pyongyang, I never would have run across my brother, who was standing in front of me in Geneva. I didn't follow his travels, but I usually heard something whenever he left the country. This time I hadn't heard a thing. Strange coincidence, us being here at the same time. I didn't like it from any angle. I didn't like being here with him, and I didn't like the coincidence.

My brother and I agreed on nothing other than that we wanted our few meetings to be carefully planned ahead of time. In some ways, he and the Man with Three Fingers were alike, nothing left to chance, though my brother was smarter and more devious.

It had not always been this way between us. Our relations had never been good, but when we were younger, there had been less poison. When it was that things changed, I could not say and had stopped trying to understand. He traveled overseas frequently, ate at restaurants with crystal wineglasses, or so he liked to say. I didn't know about the glasses that touched his lips, but I could see with my own eyes that he wore shoes with leather soles. He wouldn't say what he did on those trips, and I never tried to find out. I could have flipped a file or made a call, but I didn't want to know. My trips were simpler, easy liaison missions, cheap seats on trains, cheap meals, cheap liquor. No wonder my stomach was bad.

"Once in a while, there's something to do," I said. He looked like a prosperous Asian businessman, well-cut suit, perfectly fitted, pale blue shirt. "I do whatever there is to do, then go home. How was I to know you'd be here? If I'd known, I would have told them to get someone else." His eyes were not as dangerous as they had once been. When he was younger, he could flay a person with his eyes.

"You never make things that simple. Who sent you here? Don't bother being so secretive. All I have to do is make some phone calls."

There was never a moment to breathe; as soon as we stepped into each other's line of fire, the guns started booming. "What do you care? My orders are valid."

"They can also be canceled."

There was no sense standing in the damp evening continuing a struggle that would only end when both of us were dead. "Then get them canceled, it doesn't matter to me. It wasn't my idea to come out here in the first place."

My brother stepped around a puddle. He looked carefully at his shoes. "I have a dinner. It will probably last until midnight. We can finish this conversation later. There's a bar near a hotel on the main street that runs through Coppet, about ten kilometers up the lake." He reached down and picked a wet leaf off the tip of one shoe. When he stood upright again, he took a handkerchief from his pocket and wiped his fingers. This was his way of annoying me. It always worked. "Can you find it on your own? You'll have to take a taxi or hire a car. Meet me there at 1:00 A.M. Everything else in town will be closed but that bar; it will be hard to miss." He folded the handkerchief carefully, so that all the edges were in line, then put it back into his pocket.

"There may be a parade of people tagging along behind me. They think I'm selling missile parts."

My brother froze. It was only for a heartbeat, but I saw it. "Surely you're not peddling missile parts these days," I said. "Isn't that beneath you?"

"And surely you're not digging into other people's business these days. Oh, wait, I forgot, that's your job, isn't it?"

I turned and walked away, up the hill to the drab hotel where I was staying. The mission said it didn't have space for me, and anyway, my instructions from Sohn were to keep clear of the mission as much as possible when we weren't in talks. If I seemed to be operating outside the normal bubble, that would attract attention, he said, which is what he wanted me to do. Attract attention. From the two cars parked at either end of the street, it appeared I was succeeding. I decided not to go back to my room yet. I'd seen some beech trees that had been cut down a few streets away; maybe there would be a few chips I could pick up to bring home.

It was hard to find beechwood in Pyongyang. One year my grandfather went to great lengths to have some shipped from Bulgaria. I had imagined a whole trainload would pull up to our door, but there were only a few boards. He treasured them. The day they arrived, we celebrated as if there had been an addition to our family. For months they sat in the house, carefully leaning against the wall in the room where my grandfather sat and wrote letters. I asked if I could help saw them. The old man shook his head. It was much too soon to talk about such things, he said. The boards needed to get accustomed to the place; they weren't used to the climate, to the way we talked, to our dreams. The wood had to feel rested and comfortable, then it would be ready. Finally, on a spring afternoon nearly four months after our "guests" arrived, he said it was time. When I asked what he was going to make out of the boards, he looked surprised. "How would I know? The wood and I have to decide together, don't we? Don't think you can just impose your will on things. Don't listen to this talk you're hearing these days about man being at the center of creation. Wood doesn't know about politics. And thank goodness for that." It turned out that the beech wanted to be part of a chair. I only sat in it once, before my grandfather gave it away, a present to a friend in the army, a man with a long title and a nice office. When I went to visit him a few years after my grandfather died, he had disappeared, as had the chair.

The two beech trees had been cleared away. From the pale light of the single streetlight, I could see a little sawdust on the road, but nothing else. I walked down the hill again to town, figuring I'd sit in a quiet bar until it was time to go meet my brother. If anyone was following me, they would just have to wander around a bit or find a place to relax until I set off for Coppet. I wasn't sure where Coppet was, but I wasn't going to let my brother know that. It would give him too much satisfaction, dictating directions to me. It was bad enough he just assumed that I would accept a summons to meet him someplace out of town at 1:00 A.M. The only thing worse was that he was right.

I had been given a pocket map of Geneva before I left Pyongyang; I'd check it as soon as I found a place to sit down. It was an old map made in Hungary. Sohn had handed it to me with an odd look on his face. "What makes them think you'll find this of any use," he said, "I'll never understand. It's probably what Geneva looked like during the Austro-Hungarian Empire. Let's hope it's better than nothing."

A woman in high heels, spikes that could go through your heart, passed me when I turned onto a main street in search of a café. She was blond, Russian, a face like a fox, though I don't imagine a fox, even in a leather skirt, looks that way from the back. When she walked up to a man standing on the corner, it was clear they knew each other already. He put his arm around her waist. She drew away, just a tiny gesture, then settled against him. She doesn't like him, I thought. Maybe she'll murder him tonight, with those stiletto heels.

Chapter Two

Coppet was quiet and dark. A figure in a beret and a belted coat came out of a doorway and fell into step with me. "Lonely?"

It was M. Beret. I couldn't see his face, but the voice, even with just that one word, was unmistakable.

"No, not if you're not," I said. I kept walking.

"It would be better if you stayed in your plain little hotel, don't you think? Things can happen to people at this hour, even in Switzerland."

"I felt restless, that's all. Against one of your tidy laws?"

Another man came out from a darkened doorway, turned suddenly, and walked quickly away.

"Friend of yours?" M. Beret stopped and pulled a small pistol from his pocket. Then he spoke softly into a tiny radio. I stopped, too, and looked for a convenient place to hide if someone started shooting. Whatever this was, it wasn't my fight, not as far as I knew. "You'll remember"—M. Beret sounded somewhat annoyed—"I said that you'd be like a flower attracting bees. Well, that was a bee. You should stay off the phone; too many people on the other end."

"I wasn't on the phone, but I'll bear it in mind. You wouldn't know any bars around here, would you? Now I'm not so restless, but I'm getting thirsty. Walking at night does that to me."

"Are you kidding? Nothing is open at this hour. Your brother isn't here, if that's who you're looking for."

I digested this.

"He had too much to drink at dinner, and his friends carried him back to his hotel on Rue Puits-St-Pierre. Not a very friendly man, your brother. He seems to think highly of himself, though; keeps his clothes clean and pressed." M. Beret stared at my shoes, which were well worn. "He's staying in a pretty nice place, not like the cracker box you're in." We had resumed walking, with less of a sense of urgency. M. Beret looked at me sideways. "You mad because I'm criticizing a family member?"

"I'm just thirsty."

"I suggest you try the bottled water in your hotel. That's all my budget will support tonight."

2

"You're not bamboo, you can't just bend in the wind. You're flesh and blood, much as you hate to admit it. And you will bleed like the rest of us when it comes to that."

"I'm surprised you even recognize the concept of bending, or stopped long enough to look at bamboo, for that matter."

My brother was still pale from too much alcohol, but nothing seemed to affect his air of nasty superiority. "I found out a little about what you're doing here," he said. "It's crap."

"In contrast to your mission, no doubt one of extreme urgency—so urgent that you had to drink yourself into a coma." His hotel room was bigger than mine. The bed was large enough for a whole family. I looked into the bathroom. A nice bar of soap. A little bottle of shampoo. Fresh towels everywhere. M. Beret was right, my hotel didn't measure up to this.

"I'm not answerable to you, or to anyone that you will ever deal with. Don't forget that." My brother slumped against the wall and closed his eyes. "Did you wait for me in Coppet?"

"Briefly. I was joined not only by an unknown figure that walked quickly into the shadows but also by the Swiss service, which already knew you were falling-down drunk and wouldn't show up." I gave him an extra few seconds for that information to get past the last vestiges of alcohol before continuing. "They don't like us."

My brother laughed, softly. "No one likes us. Fuck them all."

"Yes, but they all have food. Perhaps you're too busy drinking to notice."

"Food?" His eyes opened slightly. "Is that what you're here for, to crawl and beg for food? I'll bet that bastard Sohn is behind this. Sure, he picked you for the annoyance factor. He knew you'd run into me out here. He must have planned it. This is his way of getting my goat. He didn't mention I'd be here, did he?"

"You two don't get along, I take it." My estimation of Sohn was climbing with every throb in the vein in my brother's forehead.

"Sohn has no authority to send people like you overseas. None. Pretty soon, he won't have the authority to flush the toilet. Let me see your orders."

"Impossible."

"Let me see them."

"I don't have any. Can you believe it? Completely paperless." I held up two empty hands. He didn't have to hear about Sohn's instructions to me. They weren't written down, so they weren't exactly orders. "My orders were transmitted directly to the mission, apparently. I've never seen them." This was true. "No one bothered to tell me until I arrived that I'm here as part of the delegation to the talks." Not true, but the truth was none of his business. "How do you like that? Your brother, the diplomat."

"You?" He snorted. "You? You don't know the first thing about diplomacy." The phone rang. My brother cursed and grabbed it. "What is it?" He listened. "Alright, as many loaves as you can get. Yes, bakery bread is best. Yes, immediately." He slammed down the receiver. "I can't talk to you right now. Meet me tonight." He wrote an address on a piece of paper and stuffed it in my pocket.

"This time you show up, you hear me? I'm not at your beck and call." I was at my limit. Five minutes was the maximum I could take, talking to him. "And make sure you pick a spot that won't be swarming with police." Whatever he was doing here, it was something that had to be conducted in code. My brother didn't like bread, not of any kind.

3

"Did anything happen?" The meeting had just ended. It had gone on for a little more than two hours. I spent most of the time watching the pale light from the bank of windows that stretched along the opposite wall. Curious, I thought, the way nature provided for eyelids, but not lids for the ears. Ear lids could have been hidden, so no one would have known. When you shut your eyes, it was obvious to everyone. But ear lids could have been covert. With your eyes open but your ears closed, you could have sat for hours with no one the wiser.

Short of going into a trance, it was impossible to shut out the drone of the negotiations. Their side said something, then our side said something else. Yes, no, not at all, let me repeat, just in case you misunderstand, I'll say it once again if it would help, we seem to be going over the same ground, perhaps we should take a break. If progress was a rabbit, it was nailed through both feet to the middle of the big table between the two delegations. It was going nowhere.

Mr. Roh closed his notebook. "Happen? We got through another session, and nothing went wrong. That's in the target area. It got us to lunch, which means we have a three-hour respite from more lectures about how we shouldn't be faxing blueprints to anyone the Americans don't happen to like."

"You're not telling me we're going to meet again today?"

"My, oh my, you really were tuned out, weren't you? We agreed to resume at three o'clock. Meanwhile, we're supposed to pretend to be contacting Pyongyang for instructions. They're supposed to pretend they are waiting for us to consider their latest offer. In addition, they graciously invited us to a reception at five thirty. That means more crackers and bits of dry cheese. Don't worry, we'll make excuses for your not attending."

"I'm sure no one will miss me." In the first blush of battle, I had insisted to the delegation leader I needed to attend all of the functions. Such foolishness.

"True, no one will miss you."

It was a challenge of sorts, but Mr. Roh was a puppy and I didn't have time to deal with small dogs. "I've got other things to do," I said. Going to the reception might be the opportunity I needed to pass the message, but then again, probably not. There would be no chance to speak alone to anyone on the American delegation, and I couldn't very well stand at the table with the little plate of grapes and pass a note saying, "We're crazy and will go even more nuts if you don't give us food." As far as I could tell, Sohn had been right about one thing. There didn't seem to be any danger of the talks succeeding, even if they lasted several more days. A lot of fixed stares across the table, an occasional frown, and then break for lunch, or coffee, or a trip to the bathroom. During lunch, I could write another report for Sohn. Before that, I needed to take a stroll. First things first. Geneva was boring, but at least there was plenty of air.

I set out down the narrow street in front of the mission, heading to the main road that ran beside the lake. A few reporters camped outside the gate looked up when I walked by. One of them shouted a question in Japanese and the others laughed, but no one followed me. When I reached the lake, I turned and walked along the shore in the direction of town. It would have been nice just to walk without thinking about anything, but you can't think about nothing if that's what you want to do. Things started slipping over the barriers and pretty soon they were running through my mind. At the front of the pack was my brother's appearance. That disturbed me most of all. There wasn't much doubt that he and Sohn despised each other. I didn't care if they tore each other to shreds, but I wanted to be on another continent when they did it. I never believed anything my brother said, but he was probably right about one thing—Sohn must have known we'd run across each other in Geneva. My brother was a shark; that made me, in Sohn's eyes, a tasty bit of chum. Maybe this whole story about passing a message to the

Americans was fantasy, and the real purpose of my being sent here was to get my brother to lunge at a barbed hook. Sohn seemed to have something to do with the Israelis. My brother was selling missiles. Here we were again—another tab A and slot B.

When I arrived at the statue of the naked lady, I stopped and looked up. Her backside faced the park. I took that as a sign and crossed the street. The park looked quiet, a good place to sit and think. Unlike the trees along the streets, the ones in the park were allowed to grow. The setting wasn't what you would call wild. There was a plan to it; the paths wandered in a convincingly natural way, as they were meant to. Halfway up the long slope leading to a large house, there was an enormous plane tree towering above everything else, as if all the energy of the plane trees outside, the ones whose tops had been lopped off and had been forced to grow low and squat, had concentrated into this one tree. Across the lawn, there were big oaks, big maples—it was just the sort of place my grandfather would have wanted to come for an October afternoon, when the sky was blue and the first leaves, the eager ones that did not want to wait, had begun to turn. But it wasn't October, it was mid-February and cold. Past an enormous pine tree with branches that grew just barely above the ground, I found a bench that looked out in the distance to the lake and, much nearer, a rose garden. When I sat down, I let my eyes take a slow tour around. No one seemed to be following me. M. Beret's people were somewhere nearby, but for once they stayed out of sight.

On the far side of the lake, low clouds obscured the tops of the hills. They weren't much to look at anyway. A signboard next to the bench said that farther inside the park were Roman ruins. I didn't want to see ruins. I didn't want to think about ruins. Suddenly, it was lonely in the park, and I didn't want to be there. I walked back down the hill to the street. The clouds had rolled in, and it was starting to rain.

Halfway across one of the bridges that joined the two sections of the city, I stopped and looked down into the water. Footsteps came up beside me. I wasn't in the mood to entertain guests. The rain had become serious, a winter rain that kept itself just this side of snow.

"Thinking of climbing over the side?" The Man with Three Fingers had turned so his back was against the railing. "Don't let me stop you."

"Well, if it isn't the Mexican Jumping Bean. Did you buy yourself a watch yet, or are you late for your next appointment?"

"No, I'm right on time. Right place, right time. And you, Inspector? Everything squared away?" He put the collar up on his coat. "You should check the weather forecast before you go out on these walks of yours. You're not dressed for this."

"I tell you what." I made a show of going through my pockets as the water streamed down my face. "How about I give you a detailed itinerary of my plans for the next several days? That way you won't have to hang around out in bad weather, shadowing me. You can just pick a spot and I'll be there, right on time. Twice a day should do it, don't you think? Shall we set that as the goal?"

"Goal? Inspector, my goal isn't to see you twice a day. It's not to see you at all, ever."

"And you think that's doable?"

"Oh, it's doable, alright. Just a question of time." He pushed himself away from the railing and brushed against me. "Well, take it easy, comrade. Buy a hat or something. Green felt is on sale this time of year. See you around."

He walked back in the direction I had come, toward the mission. I waited until he was out of sight. I was already so wet, it didn't make any sense to hurry. There was a café open just at the end of the bridge. It looked quiet enough. The coffee had just been set in front of me when M. Beret sat down at the next table. He had a large umbrella, which he hung on the back of his chair. "A good afternoon to you, Inspector. You look a little damp. Go ahead and drink something hot. Do you take sugar in your coffee? Of course you do, one spoonful, then you stir it slowly, counterclockwise. Usually five times, six if you are feeling pensive. You don't drink espresso. Well, once you did, but after a single sip you made a face, a very funny face, and left the rest of the cup. Brioche?" He took a croissant from his pocket and tore it in half.

"That's not a brioche. I know the difference."

M. Beret laughed. "Good for you, Inspector. Those talks, the ones that make your eyes glaze over, are almost wrapped up, I hear. Whatever you came to do, you'll have to hurry because it seems that so far, you've gotten nothing done." He pointed a finger at me. "If the talks end, then what? What is your final report going to look like? All those miles, all that travel money, all for nothing? Perhaps I could help. Should we conspire? Eh?"

I stirred my coffee, three times. "Is your service so short of things to do that the chief has time to follow me around personally? Nothing more important?"

"Three times, unusual, must be when you are agitated. Or wet." He took out a notebook and wrote something down. "It's not that I'm meticulous in all things, Inspector. But I want to take you apart like a Swiss watch, lay out all the pieces and examine them. Tick tock tick tock. What makes your machinery work? Things are grim at home these days, I take it. Tick tock tick tock. Pretty soon these talks you're in will end, and you'll be ordered back to your fatherland. Tick tock tick tock. What then?"

I took off my watch and dropped it in the coffee. "I'm sure I'll think of something," I said and walked out. The gesture made me feel good for a couple of minutes, but then I wished I had drunk the coffee. It had started to snow.

4

I spent the rest of the day in my room, trying to warm up. When I called the mission to find out whether we were on schedule for the afternoon session, they told me the "instructions" hadn't arrived yet and everything was postponed until tomorrow. I could almost hear M. Beret's listeners scratching notes on a pad: "Instructions late." The delayed arrival of nonexistent diplomatic traffic suited me. About three o'clock the maid knocked at the door, but I told her to go away. I kept the curtains shut, though it didn't much matter, there wasn't any sun anyway. Shortly before dusk the snow stopped. It drizzled for a few minutes, but then the clouds decided to call it a day and drifted off toward France. When night fell, I put on my shoes and went down the stairs to the tiny lobby. The girl behind the desk looked up. "Are you sick?"

"No. I need another bar of soap. The little one you gave me has dissolved."

"You were in your room all afternoon. Maybe you feel sick."

"No, I feel fine."

"Because if you are sick, we might have to get a doctor. I hope you don't have one of those Asian flu bugs."

"Thank you for your concern."

"Because if you do have one of those Asian bugs, we'll have to clean everything in your room, and for that we'll have to pay the maid extra. She's Romanian, and she knows the law. It could be quite a bother." I left before she could spin out the rest of the complaint.

This time my brother was waiting for me in the darkness. "There's a bench down the way, where the street bends. We can sit and talk, probably for about five minutes before the Swiss show up. That will be long enough if you don't interrupt me."

"Good, let's get it over with. Maybe we won't have to see each other again."

It was a quiet street, but then again, they were all quiet. The bench sat by itself in a small park, about thirty meters from the nearest house. The paving stones were uneven in places, but mostly the place was tidy and well kept; but then, so was almost everything in Geneva.

The night mist was just settling through the trees when I heard a car stop; the engine wheezed before it died. My brother appeared and sat down, frowning. "We don't have five minutes after all. We have two minutes. Check your watch."

"I'm listening."

"You have been sent here by people who no longer enjoy the confidence of the Center. Your mission is terminated."

"I'm still listening."

"Don't think you can ignore me on this. The talks will be broken off by the end of this week. You should return home before that. Am I clear?"

"As always."

A car door creaked. It was hard to tell how far away it was.

"My advice is that you leave immediately. Take a train tomorrow to Berlin. The embassy there will have further instructions for your return. If the Swiss ask any questions, tell them one of your relatives died."

"Of what?"

He paused and then stood up. "Don't forget what I said. You're not bamboo. You'll bleed."

"If I don't starve first, you mean."

"No, first you'll bleed. Someone is out here in this city to make sure of that. I don't know who, exactly. I can only guess why." As footsteps came up the hill, my brother crossed the street and disappeared.

5

M. Beret looked disappointed when he came close enough for me to see his face. "A pity, I wanted a picture of the two of you together." He pointed a small flashlight down the street and clicked it on and off once. "Family portraits are always precious when we get older, don't you think, Inspector?"

"I'm sorry, but I don't feel like chatting. I'm soaked to the skin from this damp air. It's the second time today I've been soaked, and there isn't a lot of heat in my hotel room. Not much soap, either. Do you know they gave me one little bar and want it to last the entire week? I thought the West was supposed to be overflowing with creature comforts."

M. Beret's laughter bounced across the paving stones. A light went on in the closest house; someone opened the window and shouted. M. Beret stood up and shouted back.

"That sounded rude," I said.

"The old man told me to be quiet or he would call the police."

"What did you say?"

"I told him I was the police." M. Beret reached in his pocket and pulled out a roll. "Hungry?"

"Yes, actually. I haven't eaten all day. But then why tell you that? You already know."

"Annoying, isn't it, Inspector? I should think you'd be used to it, where you come from."

"Hunger?"

"No, being watched."

"Believe me, we'd never approach anything like what you're doing. Much too much trouble. Eats up manpower. Not really necessary, anyway. No one could actually get lost for very long where I come from, at least, that's how it used to be."

"Now?"

"Changing circumstances, you might say. New winds blowing."

"True enough, following someone is a lot of work. Easier just to bring them in, I suppose." He was thoughtful. Then he remembered the roll in his hand; he tore it in half. "Don't ever let it be said we Swiss are not hospitable, soap notwithstanding. I don't want you to have a bad impression of my country, Inspector. I just don't want you ever to come back." He took a small bite. "I could order you out, but that would cause a diplomatic incident. Besides, then I'd be forced to order the whole pack out. We'd have to rent a bus or something." He reached into another pocket and pulled out my watch. He thumped the face once, held it up to his ear, and then handed it to me. "You forgot this. It's waterproof, but it isn't Swiss. It's counterfeit."

"Surprise," I said.

"Why don't you go across the border into France? Or Italy? Then we could deny you reentry."

"I don't think I want to do that."

"No, I didn't suppose you would. Incidentally, your mission is looking for you." He watched me put the half of the roll in my pocket. "Saving that for later?"

"Since when does the mission use you to pass phone messages?"

"If they don't start paying their phone bill, they'll have to use semaphores." He unzipped a small bag he was carrying over his shoulder and took out a book. "I bought something for you. It's in English, I hope you don't mind."

I took the book and read the title aloud. "*The Great Depression.*"

"These are difficult times in your country, I know. I apologize for waving that fact in front of your face this afternoon in the café. But many countries have gone through tough times. The hope is that they come out better, maybe learn from their mistakes. Do you know what I mean?"

"This is kind of you. I'll make sure the younger ones in the office read it." I was thinking of the girl who liked Rachmaninoff; maybe she would enjoy a book on the America her hero had missed seeing. During the Depression, he had been in Switzerland, of all places.

"You won't get in trouble, bringing that back?"

"Why would I get in trouble?"

"No reason, I suppose." He zipped up the bag and put it back over his shoulder.

"What did the mission want to tell me?"

"Inspector, I never pass on confidential diplomatic traffic; I would be betraying a sacred trust. You'll have to call them up and find out. By the way, you wouldn't have any Latin friends, would you?"

"Latin?"

"I'd watch my back if I were you."

"If you were me." I put the book under my shirt so it wouldn't get wet from the mist, which had deepened. "I'll read this tonight while I eat dinner. Could you preorder for me? That way I won't have to wait when I get to the restaurant, the one near the hotel."

"It was closed by the public health inspectors this evening. Something about Asian flu." M. Beret dug around in his pocket. "Oh, and this is for you, too. One of my men picked it up." He handed me a small piece of wood. "Do you know what it is?"

It was too dark to see and too wet to have any distinguishing feel. But I could guess. "Sure, it's beech."

M. Beret grunted. "You really are good, aren't you? Well, sleep soundly, Inspector. Please lock your door."

"I always do."

"You do? Someone told me that they don't lock hotel doors in your country."

"Really, I am disappointed. You of all people, I would have thought, wouldn't believe everything you heard. I don't suppose you have anything else for me."

"Such as?"

"I don't know. This seems to be your evening to make a pitch. First my watch, then half a roll; then a book; and finally a piece of wood.

The going rate these days must be pretty cheap for my category. Please remember, I'm not a whore, not at any price and certainly not for you."

"I repeat, Inspector, please lock your door." M. Beret bowed to me slightly. "*Au revoir*," he said and walked briskly in the direction of his wheezing car.

Chapter Three

The next morning as I left for the mission, it was hard not to notice the man waiting across the street. I could tell he was waiting for me, because after looking at him from my window for a few seconds, I knew he had genes from generations in the desert. What the hell was he doing here? Yet it didn't surprise me, somehow, to see him. Everyone was here—my brother, the Man with Three Fingers, M. Beret—and they were all waiting for me. Why shouldn't he join the crowd? Half of them wanted me to leave. The other half wanted me dead. I didn't know which half he belonged to yet. Maybe he'd tell me over a cup of coffee and a roll.

"Good morning, Inspector. How unexpected to find you here." Jenö put out his hand as I walked across the street.

"You don't really think I believe that, do you?" I put my hands in my coat pockets. "If you handed me that hundred-dollar bill right now, Jenö, I wouldn't give it back."

He shook his head. "Business has not been good, I'm sorry to say. I can't pass out money like I used to. Perhaps we can fix that. Do you have time for a cup of coffee before the talks start? You drink coffee?"

"You know about the talks? Which tab are they, A or B?"

"This is the enlightened West, Inspector. We don't keep secrets. The talks are reported in the papers, which I read every morning over coffee."

Around the corner was a café run by a Turk; I'd been there once or twice. It was close, that's all that recommended it. As we entered, Jenö nodded toward a table in the corner. Several old men were already drinking beer and arguing. The owner, in an undershirt and chewing on a cigar, looked up from his newspaper from time to time, but didn't seem concerned. It was warmer than my hotel, but that wasn't saying much.

"You find Geneva dull, no doubt." Jenö looked different sitting here in the West. He was more relaxed, perhaps. In Pyongyang, he had been guarded every moment, even though he pretended not to be. His attention had darted around. In the middle of a conversation, he had quickly glanced at someone coming through the door or moving across the lobby. Here, I had the sense that he didn't have to worry about peripheral movement, with shadows.

"I haven't seen enough to make a judgment."

"Oh, come now, Inspector. You've seen plenty. Don't tell me you haven't been walking around, taking in the sights. What is it you said to me? 'When it rains, you go out for a walk. When it's freezing, you go out for a drive.'"

"What I've seen is a lot of familiar faces, not all of them welcome."

"Surely that doesn't include me. When I heard you were here, I dropped what I was doing and came right away. I actually owe you a great deal."

The owner came up to the table. "*Gunaydun*, Jenö, my friend. *Bon jour.*" He looked at me. "*Konnichiwa.*"

"The Inspector here is not Japanese, Ahmet. He is Korean."

"I was in Korea, in 1950. We murdered the bastards good."

"He is from North Korea, Ahmet."

Ahmet didn't seem fazed. He chewed on his cigar, which even unlit smelled bad. "What do you know about that?" he said and rolled the cigar in his mouth.

"Perhaps you could bring us some coffee," Jenö said. "Leave the mud out of it if you can, and leave that thing in your mouth with the rest of the dog, would you?"

"You know him?" I watched the owner disappear behind the bar. He was a big man, big chest, thick forearms, broad hands, and eyes that had an unnatural gleam. He still had a full head of hair. When he was younger, he must have been a tank. If he had been in Korea in 1950, he'd seen a lot, none of it pleasant.

"Ahmet runs errands for me sometimes. He is dependable." Jenö said something more, but I didn't hear him, because just then a young woman stepped into view from the back room, and my heart began thudding loud enough to crowd out all other sound.

". . . daughter," Jenö hissed at me.

"What?"

"I said that's Ahmet's daughter."

"Not his granddaughter?" I took a breath, and that seemed to help my heartbeat fall back to normal.

"You look like a man who needs a drink, Inspector. Or a cardiologist."

I didn't want to see a cardiologist. Who needed doctors? There was nothing wrong with my circulation. The woman glanced my way as she moved slowly across the dining room to the kitchen. Before she disappeared, she turned to look at me, a long, caressing, lingering look. It seemed to go on and on. Somehow, I remembered to take another breath. Or maybe I didn't need one. Oxygen was irrelevant. Those eyes of hers were sustenance enough.

"You are here on assignment, I suppose." Jenö rapped the table with his knuckles. "Are you still here, Inspector?"

"Of course. You asked if I was on assignment. As opposed to what? Sightseeing? Taking a skiing holiday?" I tore my eyes away from the kitchen. Where had this princess been the other times I'd come in? I would have eaten five meals a day here if I'd realized she was in residence. I'd take up washing dishes, waiting tables, sweeping the floors. Sweeping. No, something else, perhaps.

"Would you like to go skiing?"

"I prefer your mountains at a distance." I glanced hopefully back toward the kitchen, but no one emerged.

"Dinner, then, if you can tear yourself away from that kitchen door."

"I don't think I can have dinner with you." Was there reason ever again to eat anywhere but Ahmet's? Was there reason to even go back to my hotel? I could live here, the dining room. Cigars were fine; I had absolutely no trouble with old men who smoked cigars.

"Why not?"

"If I have dinner with you, I'll have to write a report. Actually, I'll have to ask permission beforehand. It's impossible to get an answer back from my ministry for several days. Anyway, we may have a dinner as part of the talks this evening. I have to keep my schedule free."

Jenö shook his head. "I'll see you at 8:00 P.M. I assume your heart rate will have returned to normal by then. You can get permission after the fact. I do it all the time."

"Isn't 8:00 P.M. a little late for dinner?"

"Inspector, eight o'clock is still early around here to dine. Most people are only nibbling on appetizers at that hour. A car will come by to pick you up. Nothing fancy, either the car or the restaurant."

"Turkish food?"

"Forget it. Ahmet will kill you if you fool around with her. The girl's name is Dilara, if you can believe it."

"Why not?"

"It means 'lover.'"

Ahmet appeared with our coffee, an air of menace trailing him. "You would perhaps want something to eat," said Ahmet. He grinned at me. It was not a pleasant sight. His false teeth gave him a mouth much too full for the rest of his face. No matter, he didn't smile often; the scowl that regularly rode his features seemed better to keep his teeth in check.

The cigar had disappeared but was still much in evidence in the air. My mind wandered. Perhaps I could be out of the house whenever Ahmet came to visit us. I would no doubt need to go somewhere restful after a long night with Dilara, night after long night with Dilara . . . I completely forgot about breathing. Who needed to breathe? The eternal question.

"Inspector O would like something to nibble on. What do you have, Ahmet?"

Ahmet took a big knife from his belt and cut a piece of bread from a loaf he was carrying under his arm. "This is good with honey," he said and frowned at me. I had the feeling he read my mind.

2

I was picked up at seven forty-five by a plain car, driven to a plain restaurant away from the lake. That meant, I hoped, we would not be having the lake perch, which I had found after one try unpleasant to eat. No one was leaning against any lampposts on the plain street where the car stopped. I figured they might be starting their appetizers—even M. Beret's boys had to eat sometime. The driver indicated I was to get out at the only building with light leaking out from its curtained front window. There was a faded sign on the door, but it was in French—LA BELLE. I figured it said ring the bell, but there wasn't one, so I turned the handle and stepped inside. I found myself in a long hallway, barely lit by a tiny overhead bulb. Off to the right, about two meters away, was a wooden door. There was a grudging feel to the way it opened. Sometimes that can be from bad hinges, but sometimes it's the wood. "Chestnut doors," my grandfather would say, "are stubborn." The door, when it finally gave way, opened onto a dimly lit room. I could make out a few tables with chairs piled on them. A bar ran the length of the far wall, and behind the bar was a small opening, as if for a child or a dwarf, that led into another dimly lit room. I coughed, but that roused no one, so I went back into the hall and pulled the door shut. It pulled back. Definitely chestnut.

The corridor ended at a steep, narrow stairway with no banister. The stairway went up five or six steps and then disappeared into the dark. This wasn't a place I needed to hang around, I decided, but as I turned to go, the chestnut door opened and a woman appeared. She had tiny lips; it was something you were bound to notice right away, even in a dark corridor. A regular face, regular eyes, but very tiny lips. If she and Sohn somehow got together and had a baby, it would be quite a collection of miniature parts. The woman said something in a gentle voice. It was pleasant sounding, but I couldn't understand a word of it. When I didn't respond, her voice became louder, and she waved her hands. I didn't think she was explaining the dinner specials. A floorboard creaked, and Jenö came down the stairs. He said something to the woman in a language I didn't recognize. Her hands dropped to her sides, and her tiny lips gave me a tiny smile.

"Inspector, this is Margrit. She didn't know you were coming. That is to say, she didn't know you were Asian."

"What can I say?"

"Nothing." Jenö took my coat. "She is deeply apologetic. She is also very well trained, and if you had made the wrong move, you might be bleeding on the floor at this moment."

Margrit took my hand and offered what I took to be a tiny apology before turning off the hall light and disappearing again into the side room. Jenö motioned to the stairs. "Follow me, we'll eat up there. Watch your step, the stairway bulb is out. The place is closed today, so we won't be interrupted. Your M. Beret will have to wait outside. It will not make him happy, but"—Jenö shrugged—"he'll live with it. The Swiss take disappointment well. Must be in the genes."

3

We went up seventeen stairs—the five I saw, a sharp turn left, then twelve more. I pay attention to stairs; you never know when you'll have to use them in a hurry. These treads were so narrow I thought to myself that the Swiss carpenters must have tried to save all the wood they could. Maybe Swiss had tiny feet. There were two rooms at the top of the stairs. The door to one of them was shut, which is something I don't like when I'm in a strange place. The other room was brightly lit, but without much furniture. A small table with two chairs sat by a heavily curtained window.

Jenö indicated the chair where he wanted me to sit. "How about something with cheese? Fondue?" There was a black shoulder bag on the floor under the table. I kicked it to one side as I sat down.

"If you recommend it. I don't know what fondue is."

"A pot of melted cheese. You dip different things in it."

"And they come out covered with cheese, I suppose."

"That's the idea."

"Do you have another suggestion? Something simple."

"Snails."

"Simpler."

"Frog's legs."

"What ever happened to chicken? Or beef?"

"Calf. Brains."

"Pass."

"Liver."

"Pass."

"You eat dog but you won't eat calf? You eat ox knees but you won't touch liver?"

"Who says I eat dog? Perhaps some soup, a salad, bread. Fish—anything but perch."

"Let me order." He stood up and called down the stairwell. When he was seated again, he put his fingers together, one at a time. I remembered not to interrupt his thoughts. "Will you have some wine?" he asked at last.

"You didn't have me come here to eat brains and drink wine."

"Not entirely, no."

"Your black bag is clicking. Maybe you should check the mechanism. Odd placement, under the table. I wouldn't think it would pick up sound very well from there."

He reached under and pulled up the bag. "Did you kick this? You really shouldn't mess with other people's instrumentation that way. Besides, I thought things that were digital didn't click." He took out a small device and held it up for me to see. "This doesn't actually record anything. The recorders are somewhere else." He waved his hand to indicate somewhere and nowhere around the room. "Devices are not my specialty, so I don't ask where they put those things."

"Then what is that?" I pointed to the device, which was still clicking.

"I was told it was a transmitter of some sort. How it works from inside a bag I couldn't tell you. I'd turn it off, if I knew how."

Margrit came up the stairs with several plates, a basket of bread, and a bottle of wine. Jenö lifted his napkin from the table and waved it open. It looked like the pictures I'd seen of a matador waving his cape in front of the bull, which, I was once told by a Spanish tourist, is later dragged out—dead—by its tail. The matador, I seemed to recall, gets an ear.

"First we eat," said Jenö, "then we talk." He turned to Margrit, and they discussed something for several minutes. She shook her head vigorously; he shook his finger at her. Finally, she picked up the bag and heaved it out the door and down the stairs. She turned to him.

"Okay?" she asked.

"Okay," he said and picked through the breadbasket for a roll that suited him.

4

After I was back in my hotel room, I mulled over what Jenö had told me during dinner. "This shouldn't be so difficult, Inspector." He'd had several glasses of wine and was about to pour himself another. "It's straightforward, but your people keep dodging and wriggling. I argued that we should deal with you differently than we do with the Arabs, but maybe I was wrong."

"You want to give me a clue, even a little one? Because otherwise, I don't know what you're talking about." I could have pretended to go along, nodded when he said that people were wriggling. But I preferred to know who was wriggling, and why. At home I could live with ambiguity. Not here, not in this tidy country where every hedge was clipped and not a single sunbeam bounced in the wrong direction. There wasn't room for ambiguity here.

"Now that your heart rate is normal, tell me. What do you think of Dilara?" he asked. "More wine?"

"Beautiful girl," I said. "No more for me." Jenö's expression changed.

His eyebrows looked about to leap onto the table and do something with castanets. "Something wrong?" I asked. "Was that the wrong answer? You don't think she's beautiful?"

"These salted bread sticks are delicious, Inspector. Why don't you take some back to your room? They're from a wonderful bakery. Do you like baked goods?"

Chapter Four

"On your return, you will be hailed with a great ceremony at the airport. It will be thronged with press and cheering crowds, all to greet a man who had thought of abandoning the motherland but returned in its time of challenge and travail. Speakers will note that you are the grandson of a great hero; the blood lineage of the revolutionaries is always a good theme. There will be much waving of banners as you step from the aircraft stairs and plant your feet on the soil of your homeland. When they ask what made you return, you will say that Grandfather's words echoed in your heart, that you saw him in front of you constantly, that you searched your conscience and finally realized you could not betray the people. You will weep at the mistake you almost made, weep at returning to the bosom of the country, the land where your parents shed their blood."

My brother had left a message at my hotel for me to meet him again, this time in the park near the mission during the noontime break. As soon as I walked in through the gate and saw him sitting in the sun near the big pine tree, I knew I had made a mistake. Now that I heard what he had to say, I knew it was worse than a mistake.

"No. That I will not do." I clenched my jaw so hard it hurt. "I will not play that sort of fool. I will not misuse Grandfather or our parents for such a ridiculous show. I will not betray them. You know I won't do that. Why would you even suggest it? Are they so desperate at home to counter the defection in Beijing? Are they so rattled that they will grasp at anything, even this?"

My brother looked alien to me, and I thought I might despise him forever if I didn't make one last effort. "Don't you feel him near sometimes? I don't mean like a ghost, but in your blood? When you see an old man on the street who looks a little like he did at the end, walks like he did, very proud and straight, don't you think he is still around, a part of you?"

"Don't be a fool."

One more desperate attempt, one more and then I would quit. "Do you remember how Mother would sing at night, how her voice sounded in the darkness when she went down to the river to be alone? Can't you hear it on the wind, still?"

"How could you remember anything like that? You were barely more than a baby. You're romanticizing. There's no time for sentimentality."

"No, I remember. It is clear to me, her voice. I hear it sometimes."

"Do you want to know what I hear? I hear grandfather telling us that they were dead, that we had no family left but him and that we had to leave in the morning because the battle was moving our way."

"I remember her songs."

"You don't. You don't remember a thing. You didn't even cry when he told us. I don't think you knew what was happening."

"I remember Grandfather looking for someplace warm for us to sleep. I won't let you use him. It's betrayal."

"Use him? He's dead! We all have jobs to do, now and maybe after we die as well. Besides, he wasn't perfect, you know. Or maybe you don't."

"Perfect? What would you know about perfection? That's just like you, isn't it? Tearing down whatever makes you look small by comparison. Have you ever said anything decent about him? Have you ever mentioned what he did? No, you pretend as if he didn't sacrifice every-thing for us."

"This isn't about me. What I'm asking does no harm to the old man. Let him be useful again, really useful, not a musty symbol of a by-gone era. For all you know, he might have approved. He approved of al-most everything that you did, didn't he?"

That was meant to get to me. It did. "Damn you." I thought of stop-ping there, but then the words boiled over. When other people mentioned my grandfather, I could ignore them, or just walk away like I almost did in Pak's office with Sohn. That was impossible with my brother. With him it was different, exactly because he planned every word he spoke. Every word, every thought was for him part of an unending war fought against his own existence. But he did not fight on the front lines. He was a sapper who studied the structure, planned where to place the charge, and exploded it to cause maximum destruction. He thought of me as a bridge that had to be brought down to prevent the past from pursuing him.

"We aren't related anymore." I had never once thought of saying that, but there was no going back once I heard the words spoken in my own voice. "We aren't part of the same family. We don't share the same blood. From now on, we are strangers."

He was silent, but not with shock or hurt or even with contempla-tion. I knew what he was doing; he was searching even then for a way to destroy me. There was only one thing left to say, and I might as well say it. "We are nothing to each other," I said. "You and me, we have noth-ing in common, and we never did. Do you understand? Can I make it any clearer to you? We are not brothers. We are complete strangers who owe each other nothing. We will not meet. We will not talk. We will not acknowledge each other's existence. As far as I am concerned, you died and I did not mourn." He was looking out at the lake, pretending not to hear. I stopped for a moment to consider, but the words were already there, honed and dipped in poison that must have been fermenting for centuries. "Let me tell you this, if I ever find that you haven't died, if you ever work your way into my sights, if I am ever, for any reason, told to hunt down a man and kill him and it turns out to be you, I will pull the trigger. You hear me? I will pull the trigger."

That caught his attention. "No doubt you will, little brother." He got to his feet. "The only question is whether you'll live long enough to see that day."

2

I watched him walk down the hill, past the stand of oaks and the line of maples all the way out of the park. I willed myself to be calm, but I had no will left, not for that. I made it a point to draw few lines in my life. Drawing them rarely made sense. People who drew lines became trapped on the wrong side. Things changed, reality shifted, shapes became shadows and shadows faded into night. You can't see your principles in the dark. But where I did draw a line, I had no intention of erasing it.

At my grandfather's funeral, a day of bright sunshine, people I had never met before bowed their heads and murmured as they passed by that I should be true to his name. On the day he died, the radio called him the Beating Heart of the Revolution, and all at once, when I heard that, I knew what he had been trying to tell me for all the years I had been in his house. I never saw him bend.

When we were young, not long after the war, my brother came home a few times a year. Whenever he did, my grandfather would become silent. It was a great honor, my brother would say. He was attending the revolutionary school for the children of heroes killed in the war. The students were all orphans, but they had not lost their family, he told us. The fatherland was our family, the party was our future, the Great Leader was the center of our hope. No one could rest on what he had done in the past; it was to the future we owed our lives. To me, it was stirring stuff. My grandfather sat with his hands on his knees and was silent.

Once, after my brother had returned to school, the old man went out to his workroom and didn't come back, even though night had fallen. I found him sitting by the light of a single candle, holding a beautiful piece of wood he had been working on for weeks. As I stepped inside the room, he broke the wood across his knee. "Which piece should we burn first?" he asked me. I had no idea what to reply.

After my brother had disappeared outside the wall that surrounded the park, I set off for the lake. I walked, not noticing where I was or what I saw. I must have gone across one of the bridges, because the next thing I knew, I was all the way around on the western side of the lake, sitting on a bench that shared a patch of grass with a small linden tree. Out of the corner of my eye, I spotted a man jogging down the path. Barely a meter away, he stopped to tie his shoe. I knew what was going to happen next. He sat down beside me. "Nice day," he said. "You jog? Good way to get exercise and see the sights."

These people had no shame. I started to get up.

"Whoa, I didn't mean any offense," he said. "Just trying to make conversation. You look a little lonely, sitting here."

I sat back down. "Let's save ourselves a lot of time. I'll give you my answer first. No. I'll throw in an extra one for emphasis. No. And I have plenty in reserve. I brought a suitcase full of them and put several in my pocket this morning. No. Now, go ahead and ask your question."

"What question? I told you, I was jogging. I'm here on a vacation."

"Good for you. Myself, I'm here to dedicate a memorial to the Heroes of the Revolution."

"Funny man. Look, you may not know it, but there are a lot of people about to crawl up your ass. Here's my phone number." He put a piece of paper on the bench next to me. "If you get nervous or decide you want a change of scenery, just call and ask for Mr. Walbenhurst."

"Some name. I don't think I can remember it. Is it real?"

"Everything is real, Inspector. And everything is possible." He leaned over and checked his laces again. "Well, write if you get work," he smiled. "That's what my mama used to tell me."

The woman sitting three benches away waited until he jogged past before she stood up. Nothing left to chance, I said to myself. Which is why nothing was possible.

3

The talks were on and then off and then on again for the next week. Their side read talking points, we read ours, then we all stood up and stretched. Then we sat down again to read the same talking points, and to hear theirs all over again. Finally, on a rainy afternoon, the opportunity arose to pass the message that Sohn had given me. The man I had selected as the target walked up to me.

"Nice tie," he said. "Where did you get it?"

"My tie?" It wasn't what I had considered as the opening for slipping in the assassin's blade.

"You seem to have a good collection. That one looks Italian." He pointed to his own tie. "Mine are shabby by comparison, I'm afraid. I used to have one I bought in the Paris airport, but I can't find it anymore. Does that happen to you? Ties disappearing. I have the same problem with socks."

What problem? Were socks a problem? Were we exporting socks to rogue states?

"It looks like we're going to be here for another week or so. Why don't we all get together on the weekend, maybe go for a drive in the mountains? We could get a small bus. Let me know." He smiled. "Nice talking to you."

4

The idea of meeting the daughter of a Turk who worked for Israeli intelligence was not mine. I resisted up to a point, but I do not believe in taking hopeless stands. Dilara wanted to do it; she insinuated herself against me in ways that rapidly made my opposition untenable. I'd been to her father's café almost every day, and every time she served me tea and little sweets and long ravishing looks that made my heart pound on my rib cage with a fierce insistence. Thursday afternoon, during the lunch break at the talks, I hurried over to the café. Her father was away. She came outside and walked with me to my hotel.

"I'm not going up to your room," she said. "If my father caught me in your room, he'd slice you to ribbons. He doesn't trust you."

"Me? What have I done to deserve such suspicion?"

"Nothing. You're Korean, that's all, and he has bad memories of your country. You remind him of the war. He's been very strange since you showed up."

"The war was a long time ago."

"My father says time is *merde*." She smiled faintly. "Whatever that means. I try not to listen to everything he says. He doesn't like me speaking to men, by the way."

"What if I just nod my head?"

"Be serious. You aren't going to be here forever."

Such a pretty girl, such an ominous line of thought. It was unnerving. "I suppose not," I said.

"What I mean is, you won't be in Geneva forever. People show up and then fly away. It happens all the time. We need to take advantage of the time we have."

I thought so, too, though the image of my body cut to ribbons was something of a brake.

"Let's meet tonight at the Crazy Swan. It's a club. My father won't know anything about it. He doesn't even know where it is. The music is loud and the dance floor is so packed, you can barely move. Some people dance naked once in a while. It will be fun."

It wasn't exactly what I had in mind. Still, I made sure to smile.

"What? Don't you want to be with me? My father's away until tomorrow afternoon. That means tonight is free. *Carpe diem*, Inspector, don't you think?"

I didn't know what to think. I didn't know how to dance. "Yes," I said, "it will be fun."

I barely got back to the meeting room on time. The other side invited us to dinner that night. The idea of sitting and discussing where socks go instead of writhing with young bodies—some of them not wearing socks, if Dilara was to be trusted—did not appeal to me. Fortunately, fate stepped in. During a break, the delegation leader took me aside. "You slipped," he said. "You spoke English to one of them. They think they can sink their teeth into you. It probably isn't a good idea for you to be at the dinner tonight. What do you think?"

What did I think? He wanted to know what I thought? I thought the image of them as wolves pulling me down and gnawing on my throat was overdrawn. "I really think I should go to the dinner. It's important that I be there. In fact, it's critical that I be there. But if you advise against it, I have to consider that seriously." I paused long enough for serious consideration. "Please pass my regrets, won't you?"

That night, when I reached the club, there was a line at the door. "Good evening, monsieur," the doorman said. "Do you have a ticket?" He asked in French, and when I didn't respond, he repeated the question in English.

"Ticket? I'm meeting someone here." Dilara hadn't mentioned anything about a ticket. "Maybe she's inside. I'll just go in and look."

"No, pal, I don't think so." Given how big his hands were, they were surprisingly gentle on my neck. "We'll just wait over here, and maybe your friend will come out looking for you, eh?"

Jenö emerged from the club. "What are you doing here?" He looked over his shoulder into the noise and the lights beyond the door. "You're not here with Dilara, I hope. Ahmet will cut you to ribbons if he finds out. That isn't a bread knife he carries around. It's his Turkish army knife, the one he carried in the war. The last boyfriend she had was Lebanese. He disappeared."

The doorman chimed in. "He said he was waiting for a friend. Are you his friend, boss?"

Jenö shook his head. "He's not waiting for anyone. He's leaving. If he shows up again, Rudi, kick his tush down the street." Rudi nodded and stepped back inside the door.

"You give the orders around here?" I rubbed my neck where Rudi had given me a final squeeze. "You act like you own the place."

"I do. That's why Ahmet lets his sweet flower of a daughter keep coming here. We keep an eye on her."

"He knows she comes here?" Dilara had been very definite that it was a secret she kept from her father.

"Ahmet knows everything his daughter does, everyone she sees, everyone who thinks lascivious thoughts when they watch her walk away."

"I was only going to dance with her." I suppressed any thoughts Ahmet might pick up on the airwaves.

"What would you know about nightclub dancing, Inspector?"

"How hard can it be?"

"Forget about her. She'll only get you in trouble. Besides, the music in there is so loud, it could make your knees ache. Come on, we'll go get a drink someplace quiet, where we can actually hold a conversation. We need to talk."

A car pulled around the corner. The driver climbed out, and Jenö slid in behind the wheel. "Hop in, Inspector, we may have to put on a little speed to lose M. Beret's hordes." Before I had closed the door, the car jumped ahead. "Put on the seat belt, I don't want to get cited for ignoring safety regulations." We were already going 60 kph in a narrow street that seemed to be taking us rapidly out of the city. Jenö still hadn't turned on the headlamps. "Hang on for a few more minutes." He looked quickly in the rearview mirror and laughed. "Damn, they're good." The road curved sharply and the car accelerated. I thought for a moment we had left the ground. "Relax, Inspector. Enjoy the ride." Jenö took both hands off the steering wheel. "You see? The road is straight from here for the next five kilometers, and M. Beret's friends are stuck behind a garbage truck. I'm taking you to a nice place near Chamonix. You have your papers, I hope."

"No."

"Well, that's a problem. But we'll deal with it."

5

There were no other cars in the parking lot, and the inn was completely dark. Jenö pulled around back under a covered shed. "Nice and cozy," he said. "They'll figure out which road we took, but it will take them a while to find us." We walked to the back door. "I hope you like lamb, Inspector, because that's what they serve here. Lamb this and lamb that. It's a specialty of the house." Jenö opened the door with a key, waited for me to step inside, then locked the dead bolt. "The stairs to the basement are off the hall," he said. "Careful not to trip. I'll be down in a second."

Ahmet was waiting for me in the hall. It was hard to see much in the dark, but it didn't look like he was smiling. "Downstairs," was all he said, and so I went, my head suddenly full of images of ribbons. It seemed like a lot of trouble to go to over an unsuccessful effort to dance with his daughter, but you never know with some people. When I got to the bottom of the stairs, I turned to Ahmet to ask where I should go next.

6

When I regained consciousness, I was sitting in a dimly lit room, at the head of a large table. The other people were eating. "Forgive us, Inspector, but if lamb gets cold, it loses its flavor," said the man nearest me after taking a sip of wine. "We decided not to wait. Ahmet has been keeping yours warm."

"Actually, I'm not hungry." I had drooled on the tablecloth and had a slight headache.

"Have a bite, Inspector. Don't worry, we won't start dessert until you've caught up. Perhaps you'd better clean your palate first. Try some wine." He didn't offer to pour for me.

"Is this some sort of joke? You take me here"—I looked around for Jenö, but he was nowhere to be seen—"and then you knock me out. When I finally come to, you pretend I'm a welcome dinner guest." I put the napkin to my lip, which had stopped bleeding but still hurt. Pain annoys me, especially my own. "Someone has a lot of explaining to do. I don't even know who you are."

At that, the five people around the table put down their silverware. Ahmet appeared and cleared the plates, including mine.

The man nearest me sighed. "You wouldn't care for a brandy, would you?" I shook my head, which I instantly regretted. "No," he said, "I didn't suppose you would. Well, to business."

Just then there was a lot of ringing of bells from upstairs. Ahmet moved quickly to close what appeared to be a heavy wooden door—oak, probably, but I didn't think they would be happy if I went over to check. No one spoke. It occurred to me to shout to whoever was upstairs that I needed help, but on second thought it seemed hopeless, and not a sure thing that I would be any better off in all the commotion that would result. After the bells stopped, we all remained quiet for another five minutes or so. The man next to me got up and had a low conversation with Ahmet, who opened the heavy door and disappeared.

"You probably are wondering what is going on, Inspector." A man at the far end folded his napkin in a triangle and set it on the table. "You don't recognize us?"

"Should I?"

"We were on an airplane together."

I looked at each of them carefully. "You must have been in first class."

"A few of us were, actually. We are from Mossad. Does that worry you?"

"Of course not. My job description calls for me to have regular meetings with Mossad. Every Thursday night over lamb. We take turns getting knocked out."

"It was not exactly according to the script—that was Ahmet's doing. He thinks you are making eyes at his daughter. You're not, of course. She's much too young."

"Much."

The man with the triangle napkin rearranged it into a rabbit with floppy ears. "We understand that you came to Geneva on Mr. Sohn's orders. We have been trying to contact him, without success, I might add. Out of desperation, we decided to invite you to dinner."

Two lights went on in my head. I almost thought I was seeing double. "Dilara was part of the invitation. Sort of like bait?"

"She helped."

"There was never any idea of dancing with me at the disco."

"Never."

"Then why was Ahmet so upset?"

"Ahmet deals with possibilities. He likes to forestall things, especially when it comes to his virgin daughter. We don't approve of everything he does in that regard; we also don't control him."

"Getting back to Sohn." I looked at my wineglass, which was still empty. No one moved to fill it, and I was in no mood to pour for myself. This was the second light that had clicked on. They knew Sohn. That meant Sohn probably knew them, though these things are not always so symmetrical. But if he did know them, it meant the reason he picked me to come out here was welded to my bad luck in having to play host for Jenö. Unless, of course, it wasn't just bad luck. Maybe Sohn had engineered my playing host. The idea had crossed my mind before, but I had dropped it as far-fetched. I should trust my instincts, the ones that didn't touch on Turkish virgins.

"Getting back to Sohn," said the man to my right. "We have been discussing a few ideas with him over the past many months, as you no doubt know." No, I did not no doubt know. I had only entertained a bad premonition that Sohn had been working with the Israelis. Knowing and entertaining were not the same thing. "It turns out, much as he kept telling us, we do have some common ground, though as he constantly warned us, that is not a perception universally shared in your leadership."

"Or in ours," one of the other men muttered and left the table. The others did not watch him go.

The napkin man moved his chair closer to the table. "That's good, now we are only five—an excellent number for a conversation. Six is too many, don't you think?"

Ahmet walked in with a bowl of fruit and put it on the table.

"Please, Inspector, eat, have a piece of fruit." The man with the napkin took a banana and began to peel it. Ahmet found a chair next to the fireplace and sat down. His radars were turning. I tried not to think about Dilara.

"Here's what I know," I said. "First, I have a diplomatic passport; second, and in contradiction to point one, I am being held against my will in a basement somewhere in France by people who have no authority to do so."

"No, Inspector, we're not in France at all. We're in Italy. We *were* in France, but your M. Beret seems to know a lot of people in the French service. He doesn't like the Italians, however, and they don't like him. While you were resting we all drove here. Excuse my interruption—do you have a third point?"

"What about Jenö?" There was apparently a great deal of lamb going around this corner of Europe, French lamb, Italian lamb.

"He's probably sitting with M. Beret at this moment. They have a lot to talk about. As do we, Inspector. We have a message for you to give to Mr. Sohn. It is an important message, and we had quite a discussion among ourselves as to whether we could trust you with it. In the end, there wasn't much choice. Someone suggested that we pass it to your brother, but we have reason to believe that he and Sohn don't get along." A broad smile.

"And?" No question about it, they had good sources.

"And so you got the lamb dinner."

"I'm not authorized to pass messages to Sohn from you, and having disappeared for I don't know how long, I doubt if anyone in my mission will listen to anything I have to say once I get back. In fact, they probably already think I've defected." I stopped to give a short laugh, but it came out more like a bark. I should have gone to dinner with the wolves.

"Amazing, you sound just like Sohn, Inspector," said the man with the napkin. By now he had fashioned it into a hand puppet, though I didn't recognize the shape. "It's a dog," he said when he saw my questioning look, "though it appears to have lost a leg. You've never seen a three-legged dog? They seem to adapt rather well, though they can be painful to watch." I glanced around the table, but none of the others gave anything away.

"Adaptation has never been my best quality," I said. "If you want me to pass a message to Sohn, you'd damn well better have a convincing explanation for why I disappeared." I didn't need authorization to carry a message to Sohn. They knew that perfectly well.

"So, you agree to pass the message?"

"I imagine that is the only way I'll get out of here."

"Goodness, no, Inspector. We're not going to carry you away wrapped in a rug." The man to my left snorted.

"Let's get on with it." A short, bald man walked in and sat down. The others nodded at him. "I ask only that you listen closely, Inspector." He turned his full attention to me. "When I'm finished, if you have any questions about what I have said, you should ask them then. Understood?"

It wasn't an order or a threat, nothing peremptory about it. He seemed like a man under a lot of pressure and in need of a good night's sleep. "I'm listening," I said.

"Good. Sohn must have told you we have been meeting with him, or with people attached to him, for quite a while. We've been dancing around each other, but there isn't time to dance anymore." I put aside the mental picture of Sohn's little ears dancing in the desert at dusk. "Let me be blunt. We don't want our neighbors buying missiles from you." I assumed he didn't mean me personally. "You, of course, don't care what the buyers do with the missiles, as long as you are paid. You need the money from those sales, and if the sales stop, Sohn has made it very clear to us, you must have something to fill the vacuum. It's not a difficult equation to solve. We do our part, you do yours." He poured me a glass of wine, and then one for himself. "There is a little complication, however—the negotiations you are currently holding in Geneva." He took an orange from the fruit bowl, examined it closely, then put it back. "A decent orange cannot be such a difficult thing to find in this country," he said to the others in English. "Or am I wrong?" Nobody said a word.

"So far," I said when it seemed that if I didn't break the silence, we would be sitting all night contemplating fruit, "I haven't heard a message."

"That's because I'm not quite there, Inspector." The bald man rummaged through the bowl and emerged with a plum. He polished it. He held it up to the light. "Do you like plums, Inspector? Do you know what happens to a plum when it is dried? It becomes a prune. Same thing happens with countries. When they dry up, they are only good for shit."

Ahmet smiled absently into the fireplace. The others watched me with interest. I may have flushed, but I was determined not to let him win the point. "Maybe that sort of thing works with Arabs," I said evenly, "or with what's left of the Ottoman Empire. Don't try it with me." Ahmet's smile dimmed slightly, but I could tell it didn't break his concentration on which of my body parts to add to next week's lamb sausage.

The bald man bit into the plum. He said something to the others in a language that came from the back of his throat, and they nodded. "Very well, Inspector. We get down to business." The plum had dripped onto his chin. He ignored it. "The talks you are holding. I'll be blunt. They are a problem for us if they make progress."

"I don't think there's much danger of that."

"You may not think so. We do not think so. But things sometimes take an odd bounce in these talks. Do you play soccer?"

"Too much running around," I said.

"Then you know what I mean. An odd bounce in a game that seems to be going nowhere, and suddenly someone makes a goal. If your talks should suddenly make a goal, that would be a problem." He finally reached up and wiped away the drop of plum juice. "Like watching dirt on another man's face."

Sohn had sent me out to talk to the Americans in Geneva; instead I was somewhere in France—or Italy, if they were to be trusted—sharing a fruit bowl with Mossad. Sohn didn't make mistakes. I was here because he wanted me to end up here. When he played soccer, I had a feeling, the ball only bounced where he wanted it to. "If the talks succeed," I said, "it will stop our missile sales to your neighbors. I take it that isn't what you really want, even though you say that it is."

"To the contrary, it is very much what we want. And as you know, we are prepared to invest quite a bit in your country if we can be sure we are getting what we need. We want those missile transfers to stop, not slow down, not be rerouted. We want them to stop. But if the talks succeed, that will not happen. Why? Because you don't trust the Americans, your side will probe for the seams in an agreement."

Ahmet hissed through his false teeth.

"The deal will fall through sooner or later; and we will end up losing a lot of precious time on the problem. If the talks succeed, by which is commonly understood you sign something and drink a glass of champagne, we will be put on the sidelines and told not to interfere. Meanwhile, and this is our estimate, so please contradict me if you think we are wrong, your own situation will not improve. You will gain nothing from the negotiated deal, and the money you earn from sales elsewhere, even from your old customers, will become a pittance because no one will trust you anymore as a supplier. How can anyone sign a contract with someone who takes their money and then negotiates away the deal, tears it up for diplomatic gain? They barely trust you as it is. You see my point." He didn't wait for me to respond. "So it comes down to this: Would your side rather deal with someone who can deliver, or someone who can't? That's the choice. That's the message that we want you to pass to Sohn." He threw the plum pit into the fireplace and walked out of the room without saying good night.

7

"Don't turn around, but that is probably one of your M. Beret's boys who just swung in behind us."

"Why do you keep calling him 'my' M. Beret? He isn't mine. If anything he's yours. You're the one who dined with him last night. I didn't even eat." I could see headlights in the rearview mirror.

Jenö accelerated slightly and turned into the narrow street. "I'll drop you just past that warehouse, up there, on the right. You'll have to jump out while the car is moving. Are you trained for that?" It wasn't a skill we used in Pyongyang, but that was no business of Mossad.

"See you around," I said and reached for the door handle.

"You might want to release your seat belt first, Inspector."

"European sequencing," I said. Fortunately, we had slowed enough so that when I jumped out, I only stumbled against a lightpost and fell into a pile of boxes. Jenö's car disappeared; the one that had been following us squealed around the corner and roared past.

When I limped in the front door of my hotel, M. Beret was sitting with a book in his lap, dozing. He looked up when the door clicked shut.

"Ah, Inspector. Alarm bells have been ringing. Your mission is in an uproar wondering where you are. The talks were recessed and angry words have been exchanged. Your side says you have been kidnapped. Quite exciting. And you? Been skiing on the Italian side?"

"I don't ski."

"Then you must have bruised your shoulder jumping from a car. It takes practice."

"How would you know if I bruised my shoulder?"

"You're limping like a bird with a sprained wing."

"I'm tired, if you don't mind. I'd like to get some sleep. Will you do me a favor and tell my mission that I was knocked unconscious in a disco and nearly suffocated in the crush of young, sex-starved bodies, but that I'm alright now?"

"Of course, Inspector, that is probably as believable as anything." He closed his book and watched me climb the stairs. "How was the lamb, by the way?"

"Good night, monsieur."

I heard him move softly to the door.

Chapter Five

"The talks are locked up. We have no instructions; none will show up until we have sent back a good explanation for where you have been." The security man at the mission was pasty-faced and nervous. He had already smoked two cigarettes and was fumbling to light a third. The ambassador sat quietly to the side. His aide was taking copious notes, though since nobody was saying much, it was hard to see what there was to record so far. Long silences can speak volumes, but it can be tricky getting them down on paper. When I first joined Pak's section, I would polish my interrogation reports for hours, noting everything. Remarks, silences, facial tics—everything. Eventually, Pak told me that the Ministry had requested we submit something shorter. No more than one page for each report. "Boil it down," they told him. I told Pak we'd lose the nuance. He laughed. "Keep a special folder for nuance, O. Once a year we'll dump it out on your desk and sort through the pile."

"We're waiting, Inspector. You were gone for twenty-four hours. Thursday night to Friday night. Where were you?" I recognized the man talking as the driver who met me at the airport when I arrived. In this room, he didn't look like a driver anymore, or sound like one. The security man observed him sourly.

Interesting, I thought. "Turkish food," I said. "Since I was told not to attend Thursday night's dinner with the delegation, I went out for Turkish food. I think I drank too much of that ugly liquor of theirs; when I came to, I was in a pile of boxes on a street near a nightclub. It was quite bizarre, actually. Hard to believe, but there you are. Keep away from that liquor, that's my advice. If you don't mind my asking, what do my drunken wanderings have to do with holding the negotiations? It's not as if I add a lot to the discussions. I heard you accused them of kidnapping me. Why would they want to do that?"

The door opened, and a woman handed a sealed envelope to the ambassador. She waited while he signed a log. "I think this might save us some time," he said. "Give me a moment to read it." He carefully opened the envelope and looked at the single sheet of paper inside. "That's clear enough," he said when he had read it through twice. He looked at the man standing next to me. "No more questions."

"What?" The security man ground out his cigarette. "Says who?"

The ambassador's aide grimaced but didn't stop writing. The ambassador folded the paper and put it back in the envelope. "Inspector, I am going to request that you be sent home immediately. That's a formality. I don't really require approval. I have good and sufficient reason to order you out on my own authority, even before I receive guidance from Pyongyang. Your brother and I had a conversation the other day, and now I see why he warned me against letting you stay. You are disrupting my operations here. Because I do not know what you are doing or why, I consider you a menace. The Swiss are also unhappy, and if they are unhappy, so am I. The last thing we can afford is to have the Swiss snapping at us. They don't want a defection here; neither do I. It doesn't matter what airplane leaves in the next three hours, or where it goes. I want you on it."

Defection? Had my brother spread the word that I was thinking of defecting? There was a knock on the door, and the same woman came in with another envelope. The ambassador signed the log again, and this time ripped the envelope open. "Sons of bitches," he muttered. The aide put down his pen.

"I take it the inspector should not pack his bags just yet." The man who wasn't really a driver didn't sound surprised.

"Handwritten instructions from the Top." The aide and the security man glanced nervously heavenward. "He stays." The ambassador gave me a malign look. I didn't know him at all; our paths had never crossed before, and if he had passed through my sector in Pyongyang, I hadn't noticed. But he definitely didn't like me. "There are wheels spinning, Inspector. I strongly advise you stay clear of things that don't concern you." He paused. "Mountain lakes are deep, just remember that. Perhaps it would be good for you to start wearing your badge. It might help with identification." The aide closed his notebook and slipped out of the room. The ambassador turned to a young woman who had been lounging near the window. "The talks should resume the day after tomorrow. Have the delegation pass a message to the other side tomorrow morning telling them we have new instructions. Let them fuss with that idea for twenty-four hours. Don't say anything about the reappearance of the wanderer." Another malign look was flung in my direction.

In the hallway, I passed Mr. Roh. It was time for our talk. "I'm going out for some fresh air," I said. "I hear the fountain in the park, the one near the rose garden, is nice in the afternoon light." He nodded and kept walking.

2

A smart young man—that was what I concluded when I saw Roh sitting on one of the white benches beside the fountain about an hour later. Smart, a little reckless, maybe a potential security risk. That's how it would go down in his file if anyone spotted him here talking to me. A security risk because he was out meeting with a security person from another office without checking first with his own. And I knew he hadn't checked with his own, because they never would have let him come here alone to sit with me. So he was a risk, and it wasn't my worry. It meant he'd answer some questions, as long as I gave him a comfortable lead-in. His head was down and he might have been reading the book in his lap. But he wasn't; he was waiting. As soon as he heard my steps on the gravel path, he looked up.

"Nice weather," I said. "A good day to sit underneath pine trees."

"This could get me into a lot of trouble," he said. "The word going around the halls is, the ambassador doesn't like you."

"But you decided it was worth the risk. Otherwise you wouldn't be here."

"I was curious. People have been wondering about you ever since you showed up."

"Have they? And why should that be? I'm just a servant of the people, doing the people's business." He was smart and he was curious, but he knew enough not to trust me yet. That was alright. I didn't like people who trusted me too quickly. They could go the other way just as fast.

Roh closed the book. "The people's business. The people. The people."

"Our people. You know, the ones tightening their belts, again. The ones who would rather have guns than candy. I'd rather have guns than candy, wouldn't you?" I looked down at my belt. "I have at least two notches to go."

"Every day, I push aside the plate of candy in front of me. More guns, that's what I want, I tell the cook. That's why we're in Geneva, isn't it? To make sure when my mother goes for her food ration, she can be told, 'Here, have some more guns.'" He swallowed hard. "You're going to report me for that, aren't you?" He reminded me of my source on the campus back home, the girl who liked Rachmaninoff. I hadn't expected him still to have that much of an edge. I assumed being in the Foreign Ministry would have smoothed it off.

"All diplomats talk funny as far as I'm concerned. Especially inexperienced ones like you. I've stopped paying attention. But maybe you can tell me something. Why don't we go for a stroll? It's easier to talk when you're moving. I learned that somewhere. Even in a job like mine, sooner or later, you learn things. You don't realize until it's too late that you learned something; and then you don't remember where, or how, or why. There's no voice that automatically pipes up: Inspector O! Attention! Learning experience! All you can do is check for scars, or dings in the windshield. That's where lessons usually come, at 80 kph on a bad road at night with no moon."

"You sound like my father."

"I wouldn't know." We walked past the small grove of oak trees that still clung to some of last year's leaves. There is nothing to recommend old leaves; they give nothing to a tree except the mournful appearance of days past. Once, when I mentioned to my grandfather that it was odd how oak trees clung to their leaves, he snorted. "Why blame the trees? Oaks are just too kind, that's all. Not like maples." He'd pointed his cane at a maple tree. "Greediest damned tree you'll find."

"You keep looking behind us," I said to Mr. Roh. "Don't worry. No one is following." Which was almost certainly not true. I couldn't go out without someone trying to stay a respectable distance back, pretending to be birdwatching, or window-shopping, or consulting a bus schedule and wandering off curbs. But the Swiss didn't need to follow me into this park; I'd already figured that out. They had the area under constant watch. Little cameras disguised as acorns, maybe, and too bad for the squirrel who ate one. If anyone was lurking, it was the Man with Three Fingers. I didn't think he would bother with Mr. Roh, though, unless he thought he could use the youngster to club me senseless. Roh might have been followed by someone from the mission, but I'd be able to spot them soon enough.

"Where are you from?" It was an uncomplicated question, I thought, nothing he would shy away from answering.

"I was born in Pyongyang." That meant he had seen the city in better days, in the 1970s, when the streetcars ran and the lights worked.

"You get into the countryside much?" Not as simple; there were jagged edges on a question like that.

"My mother's family is from Chongjin." He paused. "I was there just before coming here. My uncle was sick." Sick. That meant he was dying of hunger, but no one would say that, certainly not this kid who was starting to wonder what I was doing, regretting he'd come out to meet me, still weighing what he said to make sure he didn't say too much.

"How were things in Chongjin?"

Mr. Roh looked at me carefully. This was the danger point, and he knew it. The question wasn't complicated; it could be deadly. If he told me what he'd really seen and if he'd misjudged me, he was finished.

"Don't worry," I said. "I'm still not planning to write anything down."

"I won't soon forget what I saw."

"Don't, don't forget. You understand me? Don't ever forget."

We fell into silence again, standing under trees with dead leaves in a dying afternoon.

"You want me to tell you something about the delegation, is that is it?" He shoved his hands in his pockets and thrust out his chin. "That's the game? Always games and countergames. I get tired of them."

"But you came out here anyway. You do have a conspiratorial frame of mind after all. I was beginning to worry." I wondered when he would get around to mentioning the delegation. I didn't want to raise it. I wanted him to open that door.

"Conspiratorial? No, just realistic. People criticize the Foreign Ministry for being unrealistic, but they don't understand. We know what's what."

"Maybe you do, maybe you don't."

"We know plenty, trust me."

"Like for instance."

"Like you can be sure the delegation leader understands perfectly well what the game is."

"Game? Whose game?"

"These talks we're in. They're part of the game at home. Some people want us to sell off the missiles to the Americans for money and food. Other people don't want us to do anything at all, just stall. And then there is a group that wants us to pretend we're making progress so another bidder will get involved."

"Really? Another bidder? Who would that be?"

He shrugged. Maybe he didn't know about the contacts with the Israelis, but it was more likely he did.

"Sure," I said. "You can't tell someone from the Ministry of Public Security, because it's a matter of security. Because you wouldn't want to get yourself into trouble, would you? Not you, or your family." It was a lousy thing to say. I wasn't going to threaten his family, even if that's what he thought.

I saw him damp down a powerful surge of anger. He waited to

speak until it had subsided, and he could trust what he was going to say. "The delegation leader goes out at night sometimes. No one knows where."

"The security man at your mission doesn't keep track?"

"The security man is busy. The delegation leader found out he likes Portuguese."

"The security man likes Portuguese girls?"

"No, he likes Portuguese boys."

We walked up the hill and then back toward the rose garden. I saw someone duck behind a tree. "Time for you to get back," I said. "I've got things to do."

3

That night, I went out for a walk. I figured I'd go down to the lake and stroll back, but I must have taken a wrong turn. One wrong turn usually leads to another. It should be simple enough to back up to the right way again, but it's not. You don't know you're lost until it's too late. By the time I realized I was lost, that I didn't know whether the lake was to my right or to my left, I was on a street that was dark and completely empty. The buildings were run-down, but that's what buildings tend to be when you're lost. The street didn't go anywhere, except to another street that was even darker and more deserted.

I didn't hear them at first, maybe because I wasn't paying attention. The footsteps behind me stopped and resumed, which told me whoever was on my tail was using sound, not sight, to keep close. There were lamps at either end of the block, but their light hung around the base of the posts. I got on tiptoe and pranced into the darkest spot I could find. From there, I sidled into a dark doorway. The door opened; I backed into a dark room. A waitress appeared, blond, in a long dress that was slit where it shouldn't have been. As soon as she said hello I knew she was Russian. "Jazz," she said. "You have ticket?"

I wasn't sure where this was going. "Ticket for what?"

"Jazz," she said. "Drink, jazz, and me. All included. Pay now."

"Thanks, I'll sit at the bar."

She shrugged. "Up to you."

There was only one person at the bar, a black man, older than I would have expected at a place like this. "Shakin' babe," he said.

"Yeah."

The lights went up slightly on the stage, and a group of four musicians began to play. It wasn't music you'd want to march to on Army Day, but it was interesting.

"Shakin' babe," the old man said. "That's shakin' stuff."

I nodded.

"You from here?" he asked.

"Nah." I'd never used "nah" before. I'd heard tourists use it, seen it in movies. It seemed like the right time. "Nah. I'm Mexican."

He lowered his head. "Cool." He lifted his glass. "Got to get me some freeholays one of these days."

"Later," I said and took my glass of beer to an empty table. The Russian girl appeared.

"Jazz," she said.

"That's cool," I said and finished my beer. The music became louder, faster, tearing apart. I reached, but it got away from me. I couldn't follow. I was lost, completely lost. Everything was moving in its own direction, the piano this way, the saxophone somewhere else, the drummer as lost as I was. How could it work? How did it happen? When did it take me to somewhere I'd never been?

I left the club a few hours later and found the way back to my hotel without much trouble. When I got to my room, I didn't even turn on the light. There wasn't anything there I needed to see.

PART IV

Chapter One

"You don't seem to be on the ambassador's good side." The Man with Three Fingers had come up behind me across the grass. I hadn't heard a thing. "You don't seem to be on anyone's good side, actually. Not that I'm surprised."

"I'm enjoying the view and the air at the moment." I resisted the urge to turn to face him. Better to act nonchalant, as if I had known the whole time he was there. "If you want to sit down, feel free. Otherwise, go get yourself a cup of espresso or something."

He walked around and stood directly in front of me. "Admit it, O, you didn't hear me creeping up behind you. I could have taken your head off and you wouldn't have known it was happening until you saw your eyes staring up from the ground." He flexed what remained of his hand. "I don't want to sit down."

"Then don't." I settled back on the bench. "Excuse me if I don't get up."

"You disappeared, but I know where you were."

"That's good, because I don't have any idea." I thought he meant the jazz club, or maybe even the place the music had taken me.

"You were chasing a delicious piece of Turkish taffy named Dilara."

"I don't know anything about Turkish taffy."

"Delicious Dilara, that's what people say. That sort of thing can get you in a lot of trouble."

"You are blocking my view, which is beginning to irritate me."

"Is that so? I don't want to irritate you. I want to grill your kidneys and feed them to the fish. Do you actually think you are walking around this city on your own, Inspector? There is a caravan behind you, everywhere you move. Swiss, Americans, South Koreans, even Chinese."

"And you. Don't forget about you."

"No, I don't follow people anymore. I just wait for them to break circuits."

I thought it over. "Is that what the trigger was, an electric eye? It could just as easily have been me that night."

"Could have been, but wasn't. I wouldn't have left you lying there."

"Maybe not. We'll never know, will we? And you're still blocking my view."

"That disappearing trick the other night was unwise. It has some people thinking you are getting ready to jump ship. It's what your brother said—that you are planning a defection. And the word is out that ship-jumpers should be stopped ahead of time, in any way necessary. Everyone's nervous because of what happened in Beijing. The Center doesn't want any more incidents."

"I seem to remember they considered the man in Beijing a traitor and his leaving good riddance. That's what they said on the radio, isn't it?"

"They don't want the garbage to blow away. They want to bury it first."

"Bury?" I moved to stand up, but he put a hand on my arm and held me in place. He might have lost a couple of fingers, but he was still plenty strong. Starting a fight on the shores of Lake Geneva had drawbacks, so I gave him a long stare.

"You seem agitated, Inspector. Something the matter?"

"Maybe it's just me, but I'm averse to being threatened. It bothers me somehow. Makes my blood boil, causes me to see white streaks and hear nasty voices. That sort of thing."

"Then don't consider anything I say as a threat."

"Friendly advice, I suppose."

"Here's the problem, Inspector. You're in someone's way, and you refuse to get out of the way. So naturally that someone thinks the only thing to do is to move you."

"That's where stories of defection come in? And deep mountain lakes?"

The Man with Three Fingers didn't answer. He stared at something behind me for a moment, then turned abruptly and walked away in the direction of town. As he passed by the last bench before the path turned away from the lake, a nondescript man in a brown coat stood up and followed him from a comfortable distance. It was so obvious it could only have been intentional. That seemed to be the Swiss style. No sense being subtle when you have so much of other people's money in your vaults.

"You must think us painfully obvious, Inspector, but your friend is way too cocky in someone else's city. I've got to do something about all these bees, don't I?" M. Beret was standing about a meter behind me, addressing the back of my head. The Man with Three Fingers must have seen him striding across the lawn.

"Is it always necessary to come up from behind? Is there a rule against approaching someone in normal fashion?"

"Well, I suppose I might emerge next time from the lake in a frogman's suit, but then we will startle the swans, don't you think?"

His hand was on my shoulder. "Still sore? I can get you a nice Indonesian masseuse if you like." He moved around the bench and sat down beside me.

The Portuguese must be fully employed. "You seem obsessed with Indonesian girls."

"No, but I was hoping you might be."

"These days my only obsession is for some time to think. Can't a man ruminate in peace? I suppose I would also like a few answers, but that is probably too much to ask. Just time to speculate will do."

"An airplane ride will give you the opportunity to sit and think, Inspector. Why don't we drive you to the airport and put you on a plane? Anywhere you want to go, just tell me, as long as it's away from here.

Your ambassador also wants you to leave, I hear. Maybe I should let him pay for the ticket."

"How can it be that I thought things were simple in Switzerland? I pictured cows wearing bells, and girls on hillsides waving at the wild-flowers."

"Fantasy. It's a very complex place, especially because people from the outside won't leave us alone."

"Alone? You don't even begin to know what it's like not to be left alone. When was the last time your country was destroyed, M. Beret?"

He sat pondering this. "Destroyed? Let me think. The Romans were here and chased the Helvetii; Napoleon stuck his nose in briefly; we've fought some battles with this duke and that one, but, no, I'd have to say we've largely avoided destruction. This city"—he swept his hand toward the buildings across the lake—"is a monument of stability. It's been here for over two thousand years, did you know?" I didn't know.

At that moment, with M. Beret pointing at a city whose only skyline was the oversized signs of jewelers, it became clear to me. This was the one chance I was going to get to pass on what Sohn had sent me to say. I might not have as good an opportunity to talk to anyone else who would be sure to understand. M. Beret was a man who listened carefully; he'd yet to ask me about lost socks or to comment on my ties. He would write down what I told him, and make sure it filtered out to the right places. He'd get it to liaison officers, and they would pass it around, if they knew what they were doing. It would end up in faraway in-boxes, just as Sohn planned.

"Good fortune shines on you," I said. "Be grateful. My land is not so lucky." As I heard myself say the words, I could barely believe my ears. This was exactly what my grandfather would say. His lectures on the sad history of Korea—overrun, bullied, forced to kneel—always filled me with rage at his self-pity. Now I was saying exactly the same thing. "We were destroyed, but don't imagine we intend for it ever to happen again."

"The Swiss are, as you know, Inspector, neutral. There is no reason to think of me as your enemy."

"Neutral? That is for the rich and fortunate. We have no time for neutrality. We are weak and poor."

M. Beret said nothing.

"That's what you think, I know, even if you won't say it. Don't worry. It's alright, we know how the world sees us. But we are not as weak as people think—or hope. What's more, we have no room left to retreat, not a millimeter. Do people want us to starve? Then they will see how desperate we can be. We will not go quietly, let me assure you. We will not starve in the shadows and die quietly out of sight."

"You are hardly in position to threaten anyone, I would think."

"Don't be too sure." That did it. That registered with him. I could see that he was already composing the memo in his head. I added an extra line for him to use. "No one should be too sure about us in this situation."

"There are people who say your country is on the verge of collapse."

"There are people who don't know their backsides from a hole in the ground."

M. Beret took a small appointment calendar from his pocket. He had one. The delegation leader had one. The entire world but me seemed to have a little appointment book. It was some sort of mark of sophistication. If you needed an appointment calendar, it meant you had appointments, which meant you were important, called upon, connected, in charge of your life. I needed to get several, one for each pocket, at least.

"This is my appointment book, Inspector. For the past two weeks or so it has been mostly blank. Do you know why? Because I have been solely focused, obsessively focused, on watching you. No luncheon dates, no dinner invitations, nothing but you. My friends think I am having an affair. Can you believe it? My entire existence is consumed. Not counting our brief stroll in Coppet, the only break I have had was the drive to Chamonix, and that was at night when there was nothing to see. Nothing! I couldn't even stop for dinner." Ah, M. Beret, I thought, you lying bastard. You had dinner with Jenö that night, whereas I had nothing to eat. "Why don't you take a trip to Montreux tomorrow? It will do us both good. You can visit the castle, ponder the dungeon, maybe. We can have lunch in a nice restaurant, separate tables for the sake of propriety, but it will be pleasant nonetheless."

"Castles? You struck me as someone interested solely in bulldozer parts."

"Of course, that's what this is all about, don't misunderstand. I know it, and so do you." He sighed and put away the notebook. "And so, we can be sure, does our mutual friend Jenö."

"I may be busy and thus difficult to follow for the next several days. I've been making it easy for you, but I do know how to slip a tail. Why don't you take time off? Go have dinner, clear your mind, read a book."

"A tempting proposition, Inspector. But I must decline. Do your best. I'll see you when I see you. Incidentally, if you like jazz, there are some good clubs around. Just ask."

2

On arriving in Geneva, Sohn had gone directly to the mission. Then, when it was still early, he came to see me. He was waiting across the street from my hotel when I stepped outside. I made a mental note to tell M. Beret to put a bench there. I don't like guests having to stand around. As soon as Sohn was sure I'd seen him, he started walking up the street, which according to the simple code we'd agreed on at our last meeting in Pyongyang meant he wanted me to walk in the other direction. The "other direction" in this case was down the hill toward town. If things went according to plan, he would double back and find me, assuming I could remember the prearranged pattern I was supposed to follow. Yesterday had been the third of March; that meant this was a morning for threes. Three blocks, then a right turn. Another three blocks, then a left turn. Three more blocks, then another right. It didn't seem to me to be the best technique for a foreign city, since we could just as easily end up in the lake with the swans, but it would have to do under the circumstances. I didn't know where all the turns would put us exactly; wherever it was, once he was there, it was up to Sohn to decide whether he wanted to go ahead with a meeting. If he saw something he didn't like, he would call it off. At some point, M. Beret would get a report that I had been out walking, but I doubted his people would know for sure who Sohn was for a couple of days at least. The Israelis, who were keeping tabs on me even though I couldn't figure out how, might imagine that I had sent their message and that Sohn had come running. If they wanted to meet with him, it was up to them to arrange the contact. I was through playing messenger boy.

My three-block dance led finally to a street with small shops, a playground, and a bar called Sunflower. The door was propped open with a box, so I went in and waited. The man behind the bar told me in French, then in German, and finally in English that they didn't open until 5:00 P.M. I shrugged. He shrugged back. I sat down on one of the barstools to wait. Five minutes later Sohn popped in. The man behind the bar started to explain again that the bar was not open, but Sohn ignored him and walked to a table in the back.

"Too bad," I said. "You just missed my brother."

"Is that so?" Sohn turned around and pantomimed drinking something to the man behind the bar.

"The place is closed," I said. "We're lucky if he doesn't kick us out."

The man walked over with two glasses of beer and set them down, not very gently, on the table. "That will be all," Sohn said, in French. I kept most of my composure.

"You speak French?" I asked when we were alone again.

"Of course I know French, Inspector, doesn't everyone in the civilized world?" He held up his glass and studied it closely. "This beer is very Swiss, I'm afraid. Don't drink it unless you have to." He took a sip and grimaced. "Now, about your brother. You saw him off?"

"No. He told me he was leaving."

"Well, he didn't go anywhere. He doesn't have tickets, and he doesn't have reservations. I think he still has shirts at the laundry, you know, those blue shirts he likes. Surprised? He lied to you."

"You want me to get his shirts for you?"

"No. Stay away from him and anything he has touched. He has things to do, and apparently he hasn't done them yet. I'm pretty sure he has an appointment to meet someone. That needs to go ahead. You've done your job."

"What job is that?"

"You rattled him. That can be fatal for someone like your brother. He can't afford that sort of emotion. He has too many enemies."

"We argued, if that's what you mean. That's what we usually do when we bump into each other. I don't think it rattled him at all."

"I think it did. I think he's off stride. At this point, it's a question of waiting to see how much. I'm almost sure he's operating on his own right now. When things are still small like this, I might be able to stop them. After that, the decisions are out of reach. People take sides, they draw big pictures. They get budgets."

"Perhaps you could be more cryptic for me."

"Later. We've got work to do."

"Me? My work here is done."

"Before I went to your hotel, I paid a call on the ambassador. He was surprised to see me."

"I'll bet."

"Actually, I thought he was going to have a stroke. No such luck. When he could finally talk, he picked up the phone and told his aide that they were leaving immediately for Zurich. A meeting, he said. I saluted him from the front steps as his car went out the gate, but I don't think he was mollified. So I went back to his office to write him a note."

"You went into his office?"

"I sat at his desk, actually. He shouldn't leave some of those documents lying around like that. The wrong people might read them. Apparently, the situation is fluid."

"Are we back to cryptic? Because if we are, I'm going to my hotel."

"Before that, you'll have to do some shopping. There are new instructions from the Center for everyone working overseas. They can be summarized as follows: Collect vegetable seeds and food, food, food. Fertilizer if it is to be had, but the first priority is food. So is the second priority. And so is the third. On ships, on trucks, on bicycles—it doesn't make any difference. For the moment, we grovel, we pander, we lick the boots of anyone who will deliver. You won't believe the catchphrase that excuses this madness." Sohn took a pen out of his pocket. "You need a pen?"

"That's the ambassador's. I saw him use it. You took the ambassador's pen."

"Don't worry, I left him his pencils, most of them, anyway. What you need to worry about is the new instructions."

"What happened to 'crazy'?" I asked. "The last time you and I spoke, that was to be my message. It was delivered, incidentally." I didn't mention to whom.

"Scratch 'crazy.' According to the new, improved thinking, it will only scare people off. 'Quietly desperate'—that's where things are now. If you already told people we're crazy, you'll have to go back and undo it." He unscrewed the pen and looked at the parts. 'They'll eat us up," he said absently. "This is exactly what the wild dogs at our door have been waiting for. It's suicide, admitting we're weak."

"I'm going to ask you a question."

"Let me ask you one first. Your brother—do you know what a menace he is, Inspector? People like him think their time has come. The Center is distracted. Every day there is more to worry about. I think we may actually be coming out of the worst of it, but there is still plenty that can go wrong. Your brother and his friends were busy last year when the sky was darkest. They used the time well, and I'm a year behind. It might as well be a lifetime."

"Do you want me to nod knowingly, Sohn? Or will you tell me what you are talking about first?"

"Imagine this. They've been digging, and planning, and putting together the pieces. A piece here. A piece there." He moved the parts of the pen around on the table. "In a month or two, if they are left alone, they'll be ready to walk into the Center and present what they've done. Then it will be too late. They'll lay out plans, sketch out scenarios. And at that point, when I am asked what I think, it's too late. Should I say: 'No! Don't do everything possible to protect the Fatherland.' Or how about: 'No! It is dangerous to go down that path, it risks everything we've accomplished, it might explode in our face.' "

I frowned. Sohn was careful with his imagery; he didn't make mistakes.

"At that point, the only answer I can offer is, 'Good for them. Hooray for them. All honor to them.' Your brother will be rewarded. He'll swagger, he'll go to the parties, he'll put his filthy fat hands—" Sohn stopped. "Forgive me."

"No, go ahead, say whatever you want. He isn't my brother anymore."

I thought Sohn would bark, but he didn't. He hadn't barked once the whole time.

"You have friends here who are anxious to meet," I said.

"If you don't mind, I'll drink while you talk."

"There isn't much else to say. I assume that with your arrival, I've become extraneous. You'll take over, and I can go home."

"Nothing of the sort. There is still a lot to be done." Sohn put his glass down and leaned toward me. Surely now, a bark. "There are things you can do that I can't."

"Such as?"

"Such as keeping a lid on the negotiations; such as watching over our diplomats and making sure none of them decide to stay out too late or forget to come home." He picked up the glass again and drained it. He wasn't going to bark, I finally realized. Overseas, he didn't do that. Overseas, he didn't walk like a bear, or clear his throat. Overseas, he was a different man.

"You don't want to meet your friends?"

"I'm too busy. It's too dangerous." He put the pen back together, the way a soldier assembles a rifle during a drill.

"But it's alright with you if I put my head in that lion's mouth."

He smiled. "Have you discovered yet what happened to the woman in Pakistan?"

"I figured you had some connection to all of that." A thought crept up on me. "Was she yours?"

"Good guess. But mine? I don't own people, Inspector. I don't like to see them murdered, either. And I don't believe for a moment that she was killed by locals. Do you?"

"Don't tell me, her murder has something to do with why I'm here." I stopped. "Next you're going to tell me my brother is tied into this as well."

He handed me the pen. "I trained her."

"You what? She was an embassy wife. What did you train her to do? Cook? Apparently, she wasn't very good at it."

"How much do you already know about her, Inspector?"

"Nothing. I think I prefer it that way. When I went to look at her personnel file, it had disappeared. All I was supposed to do was to gather a few odd facts about her and sail them on their way. I should have done that. Maybe if I had, I wouldn't be sitting here right now."

"You were destined to be here." Sohn smiled. His ears looked bigger, though maybe it was just the light. "If it's odd facts you're after, this is as odd a place as any to gather them. I thought you'd like it in Geneva."

"Here? Why would I like it here? The trees are butchered. I'm sick to death of looking at watches in store windows. And I resent like hell being tossed in front of my brother."

That rolled off Sohn's back.

"Odd, my brother's taking a sudden interest in fresh-baked bread."

Sohn perked up. "He told you that?"

"No, I heard him talking about it on the phone."

"I don't suppose you know who he was talking to?"

"I have no idea."

"Your brother hates bread."

"I know."

Sohn looked thoughtful, and I knew I wasn't part of the conversation going on inside his head.

"I'd guess your friends are going to contact you fairly soon," I said. "They seem impatient. It wouldn't surprise me if they have reserved a room for you, probably at the usual place. Maybe I'll see you around." I got up and left quickly, before he could say anything more. Halfway out the door, I realized I hadn't thanked him for the pen.

3

When I got back to the hotel, there was a bench across the street. A green felt hat sat on it, in case I had any doubt who to thank. The hotel lobby, as usual, was deserted. I walked past the desk clerk and was partway up the stairs when she called to me. "You have a message." She held up an envelope. "You want it?"

"Of course I want it if it's for me."

"It might be bad news."

I walked back down and held out my hand. "Do you mind?"

The note was from Sohn, though it wasn't signed. All it said, in Korean, was "Same place, tonight at nine." Today was the fourth, an even-numbered day. That meant I was supposed to subtract two hours from the time in the message. Or was it three? Which would mean we were supposed to meet at 6:00 P.M., assuming I remembered the code right. Sohn thought codes were indispensable. To me, they were confusing and easy to forget. Maybe a code with bread in it had advantages.

I arrived at the Sunflower at six, right on time. The bartender looked at his watch, then pointed to the same table Sohn and I had occupied a few hours earlier. I waited. People came into the bar, and left. The tables near me filled up with groups of three or four. I hadn't paid much attention to the neighborhood, but it didn't seem to be a very bourgeois crowd. A couple of women with lots of makeup and long lashes came in and surveyed the scene. One of them caught my eye. If she was Portuguese, I couldn't tell and didn't want to find out. I shook my head.

Three hours later, it dawned on me that Sohn wasn't going to show up.

4

"Tell me the truth, Inspector, do you prefer New York to Geneva? You have been to New York, haven't you?" M. Beret and I were standing in a tiny park. I didn't like being there. It was a small piece of land sandwiched between the lake and the street, the sort of thing city architects like because it meets their quota for green space. There were lots of trees—a circle of maples around a fountain, lindens along the path, a couple of big beeches off by themselves. The beeches looked like they felt crowded and wished they were somewhere else.

"Can't we find another spot?" The more I looked around the little park, the more I didn't like what I saw.

"How about the airport? I can have your bags shipped later." M. Beret sat down on a bench facing the water. I especially didn't like that. It put our backs to the street.

"What makes you think I've been to New York?"

"A friend of a friend of a friend. A very long chain of friends. They met someone who talked to someone who saw you walking down a hill to Third Avenue. You looked lost, they said."

"Small world. I had no idea you had orthodox friends."

"Given your thought patterns, I'll take that for a yes. But how am I to interpret such information? A mere police inspector, going here and there, there and here, all in the space of two or three months? It's very odd, is it not?"

"I thought so." I hadn't been walking down the hill, I'd been walking up. The other man had been walking down, the friendly man who had stopped. A friendly old man with distant connections to M. Beret?

"Again I ask, what am I to make of your frequent travels? More to the point, why is your passport so light on visas if you travel so much? Do you just slip across borders like the March wind?"

"My passport? Can we walk a bit? It's getting cold on this bench." The wind was whipping the lake into frantic wavelets that smacked against each other. In the sunlight they might have sparkled, but not under the leaden gray of the early morning clouds. When I passed by Ahmet's place on the way to meet M. Beret, it had been closed; no sign in the window, but the shades were down and the door was locked. Maybe Ahmet was out getting his knife sharpened. That meant Dilara was alone, in her bedroom upstairs. Or was she not alone? It was an interesting question, but not as interesting as the one occupying my mind at the moment. When could I get something to eat? I waited for M. Beret to produce a roll from his pocket. This was how dogs were trained, and I could see why it was so effective.

"Obviously, you've checked," I said. "Funny, I examine other people's passports with some care, but I never look at my own very closely, and it's not something I keep at home in a drawer. Surely you know that much about my country. I am handed a passport, it has my name and picture in it, a birth date. That's good enough for me. Is it the same one as last time? Who cares? Maybe they lost the last one after I handed it in. Maybe they revised the covers and had to reissue new documents to everyone. How should I know? Believe it or not, I have other things to worry about. If you want the truth, I didn't really want to come here, to this polished place under these friendless mountains. It was an order."

It took only a few minutes to walk around the edge of the park. His roll-hand stayed in his pocket the whole time. When we got back to where we started, M. Beret rested his arms on the railing that ran alongside the path. "What do you think, Inspector?" He pointed across the river.

"I've been wondering. Are those political slogans on the tops of those buildings?"

"Political slogans? No, we don't do that. They're advertisements. That one on the end is for watches."

"Then they're slogans for the rich. Ours exhort the people. Yours exhort the rich. We say, 'Victory!' You say, 'Buy!' Not a world of difference, is there?"

"Which one do you prefer?"

I was disappointed, somehow. He hadn't struck me as the type to ask that sort of question. We'd finally established good working relations, I thought. I didn't expect him to spoil things by dragging in politics. "Have you seen the trees on the street that runs alongside the lake? The street with the woman with the rump."

"Quai Gustave-Ador?"

"Is that her name?"

"The street."

"Well, those are plane trees along that street. When plane trees are free to grow, they grow tall, and the shade they produce is sweet all summer long. Those trees of yours, an entire line of them, have been butchered."

"You mean cut down?"

"They might wish they were dead. No, they have been mangled. Their tops have been hacked off. They are maimed."

"Pity the trees."

It was too snide to pass over. I went over to the bench and sat down. I wanted to be sitting when I put this knife between his ribs. "I happened to be out walking the other night. No doubt you noticed."

"I'm behind on my reports, but I'll take your word for it. Good, exercise is what you need. It helps with any lingering jet lag. Clarifies the senses." He sat down beside me. "I might wish for better weather, though. It's a bit windy. You must forgive me." There it was again—snide. That wasn't his normal style. Maybe he'd caught his fingers in a door.

"Yes, it is a bit windy, and a little chilly in the evenings. That's what I wanted to ask you about. I noticed that you seem to have an organization very similar to the Young Pioneers in my country. It seems to function after sundown."

"Is that so?" M. Beret looked at me warily. "What do you mean?"

"I happened upon several young girls. They all had on the same uniform, more or less. White boots. Long white boots."

"I see."

"Coats with fur collars."

"Yes."

"I would have thought the skirts were too short for this weather. Maybe there is a shortage of cloth in Switzerland? Or problems with distribution?"

"And did you approach one of them?"

I ignored him. "The blue light. That's what got me curious. Does it signify the headquarters of this organization for young girls?"

"You would like to investigate?"

"Some of them seemed very young."

"They do."

"I also saw a man, very short, walking behind an African woman of proportions I never even imagined."

"Indeed."

"Isn't it dangerous, that sort of thing? Do you have ambulances standing by?"

He laughed. "He visits her once a month, sometimes more."

"I saw a Korean girl, too."

"Korean? No, she is Thai."

"Thai? M. Beret, give me the benefit of the doubt, please. She may sit in a Thai café wearing those long white boots, but that does not make her Thai."

He pondered this. I could see him mentally rearranging his tidy filing system. "We shall see," he said. "Thank you. It's always good to have an informed point of view." He adjusted the belt on his coat. It was a gesture of unease, grooming behavior that police of all backgrounds lapse into when they are unsure of their footing. "We don't claim perfection. Or won't that do for an excuse?"

He might have been apologizing for mislabeling the girl. It was something I was not prepared to leave ambiguous. "I am simply observing your wide world, M. Beret. I hope you didn't think I was casting the first stone."

He smiled grimly, the way a man who has gotten the point might do. "You never really answered my original question. Out of curiosity, if you don't mind, what were you doing in New York?"

"I can't believe you of all people are asking me that." He still hadn't produced the roll, and I was beginning to think I would have to buy one for myself once I got out of this cramped park. "Is it a requirement in the West that a person must account for his movements to every police department and intelligence agency in every country he visits?"

"This isn't an interrogation, Inspector." He stood up. "I'm simply curious, and I thought you would find it a novel experience to answer a harmless question." I pretended not to notice that he had put his hand in his pocket. Dogs do that sometimes, look away when they're interested. "Your friend, the one who arrived yesterday, is in the morgue. He has a broken neck. Someone has to identify him, and your mission refuses to do it. I thought you might do the honors, seeing as how you were in a bar with him yesterday." He held out half a roll. "Please, be my guest."

That explained why Sohn didn't make the appointment at the Sunflower. The question was, when did he send me that note? Or did he send it at all? "When did you find the body?"

"I can't very well cooperate with you, Inspector, if you don't cooperate with me."

"I don't need your cooperation."

"Yes, you do. If you don't want to end up like him."

"You going to break my neck?"

M. Beret looked offended. "No, but there is someone in the neighborhood who doesn't like you, that's the impression we're getting." He paused. "Don't ask me how I know." He paused again. "I don't want anything to happen to you, not here. Having one of you in the freezer is enough."

"He had plenty of enemies."

"Then we'll have to make a list, won't we? I'll find a thick pad of paper." He dropped both halves of the roll in my lap. "Two o'clock, I'll be at the bar, the one where you met him. If you hurry, you can make the start of the morning negotiating session. It's at your mission this time, is it not? Don't worry, you won't have an afternoon session today."

Chapter Two

The morning session of the talks went nowhere, though there was a testy exchange that kept everyone awake as long as it lasted. The afternoon session was canceled; somehow, I wasn't surprised.

When I opened the door to the Sunflower a little after two o'clock, the man behind the bar was watching a small television on the counter next to the cash register. He looked up from the soccer game that filled the little screen with little figures running aimlessly. He frowned at me. I frowned back. Like I'd told the Mossad over dinner, I don't like soccer that much. They probably had already put that in my file. The man glanced at his watch, shook his head, and then pointed to an alcove in the back. M. Beret was there arranging a number of photographs on the table in front of him.

"Ah, Inspector. I knew you would make it." He pointed to the photographs. "Nothing out of the ordinary. Just an effort to connect names with faces, faces with places, that sort of thing. I'm sure you do it all the time."

There were twelve pictures, arranged in four rows of three each. The first three rows each had one clear photograph of a face; the other two were grainy or taken by cameras with fixed shutter speeds—and from a considerable distance. The last row was all landscape shots.

"We're going to do this in a certain order. All you have to say is yes or no to what I ask. Don't jump ahead; don't assume you know what I'm going to ask. Shall we begin?"

"I don't see a photo here of Sohn. I thought that's what you wanted me to do, identify him."

"Already! I make things simple, and you make them complicated." He took a deep breath. "Again, I'll go over the procedure again."

" 'Don't jump ahead.' I heard you the first time."

The man from behind the bar appeared. He and M. Beret had a brief conversation in French, in raised voices. They both looked at me. M. Beret took out his wallet and handed some money to the man, who a moment later returned with a bottle of wine, two glasses, and a small plate of cheese. There was no room on the table, so he put everything on the seat of a chair, puffed out his cheeks, and left.

"Let's get the pictures out of the way first, then we can sit." M. Beret picked up the bottle and read the label. "No hurry, actually; this won't be ready to drink for another year or so."

"I'm supposed to wait until you ask me a question."

"Good. Top row, picture on the right end. Taken at night?"

I leaned over and studied the photo. "No." It might have been, for all I knew. I just wanted to get this over with.

"Excellent. Simple answer. Continue in that vein, if you please. How about the one just below it?"

That one was taken at a distance, maybe at dusk. Two men faced the camera, although they had their heads down as if they were talking quietly. One of them was short and had sharply chiseled features; you could see that much because of the angle of the shot. In the dying light, it was hard to tell, but he seemed to have a dark complexion. I couldn't see anything of the man standing next to him. Both had on short-sleeve shirts. There were palm trees in the background. If I had to guess, I would have said it was taken somewhere tropical, but the question hadn't been where but when. I don't volunteer information unless I'm going to get something in return. There was nothing in this for me, except to find out what happened to Sohn. "You mean was it taken at night?"

"Yes."

"No. Twilight, maybe." By now I knew he didn't care when the photographs were taken, and he probably didn't care what answer I gave. He was just warming up the machinery.

M. Beret put his hands behind his back and stood on tiptoe as he leaned over the table. "Now, I want you to listen closely. Do you recognize anything in the third row of pictures? Look at them closely before you answer."

"Third row?"

"Yes."

"Third row from the top?"

"Inspector . . ."

I didn't recognize anything in the third row, but the middle picture in the second row was of my brother meeting with the short, dark man. My brother had on a hat, something stylish and worn at just the right angle. I didn't know he wore hats. From a distance, this one might make him look taller, but it didn't change his face. He looked angry, which didn't surprise me. From what little background was visible, it appeared they were in Europe, and fairly recently. I couldn't see any loaves of bread.

The last picture in the second row was of the facility in Pakistan where the Man with Three Fingers and I had botched the operation during those few minutes a lifetime ago. I had forgotten a lot of things in the meantime, but I still remembered the layout of the facility and the target building, and especially that one room, by heart. In the picture, the door was open; it hadn't been that night. The photo must have been old. All of the trees looked smaller, younger than they had been when I was there. What the hell was M. Beret doing with that picture? "No," I said finally. "I don't recognize anything."

"Not even the first picture, the one of the individual?"

I shook my head. "In the third row?" I hadn't focused on that one before. "No."

"That's Sohn when he was younger. He's changed a bit, may have had some sort of operation. I think he may have gone by another name in those days."

"Doesn't look anything like him." There was nothing wrong with the lighting or the focus. It was a good ID picture, a little old, with some of that yellow-brown that colors old pictures, but it just wasn't Sohn. The ears were too big.

"You're sure. Quite sure."

"If this is the person with the broken neck, I'm not going to be able to identify him for you, because I don't know who he is."

"Positive?"

I picked up the photograph and looked at it closely. For a moment, in the flickering light of the Sunflower's back room, it looked a lot like Pak might have appeared twenty-five years ago. "I don't know who it is. But now you have my fingerprints. Also, I suppose, my DNA. Would you like a blood sample? I could pee in a cup, if you want."

M. Beret took the photograph from me, collected the others, and put them all in a brown envelope. "I don't need your fingerprints." He moved the wineglasses onto the table. "I already have plenty. Blood samples are someone else's business. Perhaps you should visit the Red Cross headquarters, up the hill. Cheese?" I shook my head. "You must acquire a taste for cheese, Inspector. It will open up a whole new world for you."

"If it is anything like this one, I don't need it." I took three big swallows from the glass he handed me. "Do you have any other questions? Or am I free to go?" No sense hanging around; I don't like white wine.

"Have you ever broken anyone's neck, Inspector?"

"You surely don't think I killed Sohn, or whoever is in your morgue, do you?"

M. Beret took a sip from his glass. "I think many things, but I manage to winnow out most of what is untrue. You're sure you won't try some cheese? This here"—he pointed to a square piece covered with what could have been mold—"it's very good. Or this." He sliced off a small piece. "Goat cheese. Why don't you try some?"

"Excuse me, but when we first met, didn't you say that you are head of counterintelligence?"

"Not when we first met. I never do that on a first date. At some point, though, I may have mentioned something along those lines. It never hurts for the target to know whom he is talking to. What of it?"

"Why are you investigating a murder? That isn't counterintelligence business. Don't you have police for that?"

"Usually yes, but in this case no. The police have registered their firm position that this case is odd and not something they want to touch. The exact wording to me over the phone was, 'It stinks.'"

"I salute them, a police force with good judgment."

"Was Sohn a friend of yours?" You could almost hear the question snap into place. Nice technique, I thought, but the delivery was a little flat-footed.

"Friend? People here seem to use the word loosely. Where I come from, it's not a term to be tossed around. Sohn was an acquaintance, someone I'd barely met; not even a colleague, really. I wouldn't say I considered him a friend."

"Does it bother you that he is dead?"

Odd question. "Should it?" Very odd.

"I'm going to tell you something, Inspector, because I don't give a damn if you know, and maybe it will help you realize that you are about to be caught in a hurricane that will be so destructive it will probably blow your little country apart. Where it will toss you I do not know. Nor do I care."

"We're clear on one thing, anyway." Pak spoke to me of winds from odd places. M. Beret spoke of hurricanes. Maybe that was one of the differences between them and us.

"Sohn had been here before." M. Beret paused, but as I did not respond, went on. "He struck me as an intelligent man from what I saw, a bit nervous at times, and a tedious way of sitting for long periods at cafés, nursing a cup of coffee, staring at nothing."

"So far, if there is a hurricane coming, I don't even feel a breeze."

"He was here several times. He met Jenö. I know for sure he did that at least once."

"At least once? Such careful phrasing holds so many wonderful possibilities. To which conclusion would you like me to jump? Or am I free to choose on my own?" So, as soon as Sohn arrived, they already knew who he was. They were probably on him from the moment he got off the plane and entered the air terminal. More than that, they would know perfectly well if it was his body in their morgue. "Don't tell me you're unsure about something like how many times Sohn met someone as interesting as Jenö. I thought you and your teams were everywhere."

Over the lamb dinner, or maybe it was over the discussion of prunes, Mossad had told me about their exchanges with Sohn. M. Beret knew as much as I did about Sohn and Jenö; in fact, he probably knew a lot more. But he didn't seem to know for sure how much I knew. Maybe he didn't know for sure how much Jenö had told me. That suggested Jenö might be working for M. Beret, and with him, and against him all at the same time.

"Funny story, you might recognize the outlines. The two of them disappeared one evening, and then reappeared hours later. We spotted them separately, about the same time in the same part of town, near a nightclub. Sohn was nursing a bruised shoulder when I saw him next. I think he may have jumped out of a moving car. It's not something your people do very well."

"No garbage truck?"

M. Beret poured some more wine into my glass. "I don't know why, exactly, but I'm trying to help you."

"One minute you don't care if a hurricane blows me away. The next minute you're trying to help me."

"You are a smart man, Inspector."

"But what?"

"Are you so sure there is something else to that thought? Don't you take compliments, unqualified?"

"But what? M. Beret, no one begins or ends a sentence like that unless he has something else to say."

Silence for a moment. I could see he was deciding whether to let me be right or to prove me wrong.

"Very well," he said at last. "You are a smart man, so why do you stay?"

"Go on."

"That's it. That's all. *Fin.*"

"No, it's not. It might be all in some other place, under other circumstances. Not here, and not from you. Please continue, M. Beret."

He sighed. "Very well. You stay, that is, you won't leave because you are a patriot, I suppose."

"One supposes."

"Why else?" I didn't reply. "Well, then," he went on, "if it were

possible to do something, would you? Wouldn't you get out of the way
of a hurricane if you could? Wouldn't you help warn other people?"

"Go on."

"How bad do things have to get, Inspector?"

"We are back to 'you are a smart man,' aren't we?"

"No, I misspoke. I think you are a man of morality."

"No longer smart?"

"You cannot keep dodging the point. Yes, you know it, Inspector.
You cannot come outside and go back exactly the same, ever again.
Nothing can look the same when you go home. Especially now."

"But I will go home."

"Yes, we've established that, haven't we? And once there, once you
get back, what then? How will you pull up the mental drawbridge and
lock it tight? Are you going to forget everything you've learned about
the rest of the world? Empty your brain as you step across the border?"

"I can only do what I can."

He took off his beret. Without it, he looked older, but he seemed to
feel less constrained. "Compromise with evil is an awful thing, Inspector."

"Do you know, M. Beret"—I hesitated because I knew that wasn't
his name and it seemed wrong to call him that at this moment—"but
surely you must, that the starkest moral positions are the easiest to state?
Truth to be palatable cannot sit in a complex sentence. Truth must be
simple, don't you agree? It must be something that does not need to
be chewed. It should simply slip down the throat. 'Do not compromise
with evil.' Simple, easy to remember, even easier to say. Tell me, is there
a tattoo parlor nearby? It wouldn't be too painful, would it? We could
put it on your wrist, perhaps."

"My wrist?"

"Oh, I've read my history, M. Beret." I didn't give a damn what his
name was anymore. Sohn was in their morgue, and they were using that
as their opening to get to me. They'd have spent the past week arguing
how to do it, watching for an opportunity, comparing notes on where I
went, what I ate, whether I looked at the sky in the morning, trying to
figure out who I was. Go slow and sideways, that's what they'd concluded. Work his mind, find the intellectual buttons. He doesn't like
Portuguese boys, so that's out. What's left? Maybe talk to him about

morality and evil, that sort of thing. Nothing too direct, just enough to provoke him. Make him mad, confuse him, throw a little dust on his internal compass. What kind of idiot did they take me for? "I'm quite clear on the subject, as I'm sure your countrymen have always been. Compromise with evil, or just keep it over the border. Very tidy, except for the people you turn away."

He put the beret back on his head. "Sohn had eyes for Ahmet's daughter. More than eyes, actually."

They really did want to provoke me. I buttoned everything down, went right down the checklist of emotions and buttoned each one down. "I can imagine a long line of men with eyes for Ahmet's daughter, M. Beret. A few might even be Swiss, am I right?"

"She can charm the pants off of anyone she chooses. I would be very careful, were I you." No, being careful with Dilara was out of the question. But it didn't matter.

"Were you me, M. Beret, you would have a headache from the wine. You're right. It's too young."

He put his hands together and sighed deeply. "I need your help, Inspector, if that isn't too blunt. The police have warned me that they are not going to investigate the case until they have assurances that they will receive full cooperation from your mission. Although technically your mission falls under the Federal Department of Foreign Affairs, your ambassador doesn't seem to bother much with diplomacy and so the entire matter has, as the Americans like to say, fallen into my lap. I want to get rid of it, and for that, I need your help."

Helping the chief of Swiss counterintelligence was not wise, nor was it healthy. Swallowing razor blades was higher on the list of things I would consider. Still, the man seemed to know something about Sohn and his dealings with Jenö; he seemed to be working against whatever my brother was doing, and so far he had not done anything to me other than get under my skin, which was his job.

"Sohn and the ambassador didn't get along," I said. "I don't know why. I doubt very much that the ambassador killed him, though. You may think we are a little crude in our ways, M. Beret, but murder is not normally part of the routine. That's about all I can tell you, because it's everything I know."

"Really? You must know something more about Sohn. Don't tell me you were simply overjoyed to run across a compatriot in a foreign city. Overjoyed compatriots don't follow each other according to prearranged patterns."

I had to laugh. "I should have realized that people who kept such close track of their soap would be very observant about everything else. Everything and nothing. Because on this one, you'll have to brace yourself for disappointment. I really didn't know him. In case you haven't received the report yet, I did go to see the dungeon at Chillon the other day, and if you want to throw me in there you can. It would be pleasant to sit in one of those cells this summer and listen to the waves against the stone foundations. No matter what you say or how much you turn on your Swiss charm, I can't tell you any more about Sohn, because I don't know anything about him, nothing that you apparently don't already have in your files. In fact you probably know a great deal more about him than I do. I'll bet you have hollowed out an entire mountain to hold all the paper. Surely you must have other people you can ask. It seems to me that you have multiple sources, all the way to New York."

"I don't trust them. I never trust them. Besides, that's not exactly the question, is it, Inspector? I'm not asking about his patrimony. I'm not asking you for background, for his gymnasium report card. I want to know why he arrived here yesterday, and why you met him."

"You say he was here several times before. Apparently he liked the place, though I must tell you, I can't imagine why."

M. Beret pointed to the plate of cheese.

2

"You Chinese breed like monkeys, is what I hear."

I looked stoically out at the gray waters of the lake. After leaving M. Beret at the Sunflower, I'd walked to the lake to sit and be alone. Some things are not fated, even if you do your best. I did my best to ignore the woman; some people give up and go away if you pretend to ignore them. It also sometimes works if you indicate that you do not understand the language.

"Rabbits, not monkeys, that's what I meant." The woman sat down and took off her gloves. She seemed not to notice I wasn't responding. "It must be difficult for you here. Not much familiar to eat. God knows, we eat the normal things. I'll bet you wish you had something to remind you of home. I heard there are a lot of Chinese restaurants on Quai du Mont-Blanc. I wouldn't know, but you might try one of them."

"I think you are mistaken." I still didn't look at her. Maybe she'd think I was meditating in the fading afternoon light.

"No, they're over there." She pointed across the lake, her finger in front of my nose. "Of course, I've never tried one, myself. I don't eat that sort of food." She didn't stop to explain or pause before going on to the next subject. I'd met people like her before. Ideas seemed to take control of their brains in rapid-fire order. It was not good for work that required plodding persistence. But it must be good for something, maybe a survival trait, assuming it wasn't simply a loose connection. "Most Chinese girls that I've seen are okay. But a few are ugly. I'm sorry to say that, it seems unkind, but I guess if you've got a billion people, you're bound to get some real dogs. You ever eat dog? I don't think I could."

"I'm not Chinese." I finally turned to look at her. Her hands were pretty, long tapered fingers. She probably played Rachmaninoff on the piano, but I wasn't going to start a conversation on anything with her, certainly not about composers. Who knew where it would lead. I only wanted her to go away.

"Not Chinese? You could have fooled me." When I didn't reply, she tried again. "Japanese?"

"In the Orient, you are granted three guesses. You have only one guess left." She seemed to crave mystery.

"Mongolian," she said and closely examined my face. "I wouldn't have thought so; you don't have those cheekbones they have. Marvelous cheekbones. Well, no matter, it's good to see Mongolians getting out and about again. I haven't seen one in years and years. Perhaps it has something to do with the food, do you think? We have lamb in some of the restaurants, you know, though we probably prepare it differently. I hope you won't take offense at my thinking you are Chinese." She smiled and bowed slightly, as she had no doubt seen in the movies. "Mongolians are herders, isn't that right? I heard it is thanks to the Mongols that we invented croissants, though I cannot remember exactly why. Perhaps you're familiar with the story. I imagine it is taught in your schools."

"No, we have no schools. Herders have no need of education. We know only the wind in the grass and the warmth of mare's milk. We use women like cattle. Good day to you." I stood up and gave her what I imagined might be a herdsman's leer.

Chapter Three

"Somebody, surely, somebody stayed awake all the way through their presentation and took notes." The delegation head looked around the table. "If we don't have any notes, we can't send a report back. And if we don't send a report, there will be a nasty telegram tomorrow from the ministry. I don't like nasty telegrams on a Saturday."

The room was silent.

"The rule has always been that the youngest one, no matter what, fills that job. Miss Ho?"

"I got most of it."

"Most isn't all. What was the problem?"

"He was reading out loud from that document. He droned on and on. If he'd done it this morning, I might have been able to keep conscious the whole time, but after lunch . . ."

"Nobody else? What about you, Paek?"

"Paek was sound asleep," someone muttered.

"I got a good part of his opening remarks." Mr. Paek was an elderly man with a dignified bearing and doleful eyes. "But then I lost him. I think my hearing failed. I don't think I've ever been so bored. It was making me deaf."

They all laughed. "Well, patch together what you can and fill in the rest as needed." The delegation head took off his glasses. "I want the cable ready to go out before dinner. The ambassador will insist on seeing it. He's not in a good mood, and I don't want to give him any excuse to chew me out. What about you?" He turned to me. "What are your thoughts on what went on today?"

I didn't have any thoughts, at least not on today's proceedings. I was still thinking about yesterday and the morgue. I'd gone there not long after leaving the woman on the bench; she'd probably gone home and slept fitfully, dreaming of Mongolian herdsmen riding croissants, thundering across the steppes to attack the citadels of the West. M. Beret had let me in the back door of an old building, escorted me down dark corridors, and led me finally into a room with a single ceiling lamp hanging from a long cord. I didn't need more light than that to tell it was Sohn. For some reason, I was glad he was in a place with worn wooden floors.

"And what did you observe?"

"Observe?" I thought about it for a moment, until I realized the delegation leader wasn't asking me about Sohn's body. "Diplomatic fencing isn't exactly my specialty."

"Really, I would have thought human nature was something the police would follow very closely."

"It is, only we deal with people in a more natural habitat than this. We don't have to cope with quite so much honey on the lies."

"True, there is a lot of that. We honey the lies, and poison the truth. Odd, isn't it?" He idly flipped through his small notebook. "There isn't anything in here, did you know that, Inspector? I take it out and look through it when the other side starts trying to bully me. They think it has instructions in it. I select a page, remove my glasses and squint intently at this little piece of blank paper. They're not sure if I'm listening. Half the time it make them nervous. The other half, they get huffy. Once in a while, they even stop talking until I close the notebook and look up. Sometimes they're like young children, very self-important."

"Maybe you haven't frightened them enough."

"Ah, then it is true you subscribe to the position that these talks should resemble head-to-head combat, fiery speeches and table pounding? We've had some discussion among ourselves on where you stand on this question of tactics."

"Maybe a little table pounding wouldn't hurt."

"In a police interrogation, it might be perfectly well advised. Here, it must be like a rare spice—sprinkled into the pot once in a while, and then only a tiny bit at a time. If you use too much all at once, it ruins the flavor. And worse, when you need it next, there will be nothing left. At the end of the day, when we finally pack our bags, I'm supposed to get nowhere on missiles but come home with food from these people, Inspector. Food, boatloads of it. If I pound the table, what will it get me?"

"And if they think we are weak, what will it get you?"

"Very good. Some people have that talent, pointing to the dilemma at hand. Would that they had the same talent for finding solutions. The dilemma is exactly as you describe, Inspector. If it were a wild boar, you would have shot it between the eyes. What next? We have identified our dilemma with precision, with superb intellectual acumen, with a political sense of balance and a depth of understanding beyond anything seen in history. We are brilliant. What next? No one has given me an answer to that. All I receive is competing and contradictory sets of instructions on alternate weeks. If you know the answer, I'm happy to listen. I'll fill this little notebook with page after page of your ideas. I'll buy another notebook. I'll buy two. Pencils galore. But meanwhile, meanwhile, I have to proceed the best way I know how."

No one seemed to know that a senior party official was in the Geneva morgue with a broken neck. There were no odd silences, no one hurrying down the hall holding specially marked envelopes, no worried looks. The security man, who should have been shitting bricks, seemed perfectly calm. The ambassador passed me as he turned the corner into his office. The frown he gave me was normal in all respects. Maybe the Swiss hadn't said anything to anybody yet. Even the ambassador didn't know, unless he'd known all along.

2

"We're going to meet, Inspector." Most people might have said hello or feigned surprise at running into me, even though they had plotted the point where our paths would cross with great care. I was walking along the lake after the talks ended that afternoon. I could have turned right, but instead I was heading up toward the lady with the rump. I was getting too predictable. Jenö was waiting for me.

"We're going to meet, as opposed to what we are doing at the moment?" I didn't break stride when he stepped out from behind one of the butchered plane trees.

"This is just talk, passing the time. There must be three extra sets of eyes watching us."

"What makes you think they won't be doing the same the next time we meet?"

"Because we'll be somewhere other than where they imagine."

"I'm not going to get knocked out by Ahmet again."

"In this case, it will do no good if you are unconscious. Do you like pastry? I thought some Asians were not partial to bread."

Bread seemed to be on people's minds these days. Sohn especially had been interested when I told him what my brother had said on the phone. "Bread is fine," I said to Jenö, "as long as it's leavened."

"Good for you. You've been looking at an encyclopedia. How about you decide to get some pastry. Tomorrow, say about ten o'clock in the morning."

"How about after ten? I'm late rising these days."

"No, ten o'clock, on the dot, on the button. Tomorrow, you'll do everything on the button."

"Says who?"

"I know. You don't work for me. But you did work for Sohn."

"Wrong again." Jenö knew Sohn was dead. Why was I not surprised?

"Was I or was I not in your Hotel Koryo a few months ago, in the middle of winter, Inspector? Did Sohn not long afterward select you for this mission to Geneva? Are those all coincidence? Or are they beads in a wonderful necklace suggesting an elegant purpose and design?"

"I don't wear jewelry, of any description." Neither did Sohn, as far as I knew.

"In this case, I expect you to be where I tell you, at ten o'clock, with bells on. You'll love the pastry. What can it hurt?"

"And where is this best place for pastry?"

"On your side of the lake. Not too far from your mission."

"I'm not happy to hear that."

"Walk into town. Near Place du Pont there will be a cab with tinted windows driven by an Arab, a friend. Get in at nine fifty. Tell him you are looking for a good croissant."

"And he will reply?"

"He will glower at you in the rearview mirror. Ignore that. He's moody, but reliable. He'll take you up into the hills. Again, I'm reminding you, the place you're going is not far from your mission. Don't worry, your people never go up there. Never. This I know. It's in a section called Cologny. Very posh. The driver will drop you about twenty meters away from a fork in the road. The *patisserie* sits just there, aloof and alone. Go in and say politely to the nice lady you want two croissants."

"In French?"

"Don't bother. Tell her you want them to go. Nodding in a not unfriendly manner, she should ask: *au beurre ou ordinaire?* Never mind the translation. Just hold up one finger on each hand, thusly." Jenö demonstrated, using his two pinkie fingers. "However, if she tells you gruffly that the bakery has run out of dough for the weekend, it means everything is off. That is unlikely, but if it happens, leave quickly. Get back to the cab. If you don't have a bag of croissants, the driver will take off like a bat out of hell. There isn't another driver on earth that will be able to follow him. Once we figure out what went wrong, he'll drop you back in town. I'll be in touch, and life will resume its normal joyful rhythms."

"What if the nice lady says they don't have any croissants, but I see something else I like?"

"It will be the last thing you ever eat. If she says she has nothing, get out of there in a hurry. But I don't think anything will go wrong."

"Of course not."

"If we're on schedule, she'll put two in a bag for you."

"How much?"

Jenö handed me a fifty-franc note.

"I suppose now everyone has a picture of you passing me money."

"Fifty francs? We don't take pictures of anything less than a hundred. Don't be so suspicious."

"Oh ho!"

"You'll walk out with the croissants."

"How about a brioche?"

He handed over another fifty-franc note. "Now you are screwed."

I pocketed the money and smiled into the middle distance. "I don't like surveillance photos where the people are frowning, do you?"

"Walk out with the damned pastries and go back to the cab. Once you're inside, open the bag. There will be a note inside."

"A note! In a croissant? Something like a Chinese fortune croissant? This note, I suppose it will have instructions for the driver?"

"It might."

"It tells him where to take me next."

"Possibly."

"I'm to arrive at the next place at ten fifteen sharp. You want me on the bench closest to the Villa Diodati?"

"What?"

"Obviously, you want me at Le Pré Byron. It's the best place to meet around there, out in the open. You think you're the only one who has scouted meeting sites?"

"What?"

"If a red car drives by on the road below and stops, it means we proceed as planned. If it's a blue car, we abort. Sort of a double-check on the nice lady."

Jenö studied my face. "Not bad," was all he said before falling silent again. "Not bad," he said finally, "but we don't use blue cars. It will be white. And since you have plenty of money, get a brioche for me, too."

3

Saturday morning I wasn't hungry, but I didn't think Jenö would take that as an excuse to scrub his operation, so I did everything as directed. The taxi driver scowled, the nice lady in the *patisserie* popped the croissants into the bag. The note told the driver to take me to Le Pré Byron, the bench closest to the Villa Diodati. A red car, a Peugeot, stopped on the road below. I had just sat back to enjoy the view when a man appeared beside me. At first I didn't recognize him.

"Hand puppets," he said.

"Three-legged dogs." I nodded. "You look different in the light."

"You're supposed to have an extra brioche."

"You want some money back?"

"I hope you remember operational details better than you do pastry orders."

"I owe you. Do we sit here until lunch?"

"You get on a train, a local. Just past Flamatt there is a truck yard, on the left. There will be a blue truck at the far end."

"Jenö said you didn't use blue."

"Cars. We don't use blue cars. Trucks fall under different rules. Is that alright?"

"Fine."

"If the blue truck has a red flag on its antenna, stay on the train until Bern. Not a bright red, sort of dirty. Like dried blood. That means it's a go. The conductress will punch your ticket and give you the last-stage instructions. But remember, she has the final go-ahead, or not."

"And how does she let me know? A cross-eyed look?"

"She'll take your ticket, punch it, and hand it back. Might not be the same one. Look at it. Anything other than today's date, it's a bust. If she doesn't like the way things smell, if she sees someone she doesn't think belongs, she calls it off."

"Then what?"

"You get off at whatever station tickles your fancy and look around. Get some dinner. Then just come back. Nothing lost, and whoever it was that stumbled into our midst will have wasted a day."

"This is the most elaborate, complicated, irritating operation I've ever heard of. I can see twenty points where it could fall apart."

"Oh, yeah? We've been through it twenty times. It works." He stopped. "It works as long as everyone plays his part."

"Why? Why is it so complicated?"

"You want me to simplify? Someone important is coming to meet you. He's coming a long way and going to a lot of trouble. We don't want anyone else to see the meeting. No one. If we could take you to Israel it would be better. Want some sun?"

"Not on your life."

"I told Jenö you wouldn't take that option. It's not such a long flight. All the engines on the plane up to snuff."

"No."

"We could put a sack over your head, give you an injection, put you in a crate, and ship you by air freight."

"Try it, I dare you."

He shrugged.

"What makes you think I want to see a visitor? Who is he, anyway? I don't run after people I haven't been properly introduced to. Someone high up in your organization, I imagine." I didn't wait long for a response, because I didn't suppose there would be one. "Very flattering, that a mystery man would come all this way to meet me. If it's not too late, you should tell him not to bother. We could say I have a prior appointment. That would save him a trip." A blank look. "Or maybe he's already here. A shame, busy man like him, having to come all this way for nothing. The Number Two in your organization? Not the Number One; surely no organization, not even yours, would set up a meeting for your Number One without first checking that the other party was available."

"Are you going to eat both croissants?"

4

If Sohn had still been alive, maybe he would have told me to go ahead and take the trip to Flamatt to meet whoever had traveled from Tel Aviv, probably to talk about the deal to stop missile sales. But Sohn wasn't alive; he was dead. I was in Switzerland because Sohn had put me here. And even though he was dead, the orders he'd given me were not. They hadn't changed. At least, no one told me they had been changed. No one had told me anything.

So I bought a round-trip ticket and boarded the train. The scenery was fine; groomed beyond all possibility. Geneva at least had grime on some windows. The countryside looked like it was trimmed and inspected every morning. Nothing out of place; even the cows knew enough to stand in appropriate groups. An occasional farmhouse screamed out, painted in loud colors. A mark of rebellion, I thought. It surprised me that such paint was even available here; it must be smuggled in from Italy.

About thirty minutes out of Geneva, a young couple came into the car and, without a word, sat down on the seat facing mine. They looked South Asian, the woman much younger than the man. I figured the Israelis would have someone, maybe a couple of people, watching me on the train, but otherwise I thought I would be left alone. No contact, other than with the conductor. So who was this couple?

The man was striking to look at, a very dark complexion and sharply defined features. He was also well dressed. The woman seemed uncomfortable, in physical distress of some sort, and leaned on his shoulder. He paid no attention to her, but looked out the window without much interest. At last he turned to me. "You are a traveler in this country?" His English was clipped, with a bit of a singsong to it. I might have enjoyed talking to him, but I had the feeling that was something I didn't want to do. There were plenty of empty seats in the car. They shouldn't be sitting knee to knee with me. He was waiting for me to reply.

"You might say I'm a traveler. Would your companion like to stretch out on this seat? I can move."

The man ignored the offer. "From where do you come?"

Briefly, I considered the possibilities. "I'm Mexican," I said. "And you?"

"Sri Lanka." He murmured something to the woman, who picked up her head and nodded to me. "My wife is from Pakistan. She has become quite homesick and a little feverish in this place." He waved his hand at the passing landscape. "It's very neat, wouldn't you say?" The woman put her head on his shoulder again and closed her eyes. He closed his eyes as well for a moment, and then opened them suddenly. "Do you travel much?"

"Some." I realized I had seen him before. What was he doing on this train? How did he know me?

"Some." He repeated the word slowly. "Have you ever been to Pakistan?"

"Me?" From anyone else, someone who hadn't been in the second-row photo M. Beret had put on the table in the Sunflower café, someone who hadn't been standing next to my brother, this all might have passed for polite conversation between strangers on a train. If he had been a Martian, he might have been asking innocently, "Have you ever been to Pluto?" But this wasn't polite conversation. His presence was poison. I stood up. "Please excuse me; I can't ride backward for very long. I've got to find another seat."

The man gave me an odd smile and looked out the window. "Should we ever visit Mexico," he said, "no doubt we'll run across each other." I don't know what sarcasm sounds like in Sri Lanka, but that must have been it.

5

Two cars ahead, I found a seat facing forward and sat down. I had the coach to myself. I didn't bother to sit on the left side because I had a feeling there wasn't any use looking for a flag on a blue truck. The man from Sri Lanka didn't follow me. From the odd smile he gave me, though, I didn't think this was in the script for Jenö's operation. Maybe they should have gone through it twenty-one times. Jenö surely would have told me to expect the dark man. Who was he? He might be working for M. Beret, at least he was in one of M. Beret's photographs. But M. Beret's file vaults probably contained miles of photographs. I was running through the list of possibilities from habit—even though I already knew the answer. The man knew my brother. Lots of people knew my brother, to their regret I imagined, but not that many would be photographed with him. It was always possible the man worked with Sohn, more likely against him. What if the man had murdered Sohn?

Once you start making up lists of possibilities, they can go on reproducing and mutating for a while all by themselves. It's like having the flu. You get better eventually, or you don't. The last thing on the list isn't necessarily right, but it tends to stick with you.

At Flamatt, I glanced over and saw a blue truck flying a red flag, which surprised me. So they weren't going to call it off after all. The conductress came through the door in the front of the car and walked to my seat. She was blond, a long braid down her back. She wore pants, and she moved provocatively in them. I gave her my ticket and a friendly smile.

She smiled back. "Nice day to travel," she said. Small lips. It was Margrit. I remembered to avoid any sudden moves. She handed back the ticket. It was stamped with tomorrow's date. She'd scrubbed the operation. It could have been for any reason, but there was really only one that made sense. The dark man with the wistful Pakistani wife, the two of them close enough to kill me almost without moving a muscle.

"Know a good place for dinner?" I wasn't hungry, but I asked Margrit because it was something to say.

"Only if you like cheese," she said and walked away.

I watched her reflection in the window as she moved into the next car. Good wig, I thought to myself. Nice trousers, too.

6

The next afternoon, a Sunday, the delegation leader went out for a walk in the park near the mission. He was alone and moving quickly, not like someone who was trying to think, more like someone who knew where he was going and thought he might be late.

I was waiting for him. He had been nervous all morning, inattentive during most of the delegation meeting and then snapping at his deputy for lapses so minor they didn't bear mentioning. Just before the session broke up, he went around the table and dissected each person's performance. They were all going to face intense criticism when they returned home, he said. New instructions had arrived that the talks were to make progress. On what basis they were supposed to proceed had not been specified. All he had been told was that the delegation was supposed to create the proper atmosphere. He turned to Mr. Roh, who handed him a piece of paper. "Proper atmosphere," he read the term aloud. "Is there one of you with a good idea?" No one looked at anyone else when they left the room.

It was clear to me that the delegation leader wasn't planning to sit around and do nothing the rest of the day. He was anxious about something, and it wasn't about creating "atmosphere." That wouldn't bother him. He could do that, fix the atmosphere, by just readjusting his smile, or looking like he was taking notes instead of taking off his glasses and pretending to ignore what the other side was saying. There was something more serious on his mind. For a moment—a very brief, uncomfortable moment—I worried that he was planning to defect. What if he'd received a warning that when he got home he would face serious problems, something beyond the routine, and so, rather than go back to the old home, he was going to jump to a new one? That's what triggered most defections—people concerned that they'd been caught doing something they shouldn't. That's why we were constantly being warned by the Ministry to take it easy in investigations of people who were overseas. "Don't squeeze what you don't have to," the Minister famously said at one meeting.

When he came out the door and down the steps, the delegation leader didn't look around or stop to take a breath. He just pointed himself in the direction he had already decided to go, and he went. Once he was out of the compound, he picked up the pace. He might have been running, he was moving so fast, but he still managed to give the appearance of someone just out for a brisk walk.

I gave him a pretty good lead, not entirely by choice. I could barely keep up with the pace he had set. If he spotted me, it would be hard to pretend I was out for a leisurely stroll and happened to bump into him. I was panting with exhaustion; in another couple of minutes, I'd break into a sweat. My better judgment told me to break off. For once, I almost paid attention. The path turned a corner onto an unpaved track. I stopped. There was no one around, but the sound of tires on gravel was still in the air. Something large and white flashed through the trees, speeding down the road that led back out to the main avenue along the lake. I took a few deep breaths. Whatever it was, the engine was nicely tuned, though the muffler needed work.

"Going somewhere?" The Man with Three Fingers appeared from nowhere in front of me. "You seem to be out of breath."

"You do have a habit of turning up, don't you?"

"Me? If you hadn't been in such a hurry, you'd have noticed me."

"I'm busy." I turned to go, then turned back. "Were you following me, or him? People don't normally follow from in front. Or is there a new technique?"

He grinned; the effect was deadly. If a hunting spider could grin, this would be it. "I was just out for a stroll in the park and remembered you liked wood, so I thought I'd become better acquainted with some trees. But somehow, they all look the same." He walked over to a large chestnut tree. "This here, for example. I'd say in a couple of months, it will be flowering. It's an ornamental, wouldn't you say?"

"It's dead."

"Really?" He whistled and stepped back. "Dead. How do you like that? I wonder what killed it. Care to venture a guess, Inspector?"

"Why were you following him?"

"I could ask you the same thing."

"Or maybe you weren't following him. Maybe you were trying to intercept him."

"And why would I want to do that?"

"I don't know. Maybe because you were afraid he was going away and wasn't coming back."

"No, that's why *you* were following him, Inspector." He turned to look at the tree again. "What a shame. This thing happens a lot, I guess. Death, I mean."

7

I thought Jenö would be put off by the cancellation of his operation, but he seemed cheery enough, sitting on the bench across from my hotel, reading a newspaper.

"You owe me a croissant," he said, "but don't worry. We can settle later. Sit down and enjoy the spring air. Look at this light, will you? Soft as a Bedouin's handshake."

I didn't care about Bedouins. "What happened?"

"Nothing happened. We called it off, that's all."

"There was someone on the train you didn't like."

Jenö's eyebrows did a brief tango. "You picked up on that, did you?"

"Hard not to. You think he was there by accident?"

"He's never anywhere by accident. That wasn't his wife, by the way."

"How did he know I'd be on the train? You have a problem in your organization?"

"No. He just showed up. Lucky break for us. We've been wondering where he was."

"How did he know I'd be there?"

"He probably didn't. He might have seen you at the station when you got on the train. There aren't many Koreans around, and he must have been curious, sort of like a cat. He is careful where he steps, and if he sees anything new or out of place, he goes the other way."

"He didn't go the other way. He came right to me and sat down. How could he know I was Korean?"

"Well, it's a cinch you're not Mexican."

If Jenö was so happy to see the man, I figured it meant he must be a target, and that meant he had something to do with the weapons trade, missiles maybe. A perfect tab, a perfect slot. Geneva was a busy city. No wonder M. Beret looked so tired. "I hope we're not going to try this again. Once is enough."

"Don't worry, the person who was here to see you had to leave right away. You sure you won't accept a trip to the land of milk and honey? We can do the whole thing in twenty-four hours."

"Yes, I'm sure you can. But I don't like to rush my time on the beach, it's bad for my tan."

Jenö folded his paper and tucked it under his arm. "I'll be in touch."

"The man on the train, who was he going to meet?"

"Guess."

I didn't have to. What if my brother had even been sitting a few cars ahead, in the first class section? Same train, different dreams.

Chapter Four

"This is crazy," I said when I could slip out of her arms and talk again. "Your father will kill us."

"No, he loves me. Anyway, he's busy downstairs."

"Downstairs! You told me he would be away for a couple of days."

"He was going to be, but he got a rush request, so he came back. He's been working all night in the kitchen."

"Any minute he could come up and kill one of us. And something tells me it won't be you."

"Perhaps. But look at me. Look closely." She made sure that even in the moonlit room a lot was visible. "When you look at me, do you think of my father?" In case I had missed anything, she turned slightly.

"No." I took a deep breath. "I can't say that I do."

"Then come here. No more discussion." She took my hand and pulled me back to her.

2

Barely past dawn, when I was almost dressed, she opened her eyes. "You see, my little policeman, you are still alive. Take the side streets and no one will ever know you were here. Your survival instincts are probably still functioning."

I was in no shape to ask what she meant. I was more concerned with getting down the back stairs without seeing her father. Even if I made it through that minefield, there was the problem of what the day clerk in my hotel would say when I walked in, slightly rumpled. If anyone asked, the hotel staff would gladly relay the news that I had been out all night.

"Was it wonderful?" Dilara snuggled under the blanket, not really interested in the answer.

3

M. Beret was sitting in the lobby of my hotel, a cup of coffee on the table next to his chair. I was less surprised to see him than I was to see the coffee. I hadn't realized the hotel was so generous. Maybe they would part with an extra bar of soap, after all.

"Inspector, good morning."

"Wouldn't they give you a room?"

"A room? I don't sleep much these days. Too much thrashing about in the adjoining suites."

"That never bothers me," I said and started up the stairs. I wondered if M. Beret's people only got audio, or if there were pictures, too. And if so, would they get back to Pak? I knew what would happen. He would call me into his office and look at me somberly for a moment before studying a piece of paper on his desk. Then in the most exquisitely vague language he would explain that he had received "certain information," that this was potentially serious if it should develop any further but it was not his job to babysit my life in all of its facets, that he expected me to act responsibly in all ways, and that was the end of it as far as he was concerned. Then he would put the piece of paper into a folder, close the folder and put it in his desk drawer, and look up at me. "Is that clear enough?" he would ask, say he had a meeting to attend, and walk out the door.

M. Beret drank a little coffee. He replaced the cup with more than normal deliberation. "I thought you'd like to know, we threw Ahmed a very large catering job last night, with instructions that it had to be delivered by 6:00 a.m." He glanced at his watch, which was not a cheap one. "Would you like some Turkish coffee to perk you up?"

"He must be exhausted."

"I'm sure he's not the only one."

4

I would have slept past noon if the maid hadn't knocked midmorning. "Go away," I shouted, but she kept knocking. Finally, I flung open the door. "Are you hard of hearing? I told you to go away. I'm sleeping. Can I do that? Is it all right with you? Is there a regulation in your tidy land against sleeping late?"

"It's not my land. I am from Romania, and I was only checking to make sure you're not sick again. They don't want some strange epidemic coming out of this hotel. There are all sorts of health people in this city; they can be very strict sometimes. Believe me, I know."

"I'm not sick, I'm never sick." I stuck out my tongue. "You see? I'm fine."

The maid was holding a few pieces of fresh linen. She handed them to me. "Make your own bed then. I'm not going to wait around for you. My friends says I don't even have to go into your room if you've been sick."

"It's good to have friends," I said and closed the door. Just as I got back into bed, the phone rang.

"Hello, Inspector, how are you?" It was Jenö. He didn't sound happy. There were undertones of urgency flowing through his voice, the way silk sounds when it catches on a nail.

"I was trying to sleep, actually."

"It's well past noon! Your watch must have stopped. Meet me downstairs in twenty minutes. We'll have lunch."

"Nothing elaborate."

"Fine, nothing elaborate."

"Nothing that has been near a lamb."

5

Jenö was waiting, just as he said he would. He was wearing sunglasses. It was a springlike day, but not really spring; tidy clouds arranged in a blue sky, enough sun to give the grass a thrill. Technically, it was still winter, but you wouldn't hear me complain about the weather, not on a day like this.

"Let's go for a drive, Inspector. With so much sun, it would be a shame to stay in this dull town. You don't want lamb. Do you like fish? We can have lunch by the lake. Delicate fillet of perch, a bottle of white wine. Then we can smoke cigars and talk. I know just the place, in a little town called Coppet."

"Been there."

"Very well, we can try somewhere else." He seemed annoyed, which gave me some satisfaction, though not enough to make up for having to dress and come downstairs.

"Good," I said. "Somewhere else."

"Something the matter?"

"Nothing. I told you, I was trying to sleep; it was a rough night."

"So I heard."

Everyone had heard, apparently. Dilara was going to have to keep it down next time, if there was a next time. "How about a nonperch meal? Would that be possible? I realize perch is the national fish." I wasn't being difficult only out of spite. It had nothing to do with little, tasteless collections of bones. It was that Jenö was trying to put me in a grateful mood for some reason, and until I figured out why, I wasn't going to let things get cozy. "One more request. This time I exit your car in the normal fashion, after it has come to a complete stop."

"We're not using my car. Someone ran me off the road the other night and I hit a tree."

"A tree? What kind?"

"A very big tree, that's what kind. I'm borrowing Ahmet's car while mine is in the repair shop."

I felt a moment of terror as we set off down the hill. What if Ahmet was driving? There was no way he could fail to pick up what I was thinking.

"Something wrong?" Jenö asked, as he stopped next to a big, white Mercedes. It looked brand-new. The light that reflected off the hood was blinding. Maybe that explained the sunglasses. "Here we are."

"Ahmet owns this?" Ahmet was nowhere to be seen. "What else does he do, other than run a restaurant? Drugs? Centrifuges? This car must have cost a fortune."

"He told me he bought it secondhand from a friend."

"Secondhand! A hand wearing diamonds, maybe. If I were you, I'd check his friends."

"Funny, that's just what I thought."

I'd never been in a car like this one, and it was clear, neither had Jenö. He either drove too fast or too slow. His turns were too wide or too sharp. He tried adjusting the seat, tilting the steering wheel, changing the mirrors. Nothing helped. "No wonder someone sold this to Ahmet," he grumbled as we swerved to avoid a dog. "It's a lemon."

"A what?"

"A piece of garbage. The steering is off, the acceleration is off, and the braking is off. It feels like it was worked on by a mechanic who hated women."

The connection escaped me, but Jenö was driving almost on the shoulder, and I didn't want to try for too complicated a discussion. Besides, the muffler had caught my ear. "Where are we going?" The road looked familiar, close to the lake.

"Nowhere special. I invited a friend. I was sure you wouldn't mind."

6

The delegation leader stood up to greet us when we walked in the door. He looked very much at home. "Surprised to see me, Inspector?"

I was. "Not really," I said. We were in Coppet, which set my teeth on edge. "Shouldn't you be somewhere nibbling cookies?"

Jenö gestured to a chair. "Good, we all seem to know each other. That saves time. There's no assigned seating here. Very informal." Informal maybe, but not without foresight. My chair put me between the two of them, so I couldn't speak to both at the same time, or watch them. I had to turn my head from one to the other.

The delegation leader picked up a menu. "Shall we order? If we don't do that right away, they'll think we aren't here to eat. That can change the atmosphere. The waiters get aloof, and the service goes downhill from there." Atmosphere—he must have been born with an extra sensory organ that measured "atmosphere" like other people felt hot or cold. Apparently, he'd been to this place before. Obviously not on his ministry's tab, so I had to wonder who had paid the bill.

Jenö ordered. We ate in silence, and I didn't think it was a comfortable one, either. The delegation leader made annoying, exaggerated gestures with his fork as he lifted the food to his mouth. He ate slowly and occasionally closed his eyes. At one point he moaned in pleasure. That ruined what little appetite I had. It was doubly annoying because Jenö had ordered the perch for all of us. At last, with a final smack of his lips, the delegation sat back. "Quite good," he said to Jenö. He looked at my plate. "Something the matter, Inspector? This fish was excellent."

"Yes," I said. "You seemed to enjoy it."

"More wine?" Jenö looked at my glass. "You're not drinking?" How to explain to the man that I wouldn't touch anything on the table until I figured out what was going on?

"Who is doing what to whom? Isn't that the question of the hour?" I looked from Jenö to the delegation leader, and then back to Jenö. The napkin was heavy linen. I didn't think it could be folded into a rabbit. Maybe it could be made into a blunt object.

"Why don't we move out to those chairs on the patio. We can have coffee and smoke cigars." Jenö signaled the waiter. "Don't worry, Inspector, we'll find time to talk, as well. Whatever questions you have will be answered, as far as possible."

"Sure, let's talk outside, if we can hear each other over the din of cameras clicking and recorders squealing." I looked under the table. "Did you bring your black bag?"

Jenö laughed. "Remember what I told you not so long ago, Inspector? About seeing Cossacks everywhere? Don't be so jumpy. This place is perfectly clear and clean. We won't be disturbed. It's covered, believe me. It's covered."

I shrugged. "If you say so." I turned to the delegation leader. "You realize you almost didn't make it here."

"Oh?"

"The other day, when you disappeared in the white car, the one whose mechanic hates women."

"No, I knew you were behind me the whole time."

"I'm not talking about me." I watched him tighten his lips. Jenö's eyebrows did a quizzical two-step. "I don't know this for sure, but I'd say you're marked. And I don't mean for promotion."

The delegation leader twisted his napkin into a knot and put it on the table. "You're not telling me anything I didn't already know, Inspector. In fact, that's why you're here."

"Dessert, anyone?" Jenö stood up and led the way out to the patio.

7

"It's very simple, Inspector. I am working for Sohn"—the delegation leader held up one spoon—"and so are you." He held up a second spoon with his other hand. "That means we are working together. Our friend here"—he gestured at Jenö with my spoon—"has some interesting ideas that Sohn thinks should be pursued." He pursed his lips again, which I couldn't figure out. Was he just practicing on me? Maybe he was one of those people who forget the distinction between onstage and off. Some people go through the motions even when the motor is idling. "Sohn is working with Jenö," he said. He looked around for another spoon, but Jenö had picked up the third one and was stirring his coffee. "That means we work with Jenö as well. There's a certain mathematical precision to it all, don't you think? Like reducing fractions or finding a common denominator."

Reduced to essentials, everything was simple. But there were limits. It was just as Pak had said: Reduced too much, everything disappears. Not this, though. This wasn't simple. And it wasn't going to disappear.

"When was the last time you saw Sohn?" Out here, by the lake, it was easy to be casual. Everything was perfect in this spot.

The delegation leader waved his hand, a gesture to show his answer wasn't intended to be precise. "Before I left for the talks here. Last month, maybe?" He didn't give any sign of knowing that Sohn had arrived a few days ago and would be returning to Pyongyang in a metal box. "I'll see him when I get home." Again, the hand waved vaguely. If I could be casual out here, so could he. He was used to lying, but I didn't think he was used to murder.

"Let's move on." Jenö cut into the conversation. "Time is running out, and we need to get down to details. We can worry about Sohn later."

Jenö was another story altogether. Jenö could lie about anything, anytime. If I'd had the slightest doubt before, I didn't anymore. He knew about Sohn's death. He could have learned about it from M. Beret, but then again, maybe he knew because he was close by when it happened. At the moment, all I knew for sure was what Sohn had told me, which wasn't very much. One of the few things he had emphasized was that I needed to keep the delegation leader from defecting. The delegation leader had just consumed an expensive lunch of perch with a Mossad agent. As far as I knew, that wasn't a classic indicator of imminent defection, though it didn't make the negative case very well, either.

"I don't think you're clear on what we face. I don't even think you know why you're here, Inspector," the delegation leader said. "It would be very much like Sohn to send you on a mission with the tiniest part of the picture he could afford to give. Just enough to keep you from stumbling into the lake. When the time came, he'd tell you what you needed to know to do your job."

"And you? You have a full picture?" The atmospheric meter ticked down.

"Probably better than yours, though not all of it from Sohn. We're kept in the dark about a lot of things, but anything to do with foreign relations we eventually find out. Facts, rumors, crazy ideas—if they touch on foreign policy, they all swim, or float, or tumble toward our building. Sohn understood that. He even used it to his advantage. He would throw a piece of information into the air, nothing too definite—maybe nine parts fluff, one part substance—then watch it drift into our windows. That way he couldn't be accused of giving us something we weren't supposed to know."

Jenö handed each of us a cigar. "If you smoke cigars, Inspector, you'll like these. I only bring them out for special occasions."

A breeze came off the lake. It had something of spring on it, though still not much. "If you don't mind, I'll save mine for later." Maybe for a victory celebration, even a minor one, if I could figure out how to define victory. "You said time was running out. Time seems to be an obsession here. People pay a lot of attention to it in this country. They make fistfuls of money from it. If time runs out, then the world won't need watches. What will you do then?"

"My people can't hold open this deal forever, Inspector. If your people want it, they're going to have to move soon. And from what I hear, if they don't move soon, there may not be so much left of your country. The famine is growing, order is breaking down, rumors are racing around. It wouldn't take much to tip over the whole structure."

"Is that so? You think we're about to start begging?"

The delegation leader lit his cigar. "Face it, things are bad."

"Bad?" I hadn't expected him to be so direct about anything, certainly not in front of a foreigner. "Bad is nothing. Bad is normal. We've been through worse. We'll survive."

"Really?" Jenö looked thoughtfully at the mountains in the distance. They were covered with snow. "Then why turn to us?"

Fair enough, I thought. Too bad Sohn hadn't told me. Too bad Sohn hadn't told me much of anything before his head ended up at an odd angle on his shoulders. "I wouldn't know who turned to whom in this case. Maybe you came tapping at our window. You'll have to talk to someone who toils in the foreign affairs field, like him." I pointed at the delegation leader. "He might be able to supply you with some answers. You two seem to know each other. I'm just a policeman."

The delegation leader laughed. "Do you really think you'd be here if you were just a policeman? That's like saying your grandfather was just a guerrilla fighter."

"My grandfather has nothing to do with this."

"To the contrary, Inspector, I'd say he has everything to do with where we are, and where we might decide to go. You can be sure Sohn didn't pluck you out of some Public Security rabbit hole by accident."

"Plucked is the right word. I'm not here by choice." No, Sohn hadn't picked me because of my grandfather but because of my brother. "The ambassador wants me out of here. He's made that clear. I'm leaving as soon as I can. I've got no reason to stick around."

"Even before the job is done?" Jenö tapped the ash from his cigar. "Even when we're so close to the goal?"

"Goal. You want us to stop selling missiles to your neighbors. That's your goal. It's not mine. I don't have any goals that relate to missiles. Believe it or not, I don't even *think* about missiles. As long as no one carries one in my sector, missiles aren't on my list of worries." I was getting wound up. Nice weather, nice setting, but I wasn't in the mood to enjoy it. Maybe I was still tired from the night before, still smarting from Dilara's crack about her little policeman. Well, if Jenö wanted to talk about goals, that was fine with me. I could talk about goals. "Everyone in the world is allowed to sell military hardware but us, right? Big powers do it because they're big, and that means they can do whatever they want. Middle powers do it because that's how they make a lot of money. Little powers like you"—I pointed my unlit cigar at Jenö—"do it because the big powers find it useful. They let you operate on the margins where they don't want to be, or they don't want to make the effort to stop you, or they don't give a damn. But none of those conditions pertain to us." I made clear I was including the delegation leader. "We're a special case, right? You all sell missiles until you don't want to do it anymore, then you say no one else can. Too bad for you. We need the money." I didn't know if we needed the money or not, but if my brother was involved, I had to assume money was part of the mix. "If we had rich uncles to give us aid to build steel mills, or ships, or computers, we'd be happy little piglets. But we don't, we don't have anyone to shovel money at us, so we sell what we sell and you can fuck a duck if you don't like it." Little policeman! What the hell did she mean by *that*?

"No one said anything about stopping you from selling anything. If you think it's your God-given right to lug weapons around the world, be my guest." Jenö smoothed the air several times. The afternoon became calm again. The light settled on the lake. It seemed wrong for me to be here. I was taking up space I had no right to occupy. I was tired of people looking at me like I was a freak. I had roiled enough waters. I wanted to go home.

Jenö nodded at me, and his smile, the one that played on his lips most of the time, turned enigmatic. "You can sell whatever you want, it really makes no difference to us. Not one bit. Just don't sell to our enemies. That's all we ask." He was in full soothe-the-barbarian mode. You could almost hear the violins playing in the background. "And we're not just asking. We're prepared to make it worth your while, Inspector. In the long run, you'll get a lot more from good relations with us than you'll ever get from the people you're dealing with now. Do you really think they spend any time thinking about your interests, your concerns, your history? Don't be ridiculous. They only care about one thing, getting rid of us—and they'll play you for everything they can if they think it will advance that goal. That's their goal. What's yours?"

It was a little vague, his formulation, and I didn't think it was an accident. Did he mean me, in particular? Were Jenö and his colleagues prepared to make it worth *my* while? I yawned. Somewhere I'd read that was what a defeated animal did—yawned. I wasn't tired, but I was beaten. This place by the lake had defeated me. Maybe that's why they took me here. I was sure it was the two of them, together, who had carefully chosen the place. "And we're supposed to be shocked, that people thousands of kilometers away don't care about our history? Do you think we care about theirs?" I wanted to get the emphasis away from the singular and back on the collective. "Anyway, none of this is my business. How many times do I have to tell you? No one listens to me. And that includes Sohn." Which was certainly true now. I found myself yawning again.

"Someone assigned me to you when I was in Pyongyang a few months ago. That wasn't an accident." Jenö wasn't interested in signs of submission. He was poking me with a stick; he wanted to get a rise out of me.

"They just wanted someone to blame if things went wrong," I said. "That's how they work."

"Well, things are about to go wrong. I'm getting negative messages from my people: Get this done, or we pull all of it, the whole thing, off the table." Jenö looked at the delegation leader. For the first time, I sensed that they were still on separate sides of the divide. "You're going to lose it all. I have it right here." He patted his jacket pocket. "The whole deal. And you're about to see me throw it in the trash."

The delegation leader shook his head. "You trash it, then nothing will change, you still won't like your neighborhood, we'll struggle back to our feet, and life will go on. Unless Mr. Sohn has given the inspector a plan he hasn't yet revealed."

They both turned to me.

"I'll say it again, I'll say it all afternoon long if you want. I'm not the person you need to deal with."

The delegation leader put his cigar carefully into the ashtray, an oversized ceramic triangle with an abstract drawing of a fish in the center. It was spotlessly clean except for the mound of ash in the center. "Let me get this straight," he said. "Sohn sent you out here, to pass a message, I assume. You haven't done that as far as I know." Wrong, but never mind. "You probably think I've been in your way, which means Sohn didn't tell you anything about me." Wrong again. Sohn told me I'd be up to my ears in shit if you defected. "We both know how bad things are at home. Sometimes I sense the youngsters on my delegation can barely sit still. They're worried about their families, they feel guilty about being here, they can't figure out what we are doing. They're waiting, Inspector. All day long in those talks, we sit across from people who can really help us, and what do we do? We stall, because they won't give anything if we don't ask, and we won't ask because we can't afford to look weak. What are we going to do? Make more cardboard and plywood missiles? We don't even have enough plywood anymore. We probably don't even have enough screws." I heard my grandfather laugh, somewhere in the distance. "We can't sell our way out of this. We can't growl loud enough, or puff ourselves up big enough, but that is what we're going to do anyway. You want to see my instructions sometime? My job is to bluff and to stall. And when that doesn't work, I have backup instructions to stall and to bluff."

"From what I've seen, you're very good at it," I said. "If that's what you're here to do, you're doing it beyond what anyone might expect. If you ever need one, I'll write a recommendation letter."

"You don't get it, do you? One week I'm supposed to make sure nothing happens. The next week I receive instructions to make progress. I keep two files—one for angry messages asking me what the hell do I think I'm doing, the other for angry messages asking me why the hell I'm not doing more."

The ash from his cigar fell onto his trousers. As he leaned to brush it off, a shot rang out. The cushion on the back of his chair exploded. In an instant, practically before the sound died away, Jenö reached across the table, pushed the delegation leader down, shouted at me to take cover, and screamed some commands into a small radio that he pulled from his pocket—all a split second before he yanked a pistol from a holster under his jacket. Then it was over, almost as if nothing had happened, except that Jenö was breathing hard. I wasn't breathing. I wasn't scared or rattled, just amazed. I had yet to see cows with cowbells walking up a dainty Swiss hillside. The only travel calendars I could bring back home with good conscience had men with broken necks and people under a table by the lake. I started to get up. Jenö grabbed my arm and pushed me down. "Nobody moves," he said, "until I say it's okay."

"Sure, I like it under tables with black bags." I shook off his hand. "But if my pal here gets shot while I'm under a table, any table, I'll never live it down in the Ministry." I climbed to my feet and looked around. What was left of the cushion lay on the ground. It must have been hit by a tank round, judging by the hole in it. "I guess cigar smoking isn't bad for your health, after all," I said to the delegation leader.

"You're not helping things, standing there like that, Inspector," he said, looking up at me.

"You want me to go find the cannon that did that?" I pointed to the cushion.

Jenö put the earphone in his ear and listened for a moment. "Don't bother. We already have it." He put the pistol back in its holster; his eyebrows did a skeptical promenade. "That's why there wasn't a second shot."

"What took you so long to get him?"

Jenö smiled at me. He seemed genuinely amused. "I guess it's hard to be a sniper like that."

"Like what?"

"You know, with only three fingers."

That made me sit down. "Where is he?"

"The shooter? Under a tree. Must have fallen. He broke his neck."

The delegation leader picked up his cigar. "Anyone have a light?"

8

"Here are your tickets. Out of politeness, I should wish you a pleasant flight, Inspector, but really I cannot help hoping you hit rough air all of the way home, so bad the stewardesses cannot get up to serve drinks. So bad that your teeth rattle and your stomach rolls. You get the picture. I've never been in anything like the mess we have right now. This is Switzerland, for heaven's sake! Keeping it quiet is going to be a full-time job. I should have followed my first instinct and booted you out immediately. Maybe it was that green hat. It was a distraction, really."

"Perhaps," I said, "we'll meet again under better circumstances."

"Not in this lifetime, God willing."

"You're not the one who has to explain two dead countrymen to thick-necked men with dour expressions as soon as the plane lands. They probably won't even let me claim my suitcase before they start throwing questions at me. I hope that's all they throw. Oh, and did I mention, the head of my delegation—a senior diplomat, I might add—was nearly assassinated on the shores of your peaceful lake?"

"At least I'm not the only one whose career will suffer. Did you know that even the fact that your negotiations with the Americans fell apart is being pinned on me."

"Career?" I laughed. "If that's your only worry, count yourself lucky. I'm going to have to write a long and *very* convincing report about what happened to Sohn, which will be doubly difficult because I have no idea what the truth is. And that means I can't even concoct a decent story. Sohn had enemies at home, but he had friends as well. And his friends will start from the assumption that it's all my fault."

"Well, at least you can report the man with the strange hand died doing his job."

"True, but I never took him for an assassin."

"Assassin? What do you mean?"

"He tried to kill the delegation leader. That shot would have blown his head off if he hadn't dropped cigar ash on his pants at just that moment."

M. Beret looked puzzled. "Is that what you think?"

"Of course it's what I think. I was there, wasn't I? I saw it. We were both under the table."

"You were at the lake. How could you see what was going on five hundred meters away?"

"Who do you think the target was?" My blood froze.

"Yes." M. Beret spoke slowly. "It was you."

"He was trying to shoot me?"

"No, he didn't fire the shot. He disrupted it. The bullet was aimed at you. I thought you were just showing *sangfroid*."

"Pardon me?"

"Unflappable. Cold blood, literally, but that may not be the best translation under the circumstances. You knew, of course, that his job was to protect you." He watched my face. "You knew that, yes? Someone in your capital was trying to disrupt the talks, completely blow them up. The best way to accomplish that, they figured, was the death of a delegation member. They couldn't kill an American; that would get them in a lot of trouble. But murdering someone on your side . . . well, it wouldn't be the first time, eh? Apparently, the most expendable one was you. I expect that's why Sohn came out here. He had discovered elements of the plot. He needed to warn you."

Warn me? He took his sweet time about it, if that was his intent. So much time he never got around to it, someone made sure of that. "M. Beret, there's no way you could possibly know any of what you just told me. I appreciate your sense of drama, but it is pure fantasy, and if you paid for such reporting, you really should demand your money back from the source. Out of curiosity, what is the rest of the fable? Who was in the tree, trying to kill me?"

"I believe they are about to close your gate, Inspector. *Au revoir*."

"Just tell me this, what happened to him, the Man with Three Fingers? Jenö said he was dead."

M. Beret paused for a fraction longer than he should have. "We have an unidentified Mexican in the morgue, if that's what you mean. Now hurry, please. If you miss your plane I will be inconsolable."

"I will miss you, too." I kissed him on both cheeks, which I figured was a photo he might like for the files.

PART V

Chapter One

"He's dead." I was in Pak's office, squinting against the sun that bounced off the windows of the Operations Building across the way. The gingkoes in the courtyard were useless, weeks away from getting leaves that could soften the light. Worst of all, three months into the New Year, their branches had all the charm of dinosaur limbs. March is bad enough, my grandfather would say, without having to look at gingko trees.

"Really?" Shock registered in Pak's eyes. "What happened?" He wasn't feigning ignorance. I could see that he really didn't know, which meant the news hadn't gotten back here yet. Pak might be only a chief inspector, but no one had more lines out than he did. If Sohn's death had been reported, no matter in what channel, Pak would have known. Even if the news were closely held deep in the Center, Pak would find it.

"The Swiss are classifying it as an accident."

"By which I take it, you don't think so."

"I think he was murdered. That's what they suspect, too, only it would cause them too much trouble to say so."

"And why would you think this was murder?"

"For one thing, his neck was broken. That doesn't just happen. You can fall through a gallows' trapdoor, or off a horse, or out of a car, or down the stairs, but generally it isn't easy to break your neck all by yourself. If he fell, there would have been bruises. He didn't have any. None."

"How do you know?"

"I saw the body in the morgue."

"Why, the question will be asked, did Inspector O go to the Geneva morgue?"

"The mission doesn't want anything to do with bodies of any description. They said no one was missing from their roster, and they weren't going to the morgue to stare at an unidentified foreigner. In fact, they complained it was an insult, suggesting something had happened to one of the staff. The Swiss threw up their hands and asked me. I thought I owed it to Sohn. Someone did, anyway."

"So, just for the sake of argument, we'll assume you are right." I expected Pak to ask a lot of things, but not what came next. "Does that bother you, his being murdered?"

"Strange, the Swiss put the same question to me."

"And what did you reply?"

"I said I'd have to think about it. I'm still thinking, but I'm not sure I like having so many people interested in my personal reaction. What if I asked you the same thing?"

"I'd say I am bothered by it. I'd say Sohn was a good man. He grunted and barked at times, his ears were too small and the back of his head too pointed, but he was good to his people and he knew what needed to be done."

Nicely vague, that phrase—needed to be done.

"So, you knew him from before you joined the Ministry. I figured you did. There was something about the way you spoke to each other."

"It's been a while, but I don't think he had changed much."

"From what I could tell, he had a lot of enemies."

"These days, that's not hard to do. Even back then, he had the knack for it."

"The Swiss told me they saw him meeting Jenö last year."

"Good for them." Pak stood up. This time there was nothing special in his eyes. Maybe he wasn't surprised. "I feel like going for a long walk. Come along?"

As soon as we were out the gate and past the guards, it was clear Pak didn't want to talk. Silence was fine by me. I was disoriented, and it wasn't just lack of sleep. I couldn't place where I was. I'd only been away for a month, but the city had a strange feel. Everything about it was unfamiliar—the buildings, the air, the sounds. It was as if I hadn't really come back.

The afternoon was awfully cold. All of the stores were dark, and there weren't many people lined up waiting for buses. We walked for almost twenty minutes without saying a word; finally Pak stopped and turned to me. "It may not come up in the course of later conversation, so let me remind you that we are still supposed to be working on that case, the woman who was murdered."

"Welcome home, Inspector O," I said.

"No, I don't mean you have to start on it today."

"When?"

"Tomorrow. No one will call on Sunday. You can work uninterrupted."

"Anyone bother to look at the file while I was gone?" I'd come to a few tentative conclusions, but I wasn't going to share them just yet. I planned to sleep the whole day tomorrow. I could give my conclusions to Pak on Monday, tell him I'd spent all of Sunday developing them.

"We're still shorthanded. Besides, a lot happened while you were gone."

"Such as?"

"I don't know this, and because I don't know it, I would have no way of telling you about a surge of activity in Hwadae county. There haven't been enough out-of-channel orders sent to our people to suggest anything imminent. But we have noticed more visitors going up there than normal. An Iranian delegation went through Sunan about a week ago. A special Pakistani visitor flew in, too. Our nearest post has been told to keep well back and look the other way when the cars go through."

"Is that why Sohn got his neck broken?"

"Funny question. I don't think you need to generate new shoots," Pak said. "I think you need to go home and sleep long enough to get that dazed look off your face. I'll meet you tonight around nine o'clock, at the same place we had bark soup when you got back from New York. Can you find it?"

"I'm a detective, remember?"

2

"Anything but soup," Pak said to the woman.

She shrugged. "I use only the finest bark. But tonight I also have a nice piece of fish, something that is not easy to get. It was supposed to be for some military group, but they didn't show up. It's all yours."

Once the dishes had been cleared away, Pak lit a cigarette. "I'm glad you didn't bring any of these back from overseas," he said. "Cigarettes from overseas are a corrupting influence." I'd left two cartons in his office, and he'd put them in his bottom drawer. "That's what Sohn always said, before he gave us each two packs of Gitanes. He thought it was funny, us smoking French cigarettes while we went through our drills."

I hadn't been very awake a moment ago, but I was now. Wide-awake. "Sohn smoked French cigarettes?"

"See, that's just like you, Inspector. A bug on a cabbage leaf. Something wasn't right the whole time you were gone. Now I realize what it was. No sound of anyone chewing on tiny facts."

We sat in the near darkness and mulled things over. Pak ground out his cigarette. "I would smoke a second one, but it's bad for my health, everyone says." He snorted and lit another. "Can you believe it? They're telling us not to smoke because it's bad for our health! Have some more bark soup, Inspector. Now *that's* good for you."

"What about Sohn?"

"Ah, to business, always to business. The ship sinks, and Sailor O is for mending the sheets. The building burns, and Fireman O stops to polish the elevator buttons."

"I thought you wanted to talk about Sohn, that's all. Skip it. I don't care. He wasn't my friend."

"No, let's stay on that subject. You tell me he was murdered. For what? Did he stumble onto a robbery? But you don't break someone's neck in a hurry when you're running away from a robbery. You don't even break someone's neck when you're robbing him. Even in a fight . . ."

This might not be the best time, given Pak's mood, but I might as well say what I thought. "There was no fight. I think someone stepped behind him and snapped his neck. That's what they wanted to do, and that's exactly what they did."

Pak sat very still. I knew I'd touched a nerve.

"I hear they have Gypsies in Europe," he said at last.

"So?"

"Maybe they snap necks. Like the Mongols used to."

"That was backbones. The Mongols snapped backbones. I'm telling you, it wasn't a Mongol or Gypsy who broke Sohn's neck."

"Very helpful. We've narrowed the list of suspects. I can eliminate Genghis Khan. Any other ideas? Maybe Sohn saw someone he wasn't supposed to see. You were in the same city; you must have noticed something."

"I did notice one thing. I noticed someone tried to kill me."

"Anyone we know?" Pak frowned. "And don't tell me it was over a woman, either."

I sketched the events at the lakeside restaurant, Jenö's explanation, and then what M. Beret had told me.

"Maybe you shouldn't have criticized the perch," Pak said. "Okay, someone tried to kill you, but they failed. On the other hand, they finished the job with Sohn. Why? Why the hell was Sohn even in Geneva? What was going on there?"

"Nothing special. Bribery, chicanery, excess—the usual. Other than that, the city is a swamp of boredom. The most interesting thing that happens is when they execute a wristwatch in public for running slow. I don't think we need to focus on the city. We need to look more closely at Sohn."

Pak took a deep drag on his cigarette. The smoke drifted out of his nostrils.

"Cut that out, would you?" I was annoyed.

"I forgot," Pak said. "You don't like it." He took another drag, and again the smoke came from his nose; it curled out and then floated upward, tendrils of smoke like vines from a corpse's skull.

"You're murdering your sinuses. It's enough I have to breathe it."

"I've got my problems; you've got yours. Which orifice I select for blowing out my smoke is up to me. It's something I can choose for myself, and you don't get to take that away. Maybe you've forgotten, but everything isn't cheese and chocolates around here."

That brought the conversation to a halt. It was already quiet in the room. It got a lot quieter. Pak looked at me, dismayed. "I can't believe I said that. Give me a minute." He shook his head. "No, I'll need more than a minute." He pulled smoke deep into his lungs and closed his eyes. "What are the odds of smoking as much as I do and being so damned healthy? I thought these things were supposed to kill me."

Suddenly, Pak put out the cigarette and pushed the ashtray aside. "Did I do something before I joined the Ministry? Who can remember?" He moved his chair closer to the table. "Listen to me. Sohn was more dedicated than anyone you'll ever meet. He didn't believe everything they handed out. He had to be convinced, and if he had doubts, they had to be put to rest. He argued with the lecturers, he argued with the trainers, he argued with the political cadres until they turned red in the face and nearly fell over. No one touched him, though; reports against him would go flying up the chain, but no one touched him because no one doubted that once he was convinced, he would be like steel. He had no use for ideology, thought it was a waste of time. What mattered was results. When he was in charge of a team, he didn't spend time worrying about our righteousness. He wanted us to do the job and come home safe. He was always waiting for us at the dock." Pak stopped. "That tells you all you need to know about Sohn. All and everything and nothing, because I could never figure him out. None of us could."

"That was then. This is now. What did he have to do with Pakistan?"

"Who said anything about Pakistan?" Pak's voice could get a cozy lilt to it sometimes. People who didn't know him thought he was getting chummy, taking them into his confidence. I knew better.

"I never drop anything. It's all over this case. The woman was killed in Pakistan. Our foreigner is mixed up with missiles, my brother was mixed up with missiles, and Pakistan grows missiles like Mt. Paektu grows blueberries. I think there is more going on than we know."

"Thank you, Inspector." Pak smiled. "My faith in you is restored. I think you can assume there is more going on everywhere than we can know, or want to know, or dare to know. Better to be a bug on a cabbage leaf—don't worry about what's happening on the next head of cabbage. You gave some thought to the lady?"

"I did. I think she may be part of the reason Sohn was killed." This wasn't what I thought sixty seconds ago, but something Pak had said rocketed this idea out of the darkness. "The woman herself wasn't important. It was that she was working for Sohn."

"What?"

"Sohn told me that. He didn't tell me what she was doing, and it may not even be that significant. But I think her death spooked Sohn. He was afraid that someone had discovered he was watching their operations in Pakistan."

"Who?"

"Think about it."

Pak thought about it. "Your brother," he said.

"You know what I think? I think you may have asked the right question. Did Sohn see something he wasn't supposed to? Did he stumble onto a meeting that wasn't supposed to happen?"

Pak stared at me, looking inside my head.

"Something the matter?" I asked, but I already knew. My brother was the matter.

"I think you're halfway there, Inspector," Pak said finally. "It isn't just what Sohn saw, but what he knew; and more important, who he was. A lot of people might have seen the same thing, but it wouldn't have made a difference because they wouldn't know what they were looking at."

"Which means . . ."

"Which means it must have been someone who recognized him, someone who knew him. That's not a big universe, when you think about it. The number of our people abroad at any one time is small. The number in Geneva is even smaller. Either the person Sohn saw wasn't supposed to be there, or he wasn't supposed to be meeting with whomever Sohn saw him with."

M. Beret had shown me a picture of my brother with the man from Sri Lanka; the same man had sat with his knees practically touching mine on the train, on his way to another meeting with my brother, maybe in Bern. They must have decided to do it outside Geneva, because they didn't like what had just happened in the city. It hadn't been in their plans, murdering a party official. "What if the meeting Sohn witnessed was approved, but no one was supposed to know about it?" I didn't believe that, but it was a theory that had to be crossed off.

Pak shook his head. "Not likely. For that they'd only have to bring him home and tell him to keep his mouth shut. No reason to break his neck."

"Missiles. What did Sohn have to do with missiles?"

"Always roaming with a restless mind." Pak pulled out another cigarette, looked at it for a moment, then put it back in the pack.

"Heart. The line is 'roaming with a restless heart.'"

"You should know; you're the poetic one, Inspector. Care to write a poem about missiles someday? Sohn thought they were a waste of resources. Not at first he didn't. At first he was part of a program to get plans and components. He ran it."

"When?"

"Let's leave it at that."

"The man is dead; I'm interested in who killed him, especially because my own neck seems to be on the line. I'm not sure I buy the story I was handed. Besides, I thought you liked him."

"Sohn said that people would die this winter and we'd be better off without them. Or did you forget that?"

No, I hadn't forgotten.

"My mother died last night. She was thin, like a piece of paper, O. What do you think Sohn would have said to me?" He grabbed his hair in his hands and pulled until it looked like he would rip it from his head. "Worse, much worse, what would I have said to him?" Pak put his head on the table and wept. There was nothing I could do.

Chapter Two

What I had learned about the young woman murdered in Pakistan fit on a tiny piece of paper, what you might call a short list. That list was in front of me, on my desk. It bothered me that it wasn't longer. I wanted to know what happened to her. It wasn't germane to anything, but it was the start of a chain of events that had almost left me with a big hole in my head. That sort of thing piques my curiosity.

The young woman had been murdered. The murder had taken place in Pakistan. She liked music, was infatuated with Rachmaninoff. That was it; end of list. Everything else was conjecture. She might be mixed up with missiles, and she might have crossed paths with Israeli intelligence. I still didn't know how she died, but if I found out that her neck had been broken, it wouldn't surprise me. French cigarettes somewhere in the picture, too—that wouldn't have surprised me, either. I'd told Pak that her murder wasn't important, that it hadn't meant anything. Maybe so, but I hated to leave it at that. I stared at the list for a few minutes; that didn't fill in any blanks.

Early Wednesday morning Pak was called in to explain why no reporting on the case had come from his unit yet. He was gone for almost four hours. As soon as he reached the front gate, just after noon in a pelting rain, he called me from the gate phone.

"Get over to my office this instant," he said. "Have a pencil and paper; be ready to take down everything I tell you, without a single interruption." He slammed the phone down so hard I could hear it all the way to the second floor.

I was sitting with paper and pencil when Pak walked in. He threw a file onto his cabinet and tossed his coat onto a chair.

"The Minister is angry. He told me he was angry, that's how I know. He did it in an angry voice, with an angry look on his face, in case I missed the point or harbored any doubts. You might say he chewed me out. And do you know why?"

"Tell me when I'm supposed to start putting pencil to paper, would you?"

"Sure, I'll also tell you what else you can do with the pencil."

"The Minister was not happy, that's where you left off. What was the problem?"

"The problem? The problem is that a certain case that was supposed to stay very low profile has become high profile. A certain European city where we are always supposed to blend in with the landscape has decided it doesn't want to have anything to do with us anymore."

"I can't be blamed for that."

"The hell you can't." He said it slowly, without any emotion. It wasn't a threat, more like a warning, and not the sort of warning Pak threw around idly. "When Sohn picked you out, it was for a reason. Or haven't you figured that out yet? I thought when your own skin was in jeopardy it would heighten your sense of reality, but maybe not."

"One thing at a time. Forget my skin. What about the Minister?"

"The Minister wasn't happy when Sohn said he needed to borrow you. The Minister frequently is unhappy, but he doesn't brood on it. If Sohn wanted you, that was that, it didn't matter what the reason was. The Minister, as he made clear to me, expected you to do what you were told and then get back to work."

"I thought Sohn and the Minister didn't get along."

"That's not the point, not even your concern, and I'll tell you why.

It isn't your concern because it isn't my concern. It doesn't matter to me who gets along with whom these days. In fact, it's not even clear to me these days if anything matters at all."

I put down the pencil. "Strange, I never expected to hear that from you."

"Let's stay on target, shall we, Inspector? We're talking about you, not me. We're not dealing with your expectations, but with the mess you created."

"A minute ago it was a problem. Now it's a mess."

"Stick around, it's about to become a disaster. The ambassador at the mission in Geneva sent in a report. His security people asked around."

"I'll bet they did. I'll bet they found out everything they could from their Portuguese dollies."

"What?"

"I wouldn't pay attention to the security man. I'd wring his neck first."

"Wring it, or break it?"

"Don't tell me I'm being accused of murdering Sohn. Because if I am, I'm going back to my apartment. They can come for me there; I won't make you suffer the embarrassment of having me led out of your office." I stood up to go. "I know who is behind this, and so do you."

2

"Sit down, Inspector, we're not finished." Pak looked painfully grim. "You're getting paranoid. You think your brother is behind everything that happens?"

"Do we have something more to discuss?" I wasn't going to talk about a brother that I no longer had. "This whole place is on the verge of a nervous breakdown. No one is giving orders, and no one is following them. Have you seen the reports on internal travel from the countryside? None of the posts are even trying to enforce regulations anymore. They say it's hopeless, and not worth the effort. Besides, people need to eat. Our job isn't to enforce starvation, or did I miss something in the latest memo while I was away?"

"You're not focusing, Inspector. You're hip deep in someone else's business. I don't give a damn about internal travel regulations. I don't care if everyone in Yanggang skips all the way to the East Sea." He saw the expression on my face. "Alright, the question is survival—who will survive and who won't. Yes, this year is crucial. If we make it through this year, things will get better. Satisfied?"

"Says who? And more to the point, so what? I don't want to play in that arena anymore, Pak. Survival, collapse—big words, big concepts, very big. Once you warned me against reducing things to their essence. Now I'm warning you, don't stretch ideas past the point of meaning."

"Is there more to that thought, or was it just something you had to get off your chest?"

"You have something else for me. What is it?"

"Your friend Jenö. He's coming back."

I shook my head. "I don't believe it. I don't. Is he arriving on the cloak of the princess of the moon?"

"No, Inspector, everything is believable, and that will become clear when you find yourself at the airport Saturday morning, greet him, load his luggage into your car, help him check into the hotel, and sit across from him in the dining room of the Koryo."

"How did he get another visa? Three times. How? Doesn't anybody check those forms any more? What if someone tries to snatch him when he gets off the plane? He doesn't have many friends left. Without Sohn, who is protecting him?"

"Someone must be, or he wouldn't have a visa."

"So when the big burly men come up and tell him that he is supposed to go with them, what happens?"

"Simple. You will interpose your body between him and them."

"And say what?"

"That you are officially escorting a guest of the party and government of the People's Republic, that as a ranking member of the Ministry of Public Security, you will not be detained, and that there will be hell to pay if anyone interferes."

"What if they're from the army?"

"Go down shooting, Inspector! Don't worry, the army won't show its hand on this. Anyway, the army may not be opposed to his being here for all you know."

"For all I know. Nothing is all I know. What does he want to talk about?"

"I have no idea." Not likely, but I let it pass. "If he wants a meeting with someone, he won't be shy in asking. As I recall, he isn't shy. Maybe he has a message; maybe he'll give it to you. A word of advice this time—if he wants you to work for him, take the money and run."

"If I had wanted to work with foreigners, I would have been measured for a suit. Is this really our job?"

"In this situation, Inspector, there is nothing that is not our job. You are our official greeter for the next few days. Only one thing."

"I knew it."

"You're right. Not everyone is happy to see our guest."

"I'm to put my body in between, you said."

"I'm not talking about symbolic intervention. I'm being literal. I mean your body."

"Not everyone wants him back." Pak must have a clue who was in the opposition. "Anybody we know?"

"Your brother, for one, I'd guess."

"That's funny." Now who was being paranoid?

"Is there a punch line?"

"I told him to stay out of my way or I'd do something." This wasn't something I wanted to discuss with Pak.

"And he nodded agreeably."

"He said he wasn't sure I would live that long."

"In most countries, that would pass as a threat. Was it, or was it just a brotherly exchange?"

"Alright, I lost my temper with him. It wasn't the first time, but this was the worst. I told him we weren't brothers anymore. I meant it. I don't want to speak to him, or see him again."

"That isn't what I meant."

"Yes, it might have been a threat. It's hard to be sure with him. Everything he utters is nasty. I don't remember if he said it before or after I mentioned I'd shoot him if I had to."

"You said you'd shoot your own brother?" Incredulity is not in Pak's normal range, but we were getting close. "He's all the family you have left."

"I told you, I lost my temper. Not lost, actually. More like I folded it up and calmly put it in my pocket."

"Calmly," Pak said. "That's one interpretation. How about thoughtlessly? Or maybe stupidly? Your brother has plenty of ways to get at us, Inspector. He has a thousand arrows and a thousand archers. Did you think about that before crumpling up your temper and stuffing it in your pocket?"

"I didn't crumple it. Anyway, it's done, that's all I can tell you. My brother doesn't scare me."

"Wonderful! And in which pocket did you put your fear, can you tell me that? I hope it is easily retrievable, mixed with your wood chips, because it may be that fear is the only thing that will save us." Pak was building up a good head of steam. "I've heard that your brother tried very hard to block this visit. Just before I left his office, the Minister took a phone call, after which he suggested to me that you needed to do something to fix a family problem. Actually, he roared at me that if you didn't fix this, he'd skin you alive. Apologize, out of fear if nothing else. If you can still locate it."

I threw down the pencil. "This country is falling apart, and they're worrying about whether or not my brother and I are speaking?"

"You really are Korean after all, aren't you?"

"What the hell is that supposed to mean?"

"It means you can't put your temper in your pocket, because there isn't a pocket big enough to hold it. No one gives a damn whether you and your brother bash in each other's heads. Except for one thing. Your brother has influence, baleful though it is." Pak stopped and took a breath. He was furious, but I knew it wasn't just at me. It was everything, everything that was wrong, everything that was weighing on him, everything we all saw, or tried not to see, every day.

"Don't worry," I said, "nothing you could say about my brother would offend me."

"Offend! I'm not worried about offending you, Inspector. I'm trying to explain how dangerous a spot you've put us in. Us, you know?

The two of us here; you and me, followed at a short distance by the Minister. One more thing. Stay away from the school."

"I thought you wanted me to check in there once in a while to take the pulse. I was going over today, to see that girl. I have a feeling she might know the woman who was killed in Pakistan. I think they were in a Rachmaninoff club together at one point. They never got it approved, but I don't think that's a problem. Music is still an acceptable form of entertainment as far as I know, as long it doesn't involve lewdness. I don't suppose Rachmaninoff is a problem in that regard." I thought about where I had been taken by the music that night in the jazz club in Geneva. I didn't know how to describe it to Pak; I couldn't describe it to myself. "It's a compass for a heart," I said. "How else is anyone supposed to find a way through all of this?"

Pak started to say something, but then he stopped. He sat quietly for a moment. "Listen to me. We're done with the dead woman, done with Sohn. We're past it. Let someone else worry about the schools. To tell you the truth, it's making some people nervous, the idea of you among the students."

"What?"

"Stay away from the campus."

"They think I'm going to fool around with one of the students? I don't need this crap anymore. I'm taking a day off. If the Ministry objects, tell them to climb a tree." I turned to go, but then I turned back. I shouldn't have. "You know what? The Swiss asked me if I wanted to stay. Don't make me wish I had taken them up on the offer." I saw Pak recoil slightly, but there was nothing I could do about it now. M. Beret was right. Nothing would ever look the same.

Chapter Three

Tree sap smells sweet, even after a hundred years. Not like blood. When a piece of wood burns, it burns clean. Fire is pure because of the wood. Where do you think flames come from, if not from the wood?" This did not sound scientific to me, but I never said so, because when I was small and standing in my grandfather's workroom, there was no sense asking questions. Best to wait; best to listen closely because he might not alight for more than a moment on the main point. He sometimes spoke carefully, and when he did I knew I was to listen and ask nothing, nor repeat it to others. "Blood has a stench, like death. We are blood; we bleed, all of us. People talk about pure blood. No such thing. Blood stinks; it is filled with what is impure. It carries what is foul and stinks of everything that would kill us. We carry our own poisons around inside. A pure heart, people say? No, a heart is soaked in blood, every day, every minute. It is filled with what is impure, and it pumps that throughout your being. Sap is pure, wood is pure, fire is pure. You'll never walk into a forest and gag at the smell of dead or dying trees."

I didn't know what he meant then, though I listened carefully because he was speaking in a low voice. When he wanted me especially to pay attention, his voice became soft and the accent of his mountain village came out. It was hard to understand, but the worst thing I could do at such times was ask him to repeat something.

"They'll tell you about the glory of sacrificing your blood." At this I became especially alert. The reference to the ubiquitous "they," never defined, never brought into focus, it meant I should listen closely. "They have made blood glorious. The more they wade in it, the better things will be; that's what they believe, or they want you to believe." He turned away, and when at last he looked at me, I could barely sit still in the fury his look contained. "Your father, your mother—how much blood does it take?" He began to bellow like a wounded ox. "Get out! Go and walk somewhere, off by yourself, away from me. Are you going to sit there like the rest, are you going to listen with your mouth slack and then walk in line, following the one in front over the cliff? Will you bend in the wind, like some damned grove of bamboo? Don't you know the story? The prince was slain by Japs, they put his body in a room and his blood dripped to the ground, and from there grew bamboo. Is that what you want to be? Bamboo that has fed on blood, even the blood of a prince? Get out! Out! Don't come back until you find the answer. Not on your lips, but deep, deep inside where there is no one else but you."

This scared me to death. The neighbors had heard, I was sure. How could anyone not have heard for a kilometer around? They would be watching from windows and doorways, listening from where they sat under the trees. My grandfather had told me to go away. They would know what he said. I would be an orphan, no home, no family. And where would I go? What would become of me? No one would take me in, I would wander until I dropped from hunger, and then my vile blood would pollute the rice fields. I ran outside, and didn't stop running until I knew that I would never be like bamboo, never, no matter what anybody said.

2

I'd been back more than a week, and had convinced Pak I needed to go out and look around my sector. Jenö was safe in the Koryo, tired of waiting for a meeting that never seemed to happen. I was standing on a corner, looking at the willow trees along the street. It was quiet; once in a while a car went by, but even the engines seemed muffled. Most of the buildings on the main street were empty. The apartment houses that stood the next street over showed a little more life. Someone had a window open, and the lace curtains billowed in the March wind. Two women walked by, neither one a resident in my sector unless they had slipped in while I was away.

"I don't like seeing corpses on the sidewalk," the first one said.

"Sorry they offend your sensibilities."

"No, it isn't the bodies, it is the reason they are there."

"They're there because that's where people are dying these days."

"They're dying because of decisions."

"Careful." They both looked around.

"The South Koreans say we are their brothers," said the first, lowering her voice as they walked past me. "It was on a piece of paper my cousin found on the ground."

"I never pick up those things. They might have poison on them."

"It didn't seem to hurt him. But it wouldn't surprise me. The South Koreans want us to go hungry. They are willing to let the children starve. More than that, they *want* the children and the babies to starve. They think that will push us under."

"Have you noticed? There are hardly any babies being born."

"No one has the energy."

"No one has the will."

"Did you eat today?"

"Did I? I don't remember."

They turned and walked toward the river. I went the other way, for fear of what else they might say.

3

The phone call had come Tuesday morning saying that the meeting would take place that afternoon. I had to drive fast, but Jenö didn't complain. There was still a little sun left when we pulled up to the rickety bridge. The gaunt guard studied my ID for a long time. He paid no attention to Jenö's. As soon as we entered the hut, Jenö said to the general,

"I'm sorry about your brother-in-law." The major wasn't present, and there was no coughing coming from the back room.

"His brother-in-law?" I stared at them both.

"Sohn, the general's brother-in-law." Jenö sat down at the table without being invited. He relaxed.

"Always go with the cigarette butts," I said.

"Do you think you're standing here right now because I trust you?" The general shook his head. "Not a chance, Inspector. Sohn thought I should meet you. Otherwise, you would have been turned away at the gate the first time. Maybe shot."

I looked at Jenö. "How did you know Sohn's brother-in-law was in charge of this place?"

"I didn't, not until Sohn told me. He thought the military might go along with selling off the missile program if there was money in it for them, turning the production sites like this one into moneymaking enterprises." He stood up and strolled slowly around the hut. On the wall was a map of the site. He stared at it intently. "I have no idea what this place could be. It would have to be leveled. There's certainly nothing worth saving."

"Nice line of trees along the road," I said. "Poplars."

"Too bad they're not much taller than matchsticks."

The general cleared his throat. "If there is nothing else . . ."

"Somehow, you didn't strike me as a field officer." I smiled at him.

He smiled back. "Insufficiently crazed?"

"No, you move too much like a panther."

"Meaning?"

"Unerring sense of balance." I waited to see if he took that the wrong way. He didn't. "So what happens now?"

"Now?" It was my question, but the general was speaking to Jenö, as if I had disappeared from the room. "Now, we're almost out of the woods. Nothing changes, nothing stops. We test what we need to test. We spend what we need to spend. I hear something is planned for the summer in Hwadae."

"Things will get better until they get worse again." I listened to the sound of my voice. Neither of them seemed to notice. "No one understands that things can't go on like this?" It wasn't good, staying invisible too long in these situations. The trick was rematerializing in the same form that you were when you were last seen.

"I need some air." The general opened the door. "Things can always go on, Inspector. It's our curse. There is always a break in the clouds, always. Sohn knew that. It's what worried him."

"He was in a hurry," Jenö said.

"In a terrible hurry." The general stood in the doorway with his back to us. "He thought this might be the only chance."

"For what?" I remembered what Pak had said about the theory of the "only chance."

"To change course. He told me he'd move heaven and earth this time."

Jenö's right hand gripped the left. "That was his mistake. It's always fatal. He shouldn't have run out of patience."

"You can drown in patience," the general said. "Sohn didn't want to drown."

"And you?" I asked.

As the general turned to me, he adjusted his jacket. Military and police, I thought; when they get uneasy, they tug at their clothes. "It's quiet out here. None of those crazy plans going across my desk. The winds sing through the ruins. I write poetry and count the days of my life. When spring comes, I'll be transferred. The azaleas are nice in Yongbyon in April, isn't that what they say?"

"And this site?"

He shrugged. "It's not police business, I can tell you that much."

"I may see you in Pyongyang, then."

"Or in Seoul."

"Keep your balance, General."

"And you."

"If we move enough piles of dirt," Jenö said more to himself than to either of us, "sooner or later someone might notice."

Chapter Four

The phone rang just as I walked into Pak's office. Pak picked it up and frowned. "Well, tell your people to take care of it." He listened for a moment. "How many? Are you kidding? Alright, we'll be there as soon as we can. But don't blame me." He put down the phone and shook his head. "Get everybody in the building and let's go."

"Where?"

"The soccer stadium. There's a riot." Pak grinned at me. "Can you believe it? A soccer riot in Pyongyang! I never thought I'd live to see the day."

"Soccer, this time of year? Who wears shorts in this weather?"

"I guess sitting with all those people beats freezing alone in a cold apartment. Anyway, it's a championship against some team from the Middle East. Maybe the powers that be figured they couldn't function in these temperatures."

2

"That was fun." Pak rubbed his shoulder and let out a small groan. "At least it was different. I wouldn't have thought anyone could throw a bench that far." He groaned again, louder this time. "I think we did okay, Inspector. Lots of shouting. A few odds and ends onto the field. The referee cowering behind us. All sports, no politics, a little steam released and everyone happy. What do you say?"

"I say we don't let the boys in uniform have whistles anymore. The young guy next to me was blowing his the whole time. I would have killed him, but I think the sound paralyzed me."

"Probably just excited, that's all. Not something they get a lot of training for, riots."

"As will be obvious to anyone who reviews the films. Wait until the reports are filed and the comments come back from the Ministry. Someone will decide we need crowd-control gear, and then they'll decide we need training in how to use it."

"That means a lot of drills out in the cold before work. Fortunately for me, chief inspectors are exempt from field training. Unfortunately for you, inspectors are not."

"As long as it doesn't happen again for a while, maybe I'm safe."

"Don't get too comfortable, there's another match tomorrow."

"Let's hope it snows harder." Outside, a few flakes were drifting down. I liked snow late in March.

"Did you see that crowd? Magnificent, roaring like lions. Jumping up and down, a lot of yelling, and all perfectly harmless. Things are getting better, people can feel it. I don't know about you, but I never worried we'd lose control. Not once."

"I don't think we had control. I think they were just content to stay where they were and complain. If they had come onto the field, we'd have been squashed like grapes. Not one of our men had any idea what to do."

"And you did?"

"No, I just shoved back whoever was shoving me. The whole time I kept hoping nobody would call the army."

"For a soccer riot? Not likely."

"The army is sticking its nose everywhere these days. They'd like nothing better than to show we can't do our job."

"You want to know what I think? I think someone is going to have to pay for those benches. I hope it isn't us. The Ministry doesn't have the budget."

"I hate soccer. I always have. Too much running around to no purpose."

3

"You've been a good host, Inspector. I'm appreciative. Tomorrow I'll get on the plane, and you'll be free of me. Admit it, you'll be delighted." Jenö was walking beside me on the street in front of the hotel. It wasn't warm, but from the way the sun played with the wind and the clouds hurried across the sky, you could believe it might be soon.

" 'Delighted' might be a little strong," I said.

"I'm sorry about what happened at the lakeside. It was regrettable. I hope you realize I had nothing to do with it."

"M. Beret filled me in."

I detected a slight skip of the eyebrows.

"That's good."

"He said the Man with Three Fingers saved my life."

"M. Beret said that?"

"Yes, I found it curious, too."

"You still feel guilty, don't you? About leaving your three-fingered colleague all those years ago."

Somehow, Jenö had been approved for yet another visa. I had become resigned to his ability to collect visas. But that was different from being given access to my file. So who was talking to him? How would he know anything about what happened that night?

"When the Pakistanis found your colleague, they didn't know who he was. He had no identification, and no face. For some reason, they didn't leave him to die. They brought him to the nearest army hospital, and the chief surgeon—a young man who had studied in London, as a matter of fact—put him together. There was nothing to do as he recovered, so they became friends. The surgeon taught him chess. The surgeon had acquaintances. And they knew how to play chess. It was awkward for the wounded man, picking up the chess pieces with that hand. The surgeon wanted to repair it. He was advised not to."

"I sense this is not going in a good direction." The highway of possibilities was bumper to bumper from this point on.

"Then go ahead and ask. Or would you rather not know?"

"Why didn't they want his hand fixed?"

"Because they wanted him to burn with anger. Every time he lifted a chess piece, they wanted the anger to burn hotter. Eventually, during a chess game one afternoon, they casually mentioned the idea of getting even. I think he had just knocked over his queen and two or three pawns with his claw."

I didn't like one bit the detail Jenö was bringing to bear on this little tale. He hadn't just read it in a file. This was the sort of detail you got from talking to someone who had been there, or being there yourself.

"We could do something about that, they said. How so, your friend asked. A little assistance, they said. Not much. Nothing extraordinary. 'You can fix my hand?' 'Oh, no,' they said. They didn't want it fixed. They wanted him to carry it around as a reminder. 'But we can give you information now and again. Steer you in the right direction. Much more satisfying than a couple of new fingers. You know, an eye for an eye. Think about it,' they told him."

Jenö paused. I thought about it. Involuntarily, my hand went up to my eyes. I might as well ask. "How do you know all this?"

"The surgeon was a strange creature—a Pakistani Jew from Karachi. He was a student of my father, who was a surgeon in the Royal Marines before he went to Israel."

"Does anyone drive a taxi in this tale?" Of course they did.

Jenö shrugged. "Sohn took your colleague back. It had been Sohn's operation, and Sohn felt guilty."

"Sohn." I put a hand out to break my fall. "Sohn's operation." Suspicion is a leap into the unknown; you can fly away on suspicions. Confirmation is the fall to earth.

"You never saw your chief?"

"No. We weren't supposed to." I never saw my chief, the man who put us into an operation that had "hurry up" written all over it, the operation that was hung with "only chance" bunting from the walls.

"Well, Sohn, your old chief, took him back, used him as he needed. Kept him overseas mostly, edged him into the special squad when it was time. His job? You'll never guess his job."

But I already had guessed, a split second before.

"To watch and protect you."

"Funny, I thought he wanted to kill me." I laughed, one of those painful laughs that slips over the wall and gives everything away. "Can you believe it?" It would have been nice to sit down somewhere at this point, away from Jenö, away from everyone. It didn't have to be a warm place, or a place full of light. It just had to be quiet, solitary. I could feel pieces falling into place; they'd all been there, just waiting to fall into place. They'd been waiting for me to put them on leashes and take them for a nice walk. Very patient, the pieces; even when they are staring you in the face.

"Why would he want to do that? Mun didn't blame you. He blamed whoever it was that had sabotaged the operation." If this was supposed to be comforting, it wasn't. I wished Jenö would just shut up. More pieces right now I didn't need. I was on overload. Too bad, I knew what was next.

Jenö smiled. "Ready for this?"

"No."

"When he put you into the investigation of that woman in Pakistan, Sohn knew you would need protection. But he knew you wouldn't accept it. So he gave you an enemy. You felt guilty as soon as you saw Mun; that's all Sohn needed to get you back on board."

So. Sohn had set it all up. He'd kept it right at the edge of where I would figure things out. He'd even told me a story about his connection with the woman who died in Pakistan. I still didn't know what happened to her. I would never know, wasn't supposed to; more than that, it never mattered, not really. From the beginning, I'd chased that very idea up and down the lists of possibilities—maybe whoever had put us on the investigation of the woman didn't give a damn about what happened to her. Sohn was smart. He was also a son of a bitch. No wonder someone broke his neck. I backed away from loathing Sohn for a moment. "How did Mun know Ahmet was going to try to kill me?" This was a fair question; the answer wasn't obvious.

"Ahmet, of the lovely daughter?"

"You know who I mean."

"Mun knew. What difference does it make how he found out? Maybe he was tipped off." Sure, maybe he was playing chess on the lakeside in Coppet smoking a French cigarette. "However it came to pass, your three-fingered friend surprised Ahmet, deflected the shot, and then who knows what happened next? Ahmet was pretty strong for an old man. You saw him. When he got mad, he was like a bull. He also carried that knife with him everywhere he went. Maybe he sliced off Mun's cheek."

"M. Beret told me Mun had a broken neck."

"That, too."

"You don't sound so sure."

"You want me to swear an oath?"

"Why me? What did Ahmet have against me?" Other than the fact that for a few weeks, I lusted after his daughter. Ahmet's radars must have been overloaded with what I was thinking every time I saw her.

"It wasn't because of your interest in his daughter." Jenö nudged me. I would have slugged him, but it had turned cold again, a cold wind out of the north, and I knew my hand would hurt for days afterward. "Well, that wasn't the only reason. It wasn't just personal. Someone needed those missile talks to break up in confusion. They got to Ahmet. How I don't know."

"I think I can figure out the rest."

"I'm sure you can. I'd be shocked if you hadn't done it already."

"Where's Ahmet now?"

"Good question. I wish I could give you an answer."

It was such an outrageous lie, I waited to see what his eyebrows would do. They sat out the dance.

"Just out of curiosity, because it doesn't make any difference anymore and I know you're not likely to tell me anyway, how do you know so much about Sohn?"

"You might be very surprised how I know what I know, Inspector." His mind was spinning through the possibilities. I'd seen people do that, try to pick apart one of my questions at the speed of light, slam shut drawers and doors and windows in their minds before I could get there.

That might have worked on me a few months ago in the mountain hut, in the howling wind and bitter cold. Not now, not after everything that had happened. "Nice try, Jenö. But I don't think so. Sohn told people what he wanted them to know. A lot of it wasn't true, or not completely true. You believed him. You had no way to check what he told you, so you believed it. That saved a lot of trouble on your part. Belief is easy. It's doubting that causes difficulties." Jenö didn't want to say anything. He wanted to leave it at that. So did I. "Have a good flight," I said. "A driver will take you to the airport in the morning."

"One last thing. I have a present for you from a mutual friend." He reached into the pocket of his coat and handed me a soft green leather pouch.

"Shall I look inside?"

"As you wish."

"I'll wait."

"Then it's good-bye." He became very formal. "The next time we meet, Inspector, I hope it will be friendlier. Warmer."

"My regards to Margrit."

"And Dilara?"

Wonderful eyes, that girl. "Go ahead, give her my regards if you see her."

"I might." He smiled briefly. "Don't turn your back on your brother."

"Thank you."

"The enemy of my enemy . . . don't forget."

"Same to you," I said. His eyebrows didn't seem to notice.

4

"I smell smoke. What are you doing, Inspector, burning the secret papers?"

From down the hall, I heard Pak's chair creak. It did that whenever the seasons changed, as if the wood hadn't forgotten. Burning the papers—it was a joke we'd shared for years. "Imagine," Pak would say, "at the moment of the attack, when the final battle begins, we'll be caught in the middle of it, burning piles of documents of no possible use to anyone." The instructions were very firmly worded. They were circulated twice a year, and we were supposed to sign them each time they passed over our desks. No matter what, all documents were to be destroyed. There was to be no—and this was underlined or, in the years red ink was still available, marked in red—absolutely no repetition of the last time, nearly fifty years ago, when truckloads of documents fell into enemy hands.

"No, not paper," I said.

Pak stuck his head into my office. "What then? Are we installing gas grills in the desks and opening a restaurant?"

I had emptied the leather pouch Jenö had given me onto my desk. There were five pieces of wood, each one cut to show off the grain. They were all different, all perfectly sanded, perfectly stained. Each had a small, perfect initial on it—*J, A, D, S, B.*

"What kind of wood is sweet Dilara?" he asked.

"Tree of Heaven." I held it up for him to see. "Very pretty tree, but it can give you a headache."

I fed them slowly into the fire, one after the other. Each piece of wood burned differently, each according to its nature, but in the end, they all turned to ash. Pak watched the small flames without speaking. The last piece, I supposed, was M. Beret. His was a beautiful oval scrap of horse chestnut, the huge tree that sheltered the bench where we'd first met. I hesitated, gave M. Beret a swirl, and then committed him to the flames.

"No." I looked up at Pak. "Not papers. Bridges, that's all. I'm burning my bridges. You ever burn a bridge, Pak?"

He seemed surprised and thoughtful all at once, though his face was now so thin it was hard to be sure. "The gingko trees in the courtyard are thinking about spring," he said, filling the space around that moment when everything hangs in the balance. "I can always tell. Something about the way they reach for the light."

Lausanne
October 2007

May 24, 1998

To: The Files
From: Jenö M.
Subject: Operation Quince

I admit that these things rarely work out as planned. In this case, though, there is an argument to be made that we salvaged something, or that we may have salvaged something. In the end, it might not all have been a total waste of resources, though that will be the judgment of many. Much depends on how you do the tally.

On the negative side, we have lost Sohn. That is a terrible blow. He was a man of conscience, but in the end, conscience was fatal. It made him impatient. In truth, it is difficult to know how much longer we would have been able to work together. My instincts tell me that the cooperation could have continued if events had not gone so badly awry.

Less negatively, Mun is again under our protection. His knowledge is admittedly limited, but the psychological lessons we might learn through careful handling may prove valuable. My advice is not to leave him to the normal interrogators. He was never utilized fully in the first go-around, though his chess game improved considerably. What to do with him once the questioning is over cannot be settled yet. Perhaps we can send him to Canada or Japan. The story that he died under suspicious and embarrassing circumstances took hold quickly enough, so there was never an effort to press for an explanation. Whatever the Swiss know they will keep to themselves.

As for O, he might bear watching, though I feel sure we will never develop him. His brother has already been assigned a *Yam Suph* file. That will require considerable effort to maintain, but it must, at all costs, be kept current.

Ahmet's death should cause us no regret. I always thought he should have been vetted more thoroughly. If nothing else, his false teeth were too good. Where did he get the money? Moreover, it should never have come as a rude shock to learn that he had such a pathological hatred for Koreans. There was a note in his file that he fought in the Korean War, and none of us bothered to give that a second thought. It turns out his unit was overrun and suffered rough treatment, which Ahmet never forget. His daughter has been given a small stipend that should keep her in dancing shoes. An appropriate foreign service will keep an eye on her, and she will undoubtedly get frequent visits.

Most important, the effort to stop cooperation between the North and the Americans will have to be abandoned. There is no political stomach for it here any longer. The Americans say their own talks will succeed. This I doubt.

The surgeon's daughter has decided to stay where she is, driving cabs. Her father is not happy, but then, who is?

In the meantime, we have gained access to site BAMBOO. It is not the world's best piece of real estate, but it may yield some returns worth having. Work has been under way for several months. Moving dirt around can accomplish a lot if you know how to do it. The activity will no doubt eventually be noticed, especially because we have started putting the information in the usual channels, where it will find its way to where it will do us the most good. Once this seed is planted, it will grow, thanks to the fertile ground along the Potomac.